IVORY

Also by Tony Park

Far Horizon
Zambezi
African Sky
Safari
Silent Predator

Part of the Pride (with Kevin Richardson)
War Dogs (with Shane Bryant)

IVORY

TONY PARK

St. Martin's Press ≋ New York

IVORY. Copyright © 2009 by Tony Park. All rights reserved. Printed in the United States of America. For information, address St. Martin's Press, 175 Fifth Avenue, New York, NY 10010.

www.stmartins.com

Designed by Omar Chapa

The Library of Congress Cataloging-in-Publication Data is available upon request.

ISBN 978-1-250-05559-0 (hardcover)
ISBN 978-1-4668-5891-6 (e-book)

Our books may be purchased in bulk for promotional, educational, or business use. Please contact your local bookseller or the Macmillan Corporate and Premium Sales Department at (800) 221-7945, extension 5442, or by e-mail at MacmillanSpecialMarkets@macmillan.com.

First published in 2009 by Pan Macmillan Australia

First U.S. Edition: November 2015

10 9 8 7 6 5 4 3 2 1

For Nicola

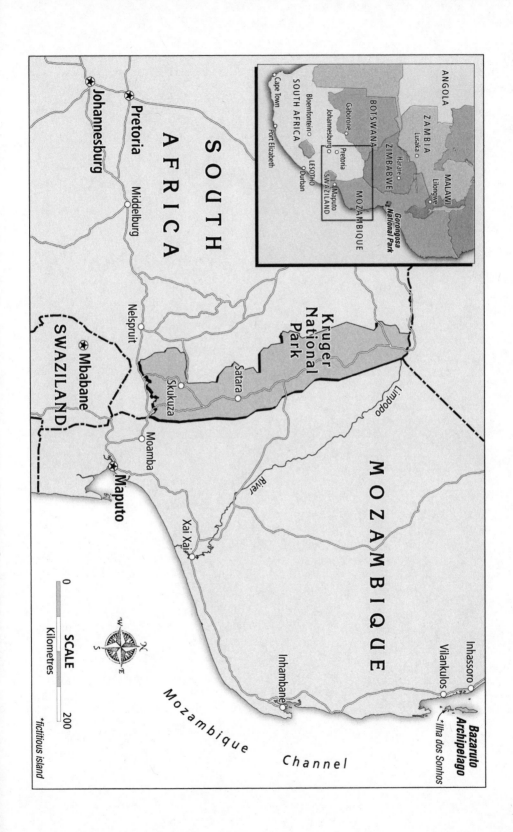

IVORY

Prologue

It was early on the morning of his fifth birthday that he saw his first elephant, and for as long as he lived he would never forget that moment.

The mist hung low over the plains, and stretched as far as he could see as he peered through the Land Rover's windscreen. The vinyl seats still gave off that oily new smell when the sun slanted in through the square windows, as it did now.

"*Ponha o seu casaco novo, Alexandre,*" his mother said. Even though it was still cold, he didn't want to pull on his new jacket. Reluctantly, he let his mother pull the scratchy garment over his arms and button it. The coat was a birthday present, but so too was his shiny new toy Land Rover—an identical miniature of his father's Series IIA. He wanted to play with the car, but his father kept telling him to look for animals.

"*Ai, não pareces elegante?*" his mother said, but Alex didn't think he looked smart at all.

"Come here, Alex," his father said. "It's time you learned how to drive." His father always spoke English and his mother Portuguese. It had always been that way and he answered each in their respective tongues. At five he was fluent in both languages, and thanks to his friend Jose, whose father worked for Alex's father at the hotel, he had a good command of the local African language, Xitswa, too.

He dropped his toy car and clambered onto his father's lap. He gripped the steering wheel and squealed with delight when his father let go.

"Donald!" his mother shrieked.

"The boy's doing fine. Look, Alex."

"Buffalo," Alex said proudly. He had seen a herd yesterday when they had arrived at the national park. His father had said there were at least a thousand buffalo in the herd, scattered like black marbles across the close-cropped green grass of the floodplain. This one was by himself, though, and he loomed out of the thinning mist like a black ghost.

"Good boy, steady as she goes. He won't hurt us."

Alex turned to watch the huge head with its curved horns that seemed as long, from tip to tip, as he was tall. The steering wheel bucked and turned in his tiny hands as the tires bounced in and out of ruts and the embedded footprints of animals that had churned the road to mud during the last rains and since dried as hard as pitted concrete.

"Maybe we'll see some lions today," his father whispered in his ear. "In the wild this time."

Alex growled in imitation of the caged beast he had seen in Vilanculos, awaiting shipment to Portugal. His father had said it was bad to keep wild animals in cages, but his mother had scoffed and said there were far too many lions in Africa as it was and they should all be shot or shipped to zoos around the world.

"*Olha, elefantes!*" his mother called.

His father took back control of the steering wheel and slowed the Land Rover to a stop. Alex turned and caught sight of the elephants. The nearest was barely twenty meters away. Alex climbed off his father's lap and onto his mother's as she was closer to the great gray beast. His father killed the engine.

"It's a female. She could be the same age as you, my boy, judging by those thin little tusks."

The elephant turned, startled, shook her head and raised her trunk, sniffing the air. Alex reached out of the open window, but his mother snatched his hand back inside. He heard a funny sound like a tummy rumble, but much, much deeper.

"They're talking to each other," his father said.

She was the biggest thing he had seen in his young life and he stared at her in silence, drinking in every detail of her wrinkled gray body. The huge head, the white tusks that shone pale gold in the growing light, the hairy tuft at the end of her tail and the pink mouth that seemed to smile at him. He found it hard to believe that she was only five, like him. "What's wrong with her ear, Papa?" There was a large V-shaped rent in the left one.

"I don't know, my boy. Perhaps a lion tried to catch her when she was a baby. If so, she's a very lucky elephant indeed."

"Can a lion kill an elephant, Papa?"

"Only a little one. Once they're this big they're safe from everything in the wild, except man."

"What do you mean, Papa?"

"People are killing elephants all over Africa, Alex, for their tusks, and it's wrong. We need to protect these animals. They're the future of our country—your future, Alex."

Alex's mother said, in Portuguese, that there were more things in Mozambique to worry about than people hunting elephants, and that his father should not fill the boy's head with such serious words on his birthday. Alex let the conversation flow over him and continued to stare, open-mouthed, at the elephant with the tear in her ear.

The elephant started to walk toward them. His mother told his father to start the engine, but his father shook his head. "She won't hurt us. She's made the decision to approach the vehicle—we'd only be in trouble if we were invading her territory."

"Donald!" his mother hissed, unconvinced.

Alex could feel his heart beating in his chest and he looked back over his shoulder at his father, who smiled at him and winked. His mother put her hands over her eyes and scrunched down so that her head was below the level of the dashboard. Alex wriggled off her lap so that he was next to the door and reached his hand out of the window again.

As the elephant drew closer, he could see the tip of her trunk was pink and that rather than being flat like a pig's snout, it had two protrusions, like funny little fat fingers. Alex could smell her musty scent and see her long eyelashes and the glistening eye that watched him.

He held his hand steady and felt the soft exhalation of warm breath on his palm as she kissed him.

1

Southampton, England

The overheated interior of the security minivan in which Jane was driven across the dock stank of the driver's body odor and the cigarette he'd obviously been smoking before she got in. The relief she got from opening the sliding door was short-lived, and the wind and rain lashed her while she struggled to drag her rucksack and day pack out. The driver had no intention of leaving his seat to help her, and was probably looking forward to relighting his smoke. Her strawberry blonde hair was plastered to her face and rivulets cascaded off the collar of her Gore-Tex parka and down the back of her neck. The bleak day matched her mood. There was no band, no streamers, no crowds of well-wishers, no tearful farewells. Just row upon row of brand-new Land Rovers, awaiting loading on a car carrier.

Her ship loomed above her. At nearly four hundred meters in length, the one hundred and thirty thousand tonne MV *Penfold Son* was hard to miss. The last of its cargo of twelve thousand steel shipping containers was being loaded by a giant crane on the dockside. It was one of the largest container ships afloat and just within the Suezmax specifications that allowed it to squeeze through the Suez Canal. It was an impressive beast, this flagship of a family-owned line; however, Jane didn't like to think of the word family when she thought of the name Penfold. It made her feel bad, and she wasn't, she told herself for the third time that morning, a bad person. Was she?

The man at the top of the gangway stared down at her as she walked up. Pale-faced and gaunt, with lank, greasy, graying hair that protruded from under his white plastic hard hat, he wore a blue boiler suit and orange safety vest.

He wiped his nose and sniffled as he took her passport from her and opened it. "Jane Elizabeth Humphries. You are from head office, *da?*"

"Yes."

"Welcome aboard." He made a note on a clipboard and handed back her passport.

She thought it a talent of the man to make the word welcome sound like an insult.

"I am engineer, Igor Putin. Name is like former president. I show you to your cabin. Come."

Another crewman, who looked Filipino, appeared and Putin handed him the clipboard. The man nodded and smiled at Jane, and took over Putin's position at the top of the gangway.

Jane wiped wet hair from her eyes and followed the Russian officer down the narrow passageway. From somewhere far beneath her came the throb of the ship's engines, vibrating up through the deck into the soles of her feet—a far more pleasant sensation than following in Igor's wake, which smelled of cheap aftershave and body odor.

"You are lawyer, yes?" Igor said without turning around to face her.

"Yes." She'd heard all the jokes and aspersions before.

"I have just got divorced from Englishwoman. I don't like lawyers. No offense."

"None taken." She didn't like smelly Russians either, but thought it wise not to upset the crew too early in the voyage.

Igor showed her to the owner's cabin. This was the crème de la crème of accommodation on board a working freighter. She'd seen pictures, but this was her first time on board one of the company's ships, though not her first cruise.

Jane hated flying. It terrified her, so she did everything—anything—she could to avoid it. If she was required to be in Paris for a business meeting on a Monday morning, she would book herself onto the Eurostar train on the Sunday afternoon and stay in a hotel, rather than risk her life on a forty-five minute flight.

She holidayed in England—something that had annoyed and, in two cases, eventually alienated past boyfriends—or took cruises. She'd been around the Mediterranean and Aegean and taken a cruise to Sydney and back on board the *Queen Mary*. She was still paying off the credit card bill from the last voyage, but that was a small price to pay, she reasoned, compared to plunging thirty thousand feet to her death.

Jane considered herself something of a seasoned sea traveler, though this would be a new adventure for her.

The owner's cabin was actually a two-room suite—a bedroom and small sitting room, with an ensuite shower and toilet. She knew it to be thirty square meters and that turned out to be about as big as a very small London flat, minus the kitchenette. There was a double bed, a bar fridge, a television with a VCR and DVD player, an AM-FM radio and an electric kettle and tea and coffee supplies on a small sideboard.

The cabin was immediately below the navigating bridge and faced forward. Through thick glass windows she had a fantastic view across the expanse of stacked shipping containers. At least the view would be fantastic when the rain cleared, she thought.

When she opened the fridge she saw six bottles of vintage Krug champagne and a punnet of strawberries. She closed the door and smiled. As she unpacked she reflected on the last two weeks at work and the way her life had been thrown into disarray.

It had been clear to her, not long after she started her new job nine months earlier, that the managing director and future owner of Penfold Shipping, George Robertson Penfold, wanted to sleep with her.

As the in-house counsel for the London-based international shipping firm, Jane could have reeled off a dozen legal and moral reasons why this would have been a bad idea, starting with the fact that George was married and had three teenage children. Had she been minded to take his increasingly unsubtle advances in a different way, she could have mounted a good case for sexual harassment. However, Jane had been attracted to George from the moment she'd entered his city office for her job interview.

He was tall, fit—he ran seven kilometers and did a hundred push-ups a day—handsome, rich, urbane, funny, intelligent and well-read. At forty-five he was young to be the MD of a company with a profit of several hundred million pounds per annum.

Of course, it didn't hurt that his father was chairman of the board, but George was a man who quite clearly could have been running a similarly sized business on his own merits. Indeed, according to company legend, he had done everything in his power *not* to inherit the business from his father.

George had run away to sea—literally—bunking out of private school at the age of sixteen to work for a rival shipping company. Being the scion of one of Britain's elite shipping families had not helped him on board a rival's vessel; in fact, it had proved a curse for his first few years. He had defended himself and his family name—even though he had earned his father's wrath—in a series of fistfights in ports around the world.

According to George, it had been his wife, Elizabeth, who had talked him into returning to the family fold. By then George was twenty-five and had more than earned his right to serve as an officer on one of his father's ships. He'd risen to captain by the age of thirty-five—no mean feat at the time—and there were few in the industry who would suggest he'd made the rank of Master Mariner by virtue of anything other than merit.

But George missed the sea, or so he'd told Jane when he'd first taken her out for a long weekend on the company yacht. There had been others aboard—the IT manager and chief financial officer—but George seemed to engineer quiet moments when it was just the two of them together. Elizabeth, George said, hated the sea and anything to do with "boats," as she insisted on calling them. She liked his family's money, George said, but not the family business.

He also suspected Elizabeth was having an affair.

Jane had been shocked to hear him make such a private admission to her. The other members of the executive team were ashore, enjoying wine and seafood in the French port in Brittany. Jane, who loved sailing, had willingly volunteered to stay behind and help George secure the yacht. Their work done, George had opened two chilled Czech pilsners, which they drank in the slanting afternoon sunshine.

"I know I'm away from home on business a hell of a lot, but I do try to be a good husband and father," George had said, looking back out to the channel.

He was a handsome man whose tan and callused hands attested to the fact he didn't spend more time than necessary in his London office. His broad shoulders sometimes looked constrained in a suit, but out on his yacht in an old T-shirt he looked free and cool, in his true element.

"Elizabeth and I have grown apart, as the Americans would say." She'd smiled at his awkwardness.

"It's been . . . well, rather too long since . . . Oh, bugger, this is what my kids would call TMI. I'm so sorry, Jane. I didn't mean to embarrass you."

"It's fine, George. I like to think we're friends, and you can talk to me about anything. Really."

He'd laid a hand on her forearm—the first time she could recall him touching her—and it had sent a ripple of electricity throughout her entire body. She'd had to catch her breath.

"God, now I suppose you expect me to say my wife doesn't understand me. I feel like a walking bloody cliché."

"Does she?" Jane had asked.

"No."

They'd had dinner ashore at a brasserie George had frequented often enough to be greeted warmly by the maître d'. Afterward, in a boutique hotel he'd booked for the evening, Jane again found herself alone with her boss, over coffee and Cointreau. There were even candles.

"I know it's wrong, but I'm attracted to you, Jane."

She'd had a moment of panic. She, too, was drawn to him, though she had never in her life been with a married or otherwise attached man. She told herself she was not the kind of woman who'd try to take another's man, though she'd never actually found herself in such a situation. She thought of Elizabeth and the children, and said, "I'm so sorry, George."

"Forgive me," he'd blurted out.

"No, no. I'm flattered, believe me, and I do like you, George. I really do. And I'm not just saying that because you pay me an inordinate amount of money."

He'd laughed it off, but she'd had the distinct feeling he would try to woo her again. She was right. Two weeks ago, after sharing two bottles of wine at a posh restaurant, she'd gone with him to the empty company flat in Soho and they had made love.

She pushed thoughts of George from her mind for the moment. There would be plenty of time to think about him on the long voyage to Africa.

The normal route from the UK to Cape Town would have taken the *Penfold Son* down the west coast of Africa, but there was nothing normal about this voyage. George had his sights set on acquisitions in Africa and north Asia. The *Penfold Son* would be taking a slow trip, through the Suez Canal, across to Mumbai and then back to Africa, stopping at Mombasa, Durban, Port Elizabeth and, finally,

Cape Town. The costly voyage was as much about public relations as it was about trade. "Britannia used to rule the waves," George had told *The Times* recently, "but in the twenty-first century it's going to be Penfold in charge." George wanted to show off his new ship and let his competitors know that he was a major player with money to spend.

Jane wasn't sailing away to forget George, so much as put some distance between them while she thought through a lot of things.

There was also a business reason for her travel to South Africa. Penfold Shipping had begun negotiations to purchase a South African company, De Witt Shipping, and Jane would play a key role in the talks. A round of intensive meetings was planned for the end of the month and George and other members of the senior executive team would be flying out to Johannesburg. Jane, of course, would rather jump out the window of her twenty-third floor London office than be stuck on an aircraft for nine hours.

The cruise on the *Penfold Son*—which had been named after George by the old man—would arrive in Cape Town three days before the meetings were due to begin. Jane would then catch a luxury train, the *Pride of Africa*, from the Cape to Johannesburg.

She'd come to an arrangement with George about taking so much time out of the office. She would, in fact, be in contact with her colleagues and boss by satellite phone and e-mail while on board. She unpacked her laptop and booted it up. Her BlackBerry beeped in her handbag, reminding her she was still very much on the job, but it would soon lose its signal. As a goodwill gesture she had offered to take two weeks' leave as well, but George had refused.

"It's high time you got a look at the sharp end of this business. Call it an extended familiarization trip. Besides, you're saving me the cost of a business class airfare by taking a slow ship to South Africa," he'd said.

There would be time to relax, though. Plenty of time, in fact. She unpacked a dozen chunky paperbacks and stacked them on the shelf next to the bed. She opened her handbag and checked the BlackBerry.

Hi. Hope you've settled in and Igor hasn't offended you too much. They're a good bunch and you'll get used to washing dishes and swabbing the decks soon enough. George. x

The kiss at the end of the message struck her as slightly improper, even in such a relaxed, abbreviated form of work communication.

Improper, but exciting. Just like George.

Indian Ocean, off the coast of South Africa

"Two targets, six miles ahead," Hans, the first mate, said.

Captain Are Berentsen put down his cup of coffee and shifted his position on the bridge of the MV *Oslo Star* so he could see the radar screen. "No AIS," he said—neither boat displayed the Automatic Identification System code that any vessel of substance would display. That wasn't unusual, though, in African waters, where the transponder was a luxury not everyone could afford. "Fishermen, I suppose."

It was the mate's watch and Are had come to the bridge to drink his coffee with his old friend, and to find an excuse to get away from the computer and the paperwork that was sadly so much a part of a master's job these days. A lookout, a Filipino able seaman, stood at the far end of the bridge.

Berentsen picked up a pair of binoculars himself and scanned the horizon. Beneath his feet the twenty-one thousand tonne deadweight Pure Car and Truck Carrier, or PCTC as it was known, was packed with row after row of new motor vehicles, tractors and earth-moving equipment. The fifteen-deck floating car park's last stop had been Port Elizabeth, where she'd taken on scores of South African-manufactured Hummer H3 luxury four-wheel drives bound for Australia. They'd take on some more cars from the Toyota plant at Durban and disgorge half-a-dozen mining trucks before the long haul across the Southern Ocean through mighty swells spawned in the empty expanses between the Antarctic and Africa.

"They're not moving." Are lowered the binoculars and rubbed his eyes. They were close to shore, less than three nautical miles, hugging the coast in order to stay out of the Agulhas current. No, it wasn't unusual to come across a couple of trawlers here. So why was the hair on the back of his neck suddenly prickling to life?

"Captain, I see them." Hans pointed to the tiny specks.

Berentsen refocused his own glasses and saw two fishing trawlers, line astern and close to each other. A streak of smoke scratched a path from the lead boat across the otherwise perfectly empty blue sky. "Orange flare. Try to raise him on the radio."

The mate repeated the *Oslo Star*'s call sign three times into the radio handset and asked the trawlers to identify themselves. There was no reply. He picked up his binoculars again. "He is flying N over C, Captain." The flags—and the orange flare—were internationally recognized distress signals.

Berentsen swore to himself. Any delay in their tight schedule meant money, but he was obliged to render assistance to any vessel at sea that needed it.

"Turn into the weather, starboard five, dead slow ahead," Berentsen said.

"Turn into weather, starboard five, dead slow ahead," Hans repeated, signaling he had understood the order to use engines and the onshore breeze to starboard to slow them down. Had they simply stopped the ship's single engine, it would have taken more than two kilometers to stop the *Oslo Star*, which had been traveling at close to twenty knots. By turning away from the stricken fishing vessels Are was using the elements to reduce his speed.

Having dropped to just six knots, Are gave the order for the mate to turn to port, back toward the fishermen. He blinked away the glare and refocused the glasses as they neared the two fishing boats. They were both sizeable trawlers, he noted. It was a sad coincidence that both vessels' diesels had given up.

"Stop engine," Are said.

"Stop engine," Hans said. "Captain, should I ready the rescue boat?"

Are rubbed his red-gold beard. Through the binoculars he could now see a white man on the lead boat waving frantically. He saw, too, the flash of sunlight on water and steel as a cable between the tow boats was pulled taut. Some instinct from generations of ancestors who had sailed the open seas since Viking days made him hesitate. "Radio MRCC. We'll stand off."

The Maritime Rescue Coordination Center at Silvermine near Cape Town in South Africa was responsible for organizing assistance for vessels in trouble. If the fishermen had been able to send a signal before losing radio communications, there could be a rescue vessel already on its way. If not, then the MRCC might task the *Oslo Star*, as the closest vessel, to render assistance.

"Smoke, sir. The rear boat's on fire!"

Are couldn't ignore the greasy black plume erupting from the towed boat's engine compartment. He focused on the trawler and saw the lick of orange flames. No mariner would be stupid enough to set fire to his own vessel as a ruse. "Hans, sound a general alarm. Ready the rescue boat and fire hoses."

The mate gave the orders while Are kept watch as the *Oslo Star* closed slowly on the stricken trawlers. He lost sight of the trawlers as smoke engulfed them.

It took his brain a few precious seconds to realize something was very wrong.

"Boat's ready to launch, Captain. Lowering now," Hans said, having just been talking on the radio to rescue crew in the forward mooring station, where the craft was stowed.

"They're moving!"

"Captain?"

Are swung to check out the lead boat again and noted a cable rising from the ocean's surface between the two craft. "That bloody fire's a fake. It hid the exhaust smoke from the lead trawler. He's moving and the fool's heading straight across our bow." He pushed the button to sound the ship's alarm and let the glasses drop so they hung from their neck strap.

"Engine full astern."

"Engine full astern," Hans replied.

Are didn't like this. The car carrier was as maneuverable as an elephant in quicksand and she couldn't take evasive action to avoid the other vessels. He punched the typhoon air horn button on the console in front of him and sent out five short blasts, signaling he couldn't understand their actions.

"Retrieve the rescue boat," Are said.

Hans looked at him. "Captain?"

"Just do as I bloody say. Get that boat back."

Are sounded five more blasts on the horn. The tow cable flickered in and out of sight between the two fishing vessels, which were set on a course to intercept them.

Something clicked in Berentsen's mind. "Engine full ahead." He pushed the general alarm signal and klaxons started blaring throughout the ship.

The mate's face had turned ashen. "Captain, if we keep on this course we'll ram them."

"That's exactly what I'm trying to do, Hans. Faster . . ." Putting the engine astern had all but stopped the ship. They were moving forward again, but painfully slowly.

The fishing boats chugged on. The lead vessel increased its speed slightly, until the tow cable was raised taut between it and the smoking boat behind. Are assumed they were in radio contact. He switched channels to try to pick up their private conversation.

" . . . *ease off. Now make fifteen knots. That's it. Hold it.*"

"Got you," Berentsen said.

"*Cut your engines in five, four, three, two . . .*"

Are looked away from the radio's speaker, which had mesmerized him for a second. Surely this couldn't be happening to him.

"Idiots. They're stopping in front of us, Captain. Why would they, now they have power? Don't they know we're going to hit them?"

"That's exactly what they want us to do. Get ready to go full astern as soon as I tell you . . ."

"But Captain, why don't we stop now, and—"

"Shut up, damn you." Berentsen turned and strode toward the rear of the bridge.

Are clapped a hand on Hans's shoulder in a gesture of apology. "Steady. Here it comes. Pray we have enough speed to cut that cable or pull them under on either side of us."

The fishing boats held steady, using their throttles to keep in position across the path of the oncoming leviathan. The tow cable's wet steel strands glittered and winked in the sunlight like a strand of dew-covered spider web.

Are Berentsen held his breath as the blunted, overhanging prow of his mighty ship obscured the cable from view. Even at this height, nearly forty meters above the water's surface, he and his crew heard the agonizing scrape of metal on metal. "Come on, my beauty," Berentsen willed his ship. For a moment the captain thought he had won.

The cable had snared the *Oslo Star*'s bulbous bow which jutted forward of the hull beneath the water and Berentsen had not been able to summon enough speed to snap the stout wire rope.

"Captain, look," said the Filipino lookout who had been wise enough to stay silent so far. "That boat's coming right toward our port side!" There were several different nationalities in Berentsen's crew but English was the common working language on board.

Berentsen knew very well what was happening without seeing for himself. Both smaller vessels would have cut their engines, allowing the onward progress of the mighty *Oslo Star* to draw them in against either side of her hull. Are tapped the keys of the Global Maritime Distress and Safety System on the control panel and scrolled down the menu on the small screen through a list of possible problems that a ship at sea could face. When he came to "piracy attack" he selected

it and hit the key that sent an emergency signal to the MRCC in Silvermine. He supposed help would come from Durban, but he had no
idea how long it would take.

"Engine stop, Hans. Astern full."

Below them the engine protested the sudden commands, sending vibrations all the way up through the car decks to the bridge high
above. "Where are you going, sir?" Hans said to his captain's back.

"To get a weapon."

"But why, sir? Who are these people?"

"Pirates."

2

Alex Tremain was more than ready for the collision of hull on hull and he rode the rocking deck of the lead trawler with practiced ease.

He buckled his custom-made ammunition vest, drew the nine-millimeter Heckler and Koch pistol from the black nylon holster low on his right thigh and cocked it. He tightened the sling of his Austrian-designed Steyr carbine so that it hung, barrel down, snug in the small of his back. A stun grenade was clipped to a webbing strap by his heart, and another, containing CS tear gas, hung from his belt.

Three other men, similarly dressed—their identities disguised by black rubber gas masks—waited beside him on the deck. The shortest of the trio, Henri, held an Assault Launch Max line launcher at the ready. The ALM resembled a futuristic rifle with a folding shoulder stock, but instead of firing bullets it was capable of sending a rubber-coated titanium grappling hook attached to a sturdy nylon line forty meters straight up into the air.

The side of the massive boxlike ship loomed above them like a sheer white cliff. Alex spoke into the microphone built into his mask. "All call signs, standby, standby . . . fire!"

At his command the grappling hook left the launcher with a whoosh as four and a half thousand pounds per square inch of compressed air was released. The folded nylon climbing rope hissed as it left the plastic container beneath the barrel of the launcher. The hook arced over the PCTC's handrail.

From the other side of the ship Alex heard the sound of gunfire. His men on the trailing fishing boat would be firing carefully aimed shots designed to miss the seamen operating the fire hoses on the top of the car carrier but scare them and any other foolhardy onlookers back inside their accommodation on deck thirteen.

Alex's earpiece crackled. "Mine missed, boss. Loading second now," Mark Novak reported from the other boat, on the far side of the target ship. No system was foolproof in battle, which was why they had spare grappling hooks, ropes and cylinders of compressed air. Novak, a burly South African former Recce Commando, was simply following the drill.

Henri tugged hard on the nylon line. "Secure."

"Go!" Alex called into the microphone.

He led the way, as always. The fact that Novak's crew would be a few seconds later meant that he would be first on board the *Oslo Star*. Adrenaline charged his body like no other drug on earth as he climbed, hand over hand, the line snaking between his boots so that he could use his feet to propel his body upward faster. Henri picked up a spare ALM and launched a second line.

"Just once I want to do this with a knife between my teeth." Mitch, the pushy American, always had to say something.

Alex ignored the bump and rasp of steel against his gloved knuckles and looked up at the approaching summit. If the captain was smart he'd be in lockdown on the bridge, his men hiding behind secured hatches.

Alex felt the vibration of the car carrier's engine and the giant ship slowly started to reverse. A glance below confirmed what he knew would be happening. The fishing boats were being gradually left behind as the *Oslo Star* freed itself of the steel snare which had entrapped it. Mitch was on the second line, climbing steadily, but if Alex couldn't get on board quickly and secure and unfurl the nylon climbing ladder he carried in his backpack, then he and Mitch would be left dangling, exposed and alone.

Captain Are Berentsen looked out from the bridge wing and cursed Leif Eriksen—the bearded giant of an engineer, who should have been with the other sixteen crewmen, locked inside the ship's mess. Instead Leif was striding along the deck, hugging the superstructure of the accommodation deck and therefore out of sight of the pirates below. Are had to duck his head back as a bullet zinged off the steel nearby.

Dressed in his grease-stained orange overalls, Leif was carrying a steel wrench almost half as long as his two-meter height. His long blond hair streamed in the stiff breeze as the ship plowed backward. He broke into a run now, hefting the spanner like a berserker.

"Security alert, Leif. I said security alert," Berentsen's voice boomed out over the ship's PA system.

Alex was within reach of the top of the railing now. The captain's voice, in accented English, warned him someone was not obeying the man's command. Taped upside down on the front of his vest was his Fairbairn-Sykes commando dagger. He drew it with his right hand as he hooked his left arm over the rail.

Alex knew that under international maritime law firearms and ammunition were not carried on board merchant vessels. The only exception to this rule was Israeli ships and he had never encountered one of those. He and his men were heavily armed in order to intimidate the unarmed crews of the ships they raided, but if there was a man on the loose on this ship then Alex would do everything in his power to subdue him without firing a shot.

Alex hauled himself up and as his head cleared the ship's steel side he was confronted with the image of a red-faced, flaxen-haired giant swinging a huge lump of metal down from a great height.

The blow was perfectly aimed and the wrench clanged down on the first two fingers of Alex's left glove. He felt nothing.

Amazement showed for a split second on the face of the oil-stained seafarer and he took a pace back as he hefted his weapon for another blow.

As Alex hauled himself over the railing he dropped to the unforgiving deck, though his perfectly executed parachute landing roll spread the impact down the right side of his body. He arrived at the feet of his opponent and stabbed down hard with the dagger, driving it through the stout leather of the man's boot, just above where he guessed the reinforced steel toecap would be.

Bellowing like a wounded buffalo, the man reeled backward and Alex had to writhe, snakelike, to avoid the falling wrench.

Alex wiped the bloody knife quickly on the leg of his flight suit and sheathed it. He swung the Steyr around from his back to cover the wounded man. Behind him, Mitch clambered over the rail—just in time. He unzipped the pack on Alex's back, took the rolled climbing ladder, fastened it to the rails with stout carabiners and hurled it overboard. The two others from his boat, Heinrich and Henri, were soon on board, making faster time on the ladder than Alex and Mitch had on the punishing rope climb.

"Bring him with us," Alex said, motioning to the scowling engineer as Henri climbed over the rail. The Frenchman and ex-Foreign Legionnaire nodded and rammed the barrel of a Glock pistol under the chin of their prisoner. "*Alive,*" Alex reminded him.

Alex checked left and right as he burst through the watertight door the engineer had conveniently left open. If the man had obeyed his captain and locked himself in, he might have bought his shipmates more time.

He was inside the ship's accommodation area, with its familiar smell of disinfectant, cooking and cigarette smoke. His rubber-soled boots squeaked on the nonslip linoleum floor as he passed the lounge. The crew, mostly Filipinos, were crouching in the mess. Alex raised his Steyr carbine and fired a burst of three rounds over their heads. The men dropped to their bellies. Behind him, Henri bustled the wounded engineer into the room with his comrades. "Stay here and guard them," Alex said, and Henri nodded. One heavily armed man was enough to keep the crew covered, as none possessed the foolhardy courage of the wounded engineer.

Alex ran along the corridor separating the lines of crew cabins and past the offices allocated to the captain and his senior officers. Ahead of him was the door leading to the bridge. He knew it would be locked. Alex opened a nylon pouch on his vest and drew out the small hunk of plastic explosive, already fitted with a detonator. He slapped it next to the lock and primed it. "Back! Fire in the hole!" he called to the others behind him. He used the three seconds of relative peace remaining to unclip the stun grenade and pull out the pin.

The hearing protectors and tinted lenses worn by Alex and his men muted the explosion to an uncomfortable bang and buffeting, but the ship's senior officers who had mustered inside the bridge had their senses assaulted by the blinding flash of light and gut-thumping bang that erupted from the stun grenade.

Alex stormed through the doorway into the smoke-filled bridge just as another blast signaled the breaching of the door leading to the port bridge wing. The other assault team, Novak, Kevin and Kufa, would be waiting outside on the port wing in order to round up any crewmen who escaped. If they entered they ran the risk of walking into crossfire if bullets started flying.

The narrow, high-intensity beam of the torch attached beneath the Steyr's shortened barrel picked out a man huddling in a fetal position on the deck below the helm, another staggering toward the far opening.

Alex heard a bang and a whoosh, and raised his left arm and staggered back a pace just in time to miss an incandescent red ball that screamed past his face. Smoke and flame seemed to fill the bridge as the hand-launched distress flare bounced off the rear wall of it, then ricocheted off the thick windows, glanced off the carpet and finally sailed out the open port door.

"*Holy fuck!*" Alex heard Novak yell in his earpiece. "That was bloody close, man." Ship's officers were coughing and crawling around the deck at his feet. Alex saw a red-bearded man at his feet holding the smoking tubular flare launcher and staring up at him with defiant rage.

Alex centered the beam of light from his rifle on the man's chest. Blood pounded in his ears, but he checked the rage he felt at the man's stupidity. Alex covered the two meters between them in a bound, leaping over the curled-up man at his feet, and swung the Steyr's plastic butt down into the side of the idiot's head. The man crumpled to the floor.

"*Clear this side,*" Novak said into his earpiece.

"Bridge secure. Get all the doors open. Clear the smoke," Alex added.

Alex scanned the control panel in front of him and found the engine controls. He knocked them out of reverse and into neutral. The ship shuddered and slowed.

The red-bearded man at his feet groaned and rolled over. Wiping blood from a split lip he looked up at Alex. "Get off my ship, you bastard."

Alex looked down at the captain, the barrel of his rifle pointing at the man. "This is *my* ship for the time being. Don't do anything stupid and you can have it back soon."

He swung the helm, changing course, and pushed the engine into full ahead.

"You're heading straight toward the coast," the captain said.

Alex ignored him. "Keep a close eye on the depth as we get closer," he said to Kevin, the Australian member of his band. "Take the helm."

"Righto, boss."

Alex undid a Velcro-flapped pouch on his vest and pulled out a portable GPS unit. He hit the go-to button and selected a pre-entered coordinate. He confirmed the ship was on the right heading and cross-checked their speed and time of arrival. He didn't use the ship's navigation system in case the captain, who now sat with his back against the wall of the bridge, saw their destination point and memorized the latitude and longitude.

"Should we send him back to the mess with the rest?" Kevin asked.

Alex shook his head. "We might need his technical advice when we get closer. Also, if he were with the rest of the crew he might try something foolish."

"What makes you think I'm going to help you?" the Norwegian asked in accented English. "You could threaten to kill me and I wouldn't assist you."

"I thought that's what you'd say." Alex kept his eye on the horizon, not deigning to face the captain. "No, if I want you to do something against your will, I'll bring your crew up one at a time and keep shooting them until you obey."

Berentsen swore in his own language.

"Speed: fifteen knots," Kevin said.

"Keep her steady," Alex said to the Australian. He turned his attention to the ship's radio, changing the frequency. He picked up the handset and pressed the "transmit" switch. "Mermaid One, Mermaid One, Mermaid One, this is Shark, over."

He paused for a few seconds then repeated the call.

"*Shark, this is Mermaid One. Have you in sight now,*" said a female voice, the accent bearing a harsh trace of Belfast.

"All set?" Alex asked into the microphone.

"*No problem here. Mermaid Two's on the other side of the dunes. She says it's a car park there, but she's in control.*"

Too much information, Alex thought to himself, mindful that their prisoner could hear Danielle's voice over the loudspeaker. "Roger, Mermaid One. See you soon, and let's stick to the facts, I've got company here."

"*Sorry,*" Danielle Reilly said to him.

"Don't be sorry, just be good," Alex said, smiling.

"*I'm always good. As you very well know.*"

Alex shook his head, returning his mind to the job at hand, which was about to get tricky. He put down the microphone and raised his binoculars. "There's the beach. Dead stop," he said to Kevin.

He could see the colors of the Indian Ocean changing closer to shore, indicating the steeply shelving seabed below. Alex and Kevin, a former member of the Australian Navy's elite clearance diver team, had dived the area and made a detailed survey of water depths at high and low tide along this deserted stretch of coastline.

The South Africans called it the Wild Coast for good reason. The sparsely populated fringes of the beach they had chosen were out of sight of any villages and accessible only by sandy tracks suitable for donkeys and four-wheel drives. They'd discounted a dozen more sites due to the strict criteria they'd imposed on themselves for this operation.

"This is madness," said the ship's captain.

"Enough from you."

Alex walked out onto the port bridge wing. Behind the narrow strip of flat white beach were dunes that surrendered to a rising landscape of rocky outcrops and hills. Through his binoculars he saw the bright orange nylon sun shelter on the beach. Danielle stepped into view from its paltry shade. She had on her blue bikini top and a brightly printed kikoi wrapped around her waist as a skirt. The hem ended halfway up her thighs, showing off her perfect pale legs.

She waved at him.

He transferred his attention to the rocky reef beside him, the top of which was only visible when a wave broke against it and receded. Alex strode back inside and walked through the bridge, past the snarling captain, out onto the starboard wing. He looked over the edge and far below saw the dark outline of the reef, not ten meters from the hull on this side.

As well as finding an ideal beach, they needed perfect weather conditions to pull this job off. Someone was smiling down on him because the sun was shining, there wasn't a breath of wind and the sea was as calm as a lake. There might be ten meters clearance on either side of the ship's thirty-two meter beam, but even a slight swell or a stiff breeze would have made it impossible to pass safely through the gap in the reef without tugs and slow, careful maneuvering with the ship's bow thruster.

Alex walked back inside the bridge, stood next to Kevin and held his breath.

"We're through!" The Australian turned and grinned at him, but Alex wasn't ready to celebrate just yet.

"Engine full ahead, hard-a-port," Alex said.

"Aye, *Captain.* Engine full ahead, hard-a-port."

"Idiot!" the Norwegian captain railed. "You're going to beach us, you fool."

"I sincerely hope so." Alex went back out to the starboard bridge wing.

The *Oslo Star* had slowly turned, so that its starboard side was almost parallel to the rapidly approaching coastline.

"Five meters, three meters, two . . ." Kevin called from inside, reading off the water's depth under the keel. Captain Berentsen looked down at the deck and shook his head.

The *Oslo Star* touched bottom. Alex looked down. The ship's massive screw churned in the water, trying to drive her closer to shore, but because of the angle at which they had beached the *Oslo Star* the dry sand still looked twenty meters or more away. He pressed the "transmit" switch on his throat microphone. "Shark Two, side ramp down, side ramp down."

"Yes, sir," Mitch said, sullen as usual. The American was in the ramp control station at the aft of the ship.

The *Oslo Star* had two ramps for disgorging her cargo of vehicles; one at the stern and one on the starboard side. Both ramps were designed for use with the ship alongside a quay. The stern ramp was angled, but reached only a little more than thirteen meters from the side of the ship, while the side ramp was twenty-five meters long. Alex knew the ramp could only be lowered twelve degrees from the horizontal. There were no guarantees they had beached the ship close enough to shore to begin unloading.

"I'm going down to check on the ramp," he told Kevin. "Take the captain back to the mess with the rest of his crew and relieve our man on guard duty, so he can help shift the vehicles. If anyone tries anything, shoot the captain first. That should put the wind up the rest of them."

"Roger," Kevin said.

Alex left the bridge and walked to the rear of the accommodation deck, past the prisoners, and got into the lift that stopped at every second deck. Stepping out onto the car deck he saw a growing dazzle of light at the ship's starboard side. Ahead of him was row upon row of gleaming Hummers, the civilian version of the American military's workhorse tactical vehicle. These models had their garish yellow, blue and shiny black flanks plastered with sheets of white stick-on vinyl film to protect their panels from scratches.

With Henri guarding the prisoners and Kevin on the bridge, the job of unloading was left to Alex and three others. Mitch would join them once the ramp was fully down. Heinrich, the German, was walking along the rows of trucks releasing the nylon straps that held the Hummers down to the deck.

The hold was filling with exhaust smoke as vehicle engines were revved to life. The ramp was almost down. Alex strode between the vehicles, making for the opening in the side of the ship.

With the captain and crew safely under guard he removed his gas mask, savoring the breeze that cooled the sweat in his unkempt mop of raven hair as he walked down the ramp. It juddered to a halt beneath his feet. He looked up at the control booth, high above.

"We're short," Mitch said into his earpiece.

"So I see." They were close—the edge of the ramp was about a meter above the water and about four meters from the exposed sand of the beach. Alex undid his assault vest, took off his radio and pulled off his boots. He dived over the edge of the ramp into the water. Surfacing, he looked up at the towering beast above him. Its engine was stopped, but he could feel the vibrations of the ship's generator in his body. He tried to stand. The water was less than half a meter above his head.

Heinrich had jogged to the end of the ramp. He leaned over the edge and held out his hand, helping Alex back aboard.

Alex picked up his radio and earpiece. "Mermaid Two, Mermaid Two. We need you down here. Now!"

"Awesome," cried the high-pitched female voice in his ear.

Alex looked to the pass through two of the sand-hills. The clatter of an old diesel engine and a cloud of black smoke told him Sarah was on her way. He pictured her, grinning madly behind the wheel of the old Series IIA Land Rover.

Sarah Hoyland was the daughter of a mechanic and she'd had a love affair with engines and cars all her life. She handled a four-by-four in loose sand better than any of them and there was air under all four wheels as Sarah crested a dune, not even bothering with the pass. They were a wild bunch, all right, but Alex loved every one of them—Sarah and Danielle more than the guys, of course. Even Mitch had his moments.

Danielle, red-haired and freckled, watched from the shelter of her sun tent. The old Land Rover landed with a cloud of sand and wincing creak of leaf springs and aging shock absorbers. Alex saw Sarah's dark curls streaming in the breeze. She and Kevin—another self-confessed petrol head—had removed the Land Rover's hard top and the pair of them had welded to the body the weird-looking array of modifications that might just save the day.

Behind Sarah was a stout roll bar of tubular steel and in front of her face was nothing, as she had folded the Land Rover's windscreen down across the bonnet. Rising up from the rear of the open pickup tray were four long lengths of flat steel ramp, strapped together in pairs, which she and Kevin had cut from a wrecked tilt bed car-carrying trailer. They protruded forward and above her, like twin prongs. The other modification was a homemade snorkel of PVC water pipe which rose from the engine's air intake, and out the side of the right front fender. Sarah had secured the towering two-meter extension to the right-hand steel ramp.

Sarah hit the flat of the beach and gunned the engine. "Yee-ha!" she screamed as she straightened and aimed for the rear of the ship, which loomed high in front of her, casting a shadow up the beach.

"She is mad, that woman," Heinrich said.

Alex nodded to the German and held his breath.

A bow wave flew up as the Land Rover entered the water. Sarah's green eyes blazed and she looked up and flashed Alex a broad, wild smile as the vehicle, then her face, disappeared below the surface of the water.

The leading edges of the steel ramps edged closer and closer to the lip of the drawbridge at the side of the ship. "Come on, come on. That's my girl," Alex whispered.

"I thought Danielle was your girl this week?" Heinrich winked, but Alex ignored the jibe.

Heinrich took a step back as the ramps connected with the ship's steel with an ear-piercing grate and clang. The Land Rover's snorkel was still clear of the water and bubbles showed its engine was still running.

Alex jumped in the water again and swam to the shallows. He unfastened a tie-down strap which held the pairs of ramps together. He slid one length free and when he pulled it toward the shoreline and locked it in place with its mate—via a simple peg-and-hole arrangement—the makeshift ramp nearly reached dry sand. He looked to where the front of the vehicle was, but there was no sign of Sarah.

"Shit," he said. He swam around the submerged Land Rover and dived beneath the water's surface. The ship's generator pounded in his ears. He found Sarah immediately. She was slumped over the steering wheel. He wrapped an arm under her breasts and pulled her clear. Once on the surface he swam sidestroke to the beach. Heinrich had stripped off his gear and was in the water as well. He waded to shore.

Together they dragged Sarah onto dry sand. Alex checked and found she had a pulse but wasn't breathing.

Alex blew two sharp breaths into Sarah's mouth and seawater erupted from her as she coughed and choked. Alex rolled her onto her side as the convulsing continued. "Jesus, you had me worried," he said, wiping his mouth.

Sarah tried to sit up and coughed again, but Alex told her to lie down. "Fuck. That was wild," she spluttered. She reached up for him and pulled his head to her and kissed him.

Alex broke free and said to Heinrich, "What are you staring at? Let's get on board and give these Hummers the only taste of beach driving they're ever going to get."

They had to sidestep as the first Hummer bounced off the main ramp onto the rickety extensions. The old Land Rover on the seabed took the strain and Alex breathed a little easier as the new four-wheel drive splashed through the shallows and carved twin ruts through the wet sand. Inside the ship, Kufa, a black Zimbabwean former merce-nary, was climbing into a vehicle. He waved at Alex, grinning broadly.

Sarah insisted she was fine and followed Alex and Heinrich back onto the ship. Alex pulled on his gear again. He went to the nearest vehicle, ripped off the shipment papers taped to the windscreen and got behind the wheel.

Alex gunned the big engine and drove across the deck to the square of light at the end. He geared down to second as he hit the ramps and felt the truck lurch as he bounced over the swaying, rising bridge. He accelerated up the beach and pulled to a halt next to Dan-ielle's beach tent. The young Irishwoman sat behind a fold-out camp-ing table, on top of which was a laptop computer and a laser printer powered by a truck battery and an inverter.

"How's Sarah?" she asked. It was, Alex thought, as though she was asking if the other woman was over a headache, rather than recovering from a near-death experience. Why was it that women said they didn't mind being in an open relationship when they didn't mean it?

"She'll live. Everything OK here?"

"Give me your engine and chassis numbers."

Alex ignored the rebuff and read the lengthy numbers from the paperwork he'd taken from the windscreen. Danielle was the antithesis of Sarah. The Irishwoman rarely made a move in life without carefully weighing the pros and cons, then setting herself a detailed plan for the way ahead.

Danielle typed the numbers into her computer and sent the document to the laser printer. The paperwork that emerged was identical to that which Alex had taken from the Hummer, except for the vehicle identification and destination details. Danielle passed the document and some tape to Alex and he fixed it to the windscreen, where the original had been.

He turned back to her. "Danielle, I . . ."

"Forget it. You're the one who kept telling us speed was essential. Now get moving. I really was worried about Sarah, and I'm pleased she's OK. I hope you'll both be happy together."

He shook his head and trod angrily on the accelerator. Alex climbed the pass through the dunes and sped along the narrow tracks that led to firmer ground. Jose waved him forward, until he was at the rear of a semitrailer, a double-deck car transporter. The vehicle's African driver hovered nearby, dragging on a cigarette.

"Everything OK, brother?" Jose asked. The Mozambican's smile showed he was enjoying himself, as ever.

Alex nodded. "So far so good." He checked his watch.

Jose had stayed aboard the second fishing boat until Alex and the rest of the men had boarded the *Oslo Star*. Once Alex had seized the ship, Jose had abandoned the trawlers and made for the coast at top speed in an inflatable boat. His job on land was to oversee shipment of the stolen vehicles. The operation on land was as slick as the hijacking at sea. Alex saw a dozen young African men trudging through the sand toward them. His contact in Johannesburg had promised him a small army of drivers to collect individual vehicles, as well as half-a-dozen car transporter trucks. The more the merrier, Alex thought. He was getting paid per vehicle at the end of the day.

"Keep 'em moving, Jose," Alex said. The command was unnecessary as the Mozambican was already in a vehicle, which he drove up onto the car transporter.

Alex climbed down from the truck, turned and ran back down the dunes to the stranded ship to get another vehicle.

The *Oslo Star* stuck out like a beached white whale. When he reached the shoreline he saw Sarah behind the wheel of the next vehicle to roll off. She pulled to a halt on the beach beside him, short of Danielle's tent.

"Feeling better?" he asked her, leaning in the window.

"This is the best job yet, Alex. I'd do you now if I could."

He leaned into the cab and kissed her hard. He felt Danielle's eyes boring into the back of his head from up the beach. "Keep moving."

"Aye aye, Captain," Sarah licked her lips and drove off.

3

George Penfold sipped freshly squeezed orange juice as he checked his e-mails.

London was waking outside in the half-light of dawn. An habitual early riser, Penfold was in his top-floor office, dressed for work, by 6:05 a.m. Other executives might travel by Rover or Rolls, but George ran through the city streets every day, regardless of the weather. His security people had told him he was at risk, but risk-taking was what had grown his father's cross-Channel shipping business into an international merchant fleet that was one of the maritime world's top ten.

The fourteenth message—how he hated e-mails—was the International Maritime Bureau's weekly piracy report, prepared by the IMB's Piracy Reporting Center in Kuala Lumpur, Malaysia. The IMB, a division of the International Chamber of Commerce, to which Penfold Shipping belonged, kept tabs on all types of maritime crime and malpractice around the world. The busy Strait of Malacca, between Singapore and Malaysia, had traditionally been the number-one hot spot for modern piracy, hence the location of the reporting center in the South-East Asian country.

Piracy hadn't been a serious problem for Penfold Shipping. Much of the company's trade had traditionally been transatlantic, though the expansion into the Far and Middle East had increased the risk of attack. Only one Penfold ship had been targeted so far, and that had been by a fairly amateurish bunch who had boarded a tanker docked in Monrovia, Liberia, for running repairs. The men, armed with machetes, had robbed the crew of their valuables and taken some navigational gear from the bridge. Thankfully, none of Penfold's people had been injured.

He read this week's report, however, with renewed interest, given his plans for expansion into African waters.

The Somali coast had been Africa's worst locale for pirate attacks in recent years, but the increased presence of U.S. and other western warships in the region following a spate of daring, high-profile attacks had forced the pirates to sail further and further from their home waters. The problem of piracy was spreading like cancer, southward down Africa's less patrolled east coast, as far down as the waters off Mozambique and South Africa. It would be an issue he would have to confront if the purchase of De Witt Shipping was successful, as the line plied all of Africa's coastal waters, as well as shipping goods to and from Asia, Europe and the Americas.

George scrolled through the list of recent incidents of piracy, stopping at one which had occurred off South Africa's so-called Wild Coast. It read:

An estimated seven men dressed in military-style uniforms and gas masks, all armed with automatic weapons, boarded the car and truck carrier MV Oslo Star. The pirates beached the ship on an isolated stretch of coast and offloaded fifty-two new Hummer H3 four-wheel drive vehicles. One member of the ship's crew was stabbed during the attack. All crew were locked in the officers' mess until the theft was complete. They then had hoods placed over their heads and their hands tied before being driven to an isolated spot ten kilometers inland, where they were abandoned with a supply of food and water.

He rocked back in his swivel chair then opened the Internet browser on his computer. He typed "pirates" and "*Oslo Star*" into the search engine. More than a dozen news stories popped up about the daring heist.

George clicked back on the e-mailed piracy report. The next item referred to a foiled raid by MEND rebels in the Niger Delta. It was believed a heavily armed gang of locals was planning to kill or kidnap foreign oil workers at a village. "Security consultants" had intercepted and ambushed the gang before it could mount its attack. Some more Googling came up with an online article based on an Amnesty International media release.

INVESTIGATION LAUNCHED INTO KILLING OF NIGERIAN NATIONALS BY "PETRO-MERCENARIES," screamed one headline. George snorted with disgust at the sensationalism.

Returning to the analysts' report on seaborne crime, George noted a summary which highlighted a number of recent incidents off the coasts of Mozambique and Tanzania, to the north. These included the hijacking of a twelve-meter luxury San Lorenzo motor cruiser, the theft of several tonnes of building materials from a coastal tramp steamer and the loss of the contents of three shipping containers from a Liberian-registered cargo freighter. In the case of the last, the pirates had made off with alcohol, television sets, DVD players and furniture. The analyst noted that these recent attacks were proof of earlier predictions that piracy would move south down Africa's eastern coast. The common thread that bound all the attacks was the reported level of organization of the attackers, their dress and their use of automatic weapons.

George pressed the intercom button on his phone.

"*Good morning, Mister Penfold.*"

"Gillian, please contact Harvey and ask him to pop in and see me. Soonest."

"Yes, sir."

"Oh, and Gillian . . ."

"Sir?"

"Get me an update on where the *Penfold Son* is right now, please."

Harvey Reynolds was Penfold's company security officer. He regularly briefed George on developments and trends in crime on the high seas. They had discussed increased security measures but had so far limited this to more sophisticated electronic tracking devices for the company's fleet.

Gillian knocked and entered. She placed a tray with a cup of freshly brewed coffee and a bowl of muesli on his desk. "Sir, the *Penfold Son*'s expected to berth in Mombasa in about twelve hours."

"Thanks Gillian. Get in touch with the master and have him fetch Jane for me. Tell him I need to discuss some confidential legal matters with her, so I'd like her to call me back from her cabin on the satellite phone."

"Yes, sir."

After a few minutes the phone rang.

"Hiya. It's Jane. Anything the matter?"

"No, no. Everything's fine. How are you enjoying the voyage?"

"It's been good, actually. I've gotten so much work done, and it's been nice to have time alone to . . . well, to think. If you know what I mean."

"Yes, I do. Same here. In fact, everything's the same here, on the home front."

"It's nice to hear your voice. Why the early call?"

"Bit of the same, really. I don't want to seem like a stalker, but I wanted to hear your voice too."

She laughed. He smiled.

"Are you alone right now?" he asked.

"Yes, I'm in my cabin. The captain told me this was going to be very important, private business."

"It is. What are you wearing?"

"George! You scoundrel."

• • •

Heinrich sprayed vodka from his mouth and held a lighter to it, sending a shower of fire over the gyrating bodies dancing on the sand. Girls squealed. Novak roared above the wail of the rock music: "Here's to us!"

Glasses, bottles, and cans were raised. Alex felt rum wash down over his wrist. "And those like us!"

"Damn few of 'em." Mitch concluded the toast. "Man, that job was a fucking buzz," he yelled in Alex's ear.

Sarah was beside him and as Alex asked Mitch to repeat himself—they were standing next to the speakers—she slipped a hand into the pocket of his shorts and felt for him. Alex tried to concentrate on Mitch's words, but his head was fuzzy. Rum did that to him.

"I said it was a fucking buzz. The car carrier. Major league now, huh? No more coastal rust buckets. How about a goddamned cruise ship next time?"

Alex shook his head. "It's not an everyday thing, Mitch. It takes planning—you know that. I wouldn't take on a liner in any case. Too much risk of innocent people getting hurt."

"Oh man, don't be such a fag."

Alex laughed off the insult. Mitch was drunk—even more so than he—and Sarah's hand had found just the right spot. "Let's dance some more," he said to her.

"Don't tell me Mitch is right?"

He pinched her bum then held her close as they swayed, barefoot in the sand, to the rhythm. Flaming torches bathed them in flickering orange as they danced. Alex caught a glimpse of Danielle in the shadows and felt bad for a moment. Fuck it, he said to himself as Sarah's mouth found his. He laid a hand on her arse and she ground against him, harder, and hooked a smooth, shapely leg around him.

It was after two in the morning, but the music still thundered down the beach and the pirates and their women kept dancing and drinking.

Lisa, Novak's wife, had even flown to Vilanculos from Johannesburg and they'd picked her up by boat from the mainland that afternoon. His two children didn't know what their father really did for a living—as far as they knew he was a diving instructor, though in truth the ex-soldier's business had gone belly-up months before.

Heinrich's Mozambican girlfriend dispensed tequila slammers from a tray while her children and half-a-dozen others from the village chased each other between the dancers and drinkers. Henri, the former Foreign Legionnaire, danced with his half-Mozambican, half-Portuguese boyfriend.

"Take me to bed," Sarah said in Alex's ear.

"Why, are you tired?"

"No."

Danielle pushed her way between Kevin, who was dancing with one of the three coffee-colored prostitutes Mitch had brought over from the mainland that afternoon, and Mark and Lisa Novak. "If you're not too busy, I need to talk to you."

Alex looked at Sarah, who shrugged and said, "No worries. I need to find a palm tree. He's all yours, Danni—for now at least."

Danielle frowned and led Alex by the arm to the beach bar. While the hotel's bar and restaurant were being renovated—one of the many jobs that had fallen behind schedule—the ramshackle thatch-and-driftwood structure was the centerpiece of social life on the island. A huge stuffed marlin, a moth-eaten relic from the seventies, had pride of place among the bric-a-brac, which included a rusted German helmet Novak had salvaged from the wreck of a U-boat, a silver-plated AK-47 Mitch had looted from one of Saddam Hussein's palaces, Henri's Foreign Legion kepi cap, and the Taliban flag Alex had captured in Afghanistan the day he lost his fingers.

The music was a few decibels less deafening by the bar. Alex ordered another rum and Coke from Jose, and a gin and tonic for Danielle.

"No thanks, Jose," she countermanded him. "I'm leaving, Alex."

He nodded.

"Aren't you going to say anything?"

Mitch bumped into him as he leaned over the bar and grabbed two frosted bottles of Laurentina beer. Alex elbowed him back into the crowd. "You said a couple of weeks ago you were thinking about it. About the time you said you wanted us to take a break, remember?"

"You don't care that I'm going, do you, Alex?"

He shrugged. "They were your rules, Danni. You were the one who said you wanted to live a little, to be wild and free. No more chartered accountant from boring Belfast. Don't tell me you're actually just a good Catholic girl after all? If so, you might need to say a few dozen Hail Marys after taking part in our grandest theft, auto."

"Don't mock me, Alex."

He held up two hands, palms out, the first and second fingers missing from his left hand.

"Wipe that bloody smile off your face, Alex. Sure, I'm trying to be serious here for five minutes. I need to get on with my life. I need to grow up, and I'd like you to be there with me when I do."

He ran a hand through his thick black hair and looked out at the dark waters and the long strip of reflected moonlight. Then he turned and stared across the beach, to the looming white concrete shell of what had once been the finest resort hotel in Portuguese Mozambique.

"That bloody monstrosity." Danni had a way of reading his mind.

"It's all I've got, Danni. It's my life, my future." He walked barefoot across the sand to the pile of timber that sat in front of the half-finished foyer. He stared up at the building in which he'd been born.

She shook her head and walked after him. "This is your problem. This gutted pile of concrete means more to you than any woman, any human being could."

He shrugged. His mother and father had owned this hotel. It was a part of his family, his childhood and, yes, he would rather lose a beautiful woman than give it up again. "You're probably right. Though you could stay here and change my mind."

She laughed without mirth. "I might, if I thought that were true, or possible. It's not just the hotel, though, Alex. It's this Peter Pan life you lead. You'll never give it up."

"Peter Pan? He wore green tights. No, I'm more Captain Hook." He held up his left hand.

"Very funny. I don't think you'll ever stop, though."

"What?" He was drunk, but he also knew what she meant.

"The theft. The piracy. You're addicted to the danger, Alex. You're fooling yourself—and all those mad bastards who follow you—that you're stealing to get enough money to open this five-star wet dream of yours. Thieving's not a means to an end for you anymore. It's become the main game."

"That's not true."

She waved his words away, as though swatting a mosquito. "The car carrier was crazy, Alex. I wish I hadn't gone along with it."

"Does that mean you want to give me back your ten grand?"

She smiled, then resurrected her grim look. "You're asking for trouble. You read the e-mails, the piracy report. You've put us on the international hot-spot map. You'll have the bloody South African Navy up here if you're not careful."

"Oooh, now I'm worried," he said, waggling his remaining fingers.

"Well, you should be. I'm going back to Ireland."

"You're serious, then."

"Of course I'm bloody serious. Jesus, Mary and Joseph, man, you're so damn infuriating, I—"

Alex moved closer and placed a hand behind her neck, drawing her face to his. "If you want to leave, no one's stopping you, but don't leave mad, Danni." He kissed her and she, though initially close-lipped, opened her mouth to him.

She broke the kiss, finally, and laid her head on his shoulder. "I've got to move on. I can't be a bloody pirate wench for the rest of my life, Alex."

He sensed movement close behind him. If it was Mitch, he'd belt him. Instead, he felt Sarah's arms encircle him and Danielle. "How about for another couple of hours then?" she whispered in Danielle's ear.

Alex waded into the warm still waters of the Indian Ocean. He smelled of booze, cigar smoke and women. It was almost a shame to lose the heady after-party aroma, but he needed to clear his head, so he dived and swam underwater for twenty meters.

He broke the surface and breathed a deep lungful of sweet African air. A rocky reef ran in a straight line parallel to the beachfront, about thirty meters offshore. With a few liberal dashes of concrete added by his father in the late sixties, a seaside swimming pool had been created. Further down the beach a perfect meter-high wave curled and broke on the sand.

He turned and floated on his back. Looking up at the hotel he recalled Danni's words. What if she really was right?

Alex's knowledge of his parents' lives was drawn from memories and whispered asides at family gatherings. What he did know was that while his father had come from good stock, his military career had not been unblemished. Back in England, Donald Tremain had been a captain in the Blues and Royals, the second son of a landed but cashless baronet. There'd been a whiff of scandal in the regiment—something about his father and another officer's wife, and the mess accounts—and Donald had resigned his commission and gone abroad, eventually landing in Portugal. With neither title nor debts to his name, he'd indulged his one true passion—other than women—and become a wine merchant working for one of Oporto's port houses, exporting the fortified wine to the United Kingdom. Soon he met and fell in love with a young ballet dancer, Estella Almeida Silva. Estella's parents were farmers in Portuguese East Africa—Mozambique—and they paid for the couple's air tickets to the colony's capital, Lourenco Marques, where the wedding could be held before Estella started to show.

"Your mother could have been a star, but she wanted to come back to Africa, and bullfights were more popular in Mozambique than the ballet," his father always used to tell him. "But on or off the stage, Alex, your mother was the most beautiful woman I ever laid eyes on."

Donald had presumed they would return to Portugal, or perhaps Britain, to start their new life, but Estella's father had a surprise in store for them. Uncertain about the long-term future of farming sugar in Africa, he had invested in a new hotel being constructed on a tiny island, Ilha dos Sonhos—the Island of Dreams—in the Bazaruto Archipelago. Tourism was booming, with Mozambique a sought-after destination for Portuguese, other Europeans and whites from neighboring South Africa and Rhodesia. Despite their complete lack of experience, Donald and Estella had jumped at her father's offer for them to manage the luxurious new hotel.

Alex's father liked to tell the story about how, just a few months later, his only child had come into the world.

"Dear God, I was nervous. I wanted your mother to go to the mainland, but she would say to me, 'Look, Donald, the women on the island have their children in their homes. It's the most natural thing in the world.' Natural, pah!"

Estella immersed herself in the running of the hotel and was overseeing the catering for a colonial society wedding of a hundred guests a week after her due date.

"The high society of Mozambique was there—even the governor. Your mother was waddling about the bloody place greeting guests with a beaming smile in public and swearing like a trooper at the staff in Portuguese behind the scenes. They loved her, you know, but there was never any doubt who was running the show."

Alex still smiled when he remembered the horrified look his father always put on when he recounted walking into the kitchen, following a breathless message from an African waiter as the wedding feast's main course was being served.

"She was on the bloody serving counter, bare to the world, a waitress holding on to each hand and the chef having a coronary trying to get the meals out while you, my boy, were served up to the world."

Alex's father told him, before he died, of the tough times and ridiculously long hours he and Alex's mother had endured to keep the hotel running and profitable. Alex, however, remembered only the good times, until it all ended.

He narrowed his eyes, and in the slanting, golden afternoon light he could mentally edit out the scorch marks, the bullet holes, the broken windows and the weeds of the overgrown garden. Instead, he saw his father in a white dinner jacket and black bow tie; his mother in a fashionably short evening gown, high heels and pearls, tying an African maid's apron in a proper bow. Waiters in starched shirts and white gloves circulated amidst a crowd of holiday-makers who seemed to speak every language on Earth. They bore silver platters piled with glasses of champagne and freshly cooked lobsters. Music played in the disco downstairs, while he and the children of the hotel's staff chased each other around the palm trees that lined the white sandy beaches.

It was a wonderful time, but it had been too good to last. There had been armed rebellion in Mozambique since the 1960s and, although life had changed little on the island, Alex and his family could not escape the inevitability of history. A bloodless coup toppled the government in faraway Lisbon in 1974 and by June 1975 Mozambicans were running their own country. Their former colonial masters were no longer welcome.

He recalled his father's mood changing from dogged optimism to barely checked rage overnight.

"No, you can't take your bloody toys, Alex!" He'd recoiled from his father's barked orders to pack one bag, and one only. He'd hidden behind his mother's skirt, but when he looked up at her, he saw she was crying.

Alex's black friend, Jose, was on the jetty as their boat pulled away from the island. Jose looked confused, but waved. Some of the hotel workers, whom Alex had only ever thought of as friends, were jeering and laughing.

Vilanculos was a crush of people and cars. There were long queues at the airport, but the Tremains were leaving Mozambique by road. Alex shivered as he recalled the *pop-pop-pop* of gunfire and the long, painful blasts of his father's hand on the car's horn as they edged through the crowds of panicky Portuguese and jubilant Africans.

A few of his parents' employees and their offspring were still living on the island, and they'd all been glad to see Alex return later in life—at least that's what they'd said. But how many of those wrinkled old men, or those once beautiful young maids and waitresses, had torched the bedding and curtains of the place where they'd once worked? How many had fired bullets from assault rifles into the bottles and glasses behind the bar; soiled the carpets and smashed every window in all of the one hundred and twenty rooms once the Tremains had left? Their revolution taught them the Portuguese were evil, colonialism was wrong and that every symbol of Mozambique's European past should be destroyed.

The resort had been profitable, but Donald had plowed most of his money back into improvements. Like many other colonials, he had never really believed he would be evicted from the glorious tropical paradise he'd come to regard as his home. In the end, they had fled across the border to Southern Rhodesia, where the whites were engaged in their own war against black nationalists.

Homeless and virtually broke, Donald had enlisted in the Rhodesian Light Infantry, the country's all-white regular army regiment, and eventually applied for and been selected for service with the elite Special Air Service.

Young Alexandre decided that when he grew up he, too, would become a soldier, and take back the country where he'd been born, and the hotel where his family had been happy. His father, away on military service for months at a time, would whisper tales of parachute raids into Mozambique, where he'd "helped even the score" for the loss of the life he'd built for his family.

Half British, half Portuguese, but African born, Alex never really felt accepted by the other white Rhodesian boys at his private boarding school. One school day that began like many others would stay in his memory forever.

"Pork and cheese, pork and cheese," two bigger, older boys taunted him as he walked to assembly. Alex clenched his fists at the local slang for a Portuguese person. His knuckles were scabbed from the last fight he'd won over his mother's heritage. He'd been about to take on this pair when the headmaster called him over.

"Tremain . . . Alex. Come with me to my office. I'm afraid I have some unpleasant news for you."

"Sir?" Alex had felt the lump rise in his throat, constricting his breathing, and the hot welling of tears even before the gaunt old man had told him.

Ironically, things got easier for him at school when the headmaster made a point at assembly the next day of reading an item from the *Salisbury Herald* about the posthumous award of the Silver Cross of Valor, Rhodesia's second highest award for bravery, to Captain Donald Tremain, Special Air Service, who had been killed in action near Mapai, Mozambique, on a cross-border raid. Tremain, already wounded by machine-gun fire, had carried a wounded comrade to safety before dying of his wounds.

After that Alex had left Africa for England where his father's family paid for him to attend Stowe private school where he completed his secondary schooling. He spent his holidays shuffled from one relative to another. None really wanted him. The legacy of his father's disgrace and his mother's profession as a dancer—Alex wondered if it really was ballet she had danced—was always whispered not quite out of earshot.

As a fourteen-year-old, Alex had read of the exploits of Britain's Royal Marine Commandos in the retaking of the Falkland Islands following the Argentine invasion. Growing up on an island, he'd been around boats since birth, although he couldn't see how naval training would equip him with the skills he'd need to see off the wild-eyed fighters armed with AK-47s and rocket-propelled grenade launchers who still inhabited his dreams. The marines seemed like a good compromise.

The thirty-two week recruit training course at Lympstone in Devon on the wind and rain swept south coast of England taught him what an easy life he'd lived so far, and if he'd thought his British background would lead to acceptance, he was disabused of such romantic notions when his corporal dubbed him "the African Spic."

In England he found himself in more than one fight with other marines in his intake, who derided his Portuguese looks and Rhodesian accent. He never lost a bout, and eventually won acceptance. But if his dark hair and eyes and olive skin were a liability in barracks, they were an asset in the local pubs and nightclubs where the young marines went in search of drink and women.

As Alex gazed up at the hotel from the water, imagining even more ambitious renovations and expansions, Danielle walked out of the hotel's foyer. When Alex was a boy a uniformed African doorman had opened heavy brass and glass doors. Now Danni picked her way through charred beams and fresh new lumber. She wore a pink T-shirt and green cargo pants and carried a bulging backpack on her shoulders.

Mitch got up from the deckchair he'd been lying in, under a palm tree in the garden. Alex swam to shore.

Alex had met Danni while shopping for fresh fruit and vegetables in the marketplace at Vilanculos. It was her smile that had drawn him to her. He'd helped her pick some tomatoes and translated for her. The stall keeper had wanted to charge her tourist prices, but Alex had bargained him down firmly and, in the end, paid for the purchase despite her protests. She told him over Manica beers at a beachside bar that she'd left Ireland a month before her thirtieth birthday. Tired of being nagged by her mother and aunties about marriage, and bored with her job as a partner in an accounting firm, she'd chucked it all in and gone in search of adventure and herself.

Danni had come to the island that day. A week later they were the last people propping up the beach bar after the other men had turned in at what passed for a reasonable hour on Ilha dos Sonhos. The rest of the gang were going deep-sea fishing early in the morning, but Alex would spend the day like most others, painting and renovating yet another hotel room.

It had been oppressively humid all day and the night was no different. Lightning marbled the dark sky and Danni moved out from under the thatch as the heavenly drums sounded.

"Come inside, you'll get wet," Alex said as the first fat drops started cratering the white sand.

"Not on your life. This is my first ever tropical thunderstorm and there's no way I'm going to watch it from under cover." She spread her arms and looked up. "It's warm. Warm rain!" She was grinning with wonder.

The storm came with the noise and ferocity of a waterfall and Alex had let Danni drag him first into the downpour and then into the warm waters of the Indian Ocean. She'd gone in still clothed in blouse and skirt, but he'd peeled them off her as they stood, waist deep, and kissed.

"Come to bed with me," he'd said into her ear over the patter of the rain.

"Now, just slow down there a minute and let me think about that, mister. We're both single, over twenty-one, and you're the most handsome man I've ever met—plus you own your own hotel and island . . ."

The bond between Alex and her had grown and she took to sharing his suite on the top floor of the hotel most nights.

Nothing was said, but Mitch would have been blind not to know that Danni was more than just a guest on the island. It made his drunken pass at her at a beach *braai* unforgivable.

"No, Mitch!"

Alex had heard Danni yell from the gloom beyond the bar and had left his seat and run into the night. She had collided with him and he'd wrapped his arms around her.

"God in heaven, that man's a pig," she'd said, breathing deep to calm herself.

"Fucking bitch tried to come on to me, then called red light," Mitch said when Alex challenged him.

"I want you to apologize to her, Mitch."

"I got a better idea. How about you fucking share her around, Alex."

Alex's first punch had broken Mitch's nose and, although the American had later split his eye and left him with bruised ribs, he'd extracted the apology to Danni he wanted—albeit a surly and grudging one.

Things hadn't been the same between Alex and Mitch since that night, and Mitch had been against letting Danni in on the secret of the Island of Dreams and the odd mix of people who lived there. Mitch wanted her gone.

Danni had asked Alex, on more than one occasion, how he was funding the slow-progressing renovations. Her curiosity was piqued when a barge laden with bags of cement, cartons of tiles, buckets of paint and a shrink-wrapped pallet of new power tools landed at the jetty two days after the island's menfolk had been away on a fishing trip.

Then Mitch had caught her in the boatshed.

Alex hadn't asked why the American had been following his girlfriend after dark, but in a way he'd been glad when things had come to a head. Danni had taken Alex's keys from the bedside drawer and, while the others were in the thatched beach bar, drinking beer and watching the rugby from South Africa on satellite television, she had freed the heavy padlock and ignored the *Danger—do not enter* signs.

Alex had told her there was only fuel and motors stored there, and that the monkey's skull and kite feathers nailed above the doors were simply to deter petty thieves from the village.

She'd found enough weapons and ammunition to wage a small war. As well as assault rifles and pistols, there were rocket-propelled grenade launchers, crates of explosives and hand grenades, and a rack of one-piece military flying suits. There was body armor and gas masks, combat boots and, in the center, two rigid-hulled inflatable boats painted in gray and black camouflage stripes.

Mitch had dragged her to the bar. "She was in the shed."

"What are you . . . mercenaries?" she'd asked, shrugging the ex-navy SEAL's hand from her forearm. "I know you're all ex-military."

"No." Alex had turned off the television.

"Drug dealers?" Danni hadn't sounded convinced. She'd seen Alex turn down a joint from Kevin and he'd told her himself, soon after she'd arrived on the island, that no one who worked for him at the hotel was permitted to use anything harder than grass or booze. "The boats . . . what are you, Alex? A pirate?"

Mitch had glared at him, shaking his head, but Alex had said, "Yes."

He didn't think she would turn him in to the authorities—not that the Mozambican police would have done anything, other than report back to him. The local police chief had been in his pay for two years. He had worried, though, that Danni would leave him. As she was finally doing now.

Alex strode from the water, running a hand through his hair.

"All packed, I see."

"Yes." She looked at him, then out over his shoulder at the endless sea for what seemed like a long time, as if imprinting the sights, smells and sounds of the beachside haven on her memory. "You're going to miss having an accountant around," she said eventually.

He smiled. "I will. I hope Sarah's been paying attention to what you've taught her."

At the bar, after she'd found out his secret, he'd offered her membership of the crew, at the same cut as everyone else. His finances were a mess. She'd accepted and soon, via Internet and phone, established offshore accounts for him in Jersey and the Cayman Islands, and produced a spreadsheet of incomings and outgoings. She'd had fun at first, she told him, working on the other side of the law, but things had changed.

"Sarah's more interested in pistons than profit and loss," Danni said now.

Sarah had shown up on the island one day, wading through the shallow aquamarine waters after jumping off a fishing dhow. She was freewheeling through Africa, catching local buses, trains and even boats, in search of thrills of any variety. She told Alex she'd heard, on the mainland, of some crazy white men who were fixing up an old hotel, and hitched a ride on the boat to come have a look for herself.

Alex was wary of visitors. He had had Danni search Sarah's clothes and backpack thoroughly while Sarah had downed cane spirit and Coke at the bar. Heinrich had been working on an outboard motor outside the boathouse, still tinkering and cursing as the sun went down; Sarah, half cut, had wandered down, drink in hand and offered to take a look. The German had scoffed, but said, "Be my guest." In fifteen minutes she'd had the motor purring.

Later, while Danielle had been tapping on her laptop in the gutted restaurant, Sarah had moved her bar stool closer to Alex and run her hand up the inside of his bare thigh.

Danni had been hinting at marriage for a while. Alex had told her he wanted her to stay on the island—indefinitely—but that he couldn't contemplate anything more permanent until he had finished renovating the hotel and become a legitimate businessman, something he fully intended on doing. Things had cooled between them and it had been two weeks since she'd slept with him when Sarah arrived.

When Danni had caught them kissing she'd shrugged the incident off, telling Alex that since he couldn't commit to her, he was free to sleep with anyone he wanted to, and that the same counted for her.

He hadn't believed her and now, seeing the set of her mouth and the bulging backpack, it was clear she wanted an all-or-nothing relationship.

"It won't be the same without you here, you know." He reached out and touched her warm cheek with the backs of the fingers on his good hand. "Come back and visit any time."

She took his other hand—the one which had been maimed and scarred in the explosion—and lightly kissed the remaining digits, one at a time. "Come find me if you ever grow up, Alex." She smiled to show there was no animosity in her words.

"Break it up, you two." Sarah's broad Australian accent was as different from Danielle's as her temperament and zest for life.

Alex smiled, consoling himself privately with the thought that at least he wasn't losing both of the women in his life. Until he looked at Sarah. She hefted a rucksack over one shoulder and carried a day pack in her left hand.

"What the . . . ?" Both these women had shared his bed last night.

"Danni told me she was leaving. I've still got more of Africa to see and I asked if she needed a traveling companion." She came up to Alex as Danielle stepped to one side, raised herself on tiptoes and kissed him on the mouth. "Bye, Captain Hook. It's been a blast."

4

The routine of shipboard life had calmed her. She had never felt so relaxed in her life—nor so bored.

Jane ran up the companionway steps two at a time, and when she reached the monkey island, the deck around the ship's single funnel, she was perspiring and breathing hard. She turned and ran back down. In London she swam three nights a week and was a keen rower on the Thames. There was a small gym for the crew on board the *Penfold Son*, but she had never been a gym junkie. She found them smelly, claustrophobic places, and the ship's was no different.

There was very little of the cargo freighter's deck that was accessible to her as a passenger. The ship was massive, but she was confined to walking around and around the superstructure. She was beginning to feel like a caged rat. There was a small swimming pool below decks, but there wasn't really enough room to get up a good rhythm, or do laps. The stairs, as she had learned, were an unforgiving place to exercise. Twice she'd slipped during rough seas and scraped her shins bloody on the hard steel. However, now the days at sea had turned into weeks she moved easily with the rocking of the massive ship, even in the roughest conditions.

She'd finished all the books she'd brought with her and caught up on all her outstanding work. The ship's satellite e-mail link was her connection to the outside world, but it was painfully slow. She wiped her brow and checked her watch. George was due to call in ten minutes, along with Penfold's chief financial officer, about the South African deal.

Jane jogged downstairs again and entered the superstructure via a watertight door. In the companionway inside she turned side on to allow Ferdinand, the Filipino steward, to pass her. He smiled a greeting.

Jane breathed deep and slow so she wouldn't sound out of breath on the phone to George—not after the way he'd left her after his last, very pervy, conversation the previous night. She'd never had phone sex before, and the thought of him sitting in his plush office while talking to her that way still provoked a reaction. George, she had come to learn in a very short time, was very adventurous in bed and even more so on the telephone. Some things he'd suggested she had balked at, telling him she'd be more open to experimentation as they got to know each other better. Much of what they had done, in the company flat in Soho and a luxury hotel suite over the course of three lunch hours, was new to her. She had enjoyed, for example, being tied to a four-poster bed with silken rope that George just happened to have stashed away in a locked cupboard in the flat. That was a first and she'd liked surrendering control to him, briefly. However, she had no desire to be spanked and he seemed to take her firm but polite "no thank you" with good humor, so she didn't feel she was in any danger with him as a lover. She felt her cheeks redden and concentrated on her breathing.

She barely noticed the smells and noises of the freighter now: the vague but ever-present odor of engine oil, which had initially made her queasy; the smell of food frying in the galley; the dull throb of the diesels far down below; music coming from an off-duty crewman's cabin somewhere nearby.

Inside her cabin was as drearily familiar as the rest of the ship. The endless expanse of ocean out through the portholes had ceased to be calming or awe-inspiring. It was just plain monotonous.

Jane pulled the band from her ponytail and teased out her hair, enjoying the cool of the air-conditioning. The satphone was on the bedside table and she took it to the small desk in the sitting room and opened and switched on her laptop in case she needed to make notes during the conversation. The phone rang, and she recognized George's private line on the caller-ID.

"Hiya," she said.

"Tell me you're naked."

"Me naked, you George. Hello, Robert, if you're there. Are you nude too?"

George laughed. "Bench is dialing in in a couple of minutes."

"I noticed you came early. I hope you're not going to be like that in South Africa."

"Who are you, and what have you done with the real Jane Humphries? The prim, straitlaced corporate lawyer I know wouldn't say such things."

"Don't tease, George. Do you really think I'm straitlaced?"

"Are you really naked?"

"No."

"Then I fear I'm right."

"Don't be so rude. I'm wearing my workout gear, actually. All hot and sweaty."

"Be still my beating—"

They cut short the banter as a recorded voice, followed by Robert Bench saying his name, told them the chief financial officer had joined their call. "How's life at sea, Jane?"

"You should try it some time, Rob," she said.

"That bad, eh? No, thanks. I get seasick in a bath. The South Africans have upped their price, George."

The CFO was all business, as usual, Jane noted. She was disappointed George had spent their brief time alone being so flippant. While the thought of him—his body, and even his words—could provoke a physical reaction in her at sea half a world away, she also had regular attacks of guilt over her new-found role as the other woman. She'd been close to calling the whole thing off on several occasions, but every time she thought of picking up a phone or willed herself to go to his office, she lost her nerve. Right or wrong, he filled a need in her that was real, however much she might fight it or hate it. From what he'd said about his deteriorating relationship with Elizabeth, Jane supposed there was the possibility that he might leave his wife for her and legitimatize what they had together. Before she'd left he'd said he wanted to talk about their future when he got to South Africa. She hadn't pushed him for anything more, as they'd lain together in bed in the flat and listened to rain drumming on the window. Jane had always assumed she would get married some day, but she had been George's lover for less than a month and, as much as he fulfilled her, she was far from certain she was ready for marriage right now.

"I thought they would," George said. "It's the whole political situation with the Yanks at the Horn of Africa. The South Africans are riding high in the short term with increased exports up and down the coast of Africa, but it's a blip. I'm happy to stall them for a while. Jane, can you think of anything that might string out the negotiations?"

She leaned back in her chair. She liked working for George not just because of their physical relationship, but also for the challenges he threw at her. It kept her on her toes. "I must admit I hadn't thought too much about things that might slow us down. Let me check out South Africa's BEE laws. We can ask for a full list of staff in every position—onshore and at sea—and tell them we want to assure ourselves the company's kosher when it comes to staffing."

"BEE?" Robert asked.

"Black economic empowerment," Jane said.

"Good thinking," George butted in. "We'll hit them with it on the first day."

"Also," Jane said, "Iain showed me the weekly piracy update. We can tell the South Africans we're waiting on estimates of revised insurance premiums from our brokers based on the recent upsurge in criminal activity off the coast of southeast Africa."

"Excellent. Although I'm less impressed with you being on first-name terms with that dour old Scottish captain, Iain MacGregor. He gave me hell as a young officer."

Jane laughed. "He's got some very interesting stories about you that I'm sure Robert would like to hear, George."

"All well and good," Bench said, "but I've got another conference call with my South African counterpart in ten minutes that I need to prepare for. If you've nothing else for me, George?"

"No, that's fine, Robert. I'm happy Jane will put the brakes on things once we get to Cape Town. We'll make the locals sweat for a while. They'll not get a better offer from anyone other than us, but just because we're big doesn't mean we'll pay anything."

Robert signed off from the conversation, but George's tone remained businesslike, somewhat to Jane's surprise. "You'll have some company tonight. Five other passengers are boarding when you get into Mombasa."

"Really?" Initially she'd enjoyed being the only passenger on board, but in the last few days she'd begun wishing there was someone else on board other than non-English-speaking stewards and seamen in greasy overalls. "Paying passengers?"

"I'm paying them. They're a specialist security team. I've hired them to conduct an assessment of the crime problem in South Africa. It's all standard risk assessment stuff for when we take over the head office in Johannesburg."

Jane twirled a strand of blonde hair in her fingers. "Harvey's already done the OH and S and security report for Jo'burg, George. I've seen it."

Penfold coughed. "Well, I've asked for another one. Also, there's the offshore crime element to contend with . . . I mean, assess."

She'd rarely, in all the time she'd worked for George Penfold, heard him stumble over a word or sentence. "By offshore crime, I take it you mean piracy?"

"I don't like that term. It trivializes what is actually theft, assault, kidnap, ransom and murder on the high seas."

"You said 'contend with,' George. Are these men a bunch of suits who'll be assessing traffic accident statistics and burglary rates in downtown Johannesburg, or are they bodyguards?"

"Security consultants."

"Why aren't they flying to Johannesburg, then?" She felt a tightness in her chest, a sure symptom of rising anger. "I hope you're not sending out a bunch of thugs to protect me, George."

"Protect you? Of course not. This is business, Jane. Look, I've got to go. I'll try and call later."

Jane ended the call and put the phone down on her bedside table. She stripped off her exercise clothes, walked into the ensuite bathroom and turned on the shower taps. She had the distinct impression that George wasn't telling her everything about these strange men who would soon be joining her on the ship.

George Penfold's intercom buzzed. "Yes, Gillian?"

"Harvey and a Mister Van Zyl, to see you."

"Show them in." It was no coincidence that the leader of the men who would be joining Jane on board the *Penfold Son* had been waiting in his anteroom while he had been talking to her. He had wanted to gauge her reaction to the arrival of the men on the ship, and see if she could guess the real reason for their imminent arrival. She had.

"Mister Van Zyl," George said, rising and extending a hand. "Take a seat."

"Call me Piet, please."

"Really, not the 'grim reaper'? Isn't that what your men called you when you served with the South African Recce Commandos in Angola?"

Penfold watched the man's face for a reaction. There was none. The pale blue eyes bored into him. With his snow-white crew cut and expensive suit he could have passed for a rock star, but George knew Piet van Zyl's fame—or infamy—was limited to a closed circle.

"You've done your research, I see," the South African said.

Harvey Reynolds had known who his employer was talking about as soon as George had mentioned the recent incident in the Niger Delta which had featured in the International Maritime Bureau's weekly piracy report. Reynolds was ex-SAS and had worked as a mercenary officer in Sierra Leone and in a management role for a security firm in Iraq, prior to being recruited to head Penfold's security arm. While the oil company in Nigeria was keeping the names of those involved a secret, despite threats of legal action from the Hague, word had already spread informally among those in the know. Harvey had crossed paths, though fortunately not swords, with Piet van Zyl in Iraq. He'd briefed George on why the South African had had to leave the Middle East in a hurry. George wanted to hear it from the man himself, so he asked him: "Tell me what went wrong in Baghdad."

"Nothing."

"But you and your men were deported, and the security firm for which you worked, Corporate Solutions, lost all its contracts and had to leave the country."

"Our work was finished there. We did what we had to do."

"Which was?"

Van Zyl shrugged and fixed George again with his piercing stare. Penfold had faced down and fought plenty of tough guys at sea and in dockside bars around the world. He didn't flinch.

"You read that my men and I shot up a car that was passing too close to a convoy we were guarding?"

"Yes, and there was an Iraqi army colonel and his two bodyguards in that vehicle. It caused a hell of a stink. I remember the news reports here in the UK. You picked the wrong car to use for target practice."

Van Zyl smiled. "We picked the *right* car, Mister Penfold. What the *media*," he made the word sound like a euphemism for excrement, "didn't report was that Colonel Hussein—no relation to Saddam— was a middleman for funds from al-Qaeda. He was equipping terrorists with arms meant for the Iraqi armed forces, and tipping off the terrs about major coalition operations. Of course, none of this could be proved, so . . ."

"So the CIA paid you to assassinate him."

Van Zyl ended the staring competition and glanced sideways at Harvey. He shrugged. "I can neither confirm nor deny that, Mister Penfold, but it's all ancient history anyway."

"So tell me about recent history. Amnesty International wants the international commission on war crimes to find out who was responsible for recent so-called atrocities in the Niger Delta. Are you going to become a liability for me, Piet?" George rocked back in his chair, steepling his fingers in front of him.

"Again, I can't comment on allegations of atrocities. One thing I've learned in other people's wars, though, is that revolutionaries, freedom fighters if you will, are not afraid to use sheer unadulterated terror to make people join the cause. The trick in counterrevolutionary warfare, Mister Penfold, is to be more terrifying than your enemies."

"Which accounts for spitting a teenage boy's head on a spear and leaving it outside his mother's hut in their village."

"Can I smoke in here?" Van Zyl asked.

"No."

The South African shrugged again. "That boy was a fighter—he hid under an upturned canoe with a light machine gun and tried to kill me. I had more respect for him than I did the men who paid me. Like you, Mister Penfold, they sat me in an air-conditioned office in a city far from Africa and got me to tell my war stories. I can read as well as kill, you know. I do my research. I know from what I read, and from that crooked nose of yours, and the small scar above your right eye, that you fought to get to where you are. You want to know if I will be a liability for you one day? Perhaps. But that depends very much on what you want me to do."

"Harvey's briefed you on the current situation, and I assume you've read online or in the financial press about my designs on a certain African shipping company?"

Van Zyl nodded.

"Maritime crime is on the rise and in particular there is a small but apparently professionally organized gang based somewhere on the coast of Mozambique. These aren't Somali brigands—they're reportedly led by a white man."

The South African shook his head. "You'd be mistaken—and racist—to think a black man can't organize a bunch of pirates, Mister Penfold. I've met Angolans and South-West Africans who turned murder and crime into an art form."

"I wasn't suggesting any such thing, what I was inferring was—"

Van Zyl held up a hand to stop him. "I know what you mean. I told Harvey on the way, so he hasn't had time to brief you, but I've already been making some calls. There are rumors of a group of ex-special-forces guys working the coast of South Africa and Mozambique. It sounded like a bit of a fairy tale to me at first, but I checked the number of attacks and modus operandi. I called the home of an ex-army acquaintance of mine, Mark Novak, in Johannesburg. He used to run a diving operation in Mozambique, near Vilanculos, but he went bust. His wife told me he was back working in Moz, but when I asked her what he was doing she was vague. When I mentioned rumors of some ex-Recce Commandos working as pirates she made an excuse to end the conversation."

Penfold was impressed. "So you've got a lead already?"

"I didn't say that. Tell me what you want me to do, Mister Penfold. What this job's really all about. I like to hear it from the man at the top, in the big office, with the big desk."

Penfold opened a drawer and pulled out three Cuban cigars. He took an antique silver cutter and nipped the end off each cigar and handed one to Harvey and to Van Zyl. "Harvey, there's some cognac in the sideboard, if you don't mind."

Reynolds walked to the bar and poured three snifters of brandy.

"I thought you didn't like smoking?" Van Zyl said.

"It's the smell of cigarettes I can't abide. In business, it's best never to assume anything."

George leaned forward and held the flame from his lighter to Van Zyl, who rotated his cigar and drew on it until the tip was glowing.

"When you board the *Penfold Son* you'll meet the only other passenger. My lawyer, Jane Humphries. If anything happens to her en route to Africa, or while she's there on business, I'll see you never get a decent contract again in your life. If you or any of your men so much as flirt with her I'll have you killed."

Van Zyl laughed out loud. Harvey sat the drinks down on the table and didn't smile. He knew when his boss was being serious. "You're not the only trained killer for hire, Van Zyl."

The South African nodded. "So, after we're finished protecting the woman?"

"You find out what you can about this gang of *pirates*, locate their base if you can, and report back to me."

Van Zyl nodded. "So you don't want me to do anything that might get you or Penfold Shipping in trouble with the court of public opinion."

"Not yet, Mister Van Zyl, not yet."

5

The five men were already on board the *Penfold Son* when Jane returned to the port at Mombasa, though they had evidently arrived not long before her.

A Hispanic man with heavily tattooed arms and his hair done in a top knot was lugging a long green plastic trunk into the guest cabin next to hers. He smiled at her and she tried not to stare at his gold tooth.

"Hey, Enrico, take bloody care with that," said a South African voice from within.

Jane paused by the opening and saw a man with the most strikingly white hair. He looked at her and smiled. "Howzit. You must be Miss Humphries." He wore black jeans and a tight black T-shirt that showed off racks of muscles.

"Jane." She leaned around Enrico, whose hands were full, and shook the other man's hand.

"I'm Piet van Zyl. Me and Enrico here and the rest of my guys will be joining you for the trip to the Cape. We'll try not to get in your way."

He seemed pleasant enough for a bodyguard, though Jane still resented the fact that George thought she needed protecting. "I don't know how to say this politely, Piet, but I'm a big girl and I don't need looking after."

He shrugged. "I go where I'm paid to. Your boss is concerned about the increase in piracy off the coast of Africa, so our primary job is to get some intel on the local situation. Don't worry, we won't be accompanying you to the ladies' room."

He laughed, but she found his last remark a bit creepy. He was quite a handsome man, but his eyes reminded her of a shark she'd seen on her cruising holiday to Australia, in the Sydney Aquarium—cold, glassy and pitiless. She wondered if he peroxided his hair.

Van Zyl and his men joined her and the captain for dinner that night. The conversation was polite but strained. Jane had become comfortable in the presence of the gruff Captain Iain MacGregor. She imagined him a man of few friends, but the arrival of the new passengers was evidently some cause of concern for him.

"It's young George's money, so he can spend it how he wishes, I suppose," MacGregor said on learning from another of Van Zyl's men, a Russian named Ivan, that their team had flown business class from London to Mombasa.

"You've had no trouble with pirates before?' Van Zyl asked.

MacGregor shook his head and speared a slice of roast beef. "I'm not too worried by gangs of Somali ruffians or petty thieves. This is a big ship."

Van Zyl raised the recent hijacking of the *Oslo Star*, but MacGregor waved off his question. "We're carrying washing machines and farm machinery. Hardly the sort of cargo modern-day buccaneers would salivate over."

Jane had read in the online weekly piracy report that a ship containing building materials and paint had been boarded, as well as another which had lost its cargo of television sets. Perhaps washing machines were exactly what this gang of cutthroat DIYers were after. She smiled to herself.

"You don't seem too worried by all this talk of piracy, miss," said Tyrone, a muscled African-American from Harlem, New York.

"I'm sure the captain knows how to stay out of trouble."

"Aye. Thank you, Jane. And in the unlikely event that anything did happen, I don't imagine they were broomsticks in those long crates you and your men loaded today."

"Tools of the trade," Van Zyl said.

The fifth member of Van Zyl's squad was a redheaded Ulsterman named Billy. He laughed at his boss's cryptic reply. He had a spider's web tattooed on the right side of his neck and when he leered across the table at Jane—not for the first time—she excused herself from the mess. On the way back to her cabin she detoured via the open deck beneath the bridge and leaned on the railing, watching the last golden rays of the sun disappear behind the horizon.

If George had thought the presence of a squad of mercenaries on board would make her feel safer, he was wrong; as a gesture of his concern for her, as his lover, it was too heavy-handed. If he'd dispatched this group of armed men because he was genuinely worried about the possibility of an attack on the *Penfold Son*, then she had cause to worry. But if the men's primary role was to gather information about a band of pirates operating from the coast of Mozambique, then surely it would have been better for them to fly to that country and liaise with the local police or maritime authorities. And why were they so obviously so very heavily armed?

Something smelled wrong to her.

The MV *Peng Cheng* stank like no other vessel he'd been downwind of.

He cut the outboard and let the rigid-hulled inflatable raider coast silently across the black waters toward the freighter, which was using its engines to maintain a stationary position about a kilometer offshore.

"I have a bad feeling about this," Kufa whispered to him.

"Me too. Masks on."

Kufa and the others on board Alex's boat, Novak and Henri, reached into the pouches strapped to their legs and drew out their gas masks. Alex looked across at the other camouflaged boat and saw Mitch, Heinrich and Kevin were doing the same. From both craft came the sound of bullets being chambered in automatic weapons.

"*Merde*," Henri said, screwing his nose in disgust before gratefully covering his face.

"Exactly. It smells of shit. Check comms," Alex said into the radio mouthpiece inside his mask. All of them checked in.

They'd seen the Chinese-registered freighter, the *Peng Cheng*, in the waters of the Mozambique Channel before—many times, in fact. Alex's curiosity about her business had been as aroused as the others," though he was less convinced of the merits of this speculative raid.

Neither democracy nor socialism ruled on the Ilha dos Sonhos. They were all ex-military men, but old ranks meant nothing on the island. Alex commanded this otherwise unruly bunch of brigands by virtue of two reasons. Firstly, the hotel—their lair—was his. At least it was his name on the ninety-nine-year lease from the government. They were there as his guests and, in the case of prying eyes from the mainland, employees. The second reason was that he was a natural leader.

Alex had been taught the theories of leadership in a classroom and had tested them on the field of battle. Here, though, with no code of military justice to make men follow him, or enforce his rules, he led by virtue of who he was.

Sometimes he missed the ability to say, "Just do this because I bloody well told you to." A reliance on rank alone didn't work with these guys, just as it rarely worked in the elite special forces units in which they had all served. With so many alpha males in one workplace, one needed to be a special breed to lead.

But Alex knew his hold was slipping.

It had started with the departure of Danielle and Sarah. While

Mitch had resented the fact that both had spurned his advances in favor of Alex, no one denied that the women had been valuable members of the crew. Alex's concern was that the others might see the women's departure as a vote of no confidence in his leadership. Mitch simply wanted to raid the *Peng Cheng* to see what loot it was carrying, but Alex knew they needed another target to hit soon to keep them focused and coherent as a team. Nevertheless, he'd tried to talk the crew out of Mitch's suggestion that they raid the Chinese freighter.

"She's up to something, man," Mitch had nagged him over drinks at the bar the night after the girls had left. "Drugs? Illegal immigrants? I don't know. She's obviously not a fishing boat and she spends too much time just hanging around off the coast, like she's waiting for a pickup."

Henri lit a cigarette and looked to Alex. "Perhaps the *Peng Cheng* is a spy ship?"

Alex had set his beer down firmly on the wooden bar top, polished smooth by generations of elbows. "The fact that we don't know her business is why we shouldn't raid her. The success of all our ops has been research, intelligence gathering and planning."

"Bullshit. What about the *Fair Lady*?" Mitch stood, ostensibly to reach for another beer behind the counter, but he remained on his feet, putting himself at the center of the seated crowd.

Mitch had been right about the seizing of the vessel Alex claimed as his own. That job had been done with no planning or forethought. They'd come across the *Fair Lady* at night, near the mainland, on their way to intercept a cargo ship bound for Beira. The cruiser was landing people and goods on a deserted beach in the middle of the night. A woman's scream, audible even above the purr of their outboards, had drawn them in. The luxury motor cruiser was running drugs and people—underage girls, as it turned out. Alex and his men had seized the *Fair Lady* and left her crew trussed on the beach. He'd called Captain Alfredo and the local police chief had basked for weeks afterward in the glory of busting the smugglers.

The *Peng Cheng* was up to no good, but then again, so was he. Alex bent to the will of his men, who lusted not for a life of legitimate normalcy but of plunder. Yet even though he was here, out on the water in the dark of the night as they wanted, he felt his hold on them had weakened by having allowed them to convince him.

As they closed on her, Alex noted the ship looked almost as bad as she smelled. Streaks of rust painted her off-white hull, and other stains, the color of raw sewage, oozed from the scuppers.

"What's that noise?" Mitch asked into his radio.

Alex held up a hand for silence. The rasping cough was a chilling memory from childhood visits to the zoo in Lourenço Marques, and bush holidays spent in Gorongosa National Park in Mozambique and Wankie in Southern Rhodesia.

A shriek carried across the calm waters. "That ain't human," Mitch said.

"I don't want to board," Kufa said.

"Shut it. All of you. We all go. Ready the grappling hooks."

Alex looked up as the stern of the *Peng Cheng* loomed large above him. The stench at her foul rear end was even worse. He swung the first of the rubber-coated hooks and it sailed up over the safety railing. It caught with an audible thud, though Alex hoped the noise of the throbbing diesel engines had masked the noise from the bridge.

Alex climbed hand over hand. As always there was the mix of excitement and dread as his hand left the rope and grasped the metal railing. He heaved himself up and over. Nothing. Memories of the brief and bloody encounter with the Norseman on the *Oslo Star* had quickened his pulse rate. He drew his pistol and crouched, covering the others as they clambered aboard. He lifted his mask and smelled smoke above the excrement. He heard voices speaking Chinese. He pointed to the bridge above them, where an Asian face was momentarily illuminated by the flaring tip of a cigarette.

Mitch raised his M4. Alex motioned for the American and the others to follow him.

He crept along the deck and paused when he heard the sawing cough again. Normally they would have gone straight for the bridge, but the two crewmen above, still smoking and savoring the balmy night air, would have seen them in plenty of time to raise the alarm.

"Let's take a look below decks first," he said into his radio. The nods from the men nearest him confirmed they were as curious as he about the *Peng Cheng*'s cargo.

A rusting handle squeaked in protest and Alex paused, making sure no one else had heard, before pulling open the watertight door. They moved silently down the narrow corridor and heard a radio blaring behind a closed hatch. "Crew's quarters. Heinrich, stay here and keep a look out," Alex whispered.

Heinrich nodded. Of all of them, the former GSG9 counterterrorist commando was the least likely to question an order, and Alex wanted someone trustworthy watching their backs.

He pressed on, descending lower into the cargo hold. Scratches and other noises, hard to distinguish over the increased volume of the engines, made him grip the pistol even tighter. His slung rifle dug into his back.

In front of him was a wooden crate, about a meter and a half high by two meters long. Several holes were drilled in the side of it. Alex removed his mask and put it back in its pouch. The others followed suit.

"Fuck, my eyes are watering," Kevin said. "What is that? Cat piss?"

Alex sniffed the ventilation holes in the crate. Kevin was right. He pulled a mini Maglite torch from one of the pouches in his vest and turned it on. Pointing the beam into the hole he knelt and, closing one eye, looked inside. The whole crate shuddered and a snarling, rasping growl from inside made Alex back off. "It's a leopard."

The others had started exploring.

"Hell, there's the biggest bloody python I've ever seen in my life here, man," Novak said.

"Birds," Henri reported. "Parrots. They're crammed into the one cage. This is inhumane."

"Lizards over here," Kufa said. "This ship is evil. We should not have boarded."

"Boss, check this out," Kevin said.

Alex moved around a wire cage containing a pangolin, an African version of the heavily armored armadillo, and found the Australian locked in a staring match with a vervet monkey. The primate started calling in a squeaky, two-part alarm.

"Shut that thing up," Mitch said.

"You want me to kill it?" Kevin raised his pistol, which had a silencer screwed to it.

"No," Alex said. "Scout around, see what else they've got in this floating zoo."

Urine and feces slopped under Alex's boots as he moved through the fetid cargo hold. Mitch whistled softly as he used a crowbar he'd found hanging on a hook to prise open a wooden crate. "Ivory. Maybe a hundred grand's worth. We're taking that."

Alex had seen Mozambique's wildlife before and after the revolution. It sickened him that the international market in animals and their body parts had been responsible for the extinction and decimation of so many species. Now was not the time to get into an argument with Mitch, though. "What else?"

"Dagga. Marijuana, boss," Novak said. "Fifty kgs' worth, at least. Dried. This place isn't just a zoo, it's a bloody goldmine."

Alex stayed away from one sack which was writhing and hissing, but cautiously opened another, which contained three rhino horns. Worth a small fortune to a Chinese herbalist who would grind it up and sell it as a cure for fever, or to an oil-rich Yemeni who would turn the matted hair into a polished handle for his dagger. He shook his head in disgust.

Henri had ventured further ahead. The darting beam of the torch fixed under his rifle barrel announced his return. "*Chef.* The next hold is full of raw timber."

"Illegally felled hardwood, I'll bet," Alex said.

"So what do we do, boss?" Novak said.

Mitch spoke first: "We take this boat and sell the loot, or ransom it back to its owners. There's millions of dollars around us, Alex."

"Sink the fucking thing," Kevin said. "This is just wrong—trading in bloody misery."

"I agree," Kufa said.

"We could take the most valuable items—the tusks and horns and the drugs," Henri ventured. "The crew haven't noticed us yet. We could just leave."

Alex's father had hunted in Mozambique and, later, in Rhodesia when on leave from the army. He'd always imagined growing up that one day his father would take him out into the bush and teach him the skills of tracking and killing. Many times he'd heard his dad rail against the evils of poaching. Later in life he'd pondered the morals of shooting big game in Africa. White men paid to hunt for sport. Black men shot what they believed was theirs, in order to feed themselves and make money.

He knew profiting from the sale of ivory or rhino horn was morally wrong, but he had become a thief, a pirate. Were there degrees of wrongness?

His head told him to leave this foul-smelling hulk at once and go back to the island. His heart told him to do something to save the endangered animals and reptiles on board. The part of his conscience that told him repeatedly that as long as no one was hurt there was nothing truly wrong with stealing goods that were covered by insurance was trying to convince him right now that the proceeds of a few rhino horns and a crate of ivory would allow him to restore a floor of the hotel and finally open for business.

Alex was still weighing his options when he heard the deep rumble of a ship's engines. It wasn't the *Peng Cheng*'s idling diesels, but another vessel. Mitch opened his mouth, but Alex waved him to silence and pointed to the direction of the noise. "Move. Quietly. Let's go topside. It sounds like this tub's rendezvousing with someone else."

Alex led his band back through the stinking hold to the metal stairs that led to clean air above. They collected Heinrich on the way and, once topside, Alex took a few deep breaths then replaced his gas mask to hide his identity in case they were spotted.

They stood at the stern of the *Peng Cheng*, hiding in the shadows as the largest freighter Alex had ever seen blocked their view of the horizon and starry night sky.

"That's the *Penfold Son*," Kevin whispered. "Seen a pic of her in a magazine. What a brute."

Voices in Chinese echoed above them and the *Peng Cheng*'s engines stopped. There was the squawk of radio static and the voice above them turned to English.

"This is *Peng Cheng*, *Peng Cheng*, out of Shanghai. We have no engine power. We are stranded. Can you assist, over?"

Alex motioned with an open palm for his men to stay put and started climbing the stairs to the bridge, to get closer. He heard the faint reply, in a Scottish-accented voice.

"*Peng Cheng*, this is the *Penfold Son*. We can't offer a tow, but I can send my engineering officer down to take a quick look if you wish."

"Affirmative, *Penfold Son*, and very much appreciated."

Jane was having trouble sleeping. She checked the digital clock-radio on her tiny bedside table. Two a.m.

She rolled over and tried to get comfortable, but to no avail. She'd been dreaming about pirates, and being forced to jump overboard at gunpoint from the stern rail of the *Penfold Son*—like being made to walk the plank. There were sharks in the water below.

It was stuffy in the cabin. The air-conditioning had been too cold. It seemed to have been stuck on the highest setting so she'd turned it off. She swung her legs out of bed and swapped her pajamas for a pair of cargo shorts and a T-shirt. She slipped on her sandals. Strictly speaking, passengers were not supposed to be on the open deck at nighttime, for safety reasons, but the first mate had seen her once before taking a stroll in the moonlight and had simply waved and smiled.

She passed the first of the cabins where Van Zyl and his men were quartered, two to a room. There was no noise from inside. If George's hired guns really were supposed to be keeping his flagship safe from pirates, it appeared they were sleeping on the job.

Jane made her way to the hatch leading to the open deck and sighed with relief at the gush of fresh air that greeted her. She walked outside and saw the sky was clear. The full moon was starting its descent toward the western horizon and as its light waned more stars were appearing above. Somewhere out there was the coast of Africa—Mozambique. She thought again about her dream and the increasing incidence of maritime attacks. She shuddered and suddenly experienced the distinct impression that she was not alone. She looked over her shoulder.

There was no one there.

Leaning out over the railing she saw the lights of another ship ahead. She didn't know about the intricacies of navigation at sea, but it looked like Captain MacGregor was heading right toward the other vessel.

"I've been watching her for a while."

Jane gave a start and turned again, and this time saw Piet van Zyl emerging from the shadows. He was dressed in black and wore a matching beanie over his white hair. "Jesus, you nearly gave me a heart attack."

Van Zyl held an overly large pair of binoculars out to her. "Take a look."

She held the glasses to her eyes and saw the lights of the other ship glare like bright green traffic lights against a luminous sea of lime. "Night vision?"

"Yes. The button on top projects an infrared beam, which provides more light. Try it out."

Jane saw the ship's bridge better with the additional invisible light source. She could even make out a man looking back at them. "Cool."

The deck shuddered under their feet. "We're slowing," Van Zyl said.

"I wonder why. Perhaps they're in trouble."

Van Zyl reached for the binoculars and she handed them back. He studied the other vessel again, but didn't reply. Instead, he took the portable radio clipped to his belt and said, "Tyrone, come topside. Bring my gear."

"Your gear? What's going on, Piet, do you think they're pirates?"

He turned to her. "I think it would be best for you to go below now, back to your cabin."

"No way. This is just getting interesting."

"Get back," Alex hissed at Mitch, swinging his arm out to force the American back into the shadows under the overhanging wing of the bridge. He'd taken the night-vision monocular from its pouch on his assault vest and removed his gas mask so he could slip the device's strap over his head. He had scanned the looming bulk of the *Penfold Son*. "Someone up there's also using a starlight scope and they just hit their infrared."

"I never worked on a ship that had night vision," Kevin said. "What do we do now, boss?"

The infrared spotlight was just one more oddity in a night that had been full of them. "There'll be crew looking down. If we move on deck they'll see us. We stay put and see what happens next."

They didn't have long to wait. The *Penfold Son*'s engines changed pitch again and the boat seemed to shudder to a near halt.

The larger freighter gleamed spotlessly white against the contrasting rust and garbage stains that camouflaged the Chinese trader.

A rigid-hulled inflatable boat was swung over the side of the *Penfold Son* and Alex could see three men on board as the ship's rescue craft was lowered to the sea. Once on the water's calm surface the crew started the outboard and cast off. It took them only seconds to bridge the gap between the two ships. A rope ladder was lowered by a Chinese crewman and one man clambered aboard. He wore overalls and carried a canvas hold-all.

"This stinks more than all that animal shit down below," Heinrich said.

"Y'all got that right," Mitch whispered.

"We should go now," Henri said, "drift away while their attention is distracted. No one would see us."

Alex shook his head. "Moon's still too high. We wait."

"Give me the binoculars," Jane said. Van Zyl ignored her, so she said, "Do you know who that man is who just got out of the inflatable boat?"

"No." The South African clearly hadn't had the chance yet to meet all the crew. Reluctantly, he handed the glasses to her.

Jane felt her heart beat faster. Tyrone, the American, was beside her. The black plastic-and-metal rifle looked like a toy in his big gloved hand. Piet, too, was now armed. His weapon was slung over his shoulder and he'd strapped a pistol belt around his waist.

"It's Igor, the chief engineer," she said, handing back the binoculars.

As the company lawyer Jane knew the carriage of firearms and ammunition on board a merchant ship was against the law. She didn't know whether to feel safe or terrified that George had arranged for Van Zyl and his men to smuggle their military-style weapons on board.

"Has the captain stopped to assist any other vessels on this journey?" Van Zyl asked.

"No. I guess they're having mechanical troubles and Igor's gone aboard to try and help out. The *Oslo Star* was hijacked by pirates pretending to have engine trouble."

"I know," Piet said. "I think you should go below now."

"Bollocks. I'm going to the bridge. You can stay here and play soldiers."

Fifteen minutes later the engineer emerged from below decks and walked back to the rope ladder with two Chinese men. One was the crewman who had helped him aboard. The other was an older man, dressed in shorts and a grubby white short-sleeved shirt. Alex thought it might be the captain. He shook hands with the European who, clutching his bag, swung over the rail and descended the ladder.

Once the inflatable boat was secured on board, the *Penfold Son* increased speed and pulled away from the poor excuse for a freighter. They felt the *Peng Cheng* start to move. She was turning toward shore and the other ship was fast disappearing to the south. "Listen in," Alex said, and all eyes turned to him as he gave his orders.

6

Alex sat on top of the wooden crate containing the captured leopard. The timbers vibrated beneath him from the noise of the big cat's rasping cough. In front of him was the captain of the *Peng Cheng*, dressed only in a pair of holey underpants and sitting on a dining chair, his hands and ankles securely bound.

"Last chance, Captain Wu." They'd succeeded in getting his name out of him, but not much else. Alex guessed that the man and his crew were more scared of their Triad masters than they were of anything the pirates could do to them. He was about to put that to the test.

Alex checked his watch. It was only a little more than thirty minutes since the *Penfold Son* had sailed away. He and his men had taken the *Peng Cheng* without a shot being fired, even though they had found AK-47s, pistols and even a crate of Chinese People's Liberation Army hand grenades in the bridge's well-stocked armory. The captain had claimed the grenades were for fishing in coastal lagoons. Given the man's disregard for wildlife, Alex almost believed him.

"It was a drop-off, wasn't it? Either you gave the engineer from the *Penfold Son* something, or he gave you something. Which was it?"

Wu, whose English was basic, had stuck to his story that the *Peng Cheng* was experiencing engine trouble and an officer from the other ship had come aboard to rectify the problem.

They'd hit the bridge hard, just minutes after the exchange had been made, but they'd found nothing of particular value or significance. When Alex had threatened to blow the ship's safe, Wu had opened it for him. Inside were ten thousand U.S. dollars, the equivalent value in rand and the ship's papers. It didn't seem enough cash for a mid-ocean criminal deal.

"I was on board before you slowed down, Wu. I know you didn't have a problem with your engines. Last chance." Alex wound the length of rope around his hand and started to heave upward, raising the trapdoor that closed the crate by a few centimeters.

Captain Wu looked down at the gap and saw a white furred paw patterned with black rosettes reach out. Yellowed claws protruded and made an agonizing screeching noise as they scratched the steel deck. The leopard snarled in anticipation and rocked the crate as it twitched its tail left and right and lowered itself to escape.

"Barbarian," Wu said.

"That's rich coming from you. This animal deserves a crack at you after the way it and the others have been treated. Say hello to the nice kitty, Captain . . ."

"OK. There was drop-off, but I not know what."

Alex gripped the rope with his other hand and began to heave. "Last chance, Captain."

A puddle appeared on the deck beneath Wu's chair, but any odor was masked by the foulness of the other fluids and solids that sluiced around the deck. "I not know! Small package. It worth one million pounds, that all I know," the Chinese man squealed.

"What?"

Wu swore in Mandarin. "One million. But small package. I not know. Diamonds maybe."

Alex held the trapdoor in place. The leopard had withdrawn its paw, though its snarling snout was now just visible as it sniffed Wu's fear with relish. "More information."

"My boss and *Penfold Son*'s boss, they trade sometime. They do business. Man come on board from other ship. I give him package. Not worth my life to check what in package."

Alex looked into Wu's eyes, trying to read him. "The man who came aboard, he gave you a million pounds?"

Wu shook his head vigorously. "No cash. That the truth. You pull this ship apart you not find any money other than what I keep in safe. My boss, his boss, they not operate like that. Money transferred to international bank account."

Alex raised the trapdoor another few centimeters. Wu yelped. "Is truth!"

Alex believed him. "What about you? What do you get out of this?"

The captain shrugged. "I get my fee when I get back to China."

Alex lowered the cage door. "If I didn't care for all these animals and reptiles, I'd scuttle this scow with you on board." He slid down from the top of the crate and, leaving Captain Wu to sit in his own filth, headed for topside and fresh air.

"All the crew are tied up in the officers' mess, boss. And a bloody mess it is too," Kevin said when Alex entered the bridge.

"Can you steer this tub by yourself, Kev?"

"Piece of piss," the Australian replied. He was the most experienced mariner in the group.

"I'll take that as a yes. The rest of you get ready to disembark. Back to the boats. Heinrich, call Jose and get the *Fair Lady* to meet us ASAP. We've got work to do."

"What kind of work?" Mitch asked.

Alex watched the looks of disappointment and fatigue vanish from their faces when he said, "Diamonds."

•   •   •

Kobus van Vuuren owed Alex Tremain his life, which is why he had left the Swedish backpacker snoring in his bed in the coastal Mozambican town of Vilanculos and driven with a hangover that would have killed a lesser man to the airport where he kept his helicopter.

A year earlier his last machine—a Russian-made Mi-8 identical to the one he piloted low over the Indian Ocean now—had suffered engine failure. He'd been on his way back from taking some French wildlife researchers—female, of course—whale spotting from the air. Kobus had auto-rotated but the landing had still been hard. He'd dragged one of the girls unconscious from the wreckage, while the other had struggled to inflate the emergency life raft. In keeping with the reliability of the rest of the machine, the raft's gas bottle wouldn't work.

As they trod water, the weight of the injured passenger sapping his strength by the minute, Kobus had replayed his life before his mind's eye. There were the wars—South-West Africa and Angola with the South African Defense Force, and the Congo and Sierra Leone in the payment of others—the women—many nationalities, many combinations, two wives—and his children—four that he knew of. It had been an interesting life, and he didn't quite feel ready to wave it all goodbye yet.

A spot on the horizon was getting larger. He'd assumed it was a mirage and hadn't even told the two Frenchwomen, but when he'd heard the rhythmic throb of the engines he'd started yelling. They had joined in, and been waving frantically when the luxurious motor cruiser pulled alongside.

Kobus had known from the moment strong, tattooed arms lifted him and the women aboard that the owner's story was bullshit. Alex Tremain had claimed he was running fishing charters and the mixed bag of nationalities aboard were all tourists. For a start, Kobus noticed only two lightweight rods amidst the bulging green vinyl military dive bags on the deck. The men had the hardened bodies, cold eyes and erect bearing of soldiers. He'd been a military man and mercenary long enough to spot one in a crowd.

"How can I thank you—repay you?" he'd asked Alex Tremain over a cold Castle Lager on the bridge, marveling at the array of computerized navigation systems. There were even cameras mounted around the boat and in the engine room, and their images flashed on a small screen in front of them. The galley was better appointed than his first wife's mansion in Sandton. The sofas were leather, the bedrooms luxurious, and there was even a jacuzzi on the rear deck which the French girls expressed a desire to try out.

"Think nothing of it," Alex had replied.

"If you ever need to charter a helicopter for any business—and I mean *any* business—come see me. I owe you one."

And here he was, hovering above the same sleek craft that had given him another chance at life. Tremain stood on the rear deck of the cruiser, dressed in a flight suit and festooned with weaponry. The call on his satellite phone had been short on detail. "I want to collect on that debt you owe me," Tremain had said. "Have you got a winch on your helo that you can operate from the cockpit?"

"Yes."

"Bring enough rope for seven men to rappel from twenty meters. Full tanks." He'd signed off with a GPS coordinate that Kobus knew without checking was somewhere in the Indian Ocean.

Kobus's satellite phone buzzed in his pocket. Answering it was a tricky business as he needed two hands to fly, but he'd wired it into his on-board system, so with a push of a button he could hear the voice in his earphones. The fact they weren't using radio confirmed his suspicion that this was a charter Tremain wanted to keep silent.

"Lower the winch," said a curt German-accented voice on the other end.

Another man stood by Alex Tremain—Kobus couldn't remember his name—holding a pole shaped like a shepherd's crook, secured to the boat with a length of cable. This was a static probe, designed to catch the hook on the end of the winch cable and discharge the significant amount of static electricity that had built up around the helicopter during the flight. It was more proof—not that he needed it—that these men were professionals.

Kobus held the lumbering military-designed cargo chopper steady and punched the button to retrieve the winch line and raise Alex. It would have been easier with a crewman on board, but Tremain had also specified that he fly alone. Tremain climbed inside the cargo compartment and took off the winch sling. He clapped Kobus on the shoulder and said, "Thanks for coming."

"What's the target?" Kobus yelled over the whine of the engines.

Tremain pulled a piece of paper from the pocket of his flight suit and showed him. It was a print-out from a website, a picture of a ship. The *Penfold Son*. Kobus just nodded.

Jane was bored again.

The small blip of excitement in the early hours—the rendering of assistance to the Chinese freighter—was hardly worth remembering now. She stood on the bridge next to Iain MacGregor, looking out over miles of sparkling blue nothingness. "Coffee?" she asked the captain.

"No thanks."

Jane unscrewed the lid of her wide-mouthed travel thermos and poured into a cup some of the delicious strong black coffee the Filipino cook had brewed for her. The coffee, she had decided, was the best thing served from the galley. She'd grown tired of greasy bacon and eggs for breakfast and bland roasts and three veg. She replaced the cap, sipped her brew and said, "Do you normally stop for broken-down vessels?"

"Depends," MacGregor said, looking out to sea, not at her. "On how far they are from a coastal port with rescue facilities. Those chaps were a fair way out to sea, and it's a pretty remote coastline along that stretch of Mozambique."

Jane nodded. "I think Piet thought they were pirates lying in wait."

The captain harrumphed.

"Aircraft on the radar screen, sir, astern of us," said the first mate.

MacGregor edged around Jane to look at the screen. "He's low. Keep an eye on him. Could be a joy-flight."

Jane picked up a pair of large binoculars lying on the instrumentation panel and wandered across to the port wing of the bridge. With nothing else to look at, an aircraft was a treat. She'd long since lost her sense of wonder at the sight of dolphins riding the bow wave, or the occasional passing whale, as impressive as they were.

She held a hand to her eyes to shield them from the sun's glare and finally made out a dark speck just above the horizon. She lifted the binoculars and focused them. "It's a helicopter."

MacGregor snatched the glasses from her. She stepped back and watched him.

"Mi-8. Russian job. What's he doing so damned low over the ocean?"

"Coming to take a look at us?" Jane ventured.

He stared at her and seemed to swallow a retort. "Turn port ninety!" he said to the first mate.

"Turning port ninety, Captain."

"He's changed course," MacGregor said, as much to himself as anyone else as he continued to watch the helicopter.

It was over them a few seconds later, hovering above the cargo deck like an enormous dragonfly, its fuselage blocking the light.

"Sound the alarm," the captain said to the mate.

Jane stood transfixed. The tips of the main rotor's blades sliced the air a scant few meters from her, beyond the thick armored glass of the bridge's windows. She could see a pilot in dark glasses and a bulbous green flying helmet that made him look more a part of the machine than a human. A door slid open in the rear compartment on the side closest to her. Men in black rubber gas masks with buglike clear plastic eyepieces were tossing out thick ropes and sliding down them.

She knew she should run, but something kept her riveted to the spot, trying to take in what was going on. Perhaps it was some kind of counterterrorist drill that she'd been kept in the dark about, a bizarre notion of George's designed to impress her. Then a man in the back of the helicopter lifted his machine gun, pointed it at her and pulled the trigger.

Jane dropped to the floor as bullets thudded into the panes above her. She screamed.

"It's too thick." MacGregor crawled across the deck and reached up for the GMDSS keyboard. He hit F8 for setup, selected "Piracy or Armed Attack," then punched the "transmit" key.

"Iain, we've got to—"

"Quiet, lassie," he said to her, his voice oddly calm and soothing, given the circumstances. The whine of the helicopter's engines was vibrating the bullet-scarred portholes above them. "I want you to do something for me, Jane."

"What?" All she wanted to do right now was run.

MacGregor crawled to a line of cabinets beneath a benchtop that ran along most of the rear wall of the bridge. Jane knew there was a small fridge behind one of the laminated doors, as she'd seen the mate take milk for the captain's tea from there. MacGregor went to the next door along from the refrigerator and opened it, still kneeling. He punched the combination into an electronic safe. The door swung open and he reached in and pulled out a padded envelope encased in a clear plastic waterproof wrapping, and Jane's passport.

"You're young George's girl, aren't you?"

Despite the commotion outside she was mildly offended and somewhat surprised by the captain's question. "His girlfriend," he said, in case she hadn't understood.

"I . . ."

He seemed to lose patience with her then and crawled to where she had left her thermos flask, near the helm. He unscrewed the lid, spilling half of the remaining coffee onto the bridge's carpet in the process. He scrunched the envelope and thrust it into the wide mouth of the container, spilling even more liquid, then screwed it shut again. "This belongs to young George. Guard it with your life. It's what these buggers have come for. I'm afraid we've been double-crossed."

"What are you talking about?"

The captain ignored her for the moment, snatching up the small day pack Jane had brought with her and zipping the flask and her passport inside it. "Put this on, head out the back to the stern and find a lifeboat. You remember how to release the boat, from the drills?"

She nodded. Somewhere outside someone was shooting again. MacGregor reached up and opened the door.

"Good girl," he said. "If they capture the ship, you'll be better off adrift in the lifeboat. There're rations and water on board. Run!" he ordered her.

Jane slipped on the day pack, stood and stumbled out the hatch and down the narrow corridor past the captain's cabin and the ship's office. As she reached the top of the stairs, which led to the rear deck below, her way was blocked by Van Zyl. He carried a rifle in addition to the pistol strapped around his waist. "Where's MacGregor?"

"On the bridge," she said. "What's happening?"

"That's what I'm going to bloody well find out. Where are you going?"

"Lifeboat. Captain said it was best."

Van Zyl nodded. "Don't let these bastards take you alive. Here, take this." He drew the pistol from the holster slung low on his right thigh. He cocked it and handed it to her.

"Oh, fuck," she said. "I want to be bored again."

He smiled and clapped her on the arm. "If they're Somalis you'll die of AIDS once they've finished with you—if they don't kill you themselves."

Jane took the stairs three at a time.

Piet van Zyl had wanted to scare the girl, to get her out of his way. It was clear he'd succeeded, though there was no way these men were like the pirates who worked the coasts of Africa and Asia. They were men like him—professionals.

He could see the rear door that led to the bridge was swinging closed. He hit it with his booted foot and heard someone reel backward in shock and pain.

MacGregor sat sprawled on the carpet, holding a revolver, which he pointed at Van Zyl.

"Put that down," the South African said. The captain lowered the weapon. "What do they want, MacGregor?"

"How the hell should I know? There's a whole ship full of stuff for them to choose from."

Van Zyl took a pace closer to the captain and held out a hand, as though offering to raise the older man to his feet. As MacGregor reached out, Van Zyl grabbed his hand, then snatched the pistol from his other hand. Before the Scotsman could protest Van Zyl raised his knee and caught him under the chin. The captain's head snapped back and hit the deck.

"I said, what do they want?" Van Zyl knelt on MacGregor's chest and thrust the captain's pistol hard into the soft skin under his jaw. He pulled back the hammer. "Tell me what's going on, quickly. You've got a revolver, even though you're not supposed to be carrying one; and Penfold organized for us to come on board with weapons and ammo. What was he expecting?"

"You don't know, do you?" MacGregor gasped, fighting for breath.

"I wouldn't be bloody well asking you if I did."

"I thought George Penfold hired you as extra security. Fat lot of good it's done if he did."

A voice hissed in the radio earpiece in Van Zyl's ear.

"That was one of my men," he told the captain. "There are at least six of them on board now." They both paused as gunshots clanged off the metal plating outside in quick succession. The helicopter peeled away over the bow, chased by bursts of automatic gunfire from Van

Zyl's men. It skimmed low over the Indian Ocean. Van Zyl looked around the bridge and noticed the open safe. "What was in there?"

MacGregor shook his head. "Bugger off. If George hasn't told you then he doesn't want you to know."

Van Zyl thought of the encounter with the Chinese freighter in the night, and then of the girl running toward him. She was wearing a day pack. What could she have that was so valuable she couldn't leave without it during a full-scale assault by pirates? Van Zyl jabbed the barrel harder into MacGregor's skin and the captain gave a yelp.

"What was in the safe?" Van Zyl pushed the barrel of the pistol harder into the captain's neck.

MacGregor hesitated, then said, "I don't know."

"What did you do with it?"

"Fuck off," MacGregor spat.

There was the sound of footsteps coming from the hallway and several bursts of gunfire. Van Zyl looked to the hatch and the speed and force of the older man's punch took the South African by surprise. MacGregor jabbed two knuckles into Van Zyl's windpipe and knocked his gun hand away. Van Zyl emitted a strangled cry as the captain delivered a Glasgow kiss, his forehead painfully squashing Van Zyl's nose.

Tyrone Washington burst into the bridge, his M4 carbine raised and ready. The former Force Recon Marine saw his commander on his knees with blood on his face and the other man raising a pistol. He fired twice and both bullets found their mark—one in MacGregor's right lung, the other in his heart.

Alex tried to shake the image of the girl from his mind, but he saw her again, wide-eyed, falling to the deck as he sprayed the armored glass windows of the bridge with the MP5. He was sure the nine-millimeter rounds from the machine pistol wouldn't penetrate and he'd deliberately fired high, but he still wasn't sure he hadn't killed her.

"*Two more amidships,*" Novak said into his radio, the report punc-

tuated with two shots in quick succession—a double tap. The South
African was conserving ammunition.

"All call signs, Alpha Fire Team's taking the bridge," Alex said
into his radio. "Henri, Heinrich, with me," he said to the men pressed
against the bulkhead next to him. "Bravo Team give covering fire.
Standby, standby . . . go!"

Alex charged up the stairs to the locked bridge door and slapped
the charge against the lock and armed the detonator.

The door blew inward and Alex ran to the opening again and
lobbed in a smoke grenade. As he entered he saw a green orb rolling
along the carpeted deck toward him. "Grenade! Back!"

He turned and dived, landing hard on Henri, who toppled back
into Heinrich, who had been ascending the stairs close behind him.
The three men hit the unforgiving metal deck hard as the hand grenade exploded above them.

"Holy fuck," Alex said, extricating himself from the pile of bodies. "You two OK?"

Henri and Heinrich nodded. Alex had slung the MP5 and now
held his Steyr out in front of him. "We're going to the stern. This is
war, boys." It was now clear to him they were up against a professional,
well-armed security force. Not only was Bravo Team taking accurate
fire from automatic weapons, but the bastards even had explosives. He
guessed the added muscle was on board because of the diamond pickup. Rather than considering abandoning the ship, the prospect of a
fight made him want the stones even more.

Alex and his team were edging down the starboard side of the
Penfold Son, one deck below the bridge. Novak, Mitch and Kufa were
on the port side, also working their way slowly toward the rear of
the ship. Kevin, the most qualified seaman among them, was on the
Peng Cheng. With the crew locked in the officers' mess, he was piloting
the ship single-handedly to the Ilha dos Sonhos. Alex regretted being
one man down.

The helicopter had started taking fire as the last man's feet touched the *Penfold Son*'s deck. Alex and his men had found half a dozen AK-47s and a pistol on board the *Peng Cheng* and, since the *Penfold Son* was involved in some sort of smuggling operation, Alex had thought it possible that the bigger ship might also be carrying an illegal weapon or two. What the pirates hadn't expected, however, was the presence of a small, well-equipped army.

Alex poked his head around a corner and then ducked back when he saw a man dressed in black T-shirt and trousers raise an M4 assault rifle. Rounds ricocheted off steel and zipped out over the ocean. Alex pulled the pin on his second-last stun grenade and tossed it. The effect would be diminished in an open space, but all he wanted was to make the man duck. As he heard the bang and saw the visible shock wave roll in front of him, Alex dived to the deck and crawled forward. He looked up and saw the man was on his knees, one hand covering his eyes, temporarily blinded by the searing light. Alex aimed and squeezed the trigger twice. The man had been trying to kill him a few seconds earlier. He felt no remorse as he saw the first of his shots punch the man in the chest and knock him backward over the railing, into the sea somewhere far below. "Move!"

Heinrich and Henri were close behind him as he rounded the superstructure. "Splash one," Alex said into his radio.

"That only leaves about another four or five guys with guns," Mitch replied. "There's two forward of us, so we can't go that-away."

"RV with us at the stern," Alex said. "Watch you don't shoot us, though." Alex guessed the ship's crew must have locked themselves away somewhere safe once the shooting started.

"Did you get to the bridge?" Mitch asked.

"Negative. They had it booby-trapped. That was the grenade going off. They must have the stones with them."

"This is turning to shit."

Much as it pained him, Alex knew Mitch was right.

"Alex, above!"

Alex turned at the sound of Henri's warning and looked up to see the flash of a muzzle and an arcing rain of spent brass cartridges. A black man was firing down on them with his assault rifle. Henri was returning fire, but as Alex lifted his rifle to join in the fusillade he saw the orb sailing down toward them.

"Grenade!" Heinrich shouted as he pushed Alex forward. The German then shoved Henri out of the path of the device. The man above them had ducked back into cover. Heinrich lashed out with his boot, trying to kick the grenade to the far end of the deck. He made contact, but the metal canister was spinning too much to move far enough away from them. Heinrich turned and ran after Alex and Henri. The grenade's explosive force threw the big German into Henri, who in turn landed hard against Alex. For the second time the three of them lay in disarray. Not all of them made it to their feet.

"Heinrich," Alex said, leaning his masked face close to the German's. He rolled the other man's body over and saw dozens of smoking holes on the backs of his legs and arms. Fortunately he'd been wearing his body armor vest, like the rest of them. "Give me a hand," Alex said to Henri. They each hooked a hand under Heinrich's armpits and dragged their barely conscious comrade between them.

"They're pushing us back," Mitch said into Alex's earpiece. "We're coming your way, ready or not."

"Lifeboat at the stern," Alex said, seeing the bright orange craft ahead of them. The hatch in the boat's stern was already open. Alex looked to his right and saw Mitch, Kufa and Novak running toward them, their boots thumping the deck.

The fully enclosed freefall lifeboat could seat forty people—more than the entire crew of the *Penfold Son* and any passengers. Rather than hanging from davits it sat in a cradle of white tubular steel that protruded out over the stern of the ship and pointed down at an angle toward the sea.

"Need a hand?" Mitch asked as he reached Alex and Henri, who were still dragging Heinrich between them.

"No."

Mitch nodded and started heading for the lifeboat.

"Wait!" Alex shouted. The hatch shouldn't have been opened. "Mitch, check the . . ."

The blonde-haired woman Alex had seen on the bridge stood in the open hatch and raised a pistol. The weapon seemed too big for her small hands. She squeezed the trigger and Mitch toppled back onto the deck. Alex let go of Heinrich, unclipped his last flash-bang, pulled the pin and tossed it straight at the woman. He charged forward, rifle at the ready, as she ducked to avoid the missile thrown at her.

Alex had one man injured and bleeding on the deck and another had just been shot in front of his eyes. His concern for the woman was gone. His finger curled around the plastic trigger of the Steyr. His mask and flame-retardant flight suit would protect him from the effects of the stun grenade, but if the woman was in any fit state to point a gun at him, he would kill her. His pulse beat loud and hard in his ears as he closed the gap to the lifeboat.

Then he saw her again. She had turned, trying to escape the grenade, and it went off in her face. The force of the blast pitched her backward into him as he reached the lifeboat. Instinctively, he lowered his rifle and reached for her, wrapping his arms around her to stop her from hitting the deck.

Bullets clanged on the bulkhead beside him. He pushed the girl back into the lifeboat and wheeled, raising the Steyr again as he did so, and pulled hard on the trigger. He sprayed a long burst of bullets, emptying the magazine in the direction of the fire, several decks above.

"Hold your fire! They've got the girl on board that boat and she's got the stuff," an unseen voice called.

That was their cue. "Get aboard," Alex roared at his men. He grabbed Mitch by the front of his vest and heaved the motionless American into the lifeboat. He stood by in the open hatch and reached for Heinrich, now staggering, and hauled him inside. Kufa and Novak followed, and Henri was still firing his M4 from the open hatch while Alex and the others strapped the unconscious woman and the two injured pirates into forward-facing seats. Henri slammed the hatch shut and was in his seat, pulling his lap and shoulder straps tight. "Head restraints!" Alex reminded them. He lifted the woman's chin from her chest and fastened a Velcro band from the seat's head-rest around her forehead. Kevin did the same for the injured and dazed Heinrich. Without the head restraints on they might snap their necks when the boat hit the water. Alex removed the safety pins from the arming device. "Ready?"

"*Oui!*"

Alex pumped the release lever, causing a hydraulic jack to begin lifting the stern of the lifeboat. The boat was held to the ship by a hook, and when the jack lifted the hook high enough the boat disengaged and they were free.

"Brace!" Alex yelled as the boat whooshed down its rails. They fell twenty meters and the force of the collision with the water slammed them forward against their restraints. The sharply profiled bow of the lifeboat had been designed to cleave through the water on impact and even before Alex had freed himself from his seat the craft was already well clear of the *Penfold Son* and still moving.

"Get the engine started," Alex said to Novak.

"What about her?" Henri asked, pointing at the woman, who was still unconscious, strapped into her seat.

"They won't shoot at us now, because of her, but they'll be coming after us."

Novak slapped a fresh magazine into his rifle and cocked it. "Let's put a lifejacket on her and dump her."

"No," Alex said. "We keep her for now. Maybe we can ransom her."

He pulled the satphone from its pouch and dialed Jose, on the *Fair Lady*. Alex gave him their position from the GPS in his watch and told him to come fetch them, quickly. They needed to put as much distance between themselves and the *Penfold Son* as possible before World War Three broke out.

7

Jane awoke to the sound of power tools.

She tried to open her eyes, but even that small movement caused her pain. Keeping them closed, she gingerly lifted a hand and found the source of the throbbing—a lump the size of an egg on the side of her head.

She blinked and saw a snowy white ceiling with soft recessed lighting. Perhaps it was all a dream—or a nightmare. But then where had the bump come from?

Her head was engulfed by a downy pillow in a starched white pillowcase. The sheets she lay on felt luxuriously textured against her skin. She was wearing a T-shirt—a long one—and briefs. She raised her head. More pain. The dark teak writing desk and chair beneath a long mirror looked like they belonged in a hotel suite. Not a lifeboat, that was for sure.

The noise brought more aching. It was a high-pitched, continuous whine. She breathed a sigh of relief when the drilling stopped. It was dark in the room as the curtains were drawn and the lights dimmed, though she could see a tiny chink of sun. Before the mechanical whine resumed she heard a bird, a seagull she thought.

Jane started to sit up, but the movement made her feel queasy, as well as bringing on another sharp stab of agony. On the bedside table, which matched the other furniture, she could see a dewy glass of water and a bottle of something called "Panado" which she hoped was paracetamol. She fought back the sickness and sat up. Her need for relief was too great. Her feet touched ribbed, camel-colored carpet. It felt like the expensive stuff in George's city flat.

George.

He would be worried about her. Jane was worried about herself too. She unscrewed the childproof cap and shook out a couple of capsules. She hesitated for a second then told herself that if someone wanted to kill her they would have done so already. Gulping down the pills and water made her feel better.

Jane padded across to a door and tested it. It was unlocked. She let herself into an adjoining sitting room. A sofa bed was unfolded, though made. There was a coffee percolator on a benchtop recessed into one wall. She opened the bar fridge beneath it and saw it was stacked with spirits, mixers and a jug of milk. The drill resumed torturing the inside of her skull and she flinched, spilling a little of the milk as the silver jug rattled against the fine china cup.

She held the cup in both hands. There were Impressionist prints on the wall and dried stems of something exotic in a terracotta amphora. Carved wooden elephants in one corner and a funky ethnic African print on the discarded sofa cushions contrasted with the latest model wide-screen plasma TV and slimline DVD recorder. Looking up and around she saw surround-sound speakers mounted on the walls.

She remembered pulling the trigger, the pistol bucking in her hands. She saw the face of the man—the shock and surprise as he keeled over backward. Then the blinding flash and deafening bang. And falling. Perhaps she'd died and gone to heaven. She'd once said to a friend that her idea of heaven would be a five-star resort with room service for eternity. If the door to the bathroom revealed a jacuzzi, miniature bottles of body oils and Moët on ice, then she'd know she was dead.

Jane moved to the curtains and parted them. She took a breath. The expanse of azure ocean, strip of wedding-white beach and garnish of palm trees were so perfect they could have been lifted from a Photoshopped travel brochure. A black fisherman in a tattered straw hat was hauling a canoe piled with nets up the sand.

She looked around her and returned to the bedroom, but she couldn't find any of her clothes. The baggy T-shirt was green. Embroidered above the left breast were a pair of black British Army parachute wings with the Roman numerals for the number three above them. Her father had retired as a major in the Blues and Royals so she knew a bit about military emblems. Odd. Acutely aware that she was naked under the shirt, she nonetheless had to find out where she was, and how she'd got there. She put down the half-drunk cup of coffee on a glass-topped table and opened the door.

In one step she went from penthouse to building site. The long corridor before her was bare concrete fogged with white dust. Electricity wires dangled from the ceiling. Barefoot, she wove her way carefully between offcuts of timber, chunks of masonry and lengths of water pipe and plastic conduit. The source of the cacophony was two doors down. She edged her way around a wheelbarrow stacked with bags of plaster and peered through the doorless entry.

The man was beautiful.

It was wrong, she supposed, to describe a guy that way, but that was her first impression. The black wavy hair, a little speckled with white dust, was too long and thick. The nose was too aquiline, the jaw too smooth. The muscles in the tight blue T-shirt were too perfectly defined, the bare skin of the arms and legs too perfectly tanned. He smiled at her, letting his finger off the drill switch as he turned, bringing silence to the room. The teeth were too perfect, the eyes too green. A canvas belt full of other tools hung from his narrow waist. It was only when he raised his left hand, to brush a lock of hair from his forehead, that he revealed his first physical imperfection, which snapped her from her reverie and reminded her she wasn't dead. Two fingers were missing and the skin on top of his hand was purpled and scarred.

"Good morning. Or should I say," looking at his watch, "good afternoon."

She tried to form the obvious questions—where am I? how did I get here?—but the words wouldn't come out. Her mouth felt as though it was full of some sticky, gelatinous substance. She felt dizzy and reached for the doorframe.

He covered the distance between them in a lion's bound, leaping over a stacked heap of white plasterboard, and caught her around the waist as she sagged. He moved her to the pile of sheeting and sat her down. She put her palms out on either side of her and tried to breathe slowly, letting the nausea subside. "Wait here," he said to her.

He returned with her coffee and a fresh glass of water. "You've had a concussion—quite a serious knock. Feeling woozy's normal."

His accent was English, though there was a hint of something else. He'd pronounced quite as *kwaart*. South African? And his skin was olive, like a Spaniard perhaps. Now that she was closer to him she could see the left side of his jaw and neck were marred by some faint pitting, like old acne scars. However the blemishing didn't extend to the other side of his face. It seemed he was perfect on one side of his body only. Human, after all, she realized. "Ta," she said as she downed half the water and returned to her coffee. "Where am I?"

"Ilha dos Sonhos. The Island of Dreams."

"Bollocks. Is this a dream?"

"No, I'm serious. We're off the coast of Mozambique, not far from Vilanculos. Do you know it?"

She shook her head. The coffee was good. "How did I get here?"

"One of my guys—one of the staff here—was out fishing and he saw an orange lifeboat on the horizon. He rowed to it and you were inside, unconscious. Badly dehydrated, too. Check your arm."

She looked down and for the first time noticed a sticky plaster in the crook of her arm. She peeled it off and saw the swollen puncture. She started to panic, and it must have shown in her eyes, because he said, "Don't worry, it was only a saline drip. One of the guys is a trained medic and it pays to be self-sufficient when it comes to health care out here. The hospital's a boat ride away and I'm afraid not quite up to scratch."

"Um, thanks. I suppose."

"You're welcome. The lifeboat said *Penfold Son*."

She switched to the water. She was incredibly thirsty, she realized, so he must have been right about her being dehydrated. "Pirates."

"What?"

"We were attacked by pirates, from a helicopter."

He smiled and collected her empty glass. "I think that knock on your head might have done you more damage than we thought."

She thought his glance might have lingered a little too long on her bare legs. She pulled the T-shirt lower. "It's true. I remember it all—well, most of it." Something else came back to her, like someone switching on a light in a darkened room, revealing an item she hadn't realized she'd misplaced. "Um, did I have a bag—a day pack—with me?"

"Yes. There was a bit of seawater and some other muck in the bottom of the lifeboat. My maid took your bag and your clothes and washed them. They're drying in the garden. By the way, Maria undressed and dressed you, not me."

"Thank you. I'm sorry, I know I should be more grateful, but this is all so bizarre."

"You're telling me. It's not every day a beautiful woman fetches up on my beach."

She felt herself blush at the naked compliment. "I'm Jane—"

"—Elizabeth Humphries. I know. I saw your passport. I wanted to wait and see if you remembered who you were. I'm Alex Tremain."

"You said 'my beach.' Do you own a whole island?"

He laughed. "No, only this hotel, and it's a long-term lease, from the Mozambican government. I grew up here. My parents owned it in the old days, during colonial times. The locals are happy for a few of us with claims on property and farms to come back and get them up and running again. I'm sorry about this," he hefted the drill, "I waited as long as I could, but we've got a span of work to do here."

"I take it that means a lot. Are you Portuguese? South African?"

"Half English, half Portuguese, and I grew up in Rhodesia—Zimbabwe to you. My first name's actually Alexandre."

"I like that better than Alex," she said. Why the hell had she said that? He smiled and she blushed again. Somewhere far off she could hear another tool running continuously, buzzing away in the background. Then it stopped.

Alex lifted his drill and pressed the trigger, but it made no sound. "Hell," he said. "Damned generator's broken again, I'll bet. My mechanic left a week ago and everything's breaking down."

"You must miss him, being stuck on an island."

"Her. And you're right, I do. I miss her a lot. I don't suppose you're any good with diesel engines, are you?"

"I'm a lawyer. Look, sorry . . . Alex, but I've got to call London immediately."

He shrugged. "No generator, no power. No power, no satellite. No satellite, no phone."

"You must have batteries, or solar, or something?"

"All on the blink, or dead, I'm afraid. We're supposedly getting a mechanic to visit tomorrow. I've got to fetch him from the mainland, so you can come with me if you like. You can call from town."

"Let's go now—today. I really can't wait. I have to be in Johannesburg in . . . What day is it today?"

"You tell me. I think you might be a bit groggy still."

"I'm fine. How long was I unconscious for?"

"About twenty-four hours. I was getting worried about you."

"Then today's Tuesday. I've got to be in Johannesburg by next Monday. I've got a train trip booked from Cape Town."

"Well, you're an awful long way from Cape Town. Is that where your ship was headed?"

She nodded, and the egg on her head hurt some more. "If I go with you to the mainland, how long would it take me to get to Johannesburg?"

"Couple of hours by plane from Vilanculos. When the power's back on you can try calling Pelican Airways. I have to go to Johannesburg myself some time in the next week or so, on business. We could go together if you like."

"I don't fly. What about a train?" She hated admitting her fears to anyone.

"There isn't one. You could try the local buses, but if you don't like traveling with chickens and goats I'd swallow my fear and fly if I were you."

"It's not funny. I don't fly."

He nodded. "Sorry. I understand. I could drive you."

He explained the journey to her in more detail. He proposed cutting across Mozambique from the coast, heading northwest to the border with Zimbabwe. From there they would head west, then south, crossing into South Africa at Beitbridge on the Limpopo River. From there, he said, it was less than a day's drive to Johannesburg. They could make it in three days, which meant if they left Thursday, she could be in the city by the weekend, in time for her meeting on Monday.

She desperately needed to call George. He would be worried sick about her, but she eventually conceded that Alex was right and she would have to wait until she got to the mainland to call him. She tried asking him if he could bring his trip forward to today, but he said some work was being done on the hull of his boat. It was frustrating.

"Cheer up. There are worse places to be stuck. I'll show you around the island if you're up to it."

"Thanks, Alex. Look, I'm sorry. You must think I'm behaving

like a spoiled city girl. I haven't even said thank you for rescuing me. It's all been a bit of a shock to the system."

A shock was what it was, all right, Alex thought as he walked downstairs, leaving Jane to change. Maria had finished ironing her clothes and had delivered them and some other things Danielle and Sarah had left behind to his room while they were chatting. He'd planned on giving the leftover skirts and blouses both women had collected during their months in Mozambique to the ladies in the small village on the island, but hadn't got around to it yet.

He stepped over beams and around piles of tiles and cans of paint. He was doing all right for materials, it was skilled labor they were short of. And money. There were some things he simply couldn't steal—like the new commercial refrigerators, stoves and ovens they would need to get the restaurant back on its feet. He stamped on a fat cockroach as he made his way through the filthy kitchen. His mother used to like telling people she'd never minded giving birth to Alex there, as it was cleaner than any hospital she'd ever seen in Lisbon.

Apart from his suite, where Jane was now dressing, there were no other rooms finished on the top floor. Each of his men had a suite, either on the first or second floor, and while these were renovated and decorated to varying degrees, there was no one of them suitable for a paying guest. If he ever did get the hotel completely renovated, and some or all of the crew stayed on, he would eventually need to find permanent accommodation for them. Alex would stay in the top-floor suite, though, where he had lived as a child. His family could have afforded a grand house elsewhere on the island, but his father had always insisted that the hotel manager's job was twenty-four hours a day, and that the only way to ensure his guests were getting top-class service was to live like one of them.

Alex walked outside into the bright light and Mitch sauntered over to him, rubbing his chest, which was badly bruised where Jane's bullet had hit his Kevlar vest. A gray sweat top covered the mark.

"You think she's got the stones?" Mitch asked, lighting a cigarette.

"I don't know. We've got until the day after tomorrow. She bought the story about the mechanic. Keep the generator switched off until we're out of earshot, then get back to work."

"Man, if she's carrying diamonds you can afford to employ a fucking army of builders to finish this place. How come we gotta work when we could be working her over?"

"Enough, Mitch. I told you, no one touches her. And we don't even know for sure it was diamonds on board."

"Yeah, but you said before, Wu's boss was getting a million pounds for whatever was in that package. No one knows she's alive, Alex. Give me half an hour with her if you're too squeamish. I talked to Henri—he agrees with me and he said he'd help me. We'll find out if she's got the rocks."

"Right. And then what would you do with her? Let her leave the island once she's healed?" Alex had expected Mitch to come up with something like this, but it worried him that Mitch had been undermining him with Henri.

"You know what I'd do with her. That bitch fucking shot me, man. It's payback. Don't mean nothing."

"I worry about you sometimes, Mitch, I truly do."

"You're just pussy-struck, man. Same as always. Every fucking broad you meet you fall for."

"Just get back to work, Mitch, as soon as we're gone. I'll find out if she's got what we're after. I'll also find out who those goons were who were waiting for us on board."

Mitch shook his head, turned and walked off.

They'd towed the *Penfold Son*'s lifeboat behind the *Fair Lady* as soon as they'd married up with Jose. Once back on the island they'd literally pulled the boat apart in case Jane had stashed the contraband on board. He'd searched Jane's meager possessions—even the inside of her thermos flask—and found nothing. Mitch, of course, had suggested checking her body while she was unconscious, thanks to the sedative their medic Heinrich had administered before connecting a saline drip. Alex had refused. As he'd told the American, if she had something of value, he'd find out, and then he'd find it.

Perhaps she didn't have the loot. He was basing his assumption that she did on the warning one of the men shooting at them had called out. "She's got 'em," the man had said. Alex presumed, or rather hoped, that meant the diamonds.

The raid had not been their finest hour. During a debrief they had gone over everything they could remember, from the helicopter-borne assault to the ignominious plummet off the stern of the *Penfold Son* in the lifeboat. The consensus was that their foes were ex-military. Their gunfire had been disciplined—two to three aimed shots at a time—and their weapons similar to the pirates'. What they'd seen of the men added to the presumption: they had military-style haircuts and were physically fit and broad-shouldered. In short, these were not merchant sailors who'd happened to be carrying an arsenal of assault rifles and hand grenades.

"The grenades worried me," Heinrich had said. "Not defensive weapons. These guys were armed and ready to assault someplace, or someone." Heinrich's back was a patchwork of wound dressings after Kevin had removed fifteen small pieces of shrapnel.

"Mercenaries?" Henri had ventured.

"Possible," Kevin conceded, "but the Penfold Line's too big to be associated with something as low rent as soldiers of fortune."

"Maybe, but don't forget someone on board was into diamond smuggling. The ship's master could have been freelancing," Alex pointed out.

There were too many questions, and these just added to the ones relating to the *Peng Cheng* and her crew. Captain Wu and his men were locked up in storage cages in the dank concrete-lined basement of the resort. He'd been given an e-mail address for the boat's owner by Wu and had sent a message, offering to start negotiations for a ransom payment. There had been no reply as yet to the anonymous Yahoo! account Heinrich had set up for the purpose.

The *Peng Cheng* and her cargo were moored at the deepwater jetty on the other side of the island, out of sight of the resort. Jane's tour wouldn't cover that part of the island. He didn't want her discovering their secret, as Danielle had. Something told him the corporate lawyer wasn't ready to drop the trappings of London life to live among a bunch of pirates. He didn't want to think about what would have to happen if she did find out the truth.

He looked out to sea, past the squeaky-clean sands of the beach and the pleasant thatched bar where they ate and drank every day, and he thought, not for the first time, that it was all worthwhile. All the risk, all the problems, all the crime, and even the blood that had been spilled. No one had been killed in any of their raids—until the day before yesterday.

Alex thought again of the man toppling backward over the railings into the sea far below. He had committed murder in the commission of a crime, even though the man in question had been trying to kill him at the time. The dead man was presumably employed to provide security, and even though Alex's crew had convinced themselves the other shooters were there to protect a criminal enterprise, Alex knew he had crossed an invisible line. It troubled him, but he forgot his worries when he saw her.

Jane had showered and piled her freshly dried hair high on her head, showing off a graceful, pale neck. She'd chosen one of Sarah's few dresses—the short blue cotton one that had never failed to arouse him whenever the Australian girl had worn it.

"I'm ready for my tour. I'm a stranger in paradise," she said.

He laughed. "No, Paradise is further north of us."

"OK, I'm ready for my geography lesson now." He pointed toward the beach and she fell into step beside him, her flip-flops slapping on the concrete veranda. Here and there were remnants of a tiled mosaic, once showing dolphins and whales. Jane paused and lifted her sunglasses to inspect the work. "They look nice."

"I'll get around to repairing that one day. If I had the money I'd bring a tiler over from Portugal. It's quite a skill. As to the geography, you're on an island in the Bazaruto Archipelago. The main islands are Bazaruto, the largest, then Benguerra, Magaruque, and Santa Carolina, also known as Paradise Island. Our island is so small it's usually omitted from maps. We're only two kilometers long, by one wide, and we're about thirty kilometers from the mainland. The bigger islands are all sand and were once part of a long peninsula joined to the mainland, but the Ilha dos Sonhos, like Paradise Island, is actually a rock island, so we have much deeper water around us than the others."

They were on the beach now, and Jane removed her sandals. Alex noticed her toenails were painted pink and she wore a tiny silver ring on the second toe of her left foot. Her feet squeaked on the white sand.

"How did you end up here?"

"I grew up here. I was born in the hotel. My parents owned this resort but were chucked out of it and the country along with all the other Europeans in Mozambique in 1975. I grew up angry, wanting to come back here and fight the people who stole our property and take it back by force."

"I take it you didn't?"

He shook his head. "I hated FRELIMO, the ruling power here in Mozambique, and for a while actively worked against them, from South Africa."

"You were in the South African Army?"

"For a few years. I'd trained in the UK as a Royal Marine then moved to South Africa in the late eighties and took a commission there. They were fighting in Angola and propping up RENAMO, the pro-democracy opposition here in Mozambique. I was involved in arms smuggling, but what I saw changed my mind."

He didn't want to go into details that might shock her. When she pushed him, he said, "Civil war brings out the very worst in people. There was wholesale destruction—of people, buildings, wildlife, you name it. I came to the conclusion that no one side was completely right or wrong and that warfare of this kind is the worst."

"There's a good kind?"

He shrugged, and stopped, pointing out to a far-off line of white water. "That's the reef. There's some fantastic snorkeling out there, if you're interested."

"So you left to find a 'good' war?"

"I went back to Britain and re-enlisted. I ended up in Afghanistan, where I felt we were doing some good, for a time, against the Taliban and al-Qaeda." He left out any mention of the two years he'd spent in special forces, in the Special Boat Service, after being promoted to lieutenant. The time in the elite maritime operations unit had taught him everything he knew about boarding and capturing ships. During the countless hours he'd spent scaling the cliff-like steel sides of HMS *Rame Head*, an old Canadian-built merchant cargo vessel moored in Portsmouth Harbor, he'd never guessed the skills he was learning would provide an income stream one day. Likewise, during his time in M Squadron, which specialized in marine counter-terrorism, he'd learned how to blow his way into locked bridges and cabins.

They started walking along the beach again, but he stopped in his tracks when she said, "You were put up for a Victoria Cross, weren't you?"

"How on earth do you know that?"

"I thought I recognized your name. It came to me a little while ago, and when you mentioned Afghanistan I knew it was you. You were in the papers—something about saving your men from blowing up?"

He said nothing, but set off again along the beach.

"I was at my parents' place. My father said he'd known your father when he was in the army. He said . . . well, he said you probably missed out on the VC because of your family, rather than what you had or hadn't done in Afghanistan."

"Ancient history," he said. "But you're right—my family name's remembered for all the wrong reasons. My old man was a bit of a scoundrel in his youth."

"Cad, my father said."

They both laughed. "He mended his ways when he met my mum. Hopefully I haven't inherited his worst traits." Although he knew he had.

"Is that how you lost your fingers, in Afghanistan?"

He nodded. He didn't really want to talk about it, but he reminded himself that what he was actually doing here, taking her around the island, was designed to get *her* talking, so he took a breath and told the story.

He skipped over the sheer unadulterated terror of what it's actually like to have someone firing bullets at you and trying to kill you. He left out the bit about one of his marines wetting himself while they were pinned down. He didn't admit what a high, what a rush it was, to raise his head above the medieval mud-brick wall, line up a Talib in the sights of his SA-80, pull the trigger and see the man's face disappear in a spray of red. The killing had given him courage. The rush, the blood-lust of war, had taken over from the cool, calculating decision-making processes they'd taught him during his officer's training. When the grenade had come over the parapet he had pushed his men aside and dived for it. He'd hefted it with his left hand—his right still holding his rifle—and just about got it away when it went off, mangling his hand and removing two fingers. The left side of his body and face had been peppered with shards of shrapnel.

One of his men had bandaged the bloody mess of his hand and then he, bellowing with pain and rage at what they'd done to him, led them out from behind the barricade to retake the village. Thankfully none of his men had been killed due to his act of madness.

"Anyone would have done the same thing," he said. "This is our beach bar—hub of all activity on the island."

Reggae played softly from speakers mounted in the thatch above them and Jose looked up from a book of cocktails. "*Inxhlecane*, Alex."

"*Inxhlecane. Mo hine cu vuka?*"

"I'm fine, man," Jose replied in English. Alex liked to stay in practice with his Xitswa, the language of the people who lived on the islands and the mainland coast around Inhassoro and Vilanculos. Alex introduced Jane to the stocky African and he shook her hand.

"We need some limes. I want to make a mojito for the lady," Jose said, consulting his book again. "I saw it on *Sex and the City*, when the satellite was still working. How about a Coke in the meantime?"

"Thanks," Alex said, shaking his head. "Jose has a degree in chemistry—a good background for any successful barman."

"*A santi wawena a sassekile*," Jose said.

"Jose says he's a better barman than he was a chemist. Don't let him near the swimming pool chemicals." Actually, Jose had just told Alex that he thought his new wife was beautiful. Alex made a face at him.

Jane laughed. "What brings you to the island, Jose?"

"I was born here," he said. Jose passed the dripping bottles of cola across the bar then walked around to join them. "This reprobate and I grew up together. His father was the owner of the resort and I was the son of the best barman north of Maputo. We played together as children. Then the war happened."

Alex saw Jane try hard not to stare at Jose's artificial leg. The prosthesis was a modern one, a Cheetah flexible running blade.

"I was recruited—forced at gunpoint, actually—into the ranks of FRELIMO. I was sent to Russia where I studied chemistry at university and bomb-making in a military camp. It was around the same time Alex was running guns to my enemies."

"What happened to you?" Jane asked.

"When I came back to Mozambique I was in the bush, fighting

RENAMO, when I stepped on an Italian-made landmine. They're plastic, so the mine detectors—even if we'd had them—wouldn't have picked it up. I hate land mines."

"But not Alex?"

Alex looked at his friend for a reaction. It was a valid question. "We got caught on opposite sides of the war. Alex hated everyone in FRELIMO for a while and I hated everyone in RENAMO and the people who backed them. But I saw my side do some bad things, as he did his. The government told me to reopen the hotel, to lure foreign tourists back, but I'm a chemist and a barman, not an hotelier, so I got the party to endorse Alex's claim on the property. The headache's all his now."

"Jose's being modest. He's my business partner."

"I can't believe we fought each other, for so long. But things are looking up now. Hopefully there will be no more killing," Jose added.

"But I thought the civil war here was long over."

"What Jose means," Alex said, finishing his Coke and setting it down firmly on the bar, "is that he hopes this country never sees conflict again."

"Exactly," Jose said.

Alex and Jose spoke briefly in Portuguese and the African nodded.

"He says he'll have a word to the cook and organize us some giant lobster for tonight. Is that OK?"

"It's sensational. Bye, Jose."

Alex led her off the beach to an old short wheelbase Land Rover, of similar vintage to the one Sarah had driven into the surf when they'd hijacked the car transport. The top had been removed and the windscreen folded flat to the bonnet, giving it the look of an off-road convertible. Alex opened and closed Jane's door for her, and she nodded her thanks.

The vehicle bounced along the sandy roads and the breeze generated from their motion kept the heat of the day at bay. It took only a few minutes of driving among low scrub and palm trees for them to arrive at a cleared area dotted with huts of thatch and woven reed walls. A fire smoked under a rack of drying fish, and a woman in a brightly printed wrap waved and smiled at Alex, without disturbing the ten-liter plastic bottle of cooking oil balanced on her head. "Most of the island's population left after the revolution, though a few, like Jose, have come back. About fifty local people live here now."

"What do they do?" Jane asked, waving at two small girls who had peeked their heads out the door of one of the huts.

"They fish, to provide for themselves and us at the hotel, and some of the men work for Jose and me as laborers. We've enticed a couple of builders to move here, and I've guaranteed employment to anyone from the village who wants it once the resort's back in business."

"That's very generous of you."

"It's their island and their wealth, as much as mine."

"That sounds a bit socialist for a former British officer and South African Army gun-runner?"

Alex smiled and nodded. "It's ironic that the people I wanted to overthrow invited me back, and that one of them was my best chum when I was a child."

"Isn't there some lingering animosity toward the former colonial regime—to you, as a Portuguese?"

"I'm Mozambican, Jane. I was born here, and so was my mother and her parents. I don't agree with everything the Portuguese did here, just as I don't agree with everything the current government does. This is my birthplace, and for people like Jose and me, living here is our birthright."

From the village Alex took a track which ran close to another beach, south of the main resort. Alex stopped near the shells of a line of eight timber buildings. Little was left of the huts other than splintered beams and dead palm fronds.

"God, this is a beautiful beach, but what happened to the houses? Were they destroyed when the Portuguese left?" Jane asked.

Alex shook his head. "No, this was my fault. When I first came back to Ilha dos Sonhos, after I'd been invalided out of the marines, I used my compensation payout to build a small holiday resort—a backpackers' place with these few huts and a campsite. My plan was to get business back to the island and make some more money before I started restoring the hotel."

"What happened?"

"A cyclone. That's what happened. It's no accident that all the remaining resort hotels along the coast look like concrete bunkers. Nothing less can withstand the force of nature. I was arrogant and I took a gamble. I've learned since then. We were only open a few weeks before the storm hit and I lost everything. I wasted a fortune."

"So what do you do for money now?"

He shrugged. "We run diving trips and fishing charters from the mainland. It's slowly-slowly now and we don't turn much of a profit. None, in fact. I put all the money back into the hotel. You can't rush Africa."

He started the Land Rover again and they deviated inland from the coastline. He shifted into low-range four-wheel drive to climb a steep hill. Sand gave way to a rough rocky road carved into the hill. Jane held tight to the dashboard as the Land Rover eased its way to the top. At times it felt like they were climbing steps. It wasn't a high peak, but from the top they could just make out the haze of the mainland, and the next island to the south of them.

"It's beautiful," Jane said. "It's not every day you meet a man who has his own island."

"I just hope I can hang onto it," he said.

They walked from one side of the clearing on top of the hill to the other and Jane shielded her eyes to take in the view.

"The pirates," he said casually, looking out over the ocean, not making eye contact with her, "what do you think they were looking for on board the *Penfold Son*?"

"I've no idea," she said quickly. "Perhaps they were just attracted to her because of her size."

"I doubt someone would go to the expense of a helicopter assault on spec," he said.

She turned and looked at him, staring straight into his eyes. "I think I killed a man, Alex."

He said nothing.

"Have you—killed, I mean?"

He nodded.

"I think he would have killed me, if I hadn't shot him first. I don't know what happened to the gun I had. At the time, it was instinctive—the only thing I could have done. I can still see his eyes, through this weird rubber mask he was wearing."

"What color were they?" Alex asked.

She didn't blink. "Green. He wasn't a Somali, or a black Mozambican. He was a white man, Alex. You tell me, what do you think they were after?"

He shrugged and walked back to the Land Rover.

8

George Penfold smashed his fist into the two-hundred-year-old oak desk and swore.

Reynolds, his head of security, had just left the office. George had ordered Harvey to get Van Zyl on the line, wherever he was. He was looking straight down the barrel of a class-A disaster.

Harvey Reynolds was the only other person in the London office who knew about the exchange. He was the fixer, the man who usually acted as the go-between in the various smuggling deals which resulted in a profit that made the handsome wage George drew from his family's company look like chickenfeed.

There were two George Penfolds.

His family, his employees and the people he did business with saw the youthful, fit, astute businessman steering the company from one successful strategic venture to another. Other men might be sated by this kind of power, but it wasn't nearly enough for George.

From an early age he'd tasted the basest, most intoxicating, most exhilarating pleasures the liveliest sea ports around the world had to offer. Outside his home and his office the other George indulged his favorite, expensive passions—gambling and women. When he gambled, he won and lost fortunes. When he was ready for pleasure the things he wanted—needed—and the women who offered them did not come cheap.

Some might say his tastes ran to the bizarre, but George knew that when it came to sex, the more he got, the more he wanted. Each new experience had to better the last, and that usually involved spending more money. His wife, Elizabeth, was conservative in her tastes, but that didn't bother him. The deceit—either with a callgirl or a pretty staff member—was half the fun.

He'd started smuggling as a cadet on board the first ship he'd sailed on, in order to supplement his income and pay for his growing menu of vices. He'd worked out early on in his career how many places there were to hide contraband on board a freighter. He didn't use drugs—anymore—but in his youth had trafficked not only grass, but also cocaine, heroin, amphetamines and ecstasy.

He wouldn't have needed the illegal money at that age if he'd stayed in the UK and got a job working in head office, as his father had wished. By turning his back on a place in the family company he'd also cut himself off from his generous allowance. He wanted freedom from his family, but he needed money.

And there was the thrill. Evading the amateurish third-world customs officials, even paying the odd bribe, was more exciting, more intoxicating than the highs of any drug. As well as living a carefree life at sea he had cash in his pocket in every port he visited. He might have been a lowly cadet on board, but ashore he ate in the best restaurants, gambled in the high-roller rooms of the best casinos, and bedded the most expensive whores in a score of foreign ports.

When he'd tired of penny-ante drug trafficking and returned to take his rightful place in the company as scion of the Penfold clan, his tastes, his needs and his greed had grown in proportion to his promotion.

In front of him was the news that Iain MacGregor, the first Penfold Line captain he'd sailed under, and one of the few others who knew the secret George, was dead. George felt little remorse for the old Scot, who had bullied him mercilessly during his time at sea. When he'd caught MacGregor smuggling gold out of Malaysia the captain had been terrified George would turn him in to his father. George had laughed. The bullying had stopped and George began to learn a few more tricks of the smuggler's trade, from a master. But MacGregor was dead and the package was gone. Failure was unforgivable.

George hadn't expected a double-cross from Chan, or his man on the high seas, Captain Wu, and he still didn't know exactly what had happened on board the *Penfold Son*. All Harvey had reported, from the South African Police Service, was what was already appearing on the Internet. The ship had entered Durban harbor, skippered by the first mate, with a dead captain on board and significant damage from an attack by pirates armed with machine guns and hand grenades.

Gillian had fielded and stonewalled calls from a dozen reporters in Africa and the UK already, and he expected more to come during the day. The IMB was badgering him for a report. He'd told Gillian to contact their public relations firm—a slimy bunch of charlatans who almost made him feel honest whenever he got their bills. However, the spin doctors would earn their money today.

And Jane was missing.

He knew he should call her parents, but news of her disappearance had not yet appeared in the media. George had already spoken to Igor Putin, the engineering officer who had been the bagman for the exchange. He'd been below when the helicopter had arrived and had taken cover when the gunfire started. Penfold couldn't blame him. The tabloid media were reporting it as World War III on board the *Penfold Son*.

"The package was missing from the safe when I got to the wheel-house," Putin had told him.

He'd told the Russian to make sure none of the crew spoke to any journalists. However, Harvey had told him that the South African police were already asking questions about passengers.

Sooner or later he would have to call them, but he wanted to hear from Van Zyl first. He'd have the man's guts on his tennis racquet.

"Call for you, sir," Gillian said when he picked up the ringing phone. "Mister Van Zyl from South Africa."

George was ready to give the man both barrels, but the South African spoke without even a greeting. "I think the Humphries woman has your property."

"What the devil are you talking about?"

"Drop the facade, Mister Penfold," Van Zyl said coolly. "It would have been nice of you to tell us we were riding shotgun over that pick-up from the Chinese freighter. You should have briefed us fully."

George was silent for a few seconds. Where had the information come from? Putin? MacGregor? Both men would have known that George had the contacts and the money to have them killed, wherever they were in the world, if they'd blabbed or tried to double-cross him. It must have been MacGregor. If the pirates had forced the location of the package out of the Scot, then how would Van Zyl have found out? A more likely scenario unfolded in George's mind while he listened to the hum of the international line in his ear.

"Did the pirates kill MacGregor, or did you, Van Zyl?"

"They did of course, but I would have thought you'd be more interested in finding the girl. She was with MacGregor when the pirates attacked."

"I told you to look after her. Is she dead?"

"I don't know," Van Zyl admitted. "When she left the bridge the safe was open and she was in a hurry, heading for a lifeboat. She was still in the boat when they escaped. One of my men was shot and nearly killed trying to stop them. I gave the woman my pistol. She hit one of the pirates, but they took him on board before we could get to him."

"Good for her." George didn't care a fig about Van Zyl's hired gun. The bottom line was that the men had failed to protect Jane, and had missed an opportunity to destroy the very gang they were supposed to be looking for. "So, despite being armed to the teeth, you and your mercenaries didn't manage to kill a single one of the criminals—although Jane may have. And you let a valuable cargo go missing and failed to protect the master of my flagship. Give me one reason why I shouldn't terminate your contract right now, Van Zyl."

"I'll give you two. I'm going to find the girl and, when I do, I'm going to kill each and every man in that gang, as well as their spouses, their children and their pets."

George snorted out a laugh, then calmed himself. Despite all that had happened, he liked the South African's style. "You do that. Bring me the girl back—intact—and the cargo. You'll get a healthy reward."

"Half the value."

"Preposterous. Ten percent, not a penny more."

"Forty percent."

"Twenty-five."

"Goodbye, Mister Penfold."

"No, goodbye and good riddance to you, Mister Van Zyl. You cocked up and you know it. Ten percent of the cash value of the cargo, and that's my final offer. There are plenty of other soldiers of fortune out there for hire."

There was a pause on the other end of the line, then Van Zyl said, "Deal."

"I'll be in Johannesburg in two days' time. Have news for me." George hung up before Van Zyl could reply and smiled to himself. No one out-negotiated him in business. He was concerned about Jane and he fantasized briefly about what he might do to the men who had kidnapped her, had they brutalized her. He wondered what privations she might be going through now.

He felt wired, pumped with adrenaline from his conversation with Van Zyl. He took his BlackBerry off his desk and scrolled through the contact numbers until he found the one he wanted—needed.

"Black Pearl, how can we satisfy you?" a female voice asked on the end of the line.

• • •

Jane followed the scent of melted butter and frying garlic and onions to the beachside bar. A pyramid of burning driftwood on the beach sent a galaxy of glowing embers into the sky, which shone a deep, dark blue from the dying light of the sun.

She rubbed the goose bumps that had risen on her bare arms despite the warmth of the evening. She couldn't believe there was no means of contacting the mainland from this island. Mobile phones, she'd read, could be charged from solar panels, and other electrical gear could be run from car batteries charged by the sun. She'd seen the glint of reflected light from the top of the hotel when they'd stood together on the hill, and the hot water in Alex's shower was scalding. He had solar power, all right. He was lying to her.

True, the generator hadn't run all afternoon, and the lights festooned around the beach bar were paraffin lanterns, but she still didn't believe him. Which was a shame, because he was so very charming.

She'd changed into another woman's swimsuit after the drive. It was odd to be wearing someone else's clothes—something she'd never do at home. She and Alex had plunged into the still waters in front of the hotel. He'd brought a mask, snorkel and fins and taken her a little way out, to where she could see bright colored fish darting away from her outstretched hands.

When they'd emerged from the water his maid was waiting with a tray of tea and sandwiches, which they'd eaten in the shade of a palm tree. It would have been all so perfect if he wasn't lying to her.

It made her spine tingle, and caused the downy hairs on her arms to stand up.

She was ravenous, so she put her suspicions and fears to one side. She'd already consoled herself with the thought that he could have killed or tortured her by now if he was, in fact, the pirate rather than the rescuer he claimed to be. Alex waved to her and she looked at the other faces around the bar. Some of the men wore painted smiles, but others barely contained their wariness of her.

"Jane, welcome. What would you like to drink?"

Music was playing—batteries she guessed, for her sake—and Jose the one-legged chemist and barman was working a cocktail shaker vigorously.

"Mojito?" Jose asked, raising an eyebrow.

She watched him pour and took a sip. "What about limes? I can't see any in there."

"Maria found a bottle of lime juice in the pantry."

She grimaced. "Just like the real thing."

"How'd you pull up?" asked a man with an Australian accent.

"Excuse me?"

"Feeling all right after your ordeal? I'm Kevin, by the way."

She said she was fine and shook hands with him.

"Evening," said the grimmest-looking man in the bunch. His drawl was American. He looked up from his drink—a double measure of straight whiskey and ice.

When Jane saw his eyes she swallowed involuntarily as the scene replayed itself in her mind. The violent, unexpected kick of the hand gun; the bright light and deafening bang of the explosion.

Alex introduced her to the rest of the men who worked for him and she learned they all had military backgrounds. She recalled reading the International Maritime Bureau's piracy update, which pointed to the organized nature of the gang that had hijacked the car carrier off the coast of South Africa.

"Don't mind Mitch, the American," Alex said as he led her away from the bar to a row of four barbecues made from two-hundred-liter fuel drums cut crossways and topped with welded metal grills. She felt the heat of the glowing coals radiating onto her bare thighs as she got closer. Alex took an enamel bowl and a brush and basted a line of cut lobsters with melted butter. Each crayfish was as long as his arm, from tentacle tip to tail. "He's actually as grim as he seems, but he means you no harm."

"I wish I could believe you," she let slip.

"What do you mean? You're perfectly safe here, Jane."

And she felt that way, for the time being, around Alex. Mitch's green eyes frightened her. She heard giggling behind her and a loud shriek and looked back to see two African women, one on either side of Mitch. He had his arms around them, but when he turned to look into the darkness between the bar and the fire, she felt him searching for her. "I know," she said to Alex, "but you can't blame me for being out of sorts."

"I understand, and I know how keen you are to get back to the mainland. I'll get you there."

She nodded her thanks. A young Mozambican girl, perhaps in her early teens, walked over, smiling.

"*Cerveja, Alexandre?*" she said.

"*Ola, Isabella. Vinho verde, por favor.*"

The girl turned and skipped back across the sand toward the bar. "Child labor, or does she just have a crush on you?"

Alex laughed. "Bit of both, I suppose."

"You're quite the lord of the manor around here, aren't you?"

He shrugged. "I love it here. The people—even those misfits at the bar—the island, the crumbling hotel. It really is the closest thing I've got to a home."

"So you're all one big happy family?"

"Mostly, yes."

She watched him chat with the girl in a mix of Xitswa and Portuguese, saying something that made her laugh hysterically, then run off to join her friends. More islanders were arriving at the *braai*, as Alex called the barbecue, and the beat and the volume of the music from the bar seemed to increase by the minute. Even somber Mitch was now dancing with his two women.

She wondered if she was right, if they really were the pirates. Alex's face was warmed by the light of the fire and when he smiled and winked at her, over the heads of two young boys playing with a football made of rags and tape in the sand, she could see he was a charmer, like his father, and probably a heartbreaker too.

They all sat together, under the stars on the beach, villagers, ex-soldiers, the young and the old at a long rickety trestle table laid with starched white linen and colonial-era silver that gleamed with the fire's reflection. Alex brought the lobsters on platters and took his place at the head of the table. Jane was on his right, and he toasted her arrival and her good fortune before they began eating. She blushed and thanked them all for rescuing her.

And the fantasy was almost a reality as she laughed at something Kevin said about a drunken brawl in Manila, her bare toes digging into the cooling sand under her feet, and the cold, crisp vinho verde cutting through the devilishly delicious lobster tail that was almost too good to swallow.

"I hope it hasn't been too traumatic for you today," Alex said to her quietly, below the hum of conversation and occasional outburst of raucous laughter.

She was about to say that no, she had had a lovely day, all things considered, but she felt the chill again. She glanced along the table: three places down on the opposite side, Mitch was staring at her with those green eyes.

9

"Where's the broad?" Mitch was picking his fingernails with the tip of his Ka-Bar as he walked into the half-renovated room that passed for the resort's office.

Alex swiveled in his chair and rocked back. He placed his hands behind his head and yawned. He was tired after last night's party, but he also wanted to show Mitch he was relaxed about Jane's presence and her movements on the island.

"She took one of the sea kayaks out. I told her to stay on the leeward side of the island, as the water's rough on the other side. Jose's watching for her return."

The air conditioner hummed above him and dripped water onto the bare concrete floor. Mitch nodded, satisfied at Alex's ruse to keep Jane away from the other side of the island, where there was actually a sheltered harbor and jetty where the captured *Peng Cheng* was currently tied up. With Jane off the island, temporarily at least, he'd ordered the generator back into action so he could catch up with some paperwork, and Heinrich, Henri and Kevin could get some more work done on the first-floor rooms.

"What if she hears the noise of the generator?" Mitch asked.

It was a valid question, as sound traveled far over water. "I'll tell her we got it fixed, but it broke down again. If she wants to call her boss I'll give her the satellite phone with the dud battery—she'll be lucky to get a minute's use out of it." They had several phones on the island, but one always had problems. "It'll make her feel better, and won't change anything."

Jane had agreed over post-dinner liqueurs and coffee to his suggestion that he drive her to Johannesburg, via Zimbabwe. If he hadn't found out what she'd taken from the *Penfold Son*'s bridge and where it was by the time they left the island, he would have several days on the road with her to get her to open up to him.

"I think she recognizes me from the ship," Mitch said, picking up a printout of a website news story from Alex's desk. "She looks at me funny. Hey, what's this?"

Alex was more concerned about the news item that Mitch was reading than he was about Jane. The article, from a South African news agency, described how the *Penfold Son* had limped into Durban harbor suffering grenade and bullet damage, and reported the death of Captain Iain MacGregor, who had been shot on the ship's bridge. There was nothing in the bulletin about the death of a security guard, which was of some relief to Alex. Perhaps the man had survived the gunfire and fall.

"We didn't get anywhere near the bridge," Mitch said. "There's no way we killed the captain."

"I know. But this is a problem for us."

"No shit." Mitch put the paper down and toyed with his knife, switching it from hand to hand.

Alex kept an eye on the blade. "If I can find that million-pound package I'm closing the operation down."

"We've had this conversation before, Alex. You do what you want, but it closes when we all say it does."

Alex sat up straight. "If you keep it going, it won't be from my island."

Mitch grasped the hilt of the Ka-Bar and drove its point down into the desktop. "Listen here, Lord Jim, this ain't your fucking island, no matter what you and Jose say. These thieves will take your precious hotel and your goddamned pile of sand as soon as they see you're making a buck. It happened here before, it happened in Zimbabwe and it's happening in South Africa, where they're forcing the whites to sell the good farms."

"I'll take that risk, but once we're cashed up, the Ilha dos Sonhos goes strictly legit."

Mitch pulled the knife free of the scarred wooden desk and walked out into the morning sunlight. He slammed the door on Alex.

Alex exhaled and ran a hand through his wavy hair, which was damp with sweat despite the struggling air conditioner. He checked his watch. Sitting in front of a computer worked for Danielle, but not for him. No amount of staring at the spreadsheets would conjure more money. He was restless and wanted to ensure all was ready on the *Fair Lady* for his trip to the mainland the next day. He grabbed the Land Rover's keys and went outside.

As he crested the summit in the center of the island—he hadn't taken the coast road in case Jane saw him from the water and decided to try to intercept him—he looked down on the *Peng Cheng* and the *Fair Lady.*

Four local fishermen from the village, who doubled as cheap stevedores when there was stolen cargo to be loaded or unloaded, were operating the *Peng Cheng*'s deck-mounted crane to raise the crated leopard out of the freighter's fetid hull. The three men charged with keeping the swinging crate steady were clearly not keen on the job.

Alex drove down the hill and onto the wooden deck of the jetty and killed the Land Rover's engine. He heard grunting and snarling from inside the crate. "Hey, careful with her, guys. Take it easy."

He climbed aboard the *Peng Cheng* via the gangway. "Quiet, my girl," he whispered to the caged cat. "Not long now."

He addressed the leader of the gang of workers, Luis, in Xitswa, asking what progress had been made on the transfer of the contraband wildlife and animal products to the *Fair Lady*.

"The snakes are aboard, Captain, all twenty-eight of them," Luis said, shuddering, "as are the birds, the monkeys, the pangolins and the lizards. All of the tusks and the rhino horns are also on your boat, Captain."

Two of the fishermen were on the *Fair Lady* and, under Alex's direction, they positioned the leopard's cage carefully on the deck.

With the cat safely stowed on board, and a tarpaulin erected over the cage to give it some shade, Alex went back inside the *Fair Lady*. He started her engines and let them idle in neutral.

He walked downstairs to the office and switched on his laptop, which, like the boat's satellite system, was now running off the engines. The air-conditioning was also humming.

He logged onto the Internet via satellite and opened the Yahoo! account Heinrich had set up. There was one message in it from "afriendofthepongli." Alex smiled and opened it.

Captain Wu had been allowed one telephone call to his master, on the condition that he spoke in English. Alex had listened in as Wu explained he and his men were being held captive but were unharmed. To the best of his knowledge the *Peng Cheng* and everything aboard it were safe. "These *gwai lo* are professional," Wu had said. Alex had snatched the satellite phone out of the captain's hand and Mitch had punched the seaman in the kidneys for his use of the Chinese term for a white barbarian. Alex had ordered the captain returned to his makeshift cell in the basement, and warned Mitch against harming him further. The damage was already done.

> Your demand of ransom is ridiculous. The Peng Cheng and her crew are not worth half of what you ask. Her cargo, however, belongs to me and I expect it to be returned. Instead of haggling for what is in the hold, I have a proposition for you. If you are the white pirate I think you are, then I have a business proposal for you. It will be worth your time, and far more

money than you have demanded for Captain Wu and my vessel. Meet me
at Emperors Palace Hotel near the airport in Johannesburg.

The message had given a date next week. Good timing, Alex
thought.

Jane rowed every weekend on the Thames regardless of the weather.
It was her favorite form of exercise. It was good to be getting a workout again, after the weeks cooped up on board the *Penfold Son*, with
only the endless metal stairs to tread.

She looked over her shoulder as she rounded the northern tip of
the island. There was no one on the water behind her, though a couple
of times she had spotted the glint of light reflected on binoculars from
the beach front bar. She imagined Alex had asked Jose to keep an eye
on her. No doubt he would say it was for her safety.

The conditions on the windward side, she soon found, were no
different to the lee of the Ilha dos Sonhos. Although she was sure these
could be dangerous waters at the wrong time of year, she was also certain she was being warned off visiting this part of the island for other
reasons.

She paddled hard, fully expecting a boat to come looking for her
at any minute. She hugged the coastline, which was rocky along this
stretch, and orientated herself by looking up to the crest where Alex
had stopped the open-topped Land Rover. From this angle she saw
that the clearing was on a slope and that Alex had shown her the
coast where she was now. Hidden from her view was the remainder of
the windward side, further to the south. That was where she wanted
to go.

With no headwind to impede her or tailwind to assist her it was
all down to her own efforts. She was perspiring, though her breathing was deep and measured as she ate up the meters. Adrenaline fed
her efforts and she was soon rounding a promontory at the foot of
the peak. She slowed and allowed the sea kayak to coast closer to the

shore. She spied a pebbly beach and aimed for it, beaching the craft with a few hard strokes.

Jane slipped on her sandals, dragged the kayak further up the beach and continued her journey southward on foot, clambering over sun-warmed boulders. Soon she had rounded the point completely and she ducked into the shadows of a massive rock when she saw what Alex had been hiding from her view on his little tour.

It was a harbor—part natural and part augmented by geometric chunks of concrete to form a breakwater. It was big enough to accommodate a small freighter and that was exactly what was parked there, next to a wooden jetty. Tied alongside the rust-stained ship was a sleek, modern motor cruiser.

The outline of the cargo ship was instantly familiar and when she gingerly made her way a hundred meters closer, to a position giving her a different perspective, she could read the name. *Peng Cheng.* It was the ship that Captain MacGregor had stopped supposedly to assist.

She'd wondered if the encounter between the vessels was related in some way to MacGregor's possession of George's mysterious package and the pirate attack. Here was the ship, tied up in Alex Tremain's private harbor, transferring cargo by crane to another vessel.

There was no doubt in her mind at all now that Alex was the leader of the gang that had stormed the *Penfold Son.* The realization made her shiver and all of a sudden she felt very frightened and very alone. No matter how kindly and handsome Alex might appear, he was a pirate.

What should she do? The safest thing, of course, would be to quickly return to the other side of the island and go on as though nothing had happened. When—if—Alex made good on his promise to ship her to the mainland, she would slip away from him at the first opportunity. It didn't matter how she got to Johannesburg.

It worried her that George might be involved in something illegal—smuggling perhaps—but there was no doubt in her mind that once Alex realized she didn't have what he was looking for she would cease to be of use to him. She thought about Mitch, with those pierc-ing green eyes. Her spine tingled with fear. When Alex eventually found a way to ask her if she had MacGregor's package, and she said no, would the urbane ex-officer hand her over to his henchman?

She'd already been gone far too long, so she turned to retrace her steps.

"Hello, gorgeous. Found what you were looking for?" Mitch held the ugly black submachine gun pointed at her one-handed, and raised the index finger of his left hand to his lips. "Hush, now. I could tell you that everything's fine, but that would be a lie."

It was cool in the basement and Jane gasped when the bucket of sea-water was thrown over her.

She could no longer feel her fingers, such was the tightness of the cold steel of the handcuffs, and the sharp pain in her wrists had been overtaken by the ache in her armpits.

Mitch, with Henri as backup, had cuffed her and forced her onto the back of Henri's waiting quad bike. Her manacled hands had been tied to the pillion rack to stop her making a run for it. Though there was nowhere to run on this tiny island of nightmares.

Back at the resort she'd been shoved in the back by the Ameri-can, down the stairs. She had fallen twice and her shins were bloody and raw and her chin was cut and grazed. With her hands behind her back, she'd had no way of breaking the falls.

She wanted to cry but bit her lip to stifle the tears as Henri re-moved the cuffs, then replaced them, running the chain through a loop of rope hanging from a ring bolt cemented into the rough concrete wall. In a gated and barred alcove a few meters away from her she heard raised voices calling in Chinese. She'd glimpsed the shadows of human forms beyond the candles as they'd hustled her into the dank cellar.

"Shut your fucking gook babble," Mitch yelled. He walked over to her, close enough for her to smell his halitosis. He lowered his voice to a near whisper. "Scared, baby doll? You ought to be."

"It is ready," Henri said. "We must be quick, Mitchell."

"Don't be such a fucking sissy. Oops, I forgot. You are." Mitch laughed.

Jane saw the momentary flash of hatred in the Frenchman's eye at Mitch's taunt, but when she glanced over at Henri she saw little compassion there for her. He shook his head, as if there was nothing he could do to alter things now.

"Ever seen these?" He held up two alligator clips attached to the ends of the insulated wires Henri had just passed him. "Kind of thing you can buy in any electrical store. But that, over there, is military issue." He nodded back to where Henri now sat on a folding chair, beside a metal camping table, on which was a chunky green plastic telephone and cradle. "It's called a field telephone. Not much used in these days of digital and satellite comms, but it's never really gone out of fashion. Know why?"

Despite telling herself she would show no sign of weakness to this man, nor comply with him in any way, she shook her head.

"I'll show you. Crank it." On his command, Henri grabbed a small handle at the rear of the base of the telephone and wound it furiously. Holding the plastic insulation, Mitch touched the two metal clips together, a few centimeters from her eyes. They crackled and sparked, dazzling her eyes with an electrical arc.

She gasped.

"And the seawater?" Mitch said. "In case you're wondering, that's to enhance the conductivity when I attach the clips." He smiled and moved one clip to her cheek. She recoiled, expecting to be shocked, but then realized both needed to be in contact with her to complete the circuit. Mitch trailed the serrated snout of the clip down her neck and over the fabric of her wet T-shirt. Despite her fear her nipple was protruding. "Cold in here, ain't it?"

"I don't know what this is all about. Please . . . I've got nothing to say to you," she managed.

He discarded the clip and slapped her, open-palmed, across the face, with enough force to turn her head and smack the opposite cheek against the concrete. "Shut the fuck up, bitch. I haven't even asked you a fucking question yet. You'll talk to me when I'm good and ready for you to say something."

Jane shook her head from the force of the blow and gingerly felt her lip with the tip of her tongue. She tasted blood, and spat.

"That won't be the last of it. You're going to bleed." Mitch reached for his belt and unclipped a wicked-looking knife, short but broad-bladed, with a T-shaped grip that he held in his palm, the sharp end protruding between two fingers. "Don't move, baby." He raised the point to the bottom of the V of her T-shirt and drew the blade back to him, so the material stretched. The blade started to slice and the shirt peeled apart.

Jane was too scared to move in case the knife connected with her skin. "What do you want?"

"Don't scream, baby. You'll wake the neighbors." Mitch laughed. "Let's not spoil the game. What I want you to do is to think, real hard, what it is I *might* want to know from you."

He took a step closer to her and she felt the point of the blade touch her throat. Her shirt was split open, revealing her bikini top. She didn't dare look down, and the pressure from the tip of the knife forced her to look straight ahead as he reached around her and unfastened the clasp.

The delicacy of his touch, the feigned tenderness, made his actions all the more terrifying. He moved the knife and cut the shoulder straps so that the bikini top fell to the ground. Her chest heaved and she closed her eyes, tight. A tear squeezed from her closed lids. This couldn't be happening to her.

Mitch grabbed her face in one hand, squeezing her cheeks tight. "Keep your eyes open, darlin'," he whispered. "Ain't no fun, otherwise."

"Hurry," Henri said from the gloom.

"Shut the fuck up. Now, Jane, do you have anything you want to say to me? Look down, baby."

He had sheathed the knife and picked up the discarded alligator clips from the wet concrete floor, where they had been sizzling and snapping away in a puddle. Mitch held one of the clips open in his right hand, its wicked serrated teeth now poised on either side of her left nipple.

"Anything at all?"

She screamed in agony at its touch and couldn't imagine how much more something could hurt. He hadn't even started with the electricity.

"Hush, breathe deep. The first shock will pass as the blood stops flowing to your nipple, baby," he said, his lips almost brushing her ear. "In the navy they taught us to focus on something—a spot on the wall maybe—and just say nothing but our name, rank, date of birth. Why don't you try that? Come on, name . . ."

Tears rolled down her cheeks and her body started to heave with her sobs. "Mitch, please . . . I'll . . . tell . . ."

"Shush." He held the other clip up to her eyes and she writhed against the restraints, trying to move out of his reach. He grabbed her hair and pulled hard, yanking her back to the position he wanted her. The sudden sharp pain overtook the throb in her breast. "I'll let you in on a secret, Jane. I don't appreciate it when someone shoots me. I don't want you to tell me anything until I've hurt you some more—it's my version of payback."

Henri moved into her sight out of the darkness. "Mitchell, don't be stupid. She was about to tell you, you stupid *cochon!* Let her speak before Alex—"

"—arrives?"

The two men looked back, into the shadows, from where Alex emerged, the nine-millimeter pistol looking like a natural extension of his right hand. "Get that thing off her body, Mitch."

The American started to protest, but dived for the floor when Alex pulled the trigger. He'd aimed high at the last second. Jane cowered away from Alex when he approached her, but he picked Mitch's knife up off the floor and used it to cut the rope binding her hand-cuffs to the wall. Realizing she was now free, she pulled the clip from her breast.

Alex picked up her sarong and tossed it to her. She caught it and held it up to cover herself.

Mitch got to his knees and said, "Alex, she was about to tell us—"

Alex squeezed the trigger again and the next bullet punched a hole through the baggy sleeve of Mitch's Hawaiian shirt.

"Holy fuck, you could have—"

"Shut up," Alex barked. "On the floor, face down, hands behind your back. You, too, Henri. I would have expected better of you," he said to the Frenchman as he sent him sprawling from the kneeling position to prone with a kick in his rear.

Jane knelt beside Mitch while Alex covered him, then reached into the American's shorts. She found the handcuff key she had seen him slip in his pocket and unlocked the bracelets. She rubbed her wrists.

"Put them on Mitch," Alex said to her, and she nodded. When she'd seen the Chinese freighter and confirmed to herself that Alex was part of the pirate gang that had attacked the *Penfold Son*, she'd been terrified about what he might do to her. Now he was her savior—though for how long, she had no idea. The thought crossed her mind that this might all be part of some elaborate ruse to make her trust Alex.

"Here," he said, tossing her a long plastic cable tie. "Do the same to Henri." She complied, although she needed Alex to press the hard black barrel of the pistol to the Frenchman's temple to force his silence and stillness. Jane's hands were shaking as she pulled the tie tight.

"Alex, don't be a fucking idiot, man," Mitch wailed. "She was going to spill the beans, and now you're going to let her get away."

"I'm taking her to the mainland, where she'll be free to do as she pleases."

"*Non*, Alex. Mitch is right this time," Henri said. "She will tell the police and that will be the end of you and the island—of all of us."

Alex looked at her, the pistol moving naturally with the direction of his dark eyes. He raised an eyebrow in silent question.

"Jesus Christ! I don't know what's going on, Alex, and that's God's honest truth. God, please don't hurt me," Jane said. Her hands still trembled as she wrapped the sarong around her and knotted it together between her breasts. "I just want to get out of this place—off this island. Please, Alex, please. If you let me go free I'll keep your secret."

Her shoulders heaved involuntarily and she sucked in lungfuls of air as she fought to keep her composure.

"Don't listen to her, man, or you're crazier than I ever thought. You'll ruin this for all of us, Alex," Mitch whined.

"No, Mitch, you've already done that. On your feet."

"Wait," Jane said. Her body had stilled now and she glared at him.

"What is it?" Alex asked.

Jane found the two alligator clips and knelt beside Mitch. "This is going to hurt you much more than it will hurt me," she whispered to him as she placed a clip on each of his earlobes. He screamed.

Alex stood by, the pistol hanging loose in his right hand. A slow smile crossed his face as he watched Jane grip the handle of the field telephone and crank it.

10

Alex lowered the binoculars and pointed. "Land." Jane kept her distance from him, at the far end of the bridge, and stood with her arms wrapped around her body. She looked across at him, then out toward the coast. She was biting her lip.

She'd been silent for most of the trip on board the *Fair Lady*, though she'd been curious initially about the menagerie lashed to the aft deck in cages, and wriggling about in safely tied hessian bags in the lounge cabin. He'd explained to her that on the way to taking her to South Africa he'd be finding a new home for the wildlife they'd captured from the *Peng Cheng*.

He'd deliberately refrained from asking her anything about the missing package, as it was clear to him she was still traumatized by her experience on the island. At one point in the voyage, when they'd crossed the wake of a speedboat, he'd reached for her elbow to steady her as the boat rocked, but she had snatched her arm away from him and moved to the stern. Even though she had returned to the bridge she was still wary of him. He couldn't blame her.

Mitch was the other passenger on board. He was in one of the staterooms below. Bound and gagged, though lying on a comfortable bed. Alex regretted the way things had turned out, but Mitch had been a festering problem for some time. Unlike the rest of the gang, Henri included, Mitch was a felon who'd found himself a job as a military man—not the other way around. The American's avariciousness and aggressiveness had been an asset in some of the attacks they'd carried out, and a liability in others. Ironically, Alex had always feared that if anyone were to kill during a raid it would be Mitch. In fact, it had been himself, on board the *Penfold Son*.

The smart thing to do would have been to kill Mitch, tie him to one of Sarah's old Land Rover engine blocks and dump his body in the clear blue waters of the Bazaruto Channel. The other smart thing would have been to kill Jane.

"Alex?"

"Yes."

"What . . . what are you going to do with me, when we get ashore?"

It was as if she was reading his mind. "I'm taking you to Johannesburg, if you still want me to, that is."

She nodded. "I think so. Aren't you worried, like Mitch and the others were, that I'll tell the authorities about you—about your secret life?"

"I'm not going to kill you, Jane. If I'd wanted to I would have already done so."

"You haven't asked me any questions yet, either. So I'm going to ask you one. Why did you and your men raid the *Penfold Son*?"

"The captain of the *Peng Cheng*, the Chinese ship you saw tied up in our harbor, confessed that he'd made a delivery to your skipper. He thought it could have been diamonds, and that was good enough for us. We had no plans at all to take on the *Penfold Son*, but my guys and I were still on board the *Peng Cheng* when the drop-off took place. It was a spur-of-the-moment thing."

"A spur-of-the-moment thing? Just like that, you decide to find a helicopter and hijack a huge cargo ship?"

He shrugged at her incredulity. "I am a pirate. How well did you know Iain MacGregor, the *Penfold Son*'s captain?"

She bit her bottom lip and paused for a few moments while she thought about her answer. "Reasonably well—as much as you get to know someone in two weeks. He was a bit dour for my liking, but professional, from what I could see."

He could tell she was holding something back. "He was killed in the attack."

"What?" She recoiled from him and stared, as if seeing him in a new light.

"It wasn't me, or any of my men. I'm a hundred percent sure of that."

"You were shooting at us from the helicopter, Alex—right at the bridge. I was there."

"Yes, but that was just to keep your heads down. I knew that on a ship like that nine-millimeter bullets would just bounce off the armored glass. It worked, too, as I saw you drop to the floor."

She nodded. "You're right, he wasn't hit then. He . . ."

"He what, Jane? Did he give you something, tell you something?"

Jane turned away from him and looked out to starboard, toward the coastline which was now visible as a low line of green through the shimmering heat haze. "I can't believe he was killed. Why should I believe you that you or your men didn't do it?"

"When you get back on the mainland and read a paper or check the Net, or talk to your boss, you're going to read that MacGregor was killed by pirates, and I want you to know, for your own safety, that it isn't true."

"What do you mean, for *my* safety?"

"Who were those men on board who were firing back at us? They weren't ship's crew, obviously. They were too well armed and well trained."

"Why the bloody hell should I tell you, Alex? You're a *pirate*, for God's sake. This is all too unreal." She started to walk aft.

"Were they in on the transfer?"

She stopped, and though she didn't look back, he knew he'd made a breakthrough. "Alex, you've been good to me, and don't think I'm not grateful to you for rescuing me from Mitch."

He stood at the helm, saying nothing, as she turned to face him.

"Are you saying that . . . that those men killed MacGregor?"

Again, he let the silence hang there, waiting for her to answer her own question.

"They didn't know anything, but perhaps . . ."

"Perhaps they worked it out, or got the information from Mac-Gregor by force? In that case, they'll be as keen to get their hands on the diamonds as I am."

"I presume you searched my gear?"

He nodded, feeling slightly embarrassed.

"And me, Alex? While you had me drugged with that "saline," did you *examine* me?"

"I swear to you, on the grave of my father, that I did no such thing, Jane, though . . ."

"Yes, I'm sure Mitch wanted to."

He nodded.

"Well, thank you for that."

"You believe me, then?"

"I do."

"Then trust what I say about MacGregor. My men didn't kill him. In fact, I'm rather ashamed to say we didn't get inside the wheelhouse as we were outgunned by a motivated, organized opponent. I expected a walkover. I did kill a man though, I think."

She looked confused.

"It was one of the men firing at us—security, mercenaries, whatever they were . . ."

"A mix of both," she said.

"I've never killed in any of the crimes I've committed. I'm not proud of it. Whatever those men were up to, none of them deserved to die. I'm being honest with you, Jane." He eased back on the throttle and checked the GPS. They weren't far from where he would make landing, a deserted stretch of sandy coastline south of Vilanculos. With his cargo on board—human and animal—he couldn't risk pulling in at the port.

She moved back closer to his side. "Why are we slowing?"

"I've got some business to attend to." He turned and walked back to the galley and unclipped and opened a drawer under the granite benchtop. He drew out a long carving knife, its blade curved from years of sharpening. He saw Jane's widened eyes and said, "Don't worry. I'm not going to give him what he deserves."

Alex went below, drawing the pistol from the belt of his tan chinos, and dragged Mitch from the bed on which he lay. "On your feet."

"Going to kill me?"

"You know I should."

He pushed him up the carpeted stairs, using the gun to prod him along. On deck, with Jane standing by watching, he motioned for Mitch to walk toward the stern.

"What are you going to do, Alex, make me walk the plank?"

"Yes." Alex, keeping the pistol trained on the American, moved to a fiberglass pod containing a self-inflating life raft. He cut the securing ties and kicked it overboard, keeping hold of a long rope that uncoiled through his hands. As soon as the container hit the water he yanked hard on the lanyard and the compressed air inside it activated and the raft blossomed into its full size. "Jump overboard, into the raft, Mitch."

"Very melodramatic. Going to cast me ashore with no provisions?"

"There's water on board. Jump in before I change my mind and shoot you."

Mitch turned and looked at Jane. He stared hard into her eyes. "You'll pay for this."

"Enough idle threats," Alex said. "Jump."

Mitch stepped off the rear deck and, despite his best efforts to retain his balance, pitched face forward into the bottom of the raft. Alex tossed the carving knife into the boat. "Use that to cut the cable ties on your wrists. Oh, and be careful not to cut yourself or stab the boat."

"Thanks a lot, *buddy*."

Alex unfastened the line securing the raft to the *Fair Lady* and returned to the bridge. He punched in a new coordinate and turned north, heading parallel to the coast, and away from Mitch—forever, he hoped. The raft was a shrinking speck on the otherwise pure blue of the Indian Ocean. It wasn't far to shore, and Mitch had a paddle. Mitch would be OK, but Alex wondered where he would end up. If Jane told the Mozambican police about what was really happening on Ilha dos Sonhos, then Mitch might actually be better off alone.

In a way, he didn't care if she did shop him to the authorities. Danielle was right about his obsession with getting the hotel up and running; but he, too, was being honest with her when he said he wanted to go straight. Perhaps this was the shake-up he needed to start afresh as an honest man.

"What are you thinking about?" Jane asked.

"Going straight."

"I thought all boys wanted to be pirates."

"Maybe it's time for me to grow up. Are you going to tell the police about me, about the island?"

"I don't know. I haven't made up my mind."

Alex nodded. He could see her predicament. She had been caught in the crossfire—literally—over an illegal act that had taken place on board the flagship of the company for which she was the legal counsel. It wouldn't be good for her career at Penfold Shipping to raise the alarm if her bosses were involved in diamond smuggling. Nor would it be good for her career as a lawyer if it were later discovered she'd been giving legal advice to a bunch of criminals.

"I really need to use a phone, you know. You must have communications from this boat—and don't give me that rubbish about broken generators."

He smiled. "Of course. But think about what you're going to say. I'm a criminal, Jane, but I don't want to see you become embroiled in something that's not your business."

She frowned at him. "It *is* my business if employees of Penfold Shipping are involved in smuggling. It's also my duty to report it to the managing director."

"As long as he's not involved. I'd play it cool if I were you."

"I don't need your advice, Alex. Why haven't you asked me where the package is?"

"I haven't got around to it, that's all."

She laughed at his honesty.

"I don't have it, but I do know where it is."

"Are you going to tell me?" he asked.

"No."

"Then I should probably feed you to the sharks. But first, make your phone call."

Alex opened a drawer under the control panel and handed Jane the satellite phone, which was like an oversized old-fashioned mobile phone. He showed her how to turn it on and returned his attention to the shoreline. "I take it you want me to make the call with you around," Jane said.

"It's your business, but it's not going to change anything. I won't harm you if you tell him the truth about me."

He was a riddle, with his softly-softly approach. By rights, and by law, she should call the police and report him and his entire pirate gang. But the seeds of doubt he had planted in her mind—about Piet van Zyl and his men, about Iain MacGregor, and even George Penfold—had taken hold.

By his own admission, Alex had killed a man in the raid on the *Penfold Son*, and for that he should be held to account and punished. However, she was inclined to believe Piet van Zyl had questions to

answer over the death of Iain MacGregor, who had entrusted something of great value to her. Alex had more information about that mysterious package than she did. Jane had not even opened the parcel
and was surprised to learn it might contain diamonds. If she had not
fallen in with Alex and his men, what would Van Zyl have done with
her? She, too, had fired a gun at a man, and had discovered that she
was capable of killing.

The way Alex had just treated Mitch had convinced her that he
was not involved in some clever plot to lever a confession from her.
He had genuinely intervened to save her from torture or worse. Ironically, Mitch's threat of pain had worked on her and she had been
about to reveal the location of the package when Alex had turned up.

She wondered what Alex's next move would be. Would he try to
charm the location out of her? He was a handsome man, but her heart
belonged to another man, even though he was married and her boss.

Her life had been so normal until a couple of months ago. And
here she was on a boat off the coast of Africa with a self-confessed
killer and would-be hotelier. Bizarre.

"George, it's me!" she said when an excited Gillian connected her.

"Jane, where are you? Are you hurt? I've been worried sick about
you."

She was pleased at his words, and the sincere tone in his voice.
"I'm fine, George. I've had a bit of a rough time, but I'm safe and on
my way to Johannesburg."

"What happened to you?"

She explained, as Alex listened in, that she had made her way to
a lifeboat when the *Penfold Son* was attacked—which was the truth—
and had lost consciousness and awoken on an island owned by the
man who had found her. That, too was the truth, though even as she
spoke she asked herself what was making her withhold important information. Alex might yet turn out to be a monster who was even
now toying with her.

"I'll fly out immediately. When can you get a flight?"

"Um, you know I don't fly, George. I'm going by road."

"Well, I'll be there to meet you, at the Melrose Arch, the hotel you were booked into. Call me again when you have a better idea of your ETA."

"Got it. It's so good to hear your voice, George."

"Yes, well, I've got company here, Jane."

She wouldn't have said anything intimate over the phone, but she thought he could have given a little hint of his feelings for her, no matter how veiled.

"Have you heard about Captain MacGregor?" he asked her.

"Yes. It's a tragedy."

"One of the security men on board was also wounded, in the arm. He fell overboard, but he'll live. Jane," George continued, "did Captain MacGregor give you anything . . . a package of some sort, before he was killed?"

And there it was. As blunt as that. Jane felt as if someone had injected ice water into her spinal column. Her heart beat faster and harder and the hair rose on her arms. Alex looked at her, and she bit her lower lip while she tried to think of what to say.

"What do you mean by a *package*, George? Papers?"

She glanced back at the pirate behind the joystick that served as the helm on the luxury motor cruiser and saw him give a slight "I told you so" nod of his head. Curse his smugness, she thought. She didn't need that now.

"Not papers. Perhaps a small packet containing something."

"Packet of what?"

"I can't talk now, Jane. I'm flying tonight and I'll be there to meet you, whenever you arrive. I'm pleased you're unharmed. Are you all right for money?"

Pleased? That was the best he could come up with? "Will you be able to call me back when you're not so busy?"

"I've a lot to get done before the flight. Can you give me a number and I'll call you when I get to Johannesburg?"

Jane put her hand over the mouthpiece and asked Alex for the number.

"You'll understand, I'm sure, if I don't give that to you."

She nodded and told George she was using a borrowed phone and the man who owned it wouldn't be with her after tomorrow. She agreed to try and call George back at his hotel the next day.

"Thanks. Goodbye, Jane. I'm pleased you're well."

Suddenly, she felt very alone.

The lighter, a flat-bottomed barge with a shallow draft, was waiting at anchor offshore, when he rounded the point.

Alex took the nine-millimeter from his waistband, cocked it and replaced it under the loose tail of his white cotton shirt. He shrugged at Jane's wide eyes. "A precaution," he told her.

He eased the throttle to neutral and coasted alongside the smaller vessel. Alfredo threw a line to him and he caught it. The two of them drew the *Fair Lady* alongside, so that she nestled against fenders made of old car tires, and tied up. The wiry African, dressed in jeans and the shiny red shirt of an English Premier League football club, jumped aboard.

"*Ola*, Alexandre, *como estas? Todo bem?*" the man said, extending his hand to Alex.

"*Estou bem*, Alfredo, *et tu?*" The African nodded that he was well. Alex turned to Jane and introduced her.

"Charmed. It is my pleasure to meet you," Alfredo said.

Alex knew Alfredo had an eye for the ladies, and more than one female backpacker had ended up staying part of her holiday at his well-appointed beachside villa south of Vilanculos. "Jane's traveling with me to South Africa," he explained in a proprietary tone.

Alfredo nodded that he had received and understood the implicit message. "I have a truck standing by on the beach for your . . . cargo, Alexandre."

"*Obrigado*," Alex said.

Alex told Jane he needed a few minutes in private with Alfredo. "Of course. How soon before we get to Vilanculos?"

"About two hours, so you've time for a shower before we dock."

"Right. I'll go downstairs then."

Alex continued to speak Portuguese to Alfredo, in case Jane was still in earshot. He pulled a roll of U.S. dollars from his trousers and counted out two thousand in hundreds. Capitao Alfredo Pereirra was the best police officer money could buy on the Mozambican coast. While Alex trusted Alfredo, he was always armed whenever cash changed hands.

Alfredo called orders in Xitswa to two men who had accompanied him on the lighter and one climbed aboard. He had no trouble starting up the small crane on the *Fair Lady*'s stern which had been designed to raise and lower a jet ski. It was now hefting the caged, grunting leopard, which Alfredo's laborers steadied with tentative fingertips as it moved over the side and onto the lighter.

"The news is bad for you, Alexandre," Alfredo said, lighting a cigarette. "Why did you have to kill the captain of the *Penfold Son*? I won't be able to protect you from a murder charge if the British government brings pressure to bear on mine."

Alex didn't bother denying knowledge of the attempted hijack. "I didn't kill him, Alfredo. There were armed men on board. I think they were there to safeguard a smuggling deal."

The policeman's eyebrows lifted in interest. "More wildlife? Ivory? Rhino horn?"

Alex shook his head. "Maybe diamonds."

Alfredo gave a low whistle. "Is the woman involved?"

"You ask too many questions, my friend."

"It's not me you should be worried about, Alexandre, but I won't go to prison for you, my friend."

"I know." Alex walked out of the air-conditioned bridge and the force of the African sun assailed him as he oversaw the transfer of the last of the crates and bags onto the lighter. "I'll see you in Vilanculos at three, Alfredo."

"Be careful, Alex."

Once they had untied from the lighter, Alex opened the throttle. He couldn't risk unloading his mammalian and reptilian cargo in the port at Vilanculos in case a policeman or customs official less corrupt than Alfredo took notice. It was a measure of the relationship he had formed with Alfredo that the policeman was not in the least surprised or perturbed about organizing at short notice a four-tonne truck to transport a wriggling, snarling menagerie of captive animals. He'd also been frank in his advice, and Alex appreciated his concern.

If Jane wouldn't tell him where she had hidden the diamonds, then he would have to follow her to them. He wasn't assuming she would fall for his charms and give up the location, but Alex was becoming more certain her employer, George Penfold, was involved in the diamond deal. She'd been unable to hide her excitement when the man had come through on the line, and Alex sensed there was more to their relationship than the purely professional. He'd also seen the way her face had dropped when he had heard Penfold, his voice faint but still understandable, ask Jane if Captain MacGregor had given her anything. "Would you like a glass of Moët?"

She looked at him wide-eyed. "You're joking."

"I never joke about champagne." He handed control of the boat to her. She was hesitant, but he showed her how to use the joystick control and keep the cruiser on the track set by the GPS. With Jane at the helm he went to the refrigerator and filled a silver bucket with cubes from the ice maker. He aimed the bottle aft and the cork flew out over the stern into the Indian Ocean. Alex poured the wine into crystal flutes and she laughed. When she smiled she was even more beautiful.

"That's delicious. Why am I accepting a drink from a pirate who kidnapped me?"

He raised a glass to hers, took back control of the boat and said,

"Fate?" They clinked and drank. "Besides, I didn't kidnap you—you fell into my arms."

Jane blushed and looked out to sea as she drank. "I was pleased you didn't kill that security man on board the *Penfold Son*," Jane said. She had already relayed the news that the man was hurt but still alive.

"Me too," he said. "Do you believe me that I didn't kill Captain MacGregor?"

She took a sip of champagne. "Yes. I don't know why, but I do believe you."

"Then you agree that . . ."

"It could have been a ricochet from all that gunfire for all I know, but . . ."

"It may have been one of those men on board. Do you think your boss knew about the diamond smuggling and that was the reason for the extra muscle?"

"Alex, I really don't want to talk to you about who may or may not have been involved in what. To tell you the truth, I'd like to wake up in my bed in London and find out this whole thing was a bad dream."

The thought crossed Alex's mind that he would like to wake up in that same bed one day. "Be careful, Jane." It was the advice Alfredo had given him, and it was good.

"There is something floating out there. A raft, I think," the woman said.

He had been studying the chart and dreaming of barbecued lobster in a beachside restaurant in Vilanculos. Their home in Frankfurt was a distant memory, as was the chain of four hardware stores he had owned for thirty years. He was living for the present now, not a care in the world that a stiff breeze and a cold beer wouldn't cure.

The boat was the love of his life—well, his second love. His first was his second wife. At thirty-five she was twenty years younger than he. She kept him young, when she wasn't trying to kill him in the cabin below. She looked wonderful in the G-string bikini and it was a shame to see her wrap the brightly printed *kikoi* she'd bought in Mombasa around her pert little arse.

He sighed and picked up the heavy rubberized marine binoculars. "Where?"

"Starboard, two o'clock. Maybe a thousand meters."

She had good eyes, as well. He focused and saw the inflatable life raft.

"We should check it out," she called back to him, brushing a strand of sun-bleached hair from her forehead.

He'd read the magazine and Internet articles about piracy. They took precautions, such as waiting to tag along with other boats when they'd sailed down the notorious Somali coast, at the recommended safe distance of two hundred kilometers from land. He carried a weapon, also. Some of the experts advised against carrying a firearm, in case it was turned on the owner. However, he was an expert shot, and had hunted boar and deer at home, and all of Africa's big five in Zimbabwe and Tanzania in years gone by.

He unlocked the cabinet beneath the helm and deftly assembled the two pieces of the double-barreled shotgun. He slipped the two fat cartridges home and snapped the weapon closed.

"Is that really necessary?" she asked.

For some reason his wife hated the shotgun.

"Yes. Take the helm, darling."

They were still in sight of the Mozambican coast, motoring slowly south in the still conditions. He hauled in the rubber dinghy, climbed over the back railing and slipped in. The fifteen horsepower outboard started first pull. "Cut the motor when I get close to the raft, Gretchen."

"You've got me worried, taking that *thing* with you." She pointed with distaste to the weapon, which cost as much as one of her diamond bracelets.

"I'll be fine. But keep watch. You know the emergency channel, yes?"

She nodded.

He let go the tender rope and gunned the outboard. The weight of the shotgun was reassuring across his suntanned knees. There was no sign of movement on board the raft and he wondered if it had been lost overboard in a storm. "Hello," he called in English.

He cut the throttle and coasted up to the raft, the inflatable sides bumping softly against each other. "Hello," he said again.

He stood awkwardly as he held the weapon in one hand and grabbed hold of the bright orange craft with the other, so he could peer inside under the nylon covering. There was a man inside, lying on his back. He wore dark sunglasses, red board shorts and a garishly printed Hawaiian shirt. "Are you all right?"

He licked his lips and looked back at his own beloved yacht and wife. He waved to her, trying to signal her to come closer. They had walkie-talkies and he wished he'd thought to bring one. Stupid, really. The man seemed unconscious. He hastily tied the tender rope to the raft and stepped on board.

He and his wife had both attended first-aid classes as preparation for their round-the-world trip. ABC—airways, breathing and circulation—he said to himself as he knelt beside the man. When he touched the man's neck the skin was warm and the pulse was beating fast.

Behind the sunglasses the eyes snapped open.

On board the yacht, Gretchen Mueller waited eighteen minutes before pushing the button to start the engine. She yelled across the water, but again there was no reply.

She put the throttle in neutral and allowed the hull to brush against the orange raft, on the far side of their own tender.

"Wolfgang?"

Engaging reverse, she stopped the yacht's drift. "Wolfgang?"

She peered down at the raft but its cover was all but closed. About thirty centimeters of zipper was unfastened, with a short length of rope protruding. Gretchen leaned over the side and grabbed the rope.

The hand darted out. It was red and sticky and it locked around her wrist with a grip that threatened to break her bones.

She screamed.

11

Alex moored the *Fair Lady* at the wharf at Vilanculos and Jane grabbed the day pack that mostly contained other women's clothes. She had showered in the spotless chrome and tile bathroom below decks in the luxurious San Lorenzo cruiser and changed into a khaki skirt and a lemon-yellow V-neck top. There had even been a hair dryer on board.

She rejoined him on the bridge and he led her down the gangway. His only luggage was a green canvas military kitbag.

Jane thought about running off and finding a bus to take her away, but she had never been a backpacker and didn't have a clue where she might find transport in Vilanculos. She was a good driver, but she was unsure about the wisdom of hiring a car and driving more than a thousand kilometers on her own, on what Alex had described as "adequate" roads.

Jane had always played it safe. She hadn't taken drugs as a teenager—her rebelliousness had been limited to lying to her parents about sleeping over with a friend and going out to a nightclub at the age of seventeen with a bunch of girlfriends who had gotten her horribly drunk on martinis. She'd been unable to stomach gin ever since. It was ironic that the safest thing for her to do now was to accept a lift from a pirate.

At college she knew she'd had a reputation as something of a prude. It didn't worry her—not then, at least—but as she'd entered her thirties she'd become restless.

There were no outward signs of it, of course. She had a good job, with a good company, a good car—a Volvo—and a mortgage. The only thing Jane Humphries had done that was completely and utterly out of order was to sleep with her married boss. And if she was honest with herself, she had loved it—the actual act of sleeping with him; the act of being bad. It didn't stop her from feeling guilty afterward, though.

It also shocked her, and she was still coming to terms with the feelings that had motivated her to keep seeing George.

The fact that he had asked her if MacGregor had given her anything had bothered her. Afterward she'd felt numb, betrayed. George was clearly involved in whatever smuggling operation had led Mac-Gregor to rendezvous with the *Peng Cheng*, and he had shown plainly that he cared more for his missing property than for her.

Setting foot for the first time in her life on mainland Africa, she took a moment to take it all in.

Vilanculos was not, at first sight, a particularly pretty town, though she could see its potential. More precisely, she could see evidence of its past glory as a tourist playground. The wharf was a crumbling finger of concrete sticking out in a wide palm-fringed bay dotted with a mix of dhows and a few rusting barges. The tide was going out and she could see sand flats appearing near the shore.

The most imposing structure in the town was right on the wharf—the gutted Dona Ana Hotel—which they walked past after leaving Alex's cruiser. A gaggle of a dozen teenage boys tailed them, offering paintings, shells and small drums for sale. Alex politely turned them down in Portuguese.

Electric drills whined from inside the hotel's angular Art Deco concrete walls and African workers pushed barrows laden with bags of cement inside to feed a churning mixer. Other tradesmen rolled pink pastel paint onto rendered walls and sanded timber window frames.

"Looks like you might have some competition," Jane said. "And their renovations are moving faster than yours."

Alex shrugged. "This was one of the grandest hotels on the coast. It was named after the wife of Senhor Joaquim Alves. He was a Portuguese tycoon who brought tourism to the Bazaruto Archipelago. He owned an airline, shipping companies and several hotels and resorts. My maternal grandfather was one of his business partners. This place was paradise in its day."

"I like your island better."

"Me too."

Alex greeted a smiling African man and the two spoke in a mix of Portuguese and Xitswa for a few minutes while Jane waited patiently. The man handed Alex a set of car keys and Alex showed her to a new Toyota Land Cruiser parked on the side of a sandy road at the end of the wharf. "Before you ask: No, it's not stolen," Alex said as he opened her door for her.

"Purchased with ill-gotten gains, though?"

"No comment," Alex said. "It's a long drive to where we're going—not in distance but in time, because of the condition of the roads," he continued, checking his watch. "We should stay here in Vilanculos for the night and get going early tomorrow."

"Will your animals be all right?"

"Alfredo's providing food and water for them. He's keeping them in a warehouse near the port overnight."

"What if the police find him driving around with a truck full of endangered creepy-crawlies?"

Alex laughed. "He *is* the police."

Piet van Zyl had found Lisa Novak's address on the Internet phone directory. He drove past the high white security wall and noted the curls of shining razor wire interspersed with the straight strands of the electric fence. As he slowed he heard the barking of dogs.

The double-cab *bakkie* he drove carried the logo of Eskom, the South African electricity company, on the side. Van Zyl and his three men all wore the blue overalls of the company. The signage on the vehicle had been forged by a former army colleague who had taken up signwriting as his legitimate career after leaving the service, and the rebirthing of stolen cars as his main source of income.

"This place is like Fort Knox," said the American, Tyrone.

"You haven't spent enough time in South Africa. This is par for the course here in Johannesburg." Van Zyl took the Sig Sauer nine-millimeter pistol from the tool bag on the floor under his feet, screwed on a silencer and cocked the weapon. He looked at each of his men, reassuring himself the resolve was still there. "Ready?"

Tyrone Washington nodded. Built like an ox, but anything but dumb, Tyrone was a man not afraid to do whatever it took to complete his mission. The fact he was black—African-American—was a bonus on this job. It would have looked suspicious for a team of all-white South African electricity workers to show up to a job. Tyrone had been a Force Recon gunnery sergeant in the United States Marine Corps, but an investigation into the shooting in Baghdad of four civilians, three women and a fourteen-year-old boy, had ended his career. The way Tyrone told it, the boy would have ended up a suicide bomber, and the time spent with one of the women, before her death, had yielded the name of a senior insurgent.

"Ready," said Billy Tidmarsh. Billy was from Portadown, Belfast, and a British Army recruitment sergeant had saved him from a stint behind bars as an eighteen-year-old petty thief. He'd served with the Parachute Regiment, in his native Northern Ireland, Sierra Leone and Afghanistan. It wasn't his drinking that stopped him from making sergeant—just the number of noncommissioned officers he had knocked unconscious in drunken pub brawls. He was steady, as long as he was off the booze. These days he drank when Piet van Zyl told him to.

Ivan was a second generation Russian Spetsnaz—special forces. His father had been killed in Afghanistan when Ivan was a baby and the son had used his two tours in Chechnya as a chance to kill as many mujahideen as he could in retribution.

Van Zyl's cell phone vibrated silently in the front pocket of his overalls. The prepaid SIM card number that flashed on the screen belonged to Enrico Alvarez, the fifth member of the team, who was on light duties because of the bullet that had passed through his right upper arm and the other one that had hit his body armor chest plate and knocked him overboard from the *Penfold Son*. Enrico would not take part in the raid, but instead was following the lady of the house, Lisa Novak. He was driving a small, nondescript rental car, an automatic as his arm was still in a sling.

"*Ja?*" said Van Zyl.

"She's just gone into the Pick 'n Pay. She's taken a list from her handbag so it looks like she'll be a while in the supermarket."

"Stay on her." Van Zyl ended the call and turned into the Novak family's driveway, stopping in front of a metal sliding gate, also topped with razor and electrified wire. He wound down his window and pushed the call button on an intercom mounted on a post.

"Hello?" said a female African voice on the other end.

Van Zyl knew, from his reconnaissance, that there was a live-in maid. He told her in Afrikaans that he was from Eskom and that he and his men were here to trim some tree branches which overhung the security fence and were too close to a power line. The idea of posing as an electricity worker had come to him as soon as he'd seen the branches, which were very close to overhead cables. It was an indication, he'd thought at the time, of a husband away from his home for too long. Mark Novak had been a model soldier—a by-the-book Recce Commando who'd made warrant officer. He was the son of a Polish immigrant and a South African mother of English descent and that made him a damned Englishman, or *rooineck*, as far as Van Zyl and the other Afrikaners in the Recces were concerned. Van Zyl had been on the receiving end of an embarrassing dressing-down from Novak when the other man had been his section commander in South-West Africa many years earlier. Van Zyl had kicked a bound SWAPO prisoner and Novak had ordered him to stop mistreating the black terrorist. The visit to Novak's house wasn't personal, however. It was business.

"The madam didn't say anything about Eskom coming today. You can call her cell phone. Here is the number . . ."

Van Zyl cut the woman off. "I don't have a cell phone. Let me come in and use yours."

"The madam will be home soon."

"Fine," Van Zyl said with an air of resignation, "we can trim from the outside, but it will mean I have to shut the power off for three hours. You can explain to the madam when she gets home why all the meat in her deep-freeze has defrosted."

The gate started to roll open. Two dogs, a massive *boerboel* and a barking Alsatian, bounded toward the *bakkie*. The maid, Van Zyl was pleased to see, had made the mistake of coming outside, drying her hands on her apron and calling the dogs to heel. Van Zyl got out first and walked toward her. As he did, he extended his hand, palm down and fist closed for the dogs to sniff. Each did so and, with the tacit approval of the maid, accepted his petting and words of greeting.

"I think you were right about calling the madam," he said to the maid. "Perhaps I should call her. Where's the phone?"

A bridge had been crossed when the woman had pushed the button opening the electric gate. She nodded and walked back inside the sprawling house, which was painted a honey tone in what Van Zyl assumed the owners would have described as Tuscan style. Once they were out of sight of the dogs he drew the Sig Sauer from his holdall, lifted it and shot the maid in the back of the head.

The rest of them moved fast, stepping over the woman's body without a second glance. The dogs, on the other side of the barred security door, barked and snarled at Tyrone, but calmed when Van Zyl walked over to them, making soothing noises and patting them. He decided to spare them.

He pulled on latex surgical gloves and pressed the start button on the laptop computer in the study. Tyrone pulled photograph albums from a bookshelf and flicked through them. As planned, Billy went past them and found the master bedroom, where he set to work emptying clothes drawers around the room, to leave the appearance of a burglar searching for hidden cash. Ivan checked the refrigerator door and magnetic noticeboard in the kitchen, then smashed bottles of condiments and splashed the contents of a carton of milk on the floor.

"Hey, I found some readies." Billy held up several thousand rand in bundles as he entered the study.

"Then the beers are on you," Van Zyl said, not taking his eyes off the computer.

"Anything useful?" Tyrone asked. "These photos are from the ark, man. Wedding stuff, baby photos. These kids must be in college by now."

"This looks interesting," Van Zyl said. The other two moved behind him. "Mozambique. When I spoke to the woman she told me her husband was working as a dive instructor somewhere on the coast, then she clammed up."

"I thought you said this guy had worked as a contractor in Iraq?" Tyrone asked.

Van Zyl nodded. "No one gives up a thousand bucks a day and then comes home and leaves a beautiful wife in Jozi to go teach backpackers how to scuba dive. Here we are."

He leaned back in the swiveling office chair so the others could see. It was a picture of Lisa Novak and six other men. They were all fit and muscled, their height and bulk dwarfing the petite, attractive middle-aged blonde. Behind them was a whitewashed building—a hotel, judging by the rows of identical balconies. Van Zyl clicked on the magnifying icon and enlarged the photo, until the name of the place, in raised black letters above the entranceway, was visible.

"Ilha dos Sonhos," he said. He clicked "print" and heard the whir of the printer next to the computer coming to life. His mobile phone vibrated again. "*Ja?*"

"She's moving. She was only in the supermarket five minutes, then she turned around and left her trolley in the middle of the aisle. Before that she was checking her handbag and cursing. I think maybe she left her pocketbook at home," Enrico said.

"Go," Van Zyl said to Billy and Tyrone. "Get Ivan and get in the *bakkie.* I'll buzz you out through the gate. Wait for me around the corner, to the south." His men obeyed him immediately.

The woman would be alarmed if she opened her gate and saw a strange vehicle inside. She might try to call the maid or, worse, Eskom or the police on her mobile phone. It was not part of the plan that she come home to find a house full of men and a dead maid. With more time Van Zyl would have found the names of the men in the photograph with Novak. There would be phone directories, or other pictures with captions, or e-mails which could be cross-referenced to holiday snaps.

He continued to search through the computer files and was checking her e-mails when he heard the metallic rumble of the gate's wheels on its track. He'd found more pictures featuring some or all of the men again, but no names. Unfortunately for Lisa Novak there was no alternative left to him.

"Trudy? Are you in there? I've forgotten my purse, please can you fetch it?"

He heard the click of her high heels on the tiles and the security door swing open and he stepped from the office into the hallway. He saw her lift a hand to her mouth when she saw the prone figure of the maid, the pool of blood spreading from one side of the corridor to the other. She looked up and saw him, recognition slowly dawning on her face.

"Hello, Lisa, remember me?" He would take her, he decided, and use her for his pleasure, either as part of the interrogation, to shame her, or afterward. It would depend on her.

The recognition widened her eyes. "You called, about Mark."

"That's right. I know what he's doing, Lisa, in Mozambique. All

I need from you are the names of the men in this photograph, and which one's in charge." He held up the glossy A4 print that was still damp to his touch.

"Why should I tell you anything, Piet? You're only going to kill me, like you did her." She looked down at Trudy.

"That's not true, Lisa. Mark's gone bad—he's a pirate. I'm not a policeman, but these men took something from my employer that doesn't belong to them. I only want it back."

She continued to look down at the dead woman. "I've got their names and numbers in my cell phone. I'll give them to you." She started to reach into the designer handbag slung over her shoulder.

"Wait! Don't move. Toss the bag to me."

But his words were too late. He was disappointed, more than anything else, when he saw the chrome work of the small automatic pistol appearing from the bag. "Drop it," he said, though he knew, and respected her for it, that she would do no such thing.

"Fuck you," she said, raising her arm.

Piet van Zyl did this sort of thing for a living. There was no way he could be outdrawn by a housewife. He fired twice.

12

After weeks cooped up on board the cargo ship, and the idyllic but simple landscape of the island's white beaches and palm trees, Jane was experiencing sensory overload on mainland Mozambique.

She'd guessed her experience of Africa, if she had arrived as planned, would be limited to boardrooms, hotel beds and perhaps a trip to the top of Table Mountain. There was nothing familiar or re-assuringly mundane about this vibrant country.

Color. It was everywhere around her. The rich, vibrant greens of a lush vegetation thriving in the humid coastal climate; the multihued blues of the sky and water; the patchwork brilliance of street markets selling the ripest, reddest tomatoes she'd seen in her life; the garish prints and colors of men's shirts and women's wraps that would have been obscene on a tourist but seemed somehow natural on the Portuguese- and Xitswa-speaking residents of this cash-poor coastal paradise.

Alex looked at ease and happy, freed of the responsibilities that weighed on him on the island. He joked and laughed with women in the street stalls, addressed barmen by their first name, and surprised small children with his knowledge of their native tongues.

They completed their shopping for the coming road trip in a

small but well-stocked supermarket, which had toiletries and food-stuffs they hadn't been able to buy at the local market. Afterward, he left her to freshen up in the simple bungalow in the spotless Palmeiras resort complex where they were staying the night.

Jane stepped from the cold shower, which was a relief after the intense beat of the sun on her head and the heavy air through which one waded rather than walked. She dried off and dressed in a short denim skirt and a white halter top. God, it would be good to get back into her own clothes.

She walked out onto the wooden deck in front of the hut and found him waiting at the foot of the three stairs. He was wearing jeans and a tight black T-shirt. He hadn't shaved and she thought the stubble suited him.

"For you," he said, holding out a bougainvillea blossom. She put it behind one ear. "Very tropical. I love these little bungalows, don't you?"

"Sure. They're nice and clean," she said.

"Simple, but elegant. Nice linen, clean, unpretentious. How do I take those ideals to a five-star international hotel?"

"Don't ask me about interior design, I'm a lawyer. Your suite was lovely, though."

"You think so? Thanks. The Royal Marines doesn't exactly qualify you as an expert in soft furnishings, but I'm enjoying turning my mind to something different."

They drove along the sandy road that ran parallel to the beach, back past the Dona Ana Hotel to a restaurant and bar that would have overlooked the bay if not for the grassy mound that blocked out the view. Jane guessed the lack of an outlook was not a bad thing during the cyclone season. The place was called Smugglers and the logo on the sign was a comical one-legged parrot dressed as a pirate and holding a tankard of beer. "How very appropriate," she said. Alex smiled.

The single-story building had a tin roof, a concrete floor and wooden stools and tables that were probably designed to be too heavy to heft during a fight. Some of the characters that started rolling into the pub as the sun sank looked as hard as the slats Jane was sitting on. Alex pointed out fishermen, charter-boat operators, ex-mercenaries turned dive instructors, and more than one criminal.

Music blared from a music station on a satellite television above the bar and a mixed group of black and white men in mobile telephone company T-shirts played round after round of pool. Outside, floodlights illuminated a sand volleyball pitch and by eight the place was full to capacity. Soon they were shouting above the music and chat and laughter of the patrons around them, just to be heard.

Jane was ravenous, and between them they quickly demolished a platter of lobster, giant prawns, crab cakes, fish and chips. They washed the food down with icy Dois M beers from big bottles.

"This is a fun place," she yelled.

Alex nodded. "It makes a change from the island. Sometimes it's good to mix with new people."

Jane looked over her shoulder and saw a raven-haired South African woman, one of a group of five girls who were attracting charter operators and divers as desperate as the four annoying kittens that mewed at their feet under the table. The woman was looking at Alex, trying to catch his eye. When Jane looked back he was looking at her, not the brunette. "I can see what you mean."

At a roared request from someone in the crowd the barman turned up the volume on the music channel. Alex leaned closer to Jane, resting his hand on the back of her stool. "What?" His fingers brushed her forearm and it felt like a jolt of electricity through her body.

"I said, 'I can see what you mean!'" She gestured back to the dark-haired woman with a flick of her head.

Alex grinned and said into her ear, "I only have eyes for you, Jane."

She laughed, but her heart was pounding fast. "You said we've got an early start. I think we should go back to the lodge now."

•   •   •

The red sun was still sluggishly freeing itself from the ocean as they left Vilanculos and drove north on the ENI, Mozambique's main coastal highway.

Behind them was the truck full of wildlife, driven by one of the Africans who had met the *Fair Lady* at the remote rendezvous site. On the bridge over the Save River they stopped to pay a toll, and then had to stop at a police roadblock. Jane couldn't help but be nervous as a policewoman in a blue uniform took what seemed an age to check Alex's registration paper, driver's license and passport. When she started asking questions in Portuguese Alex pulled a letter from the breast pocket of his safari shirt and smiled at her. She waved him through at that point, and Jane wondered if the letter had something to do with the corrupt Captain Alfredo.

"The women are the worst," he said as he checked to make sure the lorry was waved through in their wake.

"By worst, I take it you mean the most efficient?"

"The most honest."

It was a quiet road and most of the few other vehicles they saw were smoke-belching trucks laden heavily with long, dark hardwood logs, which Alex said were pod mahoganies. He swore as he pointed one out to her. "They're raping this country. That timber's destined to be made into furniture in Asian countries that have decimated their own forests. Also, the locals are still into slash-and-burn agriculture, clearing the land for peanuts and other cash crops. They don't even sell the timber they cut. It's criminal."

She saw the anger in his dark eyes. Where, she wondered, did he draw the line in terms of his own morality? Who was he, a man who used terror and military tactics to rob honest traders, to condemn other businessmen who took advantage of an African country's poverty? On the other hand, his passion for the environment touched something in her.

"Mozambique has been pillaged for centuries," he carried on, steering with one hand and waving with the other to emphasize certain points. "The province we're in now, Sofala, is named after the original Arab name for the port of Beira, from where ivory, slaves and gold were shipped. After the Arabs came the Portuguese, then we had Russian *advisers* here shooting wildlife from helicopter gunships, and now Chinese merchants. Mozambique needs a chance to heal itself, to recover properly instead of being someone else's larder, to be emptied whenever they're hungry for resources."

At the small town of Inchope Alex pulled three cans of Dois M from the car fridge while they waited in a garage for both vehicles to be topped up with fuel. He took one can to the driver of the truck, and handed the other to Jane as he got back behind the wheel and started the engine.

"You're not going to drink and drive, are you?"

"What are you going to do, report me to the police? It's not far to the national park now."

She opened her beer and had to admit to herself that it was thrilling doing something that back in England might have resulted in her getting disbarred. Alex drove slowly when they turned onto the dirt road, which was badly potholed with what looked like thousands of tiny bomb craters, each the size of a dinner plate.

"This road floods in the wet season, from October to March, and elephant move through. The indentations of their feet dry out in the winter and this is what's left," he explained as the steering wheel juddered in his hand.

"Are you going to tell me where you're taking all the animals in that truck behind us?" she asked him.

"I'm going to show you." He turned off the rutted track into an open clearing of long dry grass.

He shifted the Toyota into low-range four-wheel drive and Jane had to grip the handle on the dashboard to keep herself steady. She glanced behind them and saw the truck plodding along slowly in their wake. Alex continued on for about five hundred meters until they were out of sight of the track.

"This should do fine," he said.

Alex killed the engine and got out. Jane climbed down out of the vehicle and followed Alex back to the truck. He spoke to the driver in rapid Portuguese and the man nodded. He got out of his cab and moved to the rear of the lorry, where he undid the rope fastening the canvas tarpaulin canopy.

"Are you going to release them all here?"

"Most of them. I'll take the python and a few of the other snakes to the Pungoe River," he said in a matter-of-fact tone.

"I thought you were going to sell them to someone. I'm pleased, of course, but don't you think you should tell the park authorities?"

He looked at her and smiled. "But Jane, what I'm doing is illegal."

She laughed at the absurdity of it, but took a wary step back when Alex climbed up into the back of the truck. The African driver pushed the leopard's wooden cage to the rear. The cat, perhaps sensing its imminent release, was snarling and pawing at the slats.

"Get into the cab," Alex told Jane, and repeated the instructions in Portuguese to the driver.

Jane watched from the running board on the passenger's side as Alex fixed one end of a length of rope to a ring bolt on the top of the sliding entry to the cage. Next, he climbed up onto the roof, his weight causing the canvas to sag between the metal bows supporting the canopy. "Get inside the cab and close the doors," he said to her. The driver was already in his seat, peering out a half-closed window.

Alex hauled on the rope and the leopard exploded from its prison in a blur of black dappled fur. It growled and hissed and Jane was surprised when, instead of running off into the grass, it circled the vehicle, as if in search of human prey in revenge for its privations. Jane wound up her window and Alex slithered backward along the canopy to the cab. The old Unimog, an ex-army vehicle, had a circular hatch in the roof. Jane popped it open and Alex slid inside, half falling on her in his haste to reach safety.

Jane started laughing and couldn't stop, despite Alex's stern look.

The leopard, its tail twitching in frustration and annoyance, finally satisfied itself there was nothing it could kill, and slunk off into the long grass. Jane composed herself and watched through Alex's binoculars as the magnificent predator disappeared from view.

"I think it's safe to carry on," Alex said.

Jane found it a wonderful, liberating experience to open the cages that housed exotic African parrots, and a box full of blue-headed lizards that clucked with apparent joy as their little feet touched bare earth for the first time in a long time—perhaps in their life.

She climbed back into the cab as Alex upended wriggling hessian bags. The driver, too, refused to get out of the Unimog once he knew there were snakes slithering about in the grass below. Alex conceded defeat and walked off to the Land Cruiser, parked close by.

Jane leaped down from the other vehicle and ran after him. "You've probably got Interpol and half-a-dozen other international agencies searching for you as a result of what happened on the *Penfold Son*, but here you are risking arrest by driving halfway across Mozambique to liberate a mobile zoo full of animals. I don't understand you."

"Well, that makes two of us."

"Why did you just do that?"

He shrugged. "Because it was the right thing to do? Perhaps I'm not totally morally bankrupt, after all."

They drove back to the main track and after another deviation to the banks of the Pungoe River, where Alex prodded a giant sleepy python, with a body length twice that of a grown man and with a girth as thick as one of Jane's legs, reluctantly to freedom.

Eighteen kilometers and two hours after they'd left the sealed road they came to the entry gate and a sign that said *Bem viudo a Gorongosa*—welcome to Gorongosa National Park. An African ranger in a green uniform saluted them. Alex spoke to the man in Portuguese and whatever he said left the man laughing as he waved them through.

The sky was a hazy pale gray, which Alex explained was the result of fires lit deliberately outside the park by farmers clearing their lands. "There are farms on the slopes of Mount Gorongosa as well, which is why you can't see it, because of the burning." He said there was a push by the national park's supporters to include the mountain, with its remnant covering of Afro-Montane forest and deep, clear natural pools, in the national park. "It makes sense," he explained as he drove through the park, his eyes scanning left and right for animals and birds, "as the water collected by rainfall on the mountain feeds the floodplains, which support the park's biodiversity."

"You know a lot about this place," she said.

"This was my second home after the island. My father loved Gorongosa and its wildlife, while my mother liked coming here to spot celebrities. It was *the* safari park for the rich and famous in the old days."

In front of them wide open grasslands stretched to the horizon and the invisible mountain beyond. These, Alex said, had once looked like a verdant carpet but so many of the herbivores that had once grazed on the plains had been shot to near extinction during the Mozambican civil war. They did, however, see herds of thirty and forty waterbuck at a time and Jane took an instant liking to their shaggy gray coats and faintly ridiculous telltale markings—a white mark in the shape of a toilet seat on their rear ends. Somewhere in the long grass, he said, were about sixty buffalo, the die-hard survivors of tens of thousands that had once roamed the park.

Jane used Alex's binoculars to watch a far-off lone elephant bull ambling slowly through grass which rose above the height of its belly. He'd avoided driving closer as the pachyderms were notoriously wary of humans, who they equated with gunfire and death. Much of the park's game had been slaughtered to feed RENAMO's soldiers.

Alex took two beers from the fridge behind him and popped them open. "There's hope, though. There are people dedicated to bringing the game back."

"Can the damage ever truly be undone?"

"Come, I'll show you."

At Chitengo, the main and only functioning camp in Gorongosa National Park, he took her on a tour that showed the horrors of Mozambique's past and the promise of what the country might yet become.

They parked the Land Cruiser and he led the way to the reception building. Three ranks each of seven young men, their bare torsos glistening above green fatigue trousers, were practicing what looked like kung-fu moves, complete with loud exhalations of air at the end of each leg lunge and fist punch.

"They're rangers in training," Alex said. "In the old days they would have been doing military drill, dressed as soldiers. The new administration wants to instill discipline, but not create an army."

She nodded, though pointed to another recruit, armed with what looked like a wooden replica gun, slung from his shoulder. He waved a friendly hello to them on his way to duty. "So what's with the toy gun?"

"The rangers will be armed, once they're trained, and the wooden rifle is a way of getting them used to carrying their weapon and being responsible for it, before they get the real thing."

Chitengo was a watered green oasis amidst the still dry plains and bush. Manicured lawns surrounded tasteful chalets that looked newly painted. Alex said the camp was being progressively renovated to attract tourists, and new accommodation was being built for the park's staff, who had lived in the old guest rooms during the years when no one had visited Gorongosa.

After checking in and paying their entry fees they walked through the camping ground, which was shaded by tall Livingstone's coral trees. A couple of four-wheel drive vehicles with South African numberplates were parked side by side with fold-out tents sprouting from their roofs. Large shirtless men ensconced in deckchairs raised glasses as they walked by. Beside the swimming pool a young woman tapped away on a laptop, connecting to the rest of the world by wireless Internet, within sight of a large building that still bore the pockmarks and holes of bullets and shells.

"This was a slaughterhouse, literally, for the troops during the war. This is where so many of the park's animals ended up."

"It gives me the creeps," Jane said.

"It's meant to. The park management doesn't want to gloss over or hide Mozambique's past. They want visitors from here and abroad to see the good with the bad, in order to prevent it from happening again."

"Will it?"

"I don't know."

A group of boys aged somewhere between eight and twelve were playing soccer with a ball made from rags wrapped in rubber bands and duct tape. One ran awkwardly as he was carrying something in a woven net slung over one shoulder. It wasn't until Jane walked closer, her curiosity piqued, that she saw it was a baby.

"He's probably minding it while his mother works. Family ties are strong in Mozambique. It helps keep us together."

Late in the afternoon, after they had checked into separate chalets, Alex took her on a drive along a bumpy trail across the floodplains. The sun had entered the thick band of dust and smoke that hung just above the horizon and the contaminants turned it a deep, Bloody Mary red. They parked for a while on the shores of Lake Eurema and watched hundreds of crocodiles, which Alex said the locals referred to as sardines, because of their density. Some basked on muddy banks while others patrolled the water, nothing but nostrils and malevolent golden eyes visible.

"They say these ones thrived during the war," Alex said. Jane shuddered.

They drove on and Alex stopped at the remains of a two-story concrete building. He took a bottle of sparkling South African white wine out of the car fridge and unsnapped a leather case from which he took two crystal glasses. Jane eyed the dewy bottle with mixed emotions. They had already had a couple of beers and she was feeling a little light-headed, but she didn't want to break the magic of the sunset over the never-ending plains.

He led the way up a flight of external stairs. The building—really no more than a concrete hulk—bore the scars of wars like the others she'd seen in the camp. They took a seat, she at the top of the staircase and he two down from her, the bottle on the step between them. They were about four meters off the ground and the height gave them a commanding view.

"What was this place? It's like a fortress."

"My father always said the Portuguese were masters of cement. This is called the 'lion house.'" The cork left the bottle with a pop and the sound and sight of the golden liquid filling the glasses made her mouth water. "There used to be a bar here when I was a kid and the Portuguese elite and foreigners from around the world would gather to watch the sun go down. Funnily enough, after the tourists stopped coming, researchers would often see a pride of lions living in and around this place, as if they'd taken over the house that was named for them."

"It must have been beautiful in its day."

"It still is."

He was looking at her, searching her eyes. The last of the sun lit his face a golden bronze. He raised his glass to hers.

"What are we drinking to?"

"Africa?"

"A bit corny," she said. "Besides, you forgot the windup gramophone."

He laughed. "How about to you, then?"

"Inappropriate."

He was flirting with her, and she knew it was wrong, but she was enjoying it as well—the risk, the location, the fact that he was not her boss or married. There was no future for her with a man like Alex

Tremain. He was a criminal and a womanizer, judging by the fact she was wearing cast-off clothing from two different women.

"Your skin looks beautiful in this light."

"Alex, please."

"No, I mean it. It's just an observation, nothing more. The photographers call this time of day in Africa, the 'golden hour.' Just before dusk, and just after dawn. Beautiful."

She felt her cheeks color. Funny, that she had been thinking exactly the same thing about the way the light bathed his face. *Don't do it*, she told herself.

From far away came a low wheezing sound that rolled across the plain. It was a two-part moan rising then falling, which tailed off into a series of grunts. "What on earth was that?" She was grateful for the distraction.

"Lion." He didn't take his eyes off her. "It's not how it sounds in the movies, is it?"

"I suppose few things are the same in real life." She sipped her wine. His stare unnerved her, just as it churned her insides, in a good way.

"It's a male, perhaps calling to his mate."

She looked in the direction the sound had come from, but saw nothing. It felt as though every nerve ending in her body was tingling, from a mix of fear and excitement. The noise started again and she thought it odd how even before she knew what it was, it had raised the downy hair on her arms and brought up goose bumps. Jane started to speak, to ask how far away he thought the cat was, but he stilled her with a hand on her forearm.

"Listen. There's the female. Far off, but not as distant as you might think. Some people say a lion's roar will carry five or more kilometers, but that's rubbish. In my experience, it's no more than one at the most. They're close."

They were sitting atop a concrete ruin with no fence or gate to protect them from the lions that might decide to come and reclaim "their" house. She was nervous about the animals, but her heart was pounding because Alex hadn't moved his hand. He was blatantly trying to seduce her and her logical lawyer's brain told her that it was just a different approach to Mitch's to get her to tell him what she had done with the package Captain MacGregor had given her.

"Is it safe—here, I mean?" she said, looking down at his hand.

"I'd never let anything hurt you, Jane."

She wanted to believe him. She took a big sip of wine, breathed deep and was about to take another when he reached up and took the glass from her.

"Hey . . ."

He raised himself up on his knees so his face was level with hers, and kissed her. She leaned back, the concrete digging into her spine, but she barely noticed. She'd been surprised, and pursed her lips initially, but the warmth inside her spread like lava and she opened her mouth to him.

She thought of George and his interest in the package. Damn him and damn Alex.

She broke the kiss, despite her body's betrayal of her resolve.

"No, Alex. This isn't right."

In the gathering darkness there was silence. He looked away from her into the gloom. No frogs croaked, no birds sang, no insects chirped.

"The lions," she said, once she regained her breath. "They've stopped calling."

"They've found each other." He stood up and gathered the glasses and half-empty bottle.

13

Mitchell Reardon presented his passport to the bored-looking Mozambican official at the immigration desk at the grandiosely named Vilanculos International Airport. Alex really was a sap, he thought. If he were him he would have dealt with a dissenter with a bullet in the head.

No, that wasn't right. What Mitch would have done was cut Alex, then truss him up and drag him slowly through the water behind the *Fair Lady*, trawling for sharks. Mitch laughed to himself.

The immigration officer raised his eyebrows.

"Nothing, bro," Mitch said. "Just an old joke I remembered."

The terminal building was small—the check-in area not much bigger than a suburban home's lounge room—and Mitch was able to brush his crotch discreetly against the denim-clad rear of a slim Italian woman as he sidled his way toward the staircase. He tramped through water, muddying the work of a woman who worked the concrete with a scrubbing brush.

Upstairs, at the small snack bar, he ordered calamari and a Manica beer and took a plastic seat under an umbrella. The tops of palm trees peeked above the blurred band of heat haze that boiled up from the narrow, pitted runway. The lone Pelican Air twin turboprop aircraft sat waiting for the mixed bag of construction workers and rich foreign tourists to board.

A middle-aged couple in matching safari khaki emerged from the stairs. Mitch smiled at the woman, an attractive blonde with nice tits, but the stuck-up bitch ignored him.

He grinned behind his raised beer as he remembered the way the German woman on the yacht had begged for her life and agreed, tearfully, to everything he'd demanded of her, before he'd slashed her throat.

He felt himself start to harden in the dead man's trousers. As well as chinos and a button-down shirt he'd plundered shoes, and a set of expensive golf clubs, which were now in the airliner's hold. He couldn't help but grin as he remembered the way the bitch had directed him toward a stash of fake jewelry, a few hundred greenbacks and two imitation Rolex watches, stashed behind one of the seats in the yacht's galley. You couldn't fool a pirate that easily. He knew some pleasure sailors kept a stash of fake valuables—even wallets filled with expired credit cards—as a means of fooling bandits. That shit might work on some Somali fisherman, but not on a former U.S. Navy SEAL. No sir.

"Another beer," he said to the waitress who collected his empty.

The blonde woman's husband was in the john and Mitch smiled at her again. She continued to ignore him, pretending to read a magazine. It would have been easy, once they were in Johannesburg, to tail her and her man back to their home or hotel. But he had other business on his mind.

Revenge.

Mitch had grown tired of playing second fiddle to Alex on the island and had become increasingly disgusted at the other man's weakness. What kind of pirate limited his takings to building materials and cars? They could have made a fortune ransoming or selling the ivory and rhino horn. The leopard would have been fun to hunt. He'd hunted three others of the big five—lion, buffalo and elephant—on trips to the mainland. He would have liked to see the big cat die.

He was certain he could take command on Ilha dos Sonhos if he could get Alex out of the way for good. Damn Alex. He would have had some serious fun with that bitch, whether she'd told him the location of the diamonds or not. And then he would have done the sensible thing—killed her. Alex had no backbone, but the men respected strength. All had killed in the course of duty and none was squeamish. Novak was Alex's closest friend and ally and, while all would swear their allegiance to Tremain publicly, Mitch had already proved to himself that he could divide and conquer the gang. Henri had voiced some initial misgivings about torturing the woman, but he had also agreed with Mitch that Alex's softly-softly approach with her was a waste of time. Mitch had been able to talk the gay Frenchman around. The others would be difficult, but not impossible. The cracks were there . . . Mitch just had to bust them wide open.

Jose, as the man with some vague ancestral claim on the island, was another kettle of fish. He was intensely loyal to Alex. They were like brothers, but without an income Jose and the villagers would have to pack up and move to the mainland. Sure, they could fish for their supper, but Mitch had seen the way Jose liked to flash his gold chains, designer clothes and new BMW when he was around the ladies in Vilanculos. He'd grown used to the stream of income piracy had brought to the island. Alex had invested his share of the loot in that crumbling money pit of a hotel, more fool him, though he hadn't begrudged his local "partner" from spending his takings on material possessions. Nope, Jose had tasted western consumerism in all its glory and he would follow the dollar once Alex was dead. Kufa, the Zimbabwean, would do as he was told.

Alex's childish dream was that they would steal until there was enough money to reopen the resort and go legit. Supposedly Mitch and the others would then either retire gracefully or take up gainful employment as cabana boys and bartenders. Mitch wanted more in his old age than a redundancy payment, or the promise of tips and vacationing rich widows. He wanted it all: the island, Alex's sleek boat, and a license to rob, kill and fuck at will.

"Pelican Air Flight 401 to OR Tambo Airport, Johannesburg, is now ready for boarding," said a voice through a tinny public-address system. The aircraft's starboard engine whined and the propeller began to turn.

Mitch finished his beer slowly, unlike the tourist couple, who left their drinks half full and hurried downstairs. The man shot him a backward glance—his bitch wife must have said something. Mitch just smiled at him.

Yep, he thought, he wanted it all, and soon he'd have it.

"A photo?" George Penfold tossed the glossy print on the table of the open-air coffee shop outside the Melrose Arch Hotel. He lowered his voice to a serpentine hiss. "You kill two people, and all you bring me is a bloody photograph? I was told you were the best, Van Zyl."

On the street, an African in a Zegna suit eased himself awkwardly out of a low-slung canary-yellow Lotus and handed the keys to the hotel's valet parking attendant. George looked out across the mock-Italian cobbled square at yuppies with Bluetooth receivers in their ears, talking and gesticulating on their way to work like lunatics conversing with God. Nothing was understated in Johannesburg. The morning sunlight that glittered off a white woman's chunky gold necklace and diamante-encrusted sandals was diffused by the smoke from shantytown cooking fires somewhere beyond Melrose's border.

Melrose Arch was like an industrial estate for bankers, jewelers and insurance companies—a mini suburb with cafes and upmarket bars and restaurants rather than supermarkets and fast-food joints. It was part Milano piazza, part Manhattan rush hour, part London drab. Like most fusions it had failed to create an identity for itself, but that didn't matter. Only money did.

Piet leaned back in the sculpted white plastic chair and sipped his cappuccino. "The Novak woman pulled a gun on me. It was self-defense."

"I read the newspaper on the plane. What was the maid carrying, a butter knife?"

"I thought this was important to you, Mister Penfold, recovering your lost property and finding the English woman." He laid his cup back in its saucer and dabbed his lips with a serviette.

George pinched the bridge of his nose. He'd slept fitfully in first class on the overnight BA flight from London and he'd been up most of the previous evening, giving the blonde hooker the thrashing she so richly deserved and, he was sure, secretly craved. The sex and the punishment had not relieved his tension, nor lessened his concerns. The only bright light was that Jane was alive and would soon be joining him. She'd said on the phone that MacGregor had given her nothing, but George thought he'd detected a trace of dissembling in her pauses before answering. Time would tell. In the meantime, he was seriously doubting the wisdom of hiring Van Zyl. Not because of his ruthless disregard of human life, but because of his failure to deliver. "It is important, Mister Van Zyl. Which is why I am so monumentally unimpressed that all you bring me for the loss of two lives is a piece of paper with no names on it."

"One name. Check the sign on the front of the hotel. I enlarged the writing on my laptop. It says *Ilha dos Sonhos*—Island of Dreams."

"And where exactly is that?"

"Off the coast of Mozambique, in the Bazaruto Archipelago. It's at the epicenter of fifteen recorded acts of piracy in the last twelve months. Novak, the South African, is second from the left. I can find out who the other men are, but the important thing is we have a location."

George pursed his lips. The coffee was too cold to drink and his flight had been delayed an hour on the tarmac. Did nothing go according to plan on this godforsaken continent? "I'm listening,

Mister Van Zyl, but only because I have no one else to see for the next hour."

"My men and I take that island. We take your pirates out of the game and we find out from those we take alive what they have done with your package, since you say the woman doesn't have it."

George had read the reports of the damage done to his company's flagship—the vessel that was named after him. The criminals residing on the Ilha dos Sonhos would be an even greater thorn in his side to his legal and illegal cargo operations once he bought out the South African shipping company. They had to be dealt with. "Why should I trust you to recover my property?"

"You should have trusted me with your true agenda before sending my men and me to rendezvous with the *Penfold Son*. If you had, we could have tightened security on board. MacGregor was a fool to keep your goods in the ship's safe. It's hard to ensure the safety of something when you don't know it exists. My men and I are soldiers, Mister Penfold. We would, naturally, expect a finder's fee for goods recovered, but I'm also looking for a business partner, someone with the wealth to back other ventures I might have in mind in the future. I would think that a retainer arrangement would be of mutual benefit, now that I'm aware of, shall we say, the full suite of your shipping activities."

Bloody hell, but the man had balls. Van Zyl had failed at every turn, and here he was blackmailing him. George liked the idea of direct action against the pirates on their island lair. If he were twenty years younger and without the responsibilities of running a shipping business, he might have offered to join in the raid. The phone in his pocket vibrated. "Penfold."

"Sir, it's Gillian, good morning. I'm sorry to disturb you, but reception has just put through a call to me from a man currently in Johannesburg—an American. He wouldn't give me his name but he said he had information about the identities of the men who raided the *Penfold Son*. He said he would speak only with the owner of the company. I have a number, sir."

George took out his Mont Blanc and wrote the telephone number down on the back of a serviette. He slid it across the table to Van Zyl. "It appears I must do most of your work for you, Mister Van Zyl, now that we are prospective business partners. Call this man and tell him you're acting on my authority. Set up a meeting."

14

Jane stank.

"Would you like a beer?" said the sweating Afrikaner sitting next to her in the Toyota Hilux, not for the first time.

It was times like this—not to mention the time the ship she'd been sailing on had been hijacked by pirates—that she wished she wasn't terrified of flying. "No thank you."

At least six in the evening was a civilized hour for drinking. The three men she was sharing the vehicle with had been taking turns at driving, drinking and snoring throughout the entire grueling fifteen-hour trip. Jane had offered to drive, partly out of fear for her own safety as whoever was behind the wheel was likely to be fatigued or drunk at any one time, but the South Africans wouldn't hear of it.

They were all coal miners from Witbank, huge men with huge hands and huge beer bellies. Weynand, Christo and Dirk were gentlemen—none had made a pass at her and Christo had offered to "*klap*," which Jane assumed meant hit, "the Englishman" she had told them she was running away from. She'd assured them that it was just a tiff and that she needed her own space. No klapping was required.

They were in South Africa now and according to Weynand, who

was behind the wheel again, rubbing his reddened eyes, only three hours from Johannesburg. All the men had agreed, despite her telling them that she would catch a bus or hitch a ride from Witbank, that they would travel the extra two hours to see her deposited safely at her hotel. "You don't want to hitchhike on South African roads, hey," Christo had told her solemnly "We all go, and that way we can keep each other awake and have an extra *dop* or two before we gets home to our wives." A "*dop*" she had learned, was a drink.

"On second thoughts, I think I will have a beer please, Dirk." True to form, he popped the can of Castle Lager for her, and even slipped it into a neoprene cooler.

Jane thought about Alex as she drank, and what she would say to George when she met him in Johannesburg. She had slept very little during the evening, after she had returned to her bungalow in Chitengo Camp, alone. He hadn't touched her during or after dinner, not even a goodnight kiss, but even now in the truck she could still feel the softness of his lips on hers. She remembered the spontaneous arousal his kiss had drawn from her body and her mix of excitement and shame. It was confusing that she might feel guilty about the possibility of betraying a man who was already married. Alex had stared at her during dinner and she'd seen the desire in his eyes.

He was a criminal and she was a lawyer. She had questions for George, both as his lawyer and mistress, and no doubt there were difficult decisions to come, but a pirate could not help her, nor be her moral compass. Besides, she had to keep reminding herself, Alex had probably only wanted to bed her in order to find out what she'd done with the package.

She'd dressed, quickly, and walked to the camp ground, following the sound of clanging pots and half-muted conversations in Afrikaans. The South Africans they had seen the previous evening had been on a fishing holiday to Inhassoro and had decided, on the spur of the moment, to take an overnight detour to Gorongosa National Park. They were breaking camp when she found them, and planning on driving the long road back to Witbank in one hit. She'd told them a tale of a lover's tiff and a holiday that hadn't worked out. They'd been happy to offer her a lift.

She'd slept through a lot of the drive south on the ENI down the coast of Mozambique. When she'd woken she'd glimpsed palm trees and sugar plantations, gangly boys on the roadside holding up huge crayfish and plastic bags of cashew nuts for sale. The South Africans had stopped only to urinate and restock their cold box with ice for their beer, of which they seemed to have an unending supply. The border crossing had caused her some problems, given that she didn't have an entry stamp or visa for Mozambique. She'd concocted another story, about having two passports. She said she'd been robbed of her Australian passport and been told by immigration that she would have to report to the immigration authorities in the capital, Maputo. Weynand had whispered to her to pull out some cash, and that had settled the visa problem, though it had cleaned her out of the two hundred U.S. dollars she'd kept in her money belt for emergencies. She smiled to herself as she drank her beer. An officious Mozambican civil servant was the least worrying incident that had happened to her lately.

The Toyota's engine whined under the weight of the fishing boat it towed, yet they climbed steadily out of what the men called the Lowveld into the Highveld. It was as different to the hot, humid coast of Mozambique as could be. They sped on good roads through wide open rolling hills of crops and grazing land that stretched to the horizon. Like her travel companions, everything seemed bigger than in England. They passed a turnoff to a place called Emalahleni, which Weynand explained was the new name for his hometown, Witbank. "It means 'place of coal' in Zulu, but I'm not a Zulu, so I'm going to call it Witbank until I die," he said. The monotony of the landscape was broken by enormous coal-fired power stations, which the miners explained they supplied, and towering man-made mountains of mine waste as they neared the golden city of Johannesburg.

All the men were awake as they entered the outskirts of the city. As they passed the nondescript suburb of Benoni, which Christo explained with some pride was the birthplace of the Academy Award–winning actress Charlize Theron, Weynand said something in Afrikaans to Dirk, who then opened the glove compartment and drew out a nickel-plated hand gun. Jane thought of the moment when she had pulled the trigger and the shock in Mitch's wide eyes, distorted by the eyepieces of his mask, as the bullet punched him backward onto the deck.

"Don't worry," Weynand said to her in English, seeing but misreading her expression. He held the pistol up. "We're safe with 'the equalizer.'"

The locals called the city *Egoli*, city of Gold, and for a moment its buildings were bathed in a pale yellow as the sun slid behind a mine dump. The men said it was smoke from cooking fires and car exhaust fumes that softened the light, and the smell, when she cracked the window a little, confirmed it. She'd heard it was a dangerous place and had been warned by Harvey Reynolds, before leaving London, not to walk or sightsee by herself while staying there on business. After what she'd been through on the high seas and in Mozambique she wondered how bad it could be. The men, however, started exchanging stories of friends of friends who had been robbed, carjacked, assaulted or murdered on the streets they were now driving.

Was Alex Tremain, she wondered, in the same league as a black man who shot a white for his BMW or executed the owners of the house he robbed to eliminate witnesses? Was one less of a criminal than another? Alex had tried to explain that he and his gang used firearms as a tool to coerce cooperation from those they robbed. They would never, he assured her, fire unless to save their own lives, as had happened on the *Penfold Son.*

She shook her head, ignoring the sideways glance from Dirk, and drained the rest of her beer. Alex went on board those ships armed to the teeth and trained and ready to kill to get what he wanted. That was wrong, and she had been wrong to be tempted by his kiss, though even now she could still feel his lips on hers.

"Where are we dropping you?" Weynand asked.

"Oh, sorry. I must have been half asleep again. It's a place called Melrose Arch. Do you know it?"

"*Ja?* It's where the rich fat cats hang out. I thought you was a pommie tourist, a backpacker or something?"

"It's complicated."

"You not in trouble with the law, are you?"

"No," she assured him.

"Wouldn't have mattered if you were. We couldn't leave you stranded with that creep in Mozambique, whatever is going on."

She wanted to tell them that Alex wasn't a creep, just a pirate, but couldn't think of a way to do so without having a long complicated conversation. "Actually I'm here on business. The holiday in Mozambique was just a side trip that went wrong. This is where I'm supposed to be now. This is where I belong."

And, as the reflective glass towers of the corporate sanctuary of Melrose Arch loomed canyon-like around them, she wished to God that was true.

Alex was in a philosophical mood as he drove back to Vilanculos from Gorongosa National Park.

He tried to put her out of his mind, but failed. He told himself he should let her go, that he would be risking far too much by pursuing her and the package she had hidden. He had come to the conclusion that she had left it somewhere on the *Penfold Son* before climbing into the lifeboat. Whether she would tell him where it was or not was something he would never know. She had been concerned that her boss, George Penfold, appeared to know of the exchange that had occurred between the *Peng Cheng* and *Penfold Son*. That obviously worried her, but if her employer was involved in something criminal, what would she, as a lawyer, do about it? He'd hoped that he could get close enough to her for her to lead him, willingly or not, to the stones. That was before last night.

He'd awoken feeling as he did now, that he was more concerned for her than he was for the missing treasure.

It was something of an epiphany for him. He still missed Danielle's financial and organizational skills, and Lord knew they'd be lucky to find a diesel and marine mechanic to match Sarah, but both women were lost to him now. He hadn't thought of pursuing them, nor given a thought to whether they'd arrived at their next destination safely. He was, however, worried for Jane.

She was attractive—though so were the other girls—so there had been more to his growing attraction to her than her physical beauty. Although clearly shaken by the trauma she'd gone through on the *Penfold Son*, she had gone down fighting in the lifeboat and then set off on the kayak and discovered the island's secret. She'd also taken the time to get her payback against Mitch before leaving. She was clever and tough and she had let him take her as far as the mainland before escaping. Jane hadn't fallen for him, as other women had. She had bested him, and while he respected her for it he was still concerned for her safety. It was a long way to Johannesburg.

But he also had his men to think of, and others on Ilha dos Sonhos who relied on them. To some of the Mozambicans he was, though he felt uncomfortable about it, their *padrao*, the father figure cum employer that his own father had been in the resort's heyday. He wasn't comfortable with the almost feudal connotations, but he couldn't escape the fact that without him they had little to look forward to other than a life of subsistence fishing.

Mark and Lisa Novak wanted to retire somewhere in Mozambique, and Alex had offered the reliable former warrant officer a stake in the hotel, perhaps running the dive business or fishing charters once they went straight. Heinrich had said on many occasions that there was no way he would want to live in Germany. Henri and his lover might stay, or might move to the mainland, and Kevin was a free agent, though Alex sensed that all of them would, given the chance, make a life for themselves on the island. Jose wanted to be the richest bartender in Mozambique and Alex was quite happy to help his childhood friend's dream come true—if he could.

Removing Mitch from the team was like excising cancerous tissue. Things might be all right from now on, but the poison he'd spread might also have taken hold in some small measure. His were men of action and without it—and money—they would grow restless and either leave or try to depose him.

Money. With another million U.S. dollars he reckoned he could have two full floors renovated and the restaurant open and staffed. Then he could implement the marketing plan Danielle had written for him. There would be travel agents and journalists to be feted before paying customers were enticed back to Ilha dos Sonhos, but a quick injection of cash could see them in business before the onset of the next wet season.

Despite the Triad leader's laissez-faire attitude to the *Peng Cheng* and its crew, Alex was sure Chan would cough up at least a hundred grand for the return of his ship. That, however, would barely cover the cost of the appliances for the new commercial kitchen for the gutted restaurant. Alex needed more cash, which was why he would travel to Johannesburg and listen to Chan's offer. If it was drugs he wouldn't touch it, likewise wildlife or people smuggling, or the illegal export of timber.

He crossed the Limpopo River at Mapai. The water was low this time of year—barely ankle deep—so he waved away the boys with a span of oxen who made their money during the wet season towing South African tourist vehicles.

Alex had decided to change his route into South Africa after Jane had run off. His new route would take him cross-country to South Africa through the Mozambican extension of the Kruger National Park, the Greater Limpopo Transfrontier Park. The crossing into

South Africa would be through an out-of-the-way border post with fewer police, and if Jane had tipped anyone off about his movements then the law would most likely be lying in wait in Zimbabwe, or at the main border crossing into South Africa at Beitbridge.

On the other side of the river he paid his money to enter the Limpopo Park. It was a bubble of land—a hunting concession in the days of Portuguese rule—that had been designated as national park; however, there were still villagers living, growing crops and tending their cattle inside the area that was now shaded green on the map. It would be a long time before the Mozambican side of the reserve could boast anywhere near the same densities of wildlife as Kruger, although efforts had already been made to restock the land with elephant and buffalo from South Africa.

What Alex liked in this part of the country were the trees— towering mopanes and leadwoods which had been spared the annual feeding cycles of elephants and other game for many years. Alex's thoughts turned, briefly, as they occasionally did, to the little elephant with the tear in its ear. *What had happened to her?* he wondered. Had she migrated, with many others, across the border into Kruger to escape the guns of hunters or hungry soldiers during the civil war? More likely she was long dead.

He crossed through the quiet border post at Pafuri, in the far north of the Kruger Park, and then turned left toward the Punda Maria Gate. Once out of the park and free of its fifty kilometer an hour speed limit, he floored the accelerator. At Louis Trichardt he joined the main NI road which would take him to Pretoria and then on to Johannesburg.

As he drove one-handed, he reached under his seat and found his Glock pistol, wrapped in its oily cloth. It was loaded and cocked. It would be ironic, he thought, if he, a major supplier of stolen cars into the South African market, was stopped by a carjacker in Jo'burg. The man would regret it.

•   •   •

Over the years she had moved her family further and further south, in search of more food and water.

The terror of her younger years was a distant memory now. There had been no wholesale death, no discoveries of piles of fresh bones for many years. Some of her children had never known danger, and that, of course, was a good thing.

The only threat to her family now was food—or lack of it. It seemed she had to walk a little further, work a little harder every year, to find enough vegetation to feed herself and her offspring. Sometimes, as was the case right now, she had to destroy to care for her brood. She leaned her massive squared forehead against the trunk of the tree and pushed against it.

She took the strain, feeling it in her aging shoulders, and pushed against the bark that dug into her skin and bone. If she didn't push the tree over, her children wouldn't be able to reach the leaves and the seeds, and she would be denied the succulent treat of the newly exposed water-rich roots at the base.

Behind her the rest of the family milled about, anxiously awaiting the food their matriarch's efforts would bring. The trunk started to creak. Her baby wandered between her legs, but one of its elder sisters shooed it to safety with a swat of her trunk. She could feel the tree giving now, feel it starting to topple.

One last push.

She summoned her strength and took a step forward. One step at a time. It was how she had come from her birthplace all those years ago; how she kept her clan together and alive. The tree toppled over, sending birds squawking, squirrels scurrying and a mamba slithering from its excavated home beneath the roots.

She rested while her children and grandchildren eagerly started sorting among the leaves and the pods. Water was next. The pans to the north fed by once-turning windmills were dry—another reason for their pilgrimage southward. She looked around her and wondered where the next big tree would be found, where the next source of water lay. There seemed fewer and fewer of each every year.

One more step on another journey. She was hot and she flapped her huge ears to allow the air to cool her blood, which was filtered through a web of veins. Somewhere deep in her memory was a recollection of searing pain in one of her ears, when the lion had tried to bring her down.

She had lived, but the long ragged V-shaped rent reminded her that life was never easy.

15

Jane waved goodbye to the coal miners and promised that she would send them some money to cover her share of the fuel, but Weynand told her he would send the money back to her if she did. Their dusty *bakkie* and boat stained with fish blood and guts over the stern looked as out of place in the corporate ghetto of Melrose Arch as she did right now.

Her feet were black and her finger- and toenails encrusted with dirt. Her hair felt like straw and Alex's former girlfriend's once crisply ironed sundress was stained with perspiration patches. She'd telephoned ahead from Dirk's phone and caught George between meetings. She'd given an approximate arrival time.

A towering bald-headed man in a long coat held open a heavy glass and steel swinging door for her as she entered the airconditioned cool of the Melrose Arch Hotel. "Mister Penfold's suite, please," she said to the immaculately dressed African girl behind the reception. Jane ran her fingers through her hair and felt sand. She grimaced.

"I'm sorry, madam, there is no answer."

She frowned, but when she gave the receptionist her name she found there was a room—a luxury suite, in fact—booked for her.

The hotel's decor was a mix of funky modern interspersed with colonial decadence. The smooth lines of the minimalist restaurant to her left contrasted with the deep leather sofas and shelves crammed with antique books in the library bar to her right. Somehow it worked. Vaguely, she wondered what Alex would have thought of it. She shook her head to clear it.

While she had slept on the drive through Mozambique, it had been a fitful rest and she'd woken every time a horn blared or brakes were applied harshly. Once, to her acute embarrassment, she had found herself slumped on Dirk's shoulder. He had smiled at her when she opened her eyes, horrified to see she was linked to his T-shirt with a silvery strand of drool.

She closed her eyes and leaned against the wall of the lift, which was cool and dark, lit only by an understated blue light. The chime roused her from her micro-sleep.

Jane sighed as she scuffed down the carpeted corridor in her gritty flip-flops. She leaned her forehead against the door as the card clicked home. Bloody George, she thought. At least he could have had the decency to meet her after she'd been bloody hijacked at sea, bloody been in a gun battle, bloody shipwrecked, almost bloody tortured and nearly bloody shagged by a bloody pirate.

"My God, I don't think I've ever seen you looking so lovely."

The dimmed lights brightened and there he was, in a charcoal suit and starched white shirt and school tie, not a hair out of place, and smelling deliciously of aftershave. In one hand was a dewy bottle of Pol Roger, the other held two champagne flutes by their stems. She laughed, loud and hard, a release of fatigue, fear and dread. "Oh, George."

He set the bottle and glasses down on the receded bar and came to her, enfolding her in his arms. He nestled his face into her filthy hair and said, "Oh, Jane, I thought I'd lost you."

She felt the lump rise in her throat. She had so much she needed to tell him, to ask him. There was anger, still bottled inside her, but it was soothed by his whispered words.

"Darling, I would have died if anything had happened to you."

A tear squeezed from her closed lids and she felt him kiss it away. "George, I..."

"Hush. Come this way."

He led her to a huge bath brimming with bubbles. She smelled aromatic oils heating over a candle. Everything else could wait.

"Raise your arms," he commanded her. She dropped the day pack she still clutched and did as he told her. She slipped out of her sandals as he lifted the dress over her head. He knelt on the floor and she rested her hands on the padded shoulders of his suit jacket as he slid down her pants.

As he stood he offered her his hand, which she took as she stepped into the bath. "You don't know how much I need this."

He wrinkled his nose. "Er, yes, I do."

She laughed again and it was good to be back with him, whatever he was involved in. It was good to be back in the fold of the corporate world she knew, not at sea, not on an island full of pirates, and not bouncing around the backblocks of Africa. She could easily forget everything that had happened to her.

George left the bathroom and returned, minus his jacket and tie, with sleeves rolled up and the champagne and glasses in hand. He poured a flute for her and then one for himself. Jane slid beneath the surface of the bubbled water. When she surfaced again, he was on one knee, beside the tub. "Mmm. Are you going to scrub my back for me?"

"I'll do you one better." He set down his glass and took her soapy right hand in his. "Jane Elizabeth Humphries..."

She felt her heart start to beat faster, a jolt of adrenaline cleaving through her tiredness. As she sat up straight, water and foam sluiced over her breasts. *Oh God*, she thought.

"Will you do me the honor of being my wife?"

16

Alex fastened the second of his gold cufflinks and checked himself in the mirror. He wore a navy blazer, Oxford cotton shirt and chinos, and had buffed his leather brogues to a high sheen.

He cast an eye over the furnishings and decor of his suite in the D'oreale Grande Hotel in the Emperors Palace casino complex, and wondered how his resort rooms would compare. Here the first word that popped into his head was *extravagance*. That wasn't a bad thing for a casino hotel, he supposed, as the idea was probably to inspire punters to hit the tables and win enough money to deck out their suburban homes like one of Louis XIV's palaces. The furnishings and the colors were nice, though. He made a mental note to call the hotel's head office and find out who their interior designer was.

Chan had chosen a particularly busy, high-profile and highly defended place to meet him. Serious money changed hands at Emperors, and the camo-clad security guards at the car park entrance gate looked as though they'd have no hesitation in firing their R5 assault rifles if someone tried to break the bank in the wrong way. He had parked his Land Cruiser between a Porsche and a new Aston Martin. Did some people *want* to be carjacked? He'd liked the look of the British sports car, however, and wondered how hard it would be to boost.

He left his room and took the lift downstairs. Where was the recording studio, he wondered, that put together the soundtrack for every lift and hotel lobby in the world? It was something else to remember for the resort—no elevator music.

Alex walked past reception, returning the smile of the smartly uniformed brunette behind the counter who caught his eye, then headed left along a hallway that linked the D'oreale Grande to the main casino complex. The walls were lined with gilt-framed copies of old masters. He walked through a metal detector and set off the alarm. Alex lifted his arms while the security guard detected his cell phone and waved him through. Alex took some measure of comfort from the security—it was unlikely Chan or the henchman he would bring to the meeting had been able to smuggle in pistols.

To his right as he entered the casino was a circular room full of slot machines. He didn't care for their bleeping and chiming and he felt sorry for the people who glared at the flashing screens, hoping for a win. He was addicted to a bigger game, with bigger stakes. The complex was an odd mix of styles. Leaving the French decadence of the hotel behind him, he passed a restaurant modeled on Queen Cleopatra's barge, and then found himself in a faux Italian piazza, with a statue of Michelangelo's David in the center, surrounded by restaurants and fast-food joints.

Alex looked up and saw night was falling, the sky a darkening blue, with the first couple of stars poking through the gloom. In fact, he was looking at a roof, high above the jumble of restaurants.

Alex found the steakhouse Chan had mentioned in his e-mail. "I think I can see the people I'm meeting," Alex said to the maître d'."

He had never met Valiant Chan in person, though he had seen his picture on an Internet edition of a South African newspaper. Six months earlier, Chan had been arrested and charged over the death of an alleged drug baron called Lee. Speculation in the media, fueled by leaks from the police, had it that Lee had been hacked to pieces in an escalation of a war between rival gangs over the importation of cocaine and heroin, and the manufacture of the highly addictive Tik, the local name for methamphetamine. The unspoken inference was that thirty-eight-year-old Chan, of the well-to-do suburb of Tokai on the slopes of Cape Town's Table Mountain, was the victor in that particular battle, and that Lee's messy demise had been a way of discouraging future competitors. Chan's team of lawyers had beaten the rap, but there had been no more puff pieces about the determination of a hardworking, budding tycoon fighting off racial stereotypes.

As the slim Eurasian man rose to extend a hand, Alex wondered if Chan was being watched. Gold flashed at his wrist, and when he smiled. "Valiant Chan. You must be Mister Tremain."

The handshake was firm. The pock-faced, stocky henchman beside Chan was introduced as "Mister Wu, the brother of the man you are currently entertaining."

"No hard feelings," Alex said. The other Wu did not return the smile.

"We've already ordered drinks, Mister Tremain, or may I call you Alexandre?"

"Alex is fine."

"And you must call me Valiant." Chan called the waiter over and Alex ordered a Scotch and ice.

"I see you've come alone, Alex?"

Alex shrugged. He didn't know if pleasantries or small talk were a part of doing business in Asia, nor was he inclined to care. "Do you want your brother back alive?"

Wu stared back at him and betrayed no sign of emotion.

"This man, unlike his brother, is unfortunately mute. The fact that you raided the *Penfold Son* soon after illegally boarding the *Peng Cheng* tells me that the good Captain Wu was probably not very good at keeping his mouth shut. Am I correct, Alex, in assuming it was you who stormed the *Penfold Son*?"

Chan paused to savor and sip brandy from a snifter. Alex said nothing.

"You needn't answer that question. However, and I give you this advice for free," Chan leaned across the table and lowered his voice, "beware of George Penfold. I would not want him to think that I double-crossed him—and I am not a man who fears very much at all in this world, Alex."

Alex swallowed some Scotch and let the warmth flow through him. He didn't want his senses dulled, but he did need to appear cool and in control.

"What about your ship?"

Chan shrugged. "You're a pirate. Would you go to sea in her?"

Alex smiled.

"I thought not. Scuttle her and you'll be doing me a favor. At least that way I can make an insurance claim. I doubt, however, that Lloyds will recompense me for the loss of my cargo. What have you done with it, by the way?"

There was little point in lying, so Alex told Chan the creatures that were still alive had been released to the wild, while the horn, ivory and other animal parts destined for traditional medicines in Hong Kong and Taipei were at the bottom of the Bazaruto Archipelago.

"My, my, a pirate with a conscience? Perhaps tonight I'll meet a whore with a golden heart." Chan laughed at his own joke. "What about my mahogany?"

"Your mahogany?" Alex checked his temper. The timber belonged to the people of Mozambique and should never have been felled in the first place. "I thought it'd make a nice bar, actually."

"I like that. Perhaps we can have a drink one day to christen your fine bar."

Alex pushed back his chair and stood.

"Sit, sit, Alex. It's too early for grand gestures of dismissal. We have more things to discuss than animals and wood. I'm unimpressed by your naiveté, though your idealism is quite charming. What I've learned of your assaults on my ship and George's has piqued my interest in you and your men."

"I'm a busy man, Mister Chan."

"Valiant, remember? I don't think you are very busy at all, Alex. George Penfold's cargo is still missing—I know that because he accused me of being behind your attempt to steal it—and I feel certain that you would not be here if you had, in fact, taken what he is missing."

Alex sat. "You're talking about the diamonds."

Chan and Wu exchanged a brief glance. Wu's brother was mute, but not deaf.

"What I want to talk to *you* about, Alex, has nothing to do with George Penfold or his shipping line. You need money and I am guessing that, after your botched raid on the *Penfold Son*, you will be holding off your piratical endeavors for the next little while, correct?"

Alex leaned back in his chair and finished his Scotch. Chan was right, but he said nothing.

"You might have failed to get what you wanted on the *Penfold Son*, but a man who can organize a heliborne assault on a cargo ship in broad daylight off the coast of Africa—let alone capture my modest little craft—deserves my attention."

A waiter arrived bearing a plate. "Your steak tartare, sir."

"Thank you. Forgive me, Alex, I was ravenous. I took the liberty of ordering before you arrived. Feel free to select anything you wish from the menu."

"I'm not hungry."

"Very well." Chan took a portion of raw meat and popped it into his mouth. He closed his eyes and hummed with contentment. "Perfect."

"There is something that I want you to steal for me that will make us both very wealthy, Alex."

Alex checked his watch. "What?"

Chan leaned closer to him again. "Ivory."

Alex shook his head. "I don't kill elephant, or rhino, or anything else in Africa that lives or breathes, Valiant. I would have thought you'd have guessed by now I'm not a poacher."

Chan dabbed his mouth with a starched linen serviette. "No, no. You misunderstand. I'm not talking about a couple of spindly tusks hacked from a young bull by some poverty-stricken Mozambican poacher. I am talking about ivory by the tonne—by the truckload— from elephants killed legally, by South African National Parks rangers and accredited hunters in the name of conservation, environmental protection and sustainable land management."

Alex couldn't mask his surprise. "The cull?"

"Exactly."

Alex waved to the waiter. "I think I will eat. Lobster mornay, and let me see the wine list."

Chan smiled.

The debate had raged for years, and not just in Africa, about what to do with the increasing numbers of African elephants in some of the continent's national parks. Across the continent, total elephant numbers had fallen dramatically in the latter half of the twentieth century due to ivory poaching. In the 1930s there had been up to ten million elephants in Africa, but by 1992 that figure had dropped to around six hundred thousand. While the species was in peril in some parts of Africa, in others, such as South Africa's Kruger National Park, and Hwange in Zimbabwe, ecologists were concerned that there were too many of the animals.

Elephants, Alex knew, ate between a hundred and fifty and three hundred kilograms of vegetation and drank up to two hundred liters of water a day. They were destructive in their quest for food, clearing swathes of bush and knocking over mature trees just to nibble on a few tasty roots. Their land-clearing activities served a purpose in a balanced ecosystem—creating habitats for smaller creatures by knocking over trees; providing access to water for others by creating game trails, and propagating plant species through their dung. However, most of Africa's national parks were fenced or constrained by outside land uses, and elephants that had once roamed vast areas were now confined to finite reserves.

In years gone by, national parks rangers in South Africa and Zimbabwe—then Rhodesia—had culled elephants to keep their numbers at a sustainable level. Culling was carried out with ruthless efficiency, with teams of rangers and hunters positioned to kill entire herds driven onto their guns by helicopters and beaters. Taking out a whole family group was judged the most humane way of carrying out the grisly task. Wildlife authorities learned, through experience, that baby elephants that grew up without parental control turned into unruly, sometimes dangerous delinquents. The culls provided scientists and students an opportunity to learn more about the animals; allowed national parks rangers to manage the environment; and, as a bonus, provided huge stocks of meat, skins and ivory.

Chan savored a mouthful of raw meat and washed it down with an expensive Stellenbosch red. "You are a man who cares for the natural environment, Alex. What's your view of the cull?"

The latest elephant *indaba*, a meeting of scientists, conservationists, politicians and animal rights activists from South Africa and abroad, had heard compelling evidence for a trial reintroduction of culling, on a limited basis, in the Kruger National Park.

"Everyone seems to agree there are now too many elephants in Kruger," Alex said. "The relocation of animals is an expensive business and can't be done in volumes high enough to make a difference." Hundreds of elephants had been darted and transported across the border into the newly created Limpopo transfrontier park in Mozambique, but many had simply walked back into Kruger, where they seemed to sense they would be safer. "The verdict's still out on contraception, as far as I know. I read somewhere recently that there's an ongoing trial of immunocontraceptives going on in a private reserve outside Kruger, but who knows how soon that could be put into widespread use?"

"Whatever happens, man and nature can only coexist into the future when man takes the guiding hand," Chan said.

Alex snorted in disagreement. He paused in replying while the waiter laid the lobster in front of him. This crustacean might have come from the same place as he, from the waters of the Bazaruto Archipelago. Chan was espousing a philosophy that had seen the decimation of some species and the extinction of others, but every human, Alex included, took from nature in some way. "The transfrontier park will give Kruger's elephants room to move in time, but I agree with the scientists who say that something has to be done now, in the interim, before the animals decide for themselves it will be better off to move across the border."

Chan put down his knife and fork and spread his hands in a gesture of conciliation. "Perhaps the resumption of culling will assist that process—scare the elephants back into Mozambique, where many of their ancestors came from, yes?"

Alex nodded, grudgingly, in agreement. It was ironic that many of today's big tuskers in the Kruger Park had actually been born in Mozambique and moved into South Africa in their youth. While white South Africans were often quick to point the finger of blame at black poachers in neighboring countries, the fact was that elephant numbers had been drastically reduced by white ivory hunters in the late nineteenth and early twentieth centuries. History had shown that elephants would vote with their feet when threatened.

Elephant migrations had happened in Alex's lifetime, too, mirroring his own displacement in his youth. He'd read that between 1967 and 1976 the elephant population in Kruger had increased by more than ten percent each year—well in excess of a natural birth rate. This showed that many of the giant creatures had fled Mozambique during the escalation of troubles.

Alex's mind was racing as he sipped chilled chardonnay. The food was good and he felt himself starting to relax in Chan's company. He reminded himself to keep his wits about him. As charming as the gangster was, he would be making no offers that favored Alex over himself. Captain Wu's brother remained silent, another reminder that Alex was outnumbered.

Chan continued: "The most strident of the animal rights campaigners at the *indaba* made it quite clear they would do everything in their power to disrupt or stop the first tried cull. The shooting will be done deep in the bush, away from the eyes of tourists and protesters. South African National Parks will have two Oryx helicopters from the national defense force seconded to them for the cull, to transport the killing teams of armed rangers and accredited big-game hunters. A temporary camp with a mobile abattoir will be established in the bush to carry out the butchering of the carcasses and the ivory will be flown out by helicopter."

"You seem to know a lot about the operation."

Chan finished the last of his steak and set his cutlery down on the plate. "Delicious." He wiped his mouth. He waited while the wine waiter refilled his glass, and Alex's. When the three of them were alone Chan said, "Dates, times, GPS coordinates, flight schedules, radio frequencies, call signs, names and cell phone numbers of all the key players. I have it all, Alex."

"How?"

"That's none of your business. But my information is reliable, of that you can be sure. I have the written orders for the entire culling operation, and a mechanism in place to be notified of any changes."

"Security?"

"As tight as you can imagine. As well as the military helicopters, there will be a platoon from the South African infantry battalion at Phalaborwa assigned to protect the ivory, once it's taken. That's in addition to police service detectives from the Endangered Species Protection Unit, local uniform cops from the Kruger Park, armed rangers and the parks board's own armed investigation division members. Added to all that, there'll be a score of hunters with rifles capable of stopping an elephant."

Alex had faced worse odds in Afghanistan, in the fire fight in which he'd lost his fingers, but he'd also had air support—and he'd nearly lost his life. He finished the last of his lobster as he formulated his questions. The first was the most obvious. "How much ivory, and how much money?"

"Ah, that's what I like about doing business with westerners. No pussyfooting around. The cull will be extremely controversial and the government expects a storm of protest after it is officially announced. They are, according to my sources, so sensitive to negative public opinion that they expect the trial may even be cut short. For that reason, the plan is to kill as many elephants as possible in this first round, in order to get as close to the quota agreed at the *indaba*—two hundred animals in one operation."

Alex gave a low whistle. Many of the animals would be juveniles or babies, with little or no ivory, but others—matriarchal females—could be carrying tusks in the range of fifty to sixty kilograms. "You're talking several tonnes of ivory."

Chan nodded. "The air operations order is allowing for up to four tonnes."

Alex wasn't sure of the market value of so much ivory, or if the price would drop if so much were offloaded in one hit. He suspected Chan might keep the tusks stored somewhere safe and sell them in dribs and drabs. That way he'd minimize the risk of the theft being tracked back to him, and maintain the current high premium.

"What's to stop the South Africans from just burning the ivory in situ, in order to avoid worrying about transporting and storing it?"

Chan nodded. "The politicians want to stage a media event in Johannesburg. They want to show the world that the cull is not about stockpiling ivory in the event that the CITES regulations are relaxed further, but rather purely about environmental management and conservation."

Alex knew that CITES—the Convention on the International Trade in Endangered Species—had achieved some success in stabilizing elephant numbers on the continent by severely restricting the worldwide ivory trade. Auctions of legitimately harvested ivory—such as tusks taken from animals that had died of natural causes—were very rare and strictly monitored. It would be in Chan's interest, Alex realized, to try to ensure that the legal trade was further curtailed, or stopped indefinitely, as this would push up the price of illegal ivory. While his mind calculated the possible value of the heist, his conscience kicked him hard in the guts. "This is wrong, Chan."

The Chinese man laughed. "Excuse me, but where exactly does hijacking a ship and keeping my men imprisoned fall in your definition of wrong versus right?"

Alex lowered his voice. "Your men are criminals—like me. Those elephants are defenseless."

"I do not pretend to agree with your naive view of the world, Alex, but I respect a man who sticks to his principles. Think this through, though, before you make your decision. What would the world think of the South African government if, having finally secured a tenuous agreement to resume culling for a limited trial, it was unable to protect all that ivory?"

Alex pushed his plate away and poured himself another glass of wine. "They'd end up with egg on their face, and the cull would be regarded as a failure. Criminals—you, chiefly—would be regarded as the main beneficiaries of the slaughter of two hundred animals."

Chan grinned. "Chiefly. The man who swipes that ivory, from under the noses of the people who are planning on destroying it, and gets it to the *Peng Cheng* would also be richly rewarded."

Alex could see the headlines. The government would be backfooted into explaining how it had lost the tusks. After the fallout one of two things would happen—either there would be no more culling or, next time, the ivory taken from the slain elephants would be burned on the spot, as it should have been first time around. The initial crime would benefit Chan and the middlemen and consumers down the line, but never again would such a large quantity of ivory fall into the wrong hands. Alex felt a surge of excitement, a tingling rush like a shot of adrenaline.

Stealing ivory so that rich Japanese businessmen would have

carved seals and figurines was wrong, but so too was killing two hundred magnificent beasts that might one day take up residence across the border from Kruger if they were given a few more years' grace.

And there was the challenge.

To steal four tonnes of anything from the middle of the African bush and move it—somehow—across Mozambique and onto a ship was bigger than any job he'd ever attempted.

"How much?" Alex asked.

Chan smiled. "Again, that wonderful directness. I will not insult you with a charade of negotiating. I have read of your work off the coast of Mozambique and I am impressed. I need a man who can mount a military operation, on land and sea—and air if you think it necessary. Am I right in thinking that you are that man, Alex?"

"How much?"

"One million U.S. dollars, in cash or transferred to the bank account of your naming. Half up front—which will also secure the return of the *Peng Cheng* and her crew to me—and half on completion."

"Expenses in addition," Alex said. That was non-negotiable, as he already anticipated them to be high.

Alex did some quick mental arithmetic. He and Novak had been discussing the value of the ivory they'd found on the *Peng Cheng* and the South African had recalled that the prices fetched for ivory at the last legal auction were around the one hundred and fifty U.S. dollar mark per kilo. Chan was offering him a substantial amount more than the legitimate value of the tusks.

"You're working out the value of the ivory, yes?" Chan said, reading his mind. "If I am right—and I'm sure I am—there won't be any more legal trading in ivory for a long time if we are successful. I'll be able to name my own price for ivory on the black market. This is a long-term investment by me, Alex, and I know the allure of the magic-million price tag. Tell me, would you have said yes to less than a million dollars?"

Alex shook his head.

"So?"

"You've just bought your ship back, Valiant."

Chan beamed. "Keep it at your island hideout. Oh, yes, don't look so surprised. I know more about you than you think, Alex. Set Wu free and have him call me. I'd be obliged to you if you could accommodate the captain and his crew until you give him his orders—where and when you need him to collect the ivory."

Alex nodded. Ivory—white gold—had made Europeans rich in Africa in centuries gone by. It might just save his dream, and he wouldn't have to kill a single elephant.

17

Jane woke, slightly hungover and very confused, scrambling with her hands to escape a prison of pure cotton sheets and fluffy pillows.

She sat upright and blinked. For a second she had no idea where she was. The room was dark, though a chink of light peeping around the edge of the heavy curtains told her it was daylight. The air conditioner hummed.

She'd been dreaming of the Norman church in the village where her parents lived, walking down the aisle in an ivory dress with a lace bodice. George was waiting for her, his back to her, but when he'd turned it was Alex's face she saw. She shivered.

The bed was empty, just an indentation in the mattress beside her and the smell of his aftershave on the pillow. And on her.

She put a hand over her eyes. "Oh, God," she said aloud.

Right at that moment, Jane wanted to be back in her old room, in her parents' cottage, with a mum who'd tell her everything would be fine, and a father who'd bring her tea in bed. She wished she'd never met George Penfold or Alexandre Tremain.

She remembered George's proposal and groaned.

"George, you're already married," she'd said to him, once the shock had passed.

"She's agreed to a divorce, Jane. I spoke to her on the telephone as soon as I learned you were safe. It was hard, of course, but it'll be an amicable split, I'm sure."

"It's all so soon, George. I'm flattered, honestly, but please, I need some time to think."

He'd told her how much he had worried about her when she was missing, and how he'd come to the realization that he needed her in his life. She had been touched and had felt the tears start to well behind her eyes. It had been a very long time since she'd felt needed by anyone.

He'd told her he understood her need for time, and then dragged the upright chair from the suite's desk into the bathroom and sat and poured them both some more champagne. She'd gone over what had happened to her on the island and in Mozambique—making no reference to what had happened between her and Alex, of course—as she'd finished cleaning herself and then shaved her legs with a pink disposable razor.

When she had finished washing, George had just sat there, sipping his wine, as she'd stood. The soapy water slithered down her body as she reached across to the rail for a towel.

For a moment she wondered if his stillness and silence were signs of pouting, as if he were offended by her lack of commitment. But then she noticed his dark eyes, the only part of him showing any sign of life just then, moving from her face, to her breasts, to her lower belly.

"It's started to grow back," he said, looking at her.

She blushed, then felt a pang of annoyance. After the second time they'd slept together he'd told her he'd like it if she were bare for him. She'd gone to a beautician for a full wax. It had been painful, but the anticipation of getting it done for him, and of waiting for and receiving his approval, had been incredibly erotic. She'd read in women's magazines about people playing games of domination and submission in the bedroom and the whole idea had never really appealed to her, until she'd become intimate with George. What she liked about their liaisons was the different feelings and experiences he helped her discover.

But expecting her to maintain some bizarre standard of personal grooming while she'd been away for weeks at sea and then imprisoned on an island in the Indian Ocean was just too much. She started to speak, but he raised a finger to his lips.

"Stay there," he said, and her anger was replaced with a different emotion.

Slowly, he rolled first one, then the other of his shirt sleeves to the elbows. He still wore his suit pants and shoes. He leaned across her, the back of his hand lightly brushing one thigh, and she felt the goose bumps instantly rise on her bare flesh. George took a bar of translucent red soap, dipped it in the water and rubbed it into a lather in his left hand. With his right he took the razor she'd used on her legs and sluiced it in the bath.

Jane took a breath and held it as his fingers touched her, slowly, firmly rubbing the suds into the soft folds of her skin.

"Move your feet further apart," he commanded.

She placed her palms either side of her, against the cool, pure white tiles to brace herself as she slid her feet carefully wider on the slippery bottom of the tub. She didn't want to fall, and the effort of standing still added to the intense feelings of arousal his touch was producing in her.

"George, can't we—"

"Quiet," he'd ordered.

Jane stretched now, raising her hands past her head as she yawned in the bed. She remembered the first touch of the blade and the scraping noise it made as she dared not breathe. She lowered a hand beneath the plump duvet and felt the smoothness. Her own touch produced a repeat of the throb that had seemed to resonate through her body last night as he'd held her, in his fingers, and shaved her bare.

After he'd finished she'd turned the tables on him.

She'd stepped from the tub, placing a wet foot either side of him and forcing his legs together so she could straddle him. She noted the quick grimace as suds and water soaked the expensive pressed fabric of his trousers, but also the hardness beneath the material.

His mouth opened, hungrily, to hers as she placed her hands on his shoulders and pushed him back into the chair. She broke the kiss, amused at how quickly his cool had vanished. He looked imploringly up into her eyes.

"Please," she said.

He swallowed, licked his lips and repeated the word, as she knew he would.

She reached down between them, rocking back a little in his lap so she could undo the zipper. When he reached for her she grabbed him around the wrist and forced his hand back by his side. The memory of how slick he'd been, the slippery fluid welling from him, made her touch herself again now, in the bed.

Jane had freed him and run her hand up and down the thick shaft just twice, before standing slightly and then lowering herself down on him.

She reveled for a few pleasurable minutes in the memory of him inside her, the sense of fullness and completion. She craved that intimacy, more than she'd remembered. But now, as had happened last night, another face invaded her mind as her breathing quickened. Despite her best efforts to blank it out, she saw Alex's face.

It was no dream, though, what had happened after George had climaxed inside her. She'd stayed there, in his lap, as he'd wrapped his arms around her. As she'd laid her head on his shoulder, spent, he had whispered to her again, "Will you marry me, Jane?"

And she, feeling terribly guilty that this man, who would give up his family for her, had been supplanted in her mind by a criminal, who had been using her to find something that did not belong to him, had said, "Yes."

•   •   •

"I love you. See you at midday." George Penfold smiled to himself as he folded his mobile phone closed.

"Who's that, the little woman?" Mitch Reardon asked.

"None of your business. Tell me again why I'm taking time out of my busy schedule to see you?"

Reardon laughed, and the waitress at the Primi Piatti coffee shop in Melrose Arch was so taken aback by the ferocity of the outburst that she hovered several meters away from the table the men sat at.

Piet van Zyl waved her over. "I'll have another espresso."

Penfold waved his hand over his latte to signify he wanted nothing, but Mitch said, "Cognac, neat," and winked at the girl. Johannesburg was full of blondes. "You want to go on losing valuable cargo, and you don't want your stuff back, then just get up and leave now. But don't forget to leave enough money for the bill, and a nice fat tip for the babe in black and white."

Mitch had already said as much to Penfold's henchman, Van Zyl, over the phone before the meeting.

Van Zyl looked military. Probably an ex-Recce Commando, like Mark Novak, Mitch thought. He'd said to Mitch, "Tell me something I don't already know," and Mitch had been pleased to hear the pause at the other end when he'd replied that he could give the names and the location of all of the men who'd hijacked the *Penfold Son*.

"Well, go on, what do you have to tell me—or sell me?" Penfold said.

"Now we're talking. I know who raided your ship and where they live."

Penfold smiled, took a sip of his coffee and reached into the inside breast pocket of his suit jacket. "I know you do, Mister Reardon. Because you're one of them."

He laid the photograph on the white laminate table. Mitch saw it was a printout of a digital shot. He recalled the moment in an instant. All of them wore their black T-shirts with the skull and crossbones insignia. It had been taken with Lisa's camera. They'd all been drunk—the night after hijacking the freighter full of booze and wi-descreen televisions—and not even tight-ass Alex had prohibited Novak's wife from giving the camera to one of the Vilanculos pros-titutes to take a picture of them all.

"Where did you get this?"

"That shouldn't concern you. What *should* concern you is Inter-pol. I'm sure they'll be very interested in chatting to you, now that you've all but admitted you helped take my ship by force, damaged a significant amount of my property, and killed one of my captains."

"I didn't kill anyone."

"My heart leaped when I saw you, Mister Reardon," Penfold smiled. "My employee, Mister Van Zyl here, sourced this photo for me, but until you showed up here today we had no idea who most of these men were."

Mitch nodded. "Novak. You got it from Lisa's place." He looked at Van Zyl and saw the reflection of his own soulless eyes. The eyes of a killer. Lisa Novak had never really liked him, but he had hoped that if he ever settled with a woman she would be like her. She was no-nonsense, with a nasty mouth on her when it suited her, and she stood by her husband whatever he was doing, be it serving in the army or as a contractor in Iraq, or ripping off shipping in the Indian Ocean. And she had a sensational body. "She obviously didn't give any more away, or you stole the picture without her knowing, otherwise you wouldn't be talking to me now."

"Brilliant, Mister Reardon. Simply brilliant."

Mitch had the urge to ram his fist into the supercilious En-glishman's face and feel his nose squish under his knuckles. If they'd hurt Lisa, Novak would be worse than a grizzly woken early from hibernation. "Five hundred thousand. Dollars, not rand."

"Ridiculous," Penfold said. "I could pay a team of private in-vestigators to identify the men in this picture. It'd probably take them a week of checking out pubs and resorts on the Mozambican coast."

Mitch nodded. "It'd have to be a big team, and I'm sensing you don't have a week—otherwise we wouldn't be sitting in this little yuppie fortress. So make me an offer."

"Ten thousand dollars and you not only identify the men, you also give details of where and how to find them, any relatives living in South Africa or Mozambique, what arms they carry, and a map of their location."

"Two-fifty and I'll lead the raiding party to clean them up."

"Fifteen thousand and you'll go as part of Piet's team." Penfold looked to the South African, who had remained silent for most of the conversation. "Under his command."

Mitch scratched his chin. "I'll want a fair cut of whatever loot they've got stashed."

Penfold looked at Van Zyl, who nodded. "Then we have us a deal, though any boats the pirates have are to be burned or scuttled. I don't want you starting up an operation of your own, Mister Reardon."

Damn, Mitch thought. The guy was smart, and a tough negotiator. But fifteen grand wasn't bad for a couple of days' work. In fact, he would have paid that much himself to watch Alex Tremain die.

Alex used the hands-free car kit to talk on his mobile phone as he weaved in and out of the rolling traffic jam that was Johannesburg. He already had the beginnings of a shopping list in mind for the operation.

"Kim, hello?" said the cultured female voice, the accent that of a South African of British descent.

Just the sound of her voice did things to his body, but at that same instant he pictured Jane's face. The Englishwoman was still lurking in his mind, but he and Kim Hoddy had history. They'd been lovers before he'd left Africa to join the Royal Marines for a second time. She had wanted him to stay and marry her, but he'd thirsted for adventure, even more than he craved every long inch of Kim's supple body. She was rich—very rich—and her parents had not been sad to see the back of the half-Portuguese, half-English boy who wanted nothing more than a humble soldier's life.

"Kim, it's Alex. Howzit?"

"Alex! My God! Where are you?"

He told her, and she replied that she was getting her nails done in Sandton Mall.

That figured. She'd always been obsessed with grooming and fashion. Kim cultivated that just-stepped-off-the-yacht look and succeeded every time. Chipped nails had to be repaired as a matter of urgency and stray hairs could bring on an anxiety attack. He'd taken her to the Kruger Park once and she'd brought with her a cosmetic case the size of an artillery ammunition box.

"Aren't you still living in Mozambique?"

"Yes. I'm just here for an overnight business trip. How are Brian and the kids?"

He heard the pause on the end of the line as she thought about her answer. "Fine. Just fine. Sharna's five—she's started school now—and Brent's ten already."

She didn't say anything about her plastic surgeon husband. "Is Brian still in the army reserve?"

"Yes, and the honorary rangers. If he isn't off on maneuvers somewhere or jolling about Pilanesberg National Park in his silly ranger's uniform, he's on the golf course."

Alex smiled. "I'm close to Sandton now. Have you got time for coffee?"

"*Ja*," she said. "But how about I get the girl to put on a nice brew at home for us, rather than that American rubbish they serve in the mall?" She gave him her address and he knew how to find the house—it was in the same street where her parents lived. She might look a picture of cool elegance, but Kim had done some things in her folks' place that would have sent them to early graves if they'd known.

Alex turned off the MI and when he stopped at a set of lights he beckoned for an old woman with an armful of flowers to come to the window. Her gap-toothed smile pleased him almost as much as his fifty rand did her. He tossed the roses on the passenger seat.

Kim's house was like every other in the street—invisible behind a high rendered masonry wall topped with a multi-strand electric fence and coils of razor wire. He'd been in military compounds and safe houses in Afghanistan that weren't as well defended as the average Sandton home. However, it was justifiable paranoia as there were probably more people shot dead each year in suburban Johannesburg than in Kabul. Before he could push the buzzer mounted at window height, the electric gate started to roll open.

There was a bright yellow Chevrolet Crossfire and a British racing-green Discovery 3—whose number-plate read *BEAUTY GP*—parked on the driveway gravel, which crunched under Alex's wheels and was scattered by the galloping approach of two massive Rottweilers. The dogs had diamante collars—at least he supposed the stones were fake.

"Sunflower! Pansy!"

Alex grimaced, and hoped for the dogs' sake that they were females. Kim needn't have bothered, as Sunflower was licking his fingers and Pansy had her face buried in his crotch. Kim lifted a hand to her mouth and giggled when she saw him.

Alex waved. She was even prettier now than she had been the last two times he'd seen her, at twenty and thirty. She wore a simple white V-neck T-shirt with very short sleeves, which showed lots of cleavage and her slender arms. Her denim skirt ended above her knees and she didn't have to rise too much on her toes to kiss his cheek, thanks to the high-heeled black leather boots that encased her calves. She hugged him tight.

"You look fantastic, Kim." She'd straightened her red hair, which had been a mass of curls last time he'd seen her.

She blushed. "And you look good enough to eat, as usual."

She turned quickly and he followed her inside, across the polished Italian marble tiles. He smelled fresh coffee and the fragrance led them to a kitchen as big as one of the suites in his ruined hotel. Kim gestured to him to take a stool at the breakfast bar opposite her and poured from the percolator jug into oversized white china cups. "I've given the girl the rest of the morning off. Still just black, no sugar?"

"You remembered?" He took the cup and sipped the scalding liquid.

"All of it. I remember everything about those days. Maybe it's a symptom of my approaching midlife crisis."

"You're only, what, thirty-five, thirty-six?"

"Thirty-five!"

He laughed. "It seems like only yesterday." There were snapshots of her children on the refrigerator, and a clutter of posed studio portraits of the family together and individually on a mahogany dresser behind him in the sprawling lounge room.

"Nice house. The practice must be doing well."

"I'd rather be running a beachfront hotel in Mozambique."

He shook his head. "No, you wouldn't. I'm just about broke, Kim. You'd hate it. No electricity most of the time, no money, no nothing. Just sea and sand. You've got everything here."

Through the perfectly made-up mask her eyes betrayed her. They looked away from him, away from the comforts of her home and the real dangers of having money in a country full of poor people. "I've got nothing."

"Your kids look lovely . . ."

"It feels like a jail sometimes, Alex. Does your life ever feel like that? I don't know who I am anymore, or if I even really exist as anything more than Brian's wife and Sharna and Brent's mom."

He said nothing, but stood and walked around the granite-topped counter to her. He placed a finger under her chin and tilted her face.

"Tell me I'm beautiful and fuck me, Alex."

"Fuck me, you're beautiful, Kim."

She laughed.

• • •

Later, one arm behind her head, her hair in elegant disarray over the pillows of her marital bed, Kim said, "Are you with anyone at the moment, Alex?"

He looked up at her, from the diamond he'd been kissing in her belly button, over the recently enhanced breasts that he wasn't mad about, and thought about her question for a moment. "No. Not as such. Thought I did, but she walked out on me before I got to know her."

"Like you're going to do to me now."

He raised his eyebrows, then started kissing her belly, moving upward.

"Chase her, like you should have chased me—like I should have chased you. We're not getting any younger."

"I couldn't have given you the life you wanted," he said.

"I don't want it, believe it or not, but I want it for my children, and for that reason I'll do my time. You haven't come looking for money, have you, Alex?"

He raised his head and shook it, and she wound her fingers into his black hair and drew him to her mouth.

"I'd give it to you, if you wanted it. Anything." They kissed for a while, remembering.

"Come visit me in Mozambique some day. With Brian and the kids."

"If I come, it'll be alone."

"Not this morning."

She laughed.

"I want you in the bathtub, like the old days at your parents' place."

While Kim was in the ensuite running the bath taps he quickly dressed and went to the walk-in wardrobe. Kim's side was strewn with shoes and discarded clothes and he felt a sudden pang of guilt when he realized she'd probably changed for him as soon as she'd got home from the mall. Brian's half was laid out with military precision. Rows of designer suits and sports jackets faced off the uniforms of his part-time pursuits.

Alex pulled a green kitbag from a top shelf and stuffed in three sets of camouflaged army fatigues and two of national parks khaki. He checked Brian's shoe size and smiled. He took polished boots for the military outfit and a pair of gray *veldskoens* to complete the uniform ensembles. Riffling through a drawer he hit paydirt—two identity cards, which he pocketed.

He walked out of the house which, he thought as he looked back, had about as much charm and warmth as Colditz Castle.

Pansy the Rottweiler sidled up to him as he pushed the button for the electric gate. He took a rose from the vase where Kim had placed his flowers, stripped off the thorns and threaded it through the dog's collar. "Go look after your mom."

Alex thought about Kim as he made his way through the comparatively light afternoon traffic to Kempton Park on the eastern side of Johannesburg, near the international airport. There wasn't a lot of room for guilt in his life these days. He had used her, but she had done the same. Her life was a product of the decisions she'd made, just as his was.

They'd thought they had been in love when they were younger, but he couldn't imagine Kim married to a Royal Marine commando, living on base or in one of the gloomy coastal towns in the south of England. She'd like Mozambique, he thought, once he had the hotel renovated, though how long she'd last without easy access to her own nail artist, he didn't know.

Three military and two national parks uniforms were a good start for the plan he had in mind, but he needed more, and his next stop should make up the difference. He called Lisa Novak's number on his mobile phone but there was no answer. Perhaps she was in the garden or out shopping.

Kempton Park was down-market compared to Sandton. The modest single-story houses were set behind iron grilled gates rather than faux-Tuscan ramparts. It was an industrial suburb and the homes were interspersed among freight companies, small factories and warehouses.

Alex turned off the R21 and navigated by memory to the street where the Novaks lived. He knew something was wrong as soon as he saw the two police *bakkies* parked on the grass verge. There were two other sedans which looked like unmarked cars. He slowed as he cruised past the house. Through the gate he could see a man taking photos, the flash bouncing off the frosted glass beside the front door. If he'd been watching his front he would have seen the two cops sooner.

"Hey, pull over!"

Alex hit the brakes and the overweight white policeman scowled at him. His hand moved to the holster slung low on his right hip. The parts of his blue-gray uniform shirt that bulged from under his body armor were stained dark with sweat. His African partner carried a shotgun.

"You should watch where you're *bladdy* going, man. Get out of the car. Let me see your license."

Alex did as he was told. Fortunately his nine-millimeter was under the seat, out of sight, though even the most cursory search would find his unlicensed pistol.

"You're from Mozambique. What are you doing here?" the policeman asked.

Alex decided it was one of those occasions where the truth was the best defense. "I'm a friend of the people who live in that house." He gestured with his thumb and even that small movement made the jumpy cop with the shotgun raise his weapon a fraction. "I'm here on business. Is Lisa Novak all right?"

"How do you know her?"

There were too many cops here for it to be good news. He felt the dread creeping up his spine, and turning it cold. "I work with her husband in Mozambique. Have you contacted him yet?"

"Passport," the cop said in reply.

Alex held his slow-burning anger in check. He reached into the car, slowly, and retrieved his Mozambican passport from the glove compartment. The policeman took it from him without a thank-you, and flipped through the pages.

"Mister Alexandre Silva Tremain. You only arrived yesterday, through the Kruger Park." His eyes widened, as if the fact surprised him.

"Yes. What about it?"

The policeman ignored his retort. He closed the passport, handed it back and his whole body seemed to slump a little. It was as if he was preparing to undertake a chore he had done many times before, but regretted on each occasion. "I'm sorry to tell you, Mister Tremain, that Lisa Novak is in hospital in a critical condition, in a coma. Her maid is dead. Both were shot by intruders."

Alex said a silent prayer for Lisa and the other woman, and for his friend, Mark.

"Can you contact her husband for us? We've been looking for a number in her personal things, but there doesn't seem to be a trace of it in her cell phone or diary."

Alex knew why. The satellite phone number on the island was a closely guarded secret. If the cops had it, and they suspected anyone on the island of being involved in piracy, there were international agencies who could trace and monitor calls. There was no getting around it now though. The number would have to be compromised and a new phone and subscription paid for.

"We work on an island. I'm developing a resort and Mark—we mostly just call him Novak—is employed by me as a diving instructor. The only way to contact him is by satellite phone. I have the number. His wife would have memorized it."

The policeman looked hard at Alex, as though he were assessing every word. "Come inside with us. The detectives will probably want to talk to you, and they can call Mister Novak."

"If it's all right with you, I'd like to call him and give him the news myself."

"Ja. OK. It's a free country so I can't stop you telling him. But the detectives will want to talk to him as well."

Alex followed the two uniformed policemen through the gates, which were opened electronically by someone inside the house. He saw the dried blood.

The overweight policeman spoke in Afrikaans to a man in a golf shirt and jeans, with a Z88 on his hip and a detective's badge on a silver chain around his neck. Alex was fluent in the language and knew the cop was explaining what he was about to do.

"Go right ahead, Mister Tremain, and make your call. I'm Detective Jac le Roux."

They shook hands and while Alex waited for the call to connect he said, "Was it a robbery?"

Detective Le Roux frowned. "We don't usually give out information about a crime to complete strangers, but . . . ja, it looks that way. Place has been tossed. Looks like Mrs. Novak's purse and handbag were emptied, but nothing else seems to be missing."

"Was either woman sexually assaulted?"

"Too early to tell for sure—that'll be up to the doctor to determine—but from what we could see, no."

Henri answered the phone and Alex cut him short. "Where's Novak?" Alex nodded a couple of times, put his hand over the mouthpiece of his mobile phone and said to Le Roux, "He's busy refilling his diving tanks now. One of the other guys has gone to fetch him."

Alex looked around the Novaks' yard while he waited for Mark. The brand-new Land Cruiser Prado—bought legally, but with the proceeds of crime—was parked in the driveway next to Lisa's year-old Corolla. Both vehicles were common on the roads in South Africa, which made them appealing to carjackers and thieves. When he looked back at Le Roux, Alex saw the detective had been following his eye line.

"Why would someone shoot Mrs. Novak and her maid for a handful of cash?" Le Roux asked.

Alex shrugged. "You're the policeman. You must see violent crimes committed for little reward."

Le Roux nodded. "*Ja*, I've seen people killed for next to nothing, and because the criminals don't want witnesses around, and just because of the color of their skin. Hate crimes. But whoever did this gained entry and got past the dogs without killing them, murdered one woman and put a bullet in the head of another, picked up their spent cartridges and left without a single neighbor hearing or seeing anything unusual."

"Silencers?" Alex said, thinking aloud.

Le Roux nodded. "Again, not the mark of your average Jozi *tsotsi*. If they were disturbed by someone, then it wasn't any of the neighbors— we've canvassed them all already. One saw an Eskom van pull into the house around the time we suspect the shooting happened. We're checking with the power company. What other business are you and Mister Novak involved in apart from tourism and diving?"

"Nothing." Alex held up a hand to the detective. "Mark? I've got some bad news, man . . ."

18

Jane looked at the picture on the boardroom table and felt her heart stop.

Alex's face stared out at her, along with those of Henri, Jose, Novak, Heinrich, Kevin, Kufa, three women she didn't recognize, and the despicable Mitch Reardon. Novak had his arm around one of the women and Jane supposed it was his wife, whom she'd heard mention of while on the island, but whose name she couldn't remember.

"You've seen them before," George said.

They had started negotiations with the managing director and senior executives of De Witt Shipping, the company George had traveled to South Africa to buy. A break had been called and George had asked the rest of his team—Howard from security; his human resources manager, Penny; and chief financial officer, Robert—to give him some time alone with Jane.

He'd taken the picture from his briefcase and laid it on the table without saying anything. She looked up at him. "Yes."

"I have every reason to believe that the men in this picture are the ones who hijacked the *Penfold Son* and kidnapped you, Jane."

"I was ... I escaped, George. I told you, these are the men who rescued me from the lifeboat."

George slumped back in the reclining leather chair and clasped his fingers behind the back of his head.

Jane was confused. Since agreeing to George's proposal she had been racked with doubts, mostly concerning what she feared was her future husband's possible involvement in illegal activities. He had made no further mention of any parcel being handed over to her by Captain MacGregor and she hadn't volunteered anything about the exchange, or what had really happened on Ilha dos Sonhos. Jane wondered, too, about the timing and suddenness of his proposal. He'd told her he wanted to talk about their future when he arrived in South Africa but she thought he might have made some mention, over the phone, of how things were progressing with his wife first. It seemed odd to Jane that he would have told Elizabeth their marriage was through without even canvassing the idea of marriage with her first. However, while she had doubts about his honesty, she knew she was being equally duplicitous.

Why am I protecting a pirate? she asked herself.

"Jane, have you ever heard of Stockholm Syndrome?"

"Don't be so bloody condescending. Of course I have."

"Sorry," he said, without feeling. "Then what seems likely is that the pirates—for they are the men in this picture—pretended to be your rescuers. Did they ask you about anything or *for* anything?"

"What are you talking about?" She looked at her watch. The De Witt people were due back in the boardroom in a few minutes and she was craving the cup of coffee she'd missed out on. "No one asked me for anything."

He sighed and lowered his hands, palms down, to the heavy antique mahogany table. "Some property was stolen from the *Penfold Son*."

"What?" she asked.

George moistened his lips with his tongue and the gesture reminded Jane of a snake. "Valuable property. Taken from the captain's safe."

"Illegal property, George? Contraband?"

He leaned back again, and she could tell his reply would be evasive. "Captain MacGregor died for the contents of that safe."

She swallowed. His obtuseness was unnerving, as well as annoying. Her will wasn't as strong as his and she couldn't go on beating about the bush over something so pivotal to their future relationship. "What was transferred from the Chinese freighter, the *Peng Cheng*, to the *Penfold Son* on the night before the attack?"

He swiveled in his chair, turning to look at the closed door, as if the De Witt team were about to enter. "I don't know anything about any exchange, Jane. What happened?"

"Igor Putin, the chief engineer, crossed from the *Penfold Son* to the *Peng Cheng*, which had supposedly broken down the night before the pirates attacked. What's going on, George? Tell me."

George shook his head. "All I know is that my biggest ship was attacked and seriously damaged by pirates and I will see those men rot in jail if it's the last thing I do. Property of a significant value was stolen from the safe on the bridge and a good man lost his life trying to protect it. I was merely asking if MacGregor or anyone else on board had perhaps given you something for safekeeping, that's all. I'm sure that if they had, you would have said something by now."

His exasperation was clear and probably justified. So why did she feel even more strongly compelled to lie to him? "No one gave me anything, George."

He looked at her and she held his gaze, staring straight into the same eyes that had captured her heart just a few hours earlier. They'd been as close as two humans could be, but she felt she knew even less of him than she had before she left England. He refused to break the stare, until the opening door broke the deadlock.

Jane's heart was beating faster as Penny, breaking the silence after they all took their seats, said to Carel de Witt, "Perhaps we could look at your staffing profile, with particular reference to Black Economic Empowerment of senior executives."

Jane wasn't listening, nor even glancing at the man next to her. She was too worried.

George tuned out as Penny spoke. He knew how many people De Witt employed, what color they were, and how much each of them earned. This first round of negotiations was theater. The crunch would come in a couple of days' time in Cape Town, after he and his team had viewed the company's facilities there and those of the company's vessels that were in port.

For now, he reflected on what Mitch Reardon had told him and what Jane had not.

"We captured a broad on board," Mitch had laughed at his own clumsy alliteration. "One of your people. A lawyer." He'd said the last word as though he was talking about an insect he detested. "Of course, we asked her if the *Penfold Son*'s captain had given her anything, but she said no. Alex searched her stuff but not her, if you know what I mean."

George had been relieved at Reardon's admission. He thought of Jane's body as belonging to him. However, the gentlemanly conduct revealed a flaw in his pirate adversary's character. The man was soft. This Tremain was a professional military man, according to Reardon, but an amateur criminal. That was good.

"So she knew that you were really the men who had raided the ship and kidnapped her?" George had asked Mitch.

"Sure. I mean, it would have been a bit far-fetched for her to believe that she got clean away and we just happened to pick her up, right?"

Jane was too smart to have been duped by the pirates, so why, he pondered now, was she covering up for them? He pretended to cross-reference something Penny had just circled with her laser pointer, on the drop-down screen on which De Witt's interminably boring PowerPoint presentation about staff numbers was being projected. In reality, he was glancing again at the photo printout. He fixed his eyes on the face of Alexandre Tremain and tried to read the man's thoughts and soul.

He supposed the man was handsome, though Reardon had said his leader was partly crippled. A war hero. George silently scoffed. As a merchant seaman he'd probably been in more fights—and won more—than this half-breed dandy had had hot dinners.

George glanced beside him at Jane, who was quite plainly pretending to watch the screen. Her eyes were fixed too high to be reading the figures and digesting the pie charts. She was in a world of her own, like him. Or was her mind somewhere else—on the white sands of the Ilha dos Sonhos or, worse, in another man's bed?

He clenched his fist, then moved his shaking hand under the table to hide the emotion the thoughts provoked.

No matter what else he was leaving out of his account, Reardon had said plainly that Jane knew Tremain and his men were the pirates who had hijacked the ship she was on. So, if she was lying about her knowledge of this simple fact, was she also lying about the whereabouts of the missing property from MacGregor's safe?

George pondered how to best rid himself of Tremain and his men. If the purchase of the De Witt line proceeded as planned, he would need them scoured from the Mozambican coast for purely economic and security reasons. He'd like to think he could trust the local police or the South African or Mozambican navies to do the job, but he doubted their will and ability. Tremain, according to Reardon, had the local police in his pocket.

Van Zyl wanted to launch a lightning raid on Ilha dos Sonhos, as soon as possible, and kill the members of the gang who were living there. He wanted it done before the South African, Novak, heard about his wife and left the island for Johannesburg, as he inevitably must. Aside from the cost and logistical implications, mounting an invasion of an island posed a high level of risk. What about the islanders who presumably lived there? Would Van Zyl execute every man, woman and child in the hope that he wiped out all of the pirates and their sympathizers? Even on a remote island the massacre of an unknown number of innocents would not go unnoticed. The plan—or lack of it—revealed Van Zyl's weaknesses, but also his strengths. He was a dog of war, to be pointed in the right direction, but not unleashed until the time was right.

What George did need right now was more intelligence about the gang and its base. Van Zyl and his men could at least keep watch on Tremain's lair and its surrounds so that they were in place when the time for action was dictated.

Tremain was at large somewhere in South Africa, probably in Johannesburg by now, from what Jane had said. Yet another odd thing about Jane's relationship with the man was why she had left him midway through their trip from Mozambique. When she'd first called, Jane had told George that her "Samaritan" was giving her a lift all the way to Johannesburg, but then she had hitched a lift with some South African fishermen. What had happened, George wondered, to change her mind? According to Jane the man had business of some sort, related to his hotel redevelopment, to attend to in Johannesburg.

If Tremain learned sooner rather than later of the death of his comrade's wife he might stay in the city to meet with him and console him, or he might already be on his way back to his island. It didn't matter either way. Eventually Tremain would return to Ilha dos Sonhos and his criminal ways. If Novak had to be dealt with independently of this crew, then so be it.

Another unknown would be the reaction of the legitimate authorities to the *Penfold Son*'s hijacking. With the raid and MacGregor's death in the news media, the incident had naturally come up in his conversations with Carel de Witt. De Witt, an ex-navy man, had claimed his connections within the senior ranks of the South African National Defense Force were still strong—despite the move to black majority rule—and that if the location of the pirates' base could be found, then he was sure the South African Navy and police service would despatch a warship and officers to arrest them. He was sure the

South African government would gain the necessary approvals from the Mozambican authorities.

But George didn't want Tremain and his men arrested. He wanted them dead.

Carel de Witt had provided a driver and a sleek silver Mercedes to take Jane shopping at Sandton Mall in the afternoon. The preliminary meeting was over and De Witt and his wife were hosting George, Jane, Penny and Robert to a dinner at an expensive French restaurant in Rosebank.

Jane's heart wasn't in the shopping expedition. It rarely was. She wasn't the sort of girl to get excited over shoes or new clothes. What really irked her, however, was George's insistence that the company would pay for her evening dress. Her luggage was still in Cape Town, impounded on board the *Penfold Son*, which the South African police had decided was a crime scene as a result of MacGregor's murder. It was fair enough that the company compensate her in some way, but she didn't like being treated as George's partner or dependent. Even though that was what she might very well become.

She let the bleached-blonde sales assistant, a friendly woman who plainly lived for her work, pick out a dress for her. She sensed the woman's keenness had been aided by her "money's no object" remark. Stuff it, she thought. The whole expedition to Africa had been one nightmare after another.

"Shoes as well?" the woman queried, unable to contain her excitement.

"Why not?" Jane shrugged. "All I've got are flip-flops." Carel de Witt had laughed good-naturedly when Jane had shown him her rubber footwear at the commencement of the meeting. She'd explained that she'd bought the first gray business suit she'd seen in Melrose Arch, but had forgotten to buy shoes on her way to the meeting.

She liked the white-haired shipping owner. He, more than George, seemed not to have lost touch with the sea, despite more years in an office than a ship's bridge. His face and hands were the color of teak decking and his blue eyes misted when he talked about the fleet he would soon be losing. His hair was unfashionably long—perhaps a sign of a rebellious nature beneath the constraints of family wealth and business—and he was probably one of the few men she knew who could get away with a ponytail and a business suit. Alex's hair was almost long enough to need an elastic band.

Jane checked her watch. There wouldn't be time to stop by her hotel room and change. She looked at herself in the full-length mirror in the shop. The sales assistant beamed supportively. She climbed into the stiletto heels and turned. There was no way she would have bought a backless dress in London—it was never warm enough to wear one—but she felt different here in Africa. She wondered if her brush with violence and death in the Indian Ocean had somehow changed her.

"I'll take it," she said. "And the shoes. Don't bother wrapping them—I'll wear them."

"How late are you for dinner?"

Jane was surprised at the question, and impatient. "If I leave now I'll get there with about fifteen minutes to spare."

"Let me call Rudi at the salon two shops up. We can't send you off to dinner with your hair like *that*."

For a moment Jane felt insulted, but when she took another look in the mirror she burst out laughing. "OK."

"He's a miracle worker and he owes me big-time, hey. A lady can be fifteen minutes late for anything."

Jane sat in the chair in the salon, in her new dress and shoes, while Rudi's assistant washed her hair. She tapped her nails on the plastic arm, but she wasn't impatient with the stylist. Her mind was churning, replaying the brief discussions she'd had with George in between their interminable round of meetings.

In her purse was a cheap mobile phone, with a prepaid SIM card, which she'd bought from a shop in the mall. She took it out and scrolled through the call register to "dialed numbers" while the woman rinsed her hair clean.

The only number in the list was Alex Tremain's South African mobile. He'd given it to her in Mozambique, before she had run away from him, as she'd needed to pass it on to George, in case he wanted to call her back. She assumed George still had the number and wondered if he might use it to track Alex down. Or if he would give the number to the South African police.

She'd dialed the number once—before going to try on dresses—but hung up just as it started to ring.

Alex was a *criminal*, she told herself. A pirate. No matter how charming or altruistic he might be, or how much he had suffered from the cyclone, he had intimidated and robbed honest people. She should not be tipping him off that her boyfriend knew his identity and was after him.

"All done. Now, if you'd like to take that chair over there," the salon assistant said, "Rudi will be with you in less than a second."

"Just a minute, please." Jane's thumb hovered over the "send" button.

The phone started to vibrate in her hand and she nearly dropped it in fright. A split second later the annoying factory-installed ring tone began its monotonous melody. Jane saw the number flashing on the screen. The assistant waited patiently, looking at her, probably wondering why she wasn't answering.

Jane's heart thumped in her chest. God, what was she going to say? The easiest thing would be to let the call go through to the voice-mail service she hadn't even set up yet. Alex wouldn't even know it was her, and would most likely assume he'd been called by someone who had a wrong number.

Why had she lied to the man who was now, technically, her fiancé?

She pressed the green button. "Hello, Jane," she coughed to clear her throat, "Jane speaking."

"Jane! It's Alex. I wondered who'd called me. I thought it must have been a wrong number. Where are you? Are you all right? I've been worried about you since you ran off in Mozambique. Please tell me you're safe."

He sounded genuinely concerned, and not the least bit angry. His voice was as deep and dark as his skin and hair.

"I'm fine. I ... I didn't know whether I should call you or not. I was actually just thinking about it. You're a mind reader." She tried to laugh, but it was impossible to make light of the turmoil in her mind.

"It doesn't matter. What is important is that you're safe. How are things with your boss?"

The salon assistant was glancing at her watch and she looked up to see a man in black jeans and T-shirt and streaked hair with hands on hips, doing nothing to conceal his impatience. She ignored him.

"Alex, George ... George Penfold knows who you are. He's got a photo of you, Mitch, Novak ... everyone. He knew all your names and he didn't believe that you just happened upon me in the Indian Ocean. I tried, but—"

Alex stopped her, telling her not to worry about what she had or hadn't said to George. He was more interested in the photo. "Jane, slow down. Please. I need you to tell me exactly who was in the photo and where you think it was taken."

She took a breath and concentrated. "You're in the center, at the back. Jose and Kevin are on either side of you and Novak and his wife ..."

"Lisa."

"Yes, he and Lisa are in the middle, arm in arm. Mitch is kneeling in the sand, with Henri, Heinrich and Kufa—the picture looks like it was taken in front of your hotel—and there are two white women who I don't know, kneeling on the right-hand side."

"Shit," Alex said.

"What is it?"

"I know whose camera took that photo. We don't usually take pictures on the island, but it was her fortieth birthday so I made an exception. May God forgive me for my stupidity . . ."

"Alex?"

There was silence on the other end of the phone.

"Miss, I'm holding up a regular client for you, as a favor to Isabelle in the Ce Soir boutique. Do you want your hair done or not?"

"Oh, for fuck's sake, hold on!"

Rudi recoiled in horror and retreated behind the chair he was saving for Jane.

"Alex, what's wrong? Whose camera was it?"

"The picture was Lisa Novak's, Jane. She was shot for it. She's in hospital and might not pull through, and another woman, her maid, was killed."

Alex almost didn't recognize Jane.

He was parked outside the Melrose Arch Hotel, fifty paces from the entry with his lights switched off. The immense African security guard, who wore a long overcoat to hide whatever cannon he carried underneath, had already checked him out and Alex had explained he was waiting to pick up a guest.

No man could have ignored the elegant woman, dressed in a short black backless evening gown, who stepped out onto the entrance carpet and looked down the street. Her hair was piled high in a French roll, exposing a pale, slender neck. She lifted the cream pashmina to just below her shoulders. When she turned her head Alex, surprised, flashed his headlights and started the engine.

His breeding and training as an officer and a gentleman would have normally required him to get out of the car, but time and secrecy were more important. The doorman did the honors and Jane slid into the Land Cruiser, looking as out of place in the vehicle as a fine china doll in a wheelbarrow.

"Where are we going?" she asked as Alex pulled away from the hotel.

"Not far. What did you tell George?"

"Not that it's your business, but I told him I've got a headache, which is actually quite true. If he calls my room I'll tell him I went out to get some aspirin."

"In Johannesburg at night?" He let it ride. "Thanks for seeing me."

"I don't know what I'm doing, Alex, or why I'm doing it, so please don't thank me for anything. I'd much rather just have my old life back."

He wondered what she meant by that, and if the remark was aimed at him or Penfold.

"How's Lisa?" she asked.

"Still unconscious. Novak got in from Mozambique this afternoon and I took him to Johannesburg Hospital. How are you?"

"George asked me to marry him, and I said yes."

Alex nodded, slowly, digesting the information.

"Of course I didn't tell him about . . ."

"There's nothing to tell. It was just a kiss. Look, Jane, I wanted to see you to warn you to be careful. I know I planted the seed in your mind that George might have been up to something illegal, but I think now that you should forget all I said and not ask any questions you might not want to know the answer to."

"I'm a *lawyer*, Alex. And I'm not some bloody airhead bimbo who'll be content to be the silent, dutiful wife. For fuck's sake, I could be disbarred for not paying my speeding fines. If my future husband is smuggling drugs or diamonds or whatever out of Africa then I bloody well need to know."

She needed to vent and he decided to stay silent. Drugs or diamonds, she'd said. That was interesting, he thought. Did she not know either what was in the package Captain MacGregor had given her? If, in fact, he'd given her anything at all.

"And I don't need a bloody *pirate* telling me what questions I should and shouldn't be asking." She slumped into the car seat, raised her fingers to the bridge of her nose and squeezed. "How's Novak?"

Alex shrugged. He indicated, turned a corner and started hunting for a parking spot. It was after eleven, but the cafes and bars of the business enclave were still doing good business. "He's a soldier, but she's the love of his life. You don't see a lot of marriages survive in our business. They're looking forward to retiring early in Mozambique. His one daughter was in Namibia on holiday with her husband. Novak called her and he's staying at her place tonight. He's calm and quiet, which means he probably wants to kill whoever did it."

"It could have been random," she suggested without conviction. "It is Johannesburg after all."

Alex waited for an Audi to reverse, then claimed the car's spot. "I've only ever seen that picture of all of us on Novak's laptop—it was his screensaver—and on Lisa's camera the day it was taken. We have a strict no-camera, no-photo policy on the island—we like to protect our identities. I was drunk the day the picture was taken and I made Lisa swear she would keep the picture to herself."

"Who were the other women in the picture?" Jane asked.

Alex had opened his door and was already walking around to open Jane's, though she beat him to it. "They stayed with us a while. An Australian and an Irishwoman. They wouldn't have had copies."

Jane got out of the truck and let him close the door for her. He pressed the alarm remote. "It doesn't make sense, Alex. George has got your phone number—he even knows your name. If he suspected that you were the man who attacked the *Penfold Son* he could have tracked you down easily and had you investigated. I don't understand it."

"So you didn't tell him, then?"

She stopped in the middle of the sidewalk and turned to him. "No, I didn't. And I don't bloody well know why I didn't."

"Would you like a drink?"

She frowned at him. "Oh, all right. I hardly touched a drop during dinner."

Alex placed a hand gently on her arm to steer her toward a wine bar. She didn't protest or shrug him off. Her skin was cool and smooth, and pale like marble.

"The chardonnay's good," he said, scanning the wine list at the bar, where they took high-backed stools.

"Sauvignon blanc, please," she said to the waiter.

"Make it two," Alex said.

"He knows who you are, Alex, and he's going to get you. I've never seen him so determined, so focused, so seething with quiet rage."

Alex thanked the waiter and raised his glass to hers. She did the same, looking puzzled. "What are we toasting?"

"Life?" He shrugged. "Lisa."

"May she recover."

Alex drank some of his wine. He would stick to one glass, as there was still a long night ahead of him, and an even longer drive back to Mozambique once he'd finished his shopping. There was no way he could fly back to the island with what he needed to buy in South Africa.

"You think George paid someone to rob Lisa—to shoot her?" Jane said.

"Perhaps she resisted—stumbled upon the robbers and tried to fight them," Alex said. "She's feisty, so I wouldn't put it past her."

"Van Zyl," Jane said, as if thinking aloud.

"Who?"

She explained to him that Piet van Zyl was the head of the security detachment on board the *Penfold Son*.

"Those guys were pros," Alex said, remembering the disciplined gunfire that had foiled his attack.

"George is furious at him—at all of them—for losing . . . for losing me."

Alex raised an eyebrow, but Jane stayed silent, not wanting to elaborate on what she had let slip.

"Why? They saved his ship."

She shrugged, not rising to the bait. "All I know is he blames them for losing me and for allowing his precious ship to be damaged. There's a lot riding on this South African deal for Penfold Shipping. If he succeeds in buying De Witt's—that's the company we're trying to buy—he'll have to put you out of business. De Witt himself says he can get the South African Navy to come after you."

"Sounds like the posturing of two negotiators to me," Alex said.

Jane shook her head. "Don't underestimate George. But, God, I can't believe he'd sanction someone shooting an innocent woman."

It was time for them to stop dancing around the central issue. Jane obviously wasn't going to mention it, so he had to. There was no more time. "Jane, George Penfold didn't have someone rob and shoot Lisa Novak and murder her maid in order to get payback on a bunch of pirates."

She licked her lips, betraying her nervousness, then downed a mouthful of wine.

Alex continued: "Something went missing from the *Penfold Son* that George wants back. If you've told him you don't have it, then he thinks I do—or one of my men does. He might want us out of business, but he wants whatever belongs to him more than anything else in the world. The captain of the *Peng Cheng* told me he'd delivered something to the *Penfold Son*'s master—he thought it might be diamonds. Is that what MacGregor gave you, Jane?"

She looked out of the bar, at the passing parade of tipsy office workers looking for another drink, and tired restaurant staff heading home. "I don't know, Alex."

"What do you mean, you don't know? Wu told me it was worth a million quid. Didn't you look?"

"You forget, there was a gun battle going on—you were shooting at us from that bloody helicopter. MacGregor opened the safe and thrust a package into my hand. It was a zippered black leather pouch with something small and hard in it, about the size of a box of matches. There was nothing rattling inside. He said to me, 'Guard this with your life. It belongs to George.' Then he said something like he feared he'd been double-crossed."

Alex tried to imagine her fear and uncertainty—then and now.

"You see the predicament I'm in? I can't be a party to a crime, and I can't marry a criminal. I'm sorry, Alex, but I *wanted* George to think you had whatever it was that was valuable to him. Now I can't bear the thought that my actions caused the death of one woman, perhaps two."

Alex stayed silent a moment. He couldn't blame Jane for doing what she'd done, though right at this moment he cared far more about Lisa and the family of her maid than he did about a lawyer's principles. He forced the thoughts from his mind and said, "So, what are you waiting for? Tell him where his stuff is—whatever it is."

She looked at him now, her face resolute. "No. I want to see what it is first. I *need* to know."

Alex felt the anger surge in him, like rising bile. "If Lisa dies it'll be on your head, Jane. I can look after myself, but there are other innocents who depend on me and my men. If your fiancé's mercenaries pick a fight with me I'll happily go to hell with as many of them as I can take with me, but if they kill anyone else on my island then those deaths will be down to you as well. You've got the power to end this."

Jane picked up her purse and wrapped her shawl around her shoulders. She left her glass half full and stood. "Don't you dare lecture me. You're a fucking pirate, Alex. You take what you want at the point of a gun and you'd kill to protect *your* precious bloody men and *your* island. You think you're some kind of god to those people, but the truth is you've put them all in danger—not me. For fuck's sake, grow up and start taking some real responsibility for yourself and the people around you."

She turned on her heel and walked out. He pulled out a handful of crumpled bills and tossed them on the bar. Outside he saw her striding away, heels clicking purposefully on the pavement. "I can't guarantee your safety if you walk back to the hotel."

She laughed at him without turning around.

19

George Penfold kicked off his shoes and undid his tie. He poured himself a Scotch from the minibar and added ice from a dewy bucket.

He switched on the television remote and surfed through a few channels. The Melrose Arch Hotel didn't have a satellite adult channel, but one of the five complimentary DVDs in the drawer under the screen was an adult movie. George had wanted to bed Jane again but she had begged off with a headache. He wondered if there was more than pain on her mind.

He took the disc from the drawer and spun it on his little finger, deciding whether or not to watch it. After a commercial break the local news, in English, resumed. The Indian South African's diction was precise and cultured.

"Police have today released descriptions of four men masquerading as Eskom workers who broke into a Kempton Park home yesterday and shot dead a domestic worker and seriously wounded the owner of the property . . . Reporter Sipho Bandile has more."

George was dialing his mobile phone and only half listening to the reporter's monologue. He gulped his whiskey, the fiery liquid burning the inside of his throat.

"Van Zyl," said the voice on the end of the phone. He sounded as if he'd just woken.

"You told me both women were dead."

"They are," Van Zyl said.

"Turn on SABC 3, you bloody idiot. Why did I ever waste my time hiring you? The Novak woman's in a coma. If she regains consciousness you're finished."

There was a pause on the end of the line, then Van Zyl said, "And so are you. What hospital have they got her in?"

"Jo'burg."

"I'll take care of it."

George hung up. He was too wound up now to gain relief from masturbating to a porn movie. He picked up the hotel phone and dialed the concierge. "I need the number of an escort service. An expensive one."

"Of course, sir."

Alex attacked the city traffic.

The effort it took to concentrate on weaving in and out of the fast-moving streams did little to take his mind off his heated conversation with Jane.

She was playing both him and George Penfold.

He ignored the hooting horns and scowls of other drivers and pushed the four-wheel drive until its big diesel engine was screaming. He left the MI and made his way toward Parktown and the sprawling Johannesburg Hospital. He turned left into York from Prince of Wales, then followed the road around the bend to Jubilee and the hospital's car park which, despite the late hour, was crowded. As he walked toward the bunker-like concrete complex he realized this was probably the busiest time of day for the medicos on duty.

As if to reinforce his suspicion he had to step sharply back out of the gutter as he approached the entrance, to avoid being run down by a minibus taxi that skidded to a halt with a screech of brakes and

smell of burning rubber. The side door of the tinted-windowed vehicle slid open and two black men climbed out, carrying between them
a third man whose white T-shirt was stained purplish red with blood.
One of the men carrying him was bare-chested and the injured man
had his friend's shirt pressed against his stomach. He screamed in pain
as they tried walking him.

A medical team of a young female doctor and two nurses ran out,
the male nurse wheeling a gurney in front of him. They eased the
wounded man onto the trolley as Alex walked by.

"What happened to him?" the doctor asked, already starting her
examination as the orderly wheeled the bed.

"He got shot in the stomach. Bang, bang, these *tsotsis* opened up
on us, like, for no reason."

The doctor looked to Alex like she'd heard it all before and Alex
caught the strong scent of booze coming off the man as he spoke.

Inside the sliding doors, the emergency room looked more like a
war zone than any Alex had ever been in. He'd been one of three patients in the American military hospital in Bagram, Afghanistan,
where he'd been flown by a Black Hawk after losing his fingers in the
grenade blast. A team of U.S. Army surgeons and nursing staff had
cared for him before he was airlifted in a C-17 cargo jet to Ramstein
Air Base in Germany and then on to Stoke Mandeville in Bucking-
hamshire, England. All along the way he'd been surrounded by calm,
experienced professionals.

This, however, was barely organized chaos. Some of the people
sitting in rows of plastic chairs had makeshift bandages. There was
fresh blood on the floor and a cleaner merely smeared it pink when
she sloshed her mop through the stain.

Ambulance officers in green overalls called for doctors and nurses,
in competition with each other for priority. Gowned staff crossed the
floors and patients groaned or cried in agony. A woman was screaming abuse at a hospital staffer who simply stood in silence and nodded. A baby cried. A young man vomited on the floor.

Alex stopped an Indian woman in a white lab coat. "Excuse me, are you a doctor?"

"Yes," she said brusquely, looking at her watch.

"I'm looking for a woman who was admitted yesterday. She suffered two bullet wounds—"

The doctor cut him off. "We get eighteen thousand patients a year coming through this emergency room and too many of them are gunshot wounds."

"Her name is Novak. Lisa Novak."

"Tell the lady on reception over there. I'm sorry, I have to go."

Alex queued for ten minutes behind angry relatives and bleeding patients. Eventually, the harried African receptionist looked up Lisa's details on a slow computer and directed him down the corridor to the intensive care unit.

It was almost as crowded there as it was in the emergency room. Patients with tubes sticking out of their bodies lay side by side in the open ward, which was festooned with monitors, drips and ventilators. It looked like the aftermath of a major disaster, but this was everyday life in Johannesburg.

He heard Mark Novak before he saw him.

"You can't smoke in here, sir," said a man in Afrikaans.

"Fuck off," Novak replied in the same language, then switched to English. "I'm not leaving my wife."

Alex poked his head around a curtain and saw the face-off between the fierce looking ex-soldier and a tall African male nurse, who looked as though he could more than hold his own if it came to a fight.

"Howzit, Alex," Novak said, exhaling smoke.

"Hi, Janine," Alex said to Novak's daughter. She looked up at him and tried to smile, but he could see the tears in her eyes. Janine was twenty, and only recently married. She was sitting by her unconscious mother, holding a hand from which an IV drip protruded. "Don't get up. Novak, I need to see you—maybe outside is better."

They threaded their way through the carnage of the emergency room and Novak was lighting a second cigarette off the first by the time they stepped out into the clear night air. A siren was getting closer and somewhere in the car park an alarm was screeching. "How is she?"

Novak shrugged. "You've probably seen as many head wounds as I have. You know how they go. Sometimes they kill straightaway, other times the *oke* lives. She took one shot to her neck, a through-and-through that missed her carotid and her windpipe, so that was relatively minor, though she lost a lot of blood. The doc says the other bullet deflected partially off some bone and lodged in what they call the dura matter—it's like a tough outer layer of the bone. He oper-ated and got the bullet and skull fragments out and . . ."

He was like an engine that had run out of petrol. He leaned against the hospital's outer wall and coughed as he tried to drag on his cigarette. He raised a hand to his eyes.

"She's tough, man," Alex said.

When he moved his hand, Alex saw his eyes were red-rimmed and glistening. Novak shuddered and he drew a breath of fresh air and straightened himself. "*Ja*. I know. Anyway, like you see, she's still in a coma. The doc doesn't know when—or if—she'll come out of it, or what damage the bullet caused. He says there's a lot of brain tissue that's relatively underused and people can recover from hits to those areas. Man, I don't know, but I'm telling you, if I catch whoever did this, Alex, I'm going to peel the skin off his body while he lives."

"I think I know who's responsible."

Novak dropped his cigarette and ground it out. "Tell me."

"George Penfold."

"The *oke* who owns that ship we boarded?" Novak sounded sur-prised.

Alex nodded.

"Shit, man. We didn't even get anything and those goons of his nearly kicked our arses."

"Penfold doesn't know that. Whatever went missing from that ship, Penfold thinks we took it."

"Well if we didn't take it, who did? Was it that fucking woman?"

Alex bridled at Mark's description of Jane, though he'd been thinking similarly uncharitable thoughts during the drive to the hospital. He was still angry at the fallout from Jane's decision not to tell Penfold she knew where the diamonds were, but if he were her he would probably have done the same thing.

"You should have let Mitch get the information out of her."

Alex shook his head. "You don't mean that."

"OK. But my Lisa is the one who's been hurt, and Trudy's dead. She was part of our family. This Penfold wouldn't have done the hit himself?"

"The cops are looking for three white men and a black man who were driving a stolen Eskom *bakkie*. It was on the radio tonight. I'm betting it's the same gunslingers we ran up against on the ship."

Novak nodded. "All right. I want them, but I also want the man who pays them—this Penfold *poes*."

Novak was right, Penfold was a cunt, but Alex couldn't let him charge into the Melrose Arch Hotel with all guns blazing.

"You really want to hurt Penfold?" Alex asked, unnecessarily.

"Of course I do."

"Then what we do is get our hands on whatever it is he was prepared to kill Lisa for."

"The diamonds?"

Alex wasn't so sure that was all Penfold was missing, but he said, "Yes. I saw Jane this evening. She doesn't have them, but she's hidden them somewhere on board the *Penfold Son*. It's in dock at Cape Town."

"I want to see her."

"No. If you try and bully her she'll just go to the cops. She actually kept quiet about us being responsible for the ship hijacking. She's also worried that her boss is up to something criminal."

"But how did they know to go to my house, and what were they looking for?"

"I don't know, but I do know what they found." Alex relayed the information Jane had given him about the photo, and the fact that Penfold had been able to positively identify all the men in the picture.

Novak slumped. "So what you're saying is, we're screwed."

"What I'm saying is that we need to bring George Penfold down—not only as payback for what his thugs did to Lisa and her maid, but to keep ourselves alive."

"But not in business. I'm finished with piracy if Lisa gets better. I've already promised God."

This was a side to the South African Alex hadn't seen before, but Novak's wishes echoed his own. All he wanted was to go straight, but they couldn't run or hide from the threat George Penfold posed to them now. Even if he recovered his missing property he would still be out to eradicate the gang on Ilha dos Sonhos in order to remove the threat they posed to his shipping interests.

Novak snapped his fingers and looked as though he had just remembered something. "Hey, did you take some stuff from my wardrobe that you weren't supposed to?"

Alex had hoped Novak wouldn't notice the missing uniforms. When he'd called him in Mozambique he had offered to collect some clothes for him from his house. Novak had agreed, and had told Le Roux, the detective in charge of the investigation, by phone to allow Alex to collect a bag of clothes for him from the house, which was still being treated as a crime scene.

The car alarm that had been honking away out in the car park finally fell silent.

Novak continued: "Janine took me back to the house earlier this evening to get some more stuff. I'm staying with her—I can't be in the house without Lisa. I noticed all my old army uniforms were gone. What's going on, Alex?"

With Novak's fatigues and ones he'd stolen from Kim's husband he now had enough uniforms for what he had in mind. "I didn't think you'd care, and I didn't want to bother you, what with Lisa in hospital and all . . ."

"Bullshit. Tell me, man."

"Go back inside. Your wife needs you."

"It's for a job, isn't it? What are you hitting? Why the army uniforms?"

Alex genuinely didn't want to involve Novak in the plan to steal the ivory from the Kruger National Park. The man belonged here in Johannesburg, at his wife's side.

Novak stood straight and poked a finger at Alex's chest. "You're always saying you just need one more job. A big one. Is this it, Alex? Have you got your white whale?"

"We can handle it—me and the other guys."

Novak shook his big head vigorously. "You can't cut me out, Alex. We haven't saved enough money, Lisa and me. We have the cars to pay off, and I want to help Janine and her husband buy a house. I need that last big job as much as you do. The doctor said . . . well, he said that when Lisa wakes up she might even be paralyzed, man. I'll need money to look after her, to make things right for her."

Alex clapped a hand on the South African's muscled, tattooed forearm. "I won't see you left poor, Novak. I'll take care of it."

Novak shrugged his hand free. "Don't patronize me. And I don't want your bloody charity. The fact is that you need me if you've got a job, Alex. You're one man short now that psycho Mitch is off our hands. No one misses him, but you'll be two men down if you don't take me. Also, you saw the way Henri sided with Mitch. The Frenchy knows he was wrong and it was good of you to let him stay with the team, but we can't afford to have that sort of shit going on again— people doing things behind your back. It's not a criticism of you as a leader, Alex, but you need me to help keep them together and focused."

Alex nodded. He knew Novak was right, about everything. The

truth was that Alex *did* want out of the piracy game and Mitch and Henri had picked up on his weakening resolve.

"When's the job on?" Novak pushed.

"A week from today," Alex said.

"Tell me more."

And when Alex had finished Novak said, "You've finally gone *fokking* crazy. Count me in."

Piet van Zyl got into the driver's seat of the *bakkie* he had just broken into and popped the bonnet. He got out, opened it fully, found the car alarm and cut the wires with his pocket knife. At last the racket was over but, predictably, he could see a security guard walking toward him beneath the diffused glare of the sodium lights. The African had his right hand on his pistol and carried a large torch in his left. He shone the beam on Piet.

"It's OK, man," Van Zyl called, raising his hand to his eyes. "It's my vehicle. Bloody alarm went off by mistake." He repeated his explanation in Afrikaans, in case the guard's English was poor.

"OK, sir. But I am required to ask for identification or proof of ownership."

Piet turned around so the guard could see the red embroidered lettering on the back of the blue work shirt he wore. It said: *De Kok and Sons Plumbing*, in the same lettering as that on the side door of the pickup. The guard smiled and nodded. "OK, sir. Goodnight."

Van Zyl was winging this operation, which he wasn't happy about, but there had been no time to plan in any detail. The Novak woman needed to be silenced—tonight. The news report had said she was still in a coma, and Piet said a silent prayer of thanks for that small mercy. He was beginning to feel this whole operation was jinxed. He had put two bullets into the woman, including a head shot, but still she'd lived. He'd seen stranger things on the battlefield, but all the same, it shook him. He had thought he might try to steal a lab coat or some scrubs once in the hospital, and masquerade as a doctor or orderly, but the plumber's truck was a perfect alternative. He knew security would eventually come to investigate the blaring car alarm and he was pleased it was the gullible guard who had showed up first, rather than the vehicle's rightful owner.

The *bakkie* had yielded not only uniforms, but also a wallet, in the glove compartment, with a plumber's business cards, and a bag of tools from the floor on the passenger's side. From the center console he grabbed a sweat-grimed baseball cap, also with the business logo stitched on it. He took his pistol from the holster on his belt and the silencer from the pocket of his jeans. He screwed the attachment to the barrel and cocked it. As the weapon was now too long to conceal, he placed it in the canvas tool bag under a pile of wrenches.

As he walked through the car park he pulled the cap down low over his eyes, which remained downcast as he entered the bustling, chaotic emergency room.

There was a plan on the wall next to the receptionist's desk. The woman looked harried, explaining to a distraught mother that her child would have to wait up to an hour to see a doctor. Van Zyl noticed a plastic container full of clip-on passes which each bore a capital V followed by a number. In smaller print below it said *Visitor*. While the receptionist was pointing out the toilets down the corridor to the woman, Van Zyl quickly leaned across the counter and palmed a pass. He clipped it onto the pocket of his overall shirt and returned his gaze to the plan. He found the intensive care unit and set off down the hallway.

"Can I help you? Hey, you?" a voice said behind him.

He turned and saw a white woman in green disposable surgical scrubs. "There's a water leak in ICU," he said.

"Can I see some ID?"

Van Zyl kept his cool. He put a thumb under the visitor's pass and held it up for the woman to see, and fished in his pocket for one of the plumber's business cards, which he handed to her. "I'm a plumber, not a doctor. They don't give us fancy IDs."

"OK, sorry to trouble you, but we don't want just anyone wandering around the hospital."

He nodded. "It's good to know your security's working."

He smiled to himself as he carried on. He turned right, his shoes squeaking on the freshly washed linoleum floor. He wrinkled his nose at the universal hospital smell, the sharp odor of urine and disinfectant.

It was marginally quieter in this part of the hospital than the emergency room, though nursing staff still paced the corridors, and as he pushed open the swinging plastic doors to the intensive care unit, he saw that relatives hovered by two of the ten beds.

There was an African woman with two small daughters standing at the foot of the bed of a skinny man with a tube draining from his chest. At the far end of the ward a young woman's face was lit by the greenish glow of a monitor, attached to a patient whose head was heavily bandaged. He checked off the color, age and sex of each patient as he moved quietly between the rows of beds. The only white woman, he now saw, was the one with the head wound. It had to be Lisa Novak. Looking at the girl, who he guessed was not long out of her teens, he saw the family resemblance. A man about the same age, with bleached hair and brand-name Australian surfing shorts and T-shirt, stood beside his partner, with his hand on her shoulder.

The man looked around as Van Zyl walked past, glancing across to positively identify the Novak woman.

"Had a complaint about a leaky pipe in the bathroom. Sorry for the disturbance," he said. The man nodded, stifled a surreptitious yawn, and returned his gaze to the unconscious woman.

Van Zyl was feeling the buzz now. The adrenaline was pumping through his veins, sending little jolts of electricity to his fingertips, but he forced himself to keep his emotions in check. The woman couldn't have been placed in a better position. Her bed was right next to the door of the toilet and shower that serviced the ward. Piet opened the door and knelt down. From the bag he took one of the plumber's wrenches and set to work on the cold-water pipe that fed the washbasin. He strained, then felt the connection loosen.

As it came away from the wall he was pleasantly surprised by the force of water that jetted from the open end. Water gushed out onto the floor. To add to the realism he, too, was now drenched in water.

As he opened the bathroom door water flooded out into the ward, the flow increasing by the second. He went first to Lisa Novak's relatives. "Hey, I'm very, very sorry, but this leak's got worse and I'm going to have to ask you to move out for a couple of minutes. I'll call the nurse, as well."

"Shit, man."

"Hush, Dirk," the Novaks' daughter said to her partner. "*Ag*, what a mess. Isn't this dangerous with all the electrical machines and stuff in here?"

"*Ja*, very," Van Zyl said. "I'll have the flow turned off in a second, but I need you to wait in the corridor for just a little while, OK? Sooner we get this cleaned up, the sooner you can get back to your mom."

The girl looked at him, puzzled by something he'd said, but her heavy lids and the dark rings under her eyes betrayed her fatigue. "OK."

Van Zyl moved the African family and asked them, too, to wait in the corridor.

As soon as both sets of relatives left he returned to the bathroom and simply turned off the mains switch that supplied cold water to the toilet and washbasin. He was lucky the young man had been too stupid to question him and suggest the most logical way to stop the water flowing.

Piet took his pistol from the sodden tool bag.

Novak's mobile phone chirped in his pocket. "Hello, my girl," he said hurriedly, "any news?"

Alex stood beside Novak in the emergency room, where they had just returned, en route to ICU. Novak nodded. "OK, I'm coming now. We're back inside the hospital."

"Come," he said to Alex.

"Something wrong?"

Novak lengthened his stride and Alex jogged a couple of paces down the corridor to catch him up.

"Make way, make way!" a woman shouted. Around the corner in front of them a team of doctors and nurses ran beside a bed, which was being wheeled by an orderly. The face of the female patient was deathly white, and for a second Alex feared it was Lisa.

The party's onward rush had forced Novak and Alex to stop on one side of the hallway, to give way. The sudden burst of panic had increased Novak's own sense of anxiety and he started to run. "What's up?" Alex called.

"Something about a flood in ICU. Shit. This bloody country . . ."

"A flood?"

Alex reached for his Glock 19, concealed by the tail of his loose-fitting cream linen shirt. Checking no one was in sight, he drew the weapon, cocked it and stuffed it down the front of his pants, where it would be quicker to get to.

"Shit," Novak said, as his foot slipped in water. Janine, her young husband Dirk, and a black woman and her children were huddled outside the swinging door that led to the ICU. "Where's the nurse or the doctor?"

"I don't know, Pa," Janine said, looking up at him and wringing her hands. "It's why I called you. I've asked a cleaner to fetch a nurse. He said he didn't know anything about a problem with the plumbing."

Novak burst through the door with Alex at his heels. The lighting in the ward was dim, in consideration of the hour, and Alex reached for his pistol as he saw the door to the bathroom near Lisa's bed swing open. A man emerged carrying something in his right hand.

Time seemed to slow as Alex's eyes fed the information to his brain. The man was indoors, but he wore a hat. Why? He was wearing a tradesman's blue overalls and they were soaking wet. Did that mean he was a good plumber or a bad plumber? The thing in his right hand gleamed metallically in the diffused light of the monitor Lisa was plugged into, but it was too long to be a pistol. Or was it?

Alex's hand was already moving, independently of his thought processes. It was this primal, warrior's instinct that had kept him alive more than once. Training and experience could hone this weapon that all men were born with but not all men could wield. As he raised the pistol he called, "Novak, down!"

The South African, too, had not survived so many years in war zones by ignoring orders or allowing his reflexes to grow slow. He dived, but not to the floor. The force that drove him was protection. Like a sprinting rugby forward approaching the try line he landed across Lisa's motionless body.

Alex knew what he had seen: a silencer screwed to the end of a pistol. But even as his brain put the pieces together he was already stopping, wrapping his fingerless left hand around his right and squeezing the two-phase trigger of the Glock.

The muzzle flash, and the noise from the two shots he fired, was like a lightning strike in the dim confines of the hospital ward. Alex saw the target's right arm jerk once, from the recoil of a shot fired, and feared he'd missed, but he was rewarded with a shout of pain from the shooter. The plate-glass window behind the gunman shattered into a thousand glittering shards from Alex's second bullet. Something clattered heavily to the floor.

Novak was groaning too, and Alex glimpsed a spreading bloodstain on Lisa's white bedspread as Novak tried to stand.

Some piece of hospital equipment had short-circuited from a bullet or Novak's crashing fall onto his wife. The lights flickered and went out and a piercing alarm sounded from Lisa's monitor.

"Stay down, Mark!" Alex shouted. The South African was between him and the gunman, who had dropped down, perhaps to retrieve his fallen pistol.

Alex moved forward and cuffed Novak down with his left hand and fired two more shots at the shadowy figure who jumped up onto the windowsill then out into the night.

"How bad are you hit?"

"Through and through," Novak said, lifting his right arm. The bullet had pierced his forearm and he was bleeding profusely. Novak winced and touched his arm. "Bone's OK."

Alex looked down at the bed and as lights flickered back on he saw where the stuffing had exploded from the mattress an inch from Lisa's left shoulder. She was as safe as a woman in a coma with bullet damage to her brain could be. "Stay here with her."

Janine and Dirk burst into the room. The girl was screaming incoherently and the hospital seemed filled with the clangor of alarms and raised voices. "Give me your 38 Special," Novak growled at his daughter. The girl, lower lip quivering, reached into her handbag and handed the snub-nosed pistol to her father. "Go, Alex. I'm fine. Cops will be here any minute—there's always plenty of them hanging around this place at night."

Alex peeked over the window ledge and saw the gunman running along the awning roof over the entryway to the hospital. The drop was about three meters. He leaped out into the cool night and landed, feet together and knees bent.

Although he landed upright he immediately rolled and dropped to his belly. He heard the crack and thump of air being displaced a few centimeters above his head as the man turned and fired a silenced shot at him. Alex stretched his hands out in front of him and fired twice, but the man had already leaped over the far end of the awning. Alex pulled himself to his feet and sprinted, his feet clanging on the tin roofing.

At the edge of the awning he paused. Below him was a rubbish skip and he prayed it wasn't full of disposed needles and scalpels as he jumped over the edge. Foul-smelling garbage spattered up over his shirt and face, but he kept his pistol raised and out of the muck. The steel sides of the bin probably saved him, as he heard a bullet clang off the side. When he poked his head over the top he couldn't see the man, so he vaulted out and ran into the car park.

"Stop, police!"

Alex ignored the shout from behind him. He didn't want to talk to the police about the night's events, but nor did he want to be mistaken for the perpetrator and shot in the back. He doubled his body as he ran between the rows of parked cars.

Ahead of him he heard a squeal of rubber and the screech of poorly lined brakes as a car skidded to a halt. A horn was hooted and then a man started yelling abuse, but shut up quickly. Alex guessed the fugitive had pointed his pistol at the angry driver. Alex raised his head above the roofline of a Corolla and saw where the car had stopped. The driver had his hands held high and was backing away. "Sorry, sorry, man," the now terrified citizen was saying. "Take the *bladdy* car, just don't kill me. I've got a wife and a sick kid in the hospital."

Alex saw the hatted figure behind the wheel and cut through two rows of cars so that he was closer to the car park exit than where the hijacking had just taken place. The bastard would have to drive right past him.

As he heard the Corolla slide into the corner and the driver gun the engine into the straight, Alex stepped out from the protection of a BMW four-by-four and fired twice at the oncoming vehicle. The windscreen starred, obscuring his aim, but he pumped another two bullets into the driver's side. Instead of slowing, the car accelerated and veered toward him. Side panels were dented and scratched with the sound of screeching metal as the driver glanced off the rear bumpers of three of four cars close to Alex, who had to step back further into cover as the car raced past him.

"Shit." Alex realized the man must have ducked beneath the dashboard and driven by instinct. Charging full-pelt toward the enemy was, paradoxically, the best way to get through an ambush, and it had worked for Alex's quarry.

Alex ran as fast as he could across another four rows of parked vehicles to his Land Cruiser. The vehicle had a powerful four-liter engine, but it was diesel and slow to reach its top speed. He'd have little hope of catching the nimble smaller sedan before it got out of the hospital grounds and into the maelstrom of Johannesburg's fast-moving nighttime traffic. That is, if he stuck to the road.

Alex started the engine and turned in the opposite direction to the car park exit signs. Between him and the road onto which the car park fed was a raised earthen berm, covered in grass and flowerbeds. It acted as a partial noise and visual barrier between the hospital and the traffic outside. Alex shifted into low-range four-wheel drive and lurched over the concrete curb. The Land Cruiser's wide, knobbly tires bit hard into the landscaped topsoil, spun for an instant, then propelled him up and over the barrier with effortless ease. As he coasted down the other side he shifted back into high range and floored the accelerator.

The Corolla whizzed by him as Alex hurtled down the hill. As he left the high-raised curb there was air under all four wheels momentarily. Horns blared around him as he veered out into the middle lane while wrenching the steering wheel around to the left. The Corolla was two cars ahead of him, but couldn't accelerate away as there was a semitrailer trying to pass another truck carrying a shipping container. The gunman leaned on his horn, but to no avail. Alex geared down to third, tortured the engine and transmission with another heavy burst of diesel, then shifted to fourth and narrowed the gap.

He saw the man's white face for the first time as he turned and looked through the rear window. Alex accelerated harder, bringing his bumper almost to the rear of the Corolla. The man raised his hand and Alex flinched, expecting a shot, but to his surprise he saw the man was bringing a cell phone to his ear. That could mean reinforcements. Alex shifted up into fifth and the extra boost of speed on the slight downhill slope pushed him into the rear of the sedan. Alex heard the other car's bumper shatter. The man braked instinctively, but Alex accelerated harder. Other cars hooted and sped around them, trying to escape the madness.

The man veered sharply to the right, into the oncoming traffic. His high-risk, gutsy move paid off. Alex braked and the Corolla weaved in and out of the erratically swerving parade of cars.

Alex wanted this man dead. He gritted his teeth and followed the gunman's lead, swinging out around the lorry in front of him, into the oncoming stream. Cars jinked out of his way as he pushed the big diesel engine beyond its limits.

He was again closing on the Corolla, which had been slowed by some unseen obstacle up ahead which was reducing the traffic to a crawl. If the Corolla couldn't find an exit soon, Alex would have him trapped. However, there would be innocents all around them. Alex nipped out into the wrong lane again, past the last car between him and the man he wanted, then darted back in behind his target. Although he saw the sedan's brake lights flash, he touched the accelerator pedal harder with his toe and braced for the inevitable collision.

Gunfire erupted.

Too late, Alex glanced up into his rearview mirror. A BMW 3 Series sedan was behind him and a black man was leaning out the passenger side, holding a Heckler and Koch MP5 machine pistol. Alex saw the muzzle winking in the darkness and heard the rattle of bullets on the rear bodywork of his vehicle.

Suddenly, he was weaving. The steering wheel went slack in his hands and he turned hard, overcorrecting. The Land Cruiser had been sitting on close to a hundred kilometers per hour and it nearly rolled before he wrestled the wheel back the other way. He started to slow, and heard the slap of burst rubber beneath him. The gunman in the other car had shot out at least one of the rear tires. Alex pressed on despite the deafening shriek of his bare left rear rim cutting into the tar of the road, but he could gain no further ground on the Corolla when the traffic ahead started to pick up speed once more. To seal his defeat the right rear tire exploded after another burst of gunfire.

Alex veered to the left onto a steep grassy embankment. Once more the four-wheel drive would go where no town car could follow. The brakes seemed useless as he careened over the lip and hurtled down the near-vertical drop.

The phone in George's suite rang and rang, but there was no answer.

It was one o'clock in the morning. Hardly a civilized time to be calling someone, but Jane had known George to take calls far later than this from the UK. He'd told her he was a borderline insomniac. Perhaps he had turned down the volume on the phone's ringer in order to try to get some sleep. Not like George, but possible.

Despite the hard line she'd taken with Alex, she felt terrible about what had happened to Lisa Novak. Still dressed, and fortified by a half-bottle of white from the minibar in her hotel room, she had resolved to tell all she knew to George, and to hear, from him, just what was in the package that Iain MacGregor had entrusted to her.

She could no longer afford to give him the benefit of the doubt, nor wait to check for herself what was in the pouch she had hidden on board the *Penfold Son* before the pirates seized her. Too many lives were at risk.

She didn't regret standing up to Alex, though. He had charmed her, and she was a little disturbed at how easily she had fallen for his advances, but he had also abducted her and held her on the island against her will.

Jane put her high heels back on and checked her hair in the mirror, tidying a couple of loose strands. On impulse, she decided to try the phone one more time before knocking on his door.

This time it was busy. "Oh, bugger it," she said aloud. She hung up and marched out of her room to the lifts. At least he was in his room now.

George was staying a floor above her. She imagined he had avoided booking her next door to him so as not to give the other company executives anything to gossip about. They were staying on the same level as her. The lift doors opened and Jane followed the room numbers down a corridor to her right.

Counting the doors ahead, she had already identified George's, but thought she must have made a mistake when it opened and a woman emerged. She was early thirties, Jane guessed, with a jet-black bob and breasts that seemed out of proportion to her skinny build. She wore a red lycra singlet top and a black miniskirt. She tottered into the hallway on impossibly high stilettos. Dressed like that, Jane thought she was either going to a rave or else she was a prostitute. She couldn't hear any house music coming from the room, which, as she got closer, she saw was definitely George's suite.

Jane stopped in front of the woman as she was pulling the door closed. She was thumbing through a wad of red two-hundred rand notes. Jane was rewarded with a look of shock and surprise on the woman's face when she looked up.

Jane stood there, hands on hips in the hallway, staring at the stranger.

The woman regained her composure and tossed her head, flicking her hair out of her eye. "Hello . . . I'm afraid I got my room number wrong. All these doors look alike, don't they?"

Jane thought it a pathetic attempt at covering up. She could hear George talking from inside the room. The door was still not pulled closed and she didn't want to cause a fuss and alert him just yet. Her mind raced. Perhaps the woman was telling the truth, although the handful of cash that she hurriedly stuffed into a large patent leather shoulder bag indicated otherwise. "Don't worry." Jane winked. "I'm not the wife, just a friend. He told me you'd be coming and invited me to join you if I made it back to the hotel early enough."

The woman let out an audible hiss of air. "God, you had me worried there for a moment. Thought you might have been a work colleague or something. I knew you weren't the wife," she nodded back toward George's room, "because she's on the phone."

Jane smiled, even though she felt dizzy. She thought she might throw up, so she swallowed hard.

The woman flicked her hair from her face. "He didn't mention anything about anyone joining us. I'd be happy to stay for a bit, if you like, though it'll cost him extra." She looked Jane up and down and ran the tip of her tongue around her full red lips.

If the gesture was meant to turn her on, it had precisely the opposite effect. Jane hid her revulsion and said, "No, thanks anyway."

The woman shrugged. "Maybe next time?"

"Perhaps. Just out of interest, how was he?"

"Rough. Nasty. I've got bruises that'll last a week, but he got what he paid for. But I suppose you know all about that side of him?"

"Yes, of course," Jane said. "Night."

Jane waited in the shadow of the doorway until the woman had rounded the bend in the corridor and she heard the lift bell chime. She stood there, leaning against the door frame for support, listening to George talking to his wife.

"No, I told you before, you can call any time, day or night, my love," he said. "Especially when it's about the kids. I'm glad she's all right now, though. Poor pet. Give her all my love."

Jane frowned. This was supposedly a woman George had blazing rows with every night, and who made him sleep in a separate room. The same woman who had supposedly granted him a divorce.

"I love you too, Liz," he said. "And I miss you terribly." He chuckled loudly. "Yes, you naughty minx, I miss *that* too. I can't wait to get home and give you a jolly good seeing-to, my bad girl. Love you. Night night."

It amazed her that George would risk sneaking a hooker into the hotel when she—the woman he had proposed to—was staying in the same hotel. Maybe risky two-timing was part of the sexual thrill for him. If that was the case, then he probably got the same kick out of sleeping with her back in the UK.

Jane felt sick to her stomach. She pulled the door closed softly and turned and walked down the hotel corridor.

20

Alex called Janine Novak's cell phone and told her to ask her father, quietly so that the police officers couldn't hear, to call him when he had a chance. He hung up, ran some water in the hotel bathroom's washbasin and shaved, carefully and painfully, with a disposable razor.

His seat belt had saved his life, though his chest felt as though it had been kicked by a horse and his face was flecked with dried blood from where the windscreen had shattered and sprayed him when the Land Cruiser had landed, nose first, in the bottom of the deep concrete stormwater culvert.

He'd passed out—for how long he didn't know—and when he came to he was surprised to find himself alive. He guessed that the police had probably been hot on his tail after he'd left the hospital, and the man who had shot out his rear tires had not had the chance to stay and finish the job.

The men in the BMW had probably been hiding elsewhere in the hospital car cark, waiting to pick up the gunman; but the shooter had had to change his plan quickly when Alex followed him out of the ICU window. Alex recalled, as he shaved, how the man had been talking on a mobile phone while driving.

Almost as miraculous as the fact that he had survived the shootout and the totaling of his four-by-four was that someone had stopped to assist him soon after his crash. Good Samaritans were a rarity in a country where hijackers often pretended to be roadside breakdown victims. The man who had come to Alex's rescue was a security guard on his way home. He had perhaps been more willing to stop than the average motorist by virtue of the semiautomatic shotgun he toted with him to the crash scene.

The guard, a Zulu named Doctor—whose parents presumably had loftier career goals in mind for him—gave him a lift to the Garden Court Hotel near OR Tambo International Airport, in the industrial suburb of Isando. When Doctor had asked Alex if he wanted to call the police, Alex had said no, and the security guard had just shrugged. He'd also said nothing when Alex had searched the floor of his Land Cruiser until he found his pistol.

Alex smiled in the mirror as he remembered Doctor's thanks for the handful of rand notes Alex had palmed him as they shook hands in the hotel car park at two in the morning. "One more thing," Alex had said.

"What's that, my brother?"

"Have you got any spare nine-mill ammo on you, *bru*?"

"The company counts all my rounds, man, for my service pistol." He patted the Browning slung low on his right thigh. "But fortunately I always carry a backup." He pulled his second pistol from the rear of his trouser waistband, thumbed the magazine release catch and emptied ten bullets into his palm. "*Hamba gahle*," he said to Alex as he handed him the glittering pile of brass and copper.

"And you go well yourself, Doctor."

Alex gingerly fingered the sash-like bruise across his chest. Fortunately there were no ribs broken. His mobile rang and he picked it up without checking the caller identification on the screen. "Novak?"

"It's Jane."

"Oh."

He was tempted to hang up on her. He told himself he was finished with her, and didn't care what happened to the selfish bloody woman. But something made him hold on. He waited through four long seconds of silence.

"I was wrong," she said.

Again, he said nothing.

"And I feel terrible for Lisa. How is she? Any better?"

He broke his silence and told her about the second attempt on Lisa's life during the night, and his wounding and pursuit of the unknown gunman. Alex walked out of the bathroom and sat on the bed, a towel around his waist.

"Which arm did you shoot the man in?" Jane asked.

The scene replayed itself in his mind. The shooter was right-handed and had dropped his pistol on the ICU ward floor, before retrieving it and jumping out the window. "Right. But it couldn't have been a serious hit as the guy was up and firing back at me a couple of minutes later."

"The man who headed the security detachment on the *Penfold Son*, Piet van Zyl, had a breakfast meeting with George this morning. I didn't speak to him, but he looked pretty ropey—like he'd been up all night. He had a bandage around his right wrist, just behind the thumb, and some scratches on his arms and face."

"I must have grazed him before he jumped through the window."

"How's Novak?"

Alex had told her about Novak being shot while protecting his wife. "He's OK. The police have given him a grilling, but your boss can rest assured Novak hasn't said anything about hijacking Penfold's ships in the Indian Ocean. Lisa has got a round-the-clock police guard in an isolated ward and Novak is sitting next to her with two guns. One thing's for sure: if Penfold's hired guns go into that hospital again, they won't come out alive."

Alex didn't tell her the best news of the night—the only good news, in fact. The force of Novak's fall on his wife had pushed her body toward the metal bed-head and she had bumped the tubular steel hard. A few minutes after Alex and the gunman had exited via the window, Lisa had opened her eyes. The blow had caused her to regain consciousness. Lisa was talking, but was having trouble remembering anything about either shooting.

"Do you know where Van Zyl is now?"

"No, although I do know he and his men are flying somewhere. After breakfast they checked out and I overheard them booking a car from the hotel to the airport."

"Did they have any firearms with them, any gun bags?"

"No. Not that I could see. All my stuff is still stuck on board the *Penfold Son* in Cape Town. The local customs and police people wouldn't allow access to it—so I imagine Van Zyl's arsenal is on board too. George says he expects workmen to be allowed on board in a couple of days' time. He told them he wants her ready to sail ASAP, so perhaps Van Zyl's flying to Cape Town. We're all going down there to continue the negotiations and inspect the De Witt fleet before the takeover. It's why I called you."

"What's that got to do with me?"

"I hid the package Captain MacGregor gave me somewhere on the *Penfold Son*."

"I guessed as much. So why don't you just get it, have a look at it and confront George once and for all."

"I want to get it before George and the others board the ship and I can't do that by myself. It's berthed at the Duncan Dock at Cape Town and with security the way it is these days I can't just walk on board. If I use my Penfold ID, George will find out about it."

"What's in it for me?" Alex asked. As he sat on the hotel bed next to the dive bag he'd salvaged from his wrecked Land Cruiser, a plan was already forming in his mind.

She paused. "If there's stolen property, or something else illegal in that package, I can't be a party to its sale or profit from its disposal."

"Spoken like a true lawyer. Why don't you just tell George where the package is, so he and his goons can lay off my guys?"

"For the same reason you won't go to the police and tell them Piet van Zyl probably shot Lisa Novak. Because you want to get even yourself, and you want to know what's in that package as much as I do."

"You're right. What made you change your mind about George?"

"I found out some stuff about him. He's been lying to me since I met him. At least you came clean about being a criminal."

"Thanks. I think. OK, I'll come to Cape Town and help you find the package." There was another reason he would go with her, instead of returning to Mozambique immediately and planning the ivory heist. He wanted to see her again.

Alex no longer had a car, so he couldn't drive to Cape Town, and as he was carrying a pistol and had no contacts in the Mother City who could sell him some hardware at short notice, he couldn't fly. Jane, with her pathological fear of flying, was catching the train. And not just any train.

She and George Penfold were traveling in luxury, on board the *Pride of Africa*, a rolling five-star hotel that would take the best part of three days to reach Cape Town. Alex had called Rovos Rail's bookings office and been lucky enough to get a berth on the train. It was expensive, but he had some fat in the expenses budget he'd drawn up for Valiant Chan.

It was raining as he stepped out under the portico in front of the hotel after settling his account, with cash. The taxi the concierge had arranged flashed his lights and pulled up. Although summer was approaching, the Highveld rain had a chill to it. Alex was wearing a brown leather suit coat to hide the Glock tucked in his jeans, as well as to ward off the cold.

"Alexandra," he said.

The driver raised his eyebrows with a "you're *sure?*" look, but then just said, "*Yebo.*"

The driver cut through the back streets of Edenvale and eventually navigated his way onto the multi-lane N3 for the short hop to London Road, the entrance way to Alexandra.

More commonly known as "Alex," the township was set up to house the black workers of northern Johannesburg. These days more than three hundred thousand souls lived there in shanties, modest houses and imposing multistorey hostels that loomed like prison blocks over the bustling eight hundred hectares of humanity.

Few whites had business here, but Alex had visited a man he knew only as Sipho on half-a-dozen occasions. He gave directions to the driver as they crossed the Jukskei River. Things were changing here, slowly but for the better, and the Alexandra Renewal Program had had a few wins since his last visit. There were more new houses, a new primary school he hadn't noticed last time, and the stadium was coming along. Even the river didn't smell as bad.

He had to call Sipho's mobile phone to make sure he had the right house.

"Yes, this is my home. You are welcome. I can see your car and I am coming now," Sipho said into the phone.

Alex recognized the short, hunchbacked African man waving to him from behind a stout grilled security door, but not the house around him. What had once been a drab single-story gray house with a flat iron roof was now a two-story dwelling with angular, sloping lines, its walls painted a bright ochre. There was the struggling beginnings of a garden in front, which looked like it could desperately use the fat drops of rain that were now pinging the top of the Mercedes. "Wait here," he told the driver. The man looked up and down the narrow street. Half-a-dozen young men were sitting in the gutter opposite them, eyeing the shiny black sedan, but Alex said, "Don't worry. Once they see where I'm going, no one will touch you." The driver nodded, though he plainly wasn't convinced.

Sipho held open the security door for Alex, looked left and right, and across to the youths, who nodded back at him. Alex guessed they were his lookouts. They shook hands in the African way, raising their palms to interlock thumbs halfway through. "How are you, my friend?" Sipho asked.

"Fine, and you? You seem to have prospered since my last visit."

Sipho smiled, following Alex's gaze around his new home. The house was starkly furnished, though spotlessly clean, and Sipho proudly showed Alex the three bedrooms and the indoor flushing toilet, which he also demonstrated with obvious pride. "You probably take these things for granted."

"Not in Mozambique, believe me."

"What can I do for you, my friend?"

Sipho already knew why he was here, even though they hadn't discussed it over the phone, and he led Alex into the backyard, where there was a much smaller brick building, with a flat roof like Sipho's old house. It had a solid steel door, which squeaked noisily when Sipho unlocked a padlock as big as Alex's fist. The windows, he saw, were blocked with more steel plate behind the original burglar bars.

Not everyone in the neighborhood was as prosperous as Sipho. Despite the rain the smell of wood smoke and raw sewage was strong. On one side he heard a child screaming from a house, while somewhere else nearby a man raised his voice in anger.

Sipho closed the door behind him and they were in darkness. Alex casually brushed open his coat, the fingers of his good hand resting on his pistol. Sipho pulled a cord and a bare electric light came on, revealing enough weapons, ammunition and explosives to equip a hundred soldiers.

Alex went to the homemade wooden gun rack and selected one of more than a score of R5 military assault rifles.

"A good choice," Sipho said, not that he had any idea why Alex was interested in such a weapon.

The weight and feel of the rifle were familiar in his hands, like an extension of his own body. Thanks to his service with the South African Army he could strip and assemble one of these blindfolded. He pulled back the slide, checking the breech was empty at the same time as cocking it. He aimed at a fly speck on the wall and squeezed the trigger. The hammer clicked. The R5 was a copy of the rugged Israeli Galil. On full automatic it could fire more than six hundred bullets a minute.

"Ex-army?"

Sipho shrugged. "The defense force themselves estimate they've misplaced nearly five hundred rifles in the last few years."

"I need six, plus twenty-five thirty-five-round magazines," Alex said, replacing the rifle and wandering slowly down the rack of assorted guns, knives and explosives. Sipho's place was a veritable supermarket of death. It was surprising he didn't have a few stolen shopping trolleys as well. "And ten of these," he said, hefting a fragmentation hand grenade. He smiled as Sipho winced when he tossed the grenade and caught it. "Don't trust your own merchandise?"

"Hey, there are kids living next door."

Alex was tempted to say something about Sipho's apparent concern for his neighbors, while dealing in products that would leave children fatherless and motherless across the country. Alex knew very well why Sipho was doing such a good trade in R5s. Johannesburg's street crime was an escalating arms race. When the security guards started carrying semiautomatic shotguns and wearing body armor, the crooks needed weapons that would punch a hole through Kevlar and outgun their opposition.

If all went according to plan no one would be injured by Alex's purchases and the guns, he promised himself, would end up at the bottom of the Indian Ocean, along with his other weaponry, once he went legit. With luck, that would be very soon.

"Shit, Sipho, what don't you have here?" Alex picked up a grenade the shape and size of a beer can. He whistled. "Thermite?"

Sipho nodded.

"Who uses these?"

"You can burn through the top of a safe with one of those."

Alex nodded. Pulling the pin of an ANM 14 thermite grenade

set off a chemical reaction between the aluminum and iron oxide inside, producing temperatures in excess of two thousand degrees. The grenades were designed to sabotage equipment and could melt through a vehicle engine block or the breech of an artillery gun in minutes.

"I'll take four. What's in these boxes?"

Sipho shuffled along and opened a cardboard carton. From it, he pulled a tan army load-bearing vest. "Brand new. Straight from the factory."

"Perfect," Alex said. He'd thought he would have to stop at an army surplus store. "Six sets."

They haggled over the price for a few minutes, but met, as they usually did, in the middle. Oddly, Alex trusted Sipho, and he knew he was getting a good deal on the equipment. He hoped, though, he would never meet the man again in his life.

"You want to take all this now?" Sipho asked.

"No." He gave Sipho the address of a self-storage place in Nelspruit, the last major town on the N4 tollway between Johannesburg and the Mozambican border. Alex had used the garage there to store stolen goods that he'd moved from Mozambique into South Africa. In an adjoining unit there was also a stolen Nissan *bakkie*, which would soon be getting resprayed in South African Army tan brown. "Three days from now?" Alex pulled a key to the storage garage off his key ring.

"*Yebo*, Alex. A pleasure doing business with you, as always."

Not for long, Alex told himself.

21

Jane and George said little to each other for most of the journey by limousine from Melrose Arch to Pretoria's Capital Park Station, where they would board the train for their trip to Cape Town.

George had a list of calls to make, mostly to the UK, which was fine by Jane. The air-conditioning in the Mercedes was icy and Jane asked the driver to turn the temperature up and the radio down.

She hadn't confronted George about the prostitute in his room and nor would she, until she knew exactly who she was dealing with. What was clear to her now was that George had lied to her about his relationship with his wife and was sleeping with other women as well. She now doubted he had any intention of divorcing Elizabeth. His actions, while despicable, were not criminal. However, once she found out what was in the package she had hidden on board the *Penfold Son* she might clarify that assumption.

The countryside between Johannesburg, South Africa's largest city, and Pretoria, its capital, had once been open farm and grazing land, but it was being increasingly filled with housing developments. Wealthy citizens were seeking escape from Johannesburg's violent crime.

Jane wore a cream linen jacket and skirt and matching heels that she'd bought that morning. She was on first-name terms now with the lady at the boutique at Melrose Arch. She looked out of the tinted window so George wouldn't see the concern on her face. Not that he would notice.

What, she asked herself yet again, was she doing? From what she had learned in the past twenty-four hours the handsome, urbane millionaire businessman next to her had a predilection for hitting prostitutes, and had quite possibly paid a man to try to kill an innocent woman. She wondered if the mildly kinky sex she and George had already engaged in would have been a precursor to something much more violent and dark.

Jane glanced at George, then back out the window. She was still having trouble believing all of this—any of it—was true. She wished there was some plausible explanation for the way he'd spoken to his wife and the horrible things the prostitute had said he'd done to her. At the same time, the revelations had confirmed to her that she'd made the right choice in not telling George about the package MacGregor had given her. Aside from the terrible consequences for Lisa Novak, which Jane felt genuinely sorry for, she'd put at least one of George's dishonest pursuits on hold. What she needed to do now was find out what was in that package.

Pretoria's streets were busy with civil servants on their lunch breaks. The traffic, however, didn't seem as heavy, or as fast, as Johannesburg's. They skirted the center of the city but rejoined its main thoroughfare, Paul Kruger Street, near the zoo.

Like the train they would be traveling on, Capital Park Station was a lovingly restored relic of the golden years of rail travel. Green-liveried African porters took their bags and a hostess led Jane and George, who was still talking on his mobile phone, into the high-ceilinged station building. There were no tickets to hand over or boarding passes to collect. Nor were there metal detectors or X-ray machines to scan their baggage. This was yet another reason why Jane preferred terrestrial travel to airplanes. That, and the fact a waiter in a bow tie and silk vest was approaching with a tray of champagne and orange juice.

George waved his hand dismissively, but Jane took a glass to steady her nerves. She looked around for Alex, wondering if he would show up. She couldn't see him.

The hall was filling with passengers. The accents were a mix of German, British and American. It was the sort of train where men were expected to wear a jacket and tie to dinner. Jane had worried briefly, despite the bigger concerns in her life at the moment, if she would be underdressed in her work suit. In fact, looking around the room she thought most of the women looked pretty shabby. If anything, she was overdressed. A South African matron in her fifties was wearing a cropped top and three-quarter length camouflage trousers that would have looked bad enough on a teenager—ditto the piercing that one woman wore in her belly button. An elderly couple speaking a Nordic language arrived in matching khakis, their faces reddened from an arduous few days at some luxury safari lodge, no doubt.

A steam whistle blew outside, loud enough to make her flinch. Jane left George on his phone and threaded her way between chintz armchairs and steamer trunk tables bearing silver platters of triangular sandwiches with no crusts. She was too tense to eat, but exchanged her empty champagne flute for a full one from a passing waiter. From the French doors leading to the platform outside she could see the locomotive. It was long and sleek, painted dark green and wreathed in steam. She'd read that while the train would actually be pulled by a diesel or electric engine for most of the trip, departures and arrivals were always done with a steam loco. It was all for show, not unlike her presence in Africa at George's side, she thought bitterly.

If she hadn't been so worried about what was going to happen at the end of the journey she might have enjoyed the build-up more. Now she was just anxious to get on board and underway. She checked her watch and tapped her foot on the ornately tiled floor while she waited for boarding to commence. Outside on the platform millionaires with tiny digital cameras snapped pictures of each other on the locomotive's footplate.

George finished his call, made his way to Jane, then said he was going to find the bathroom. Jane turned and caught sight of Alex.

She recognized him even before she saw his face.

He was looking away from her, but the thick, longish black hair and the broad shoulders that filled his black suit jacket gave him away immediately. He wore tight-fitting jeans and fashionable brown leather shoes. Alex seemed completely at ease in this world of moneyed shabby chic.

She felt oddly comforted, seeing him. He was talking to an African porter and as Jane threaded her way toward him she could hear it was in the man's native language. She glanced over her shoulder and saw George disappear into the gents at the far end of the station hall. As Jane came up behind Alex the porter laughed out loud at whatever Alex had said to him.

He turned, as if sensing she was behind him, and when he smiled her mind flashed back to the moment they had shared on the stairs of the ruined building in the middle of Gorongosa National Park. She felt safer now that he was here, which was ridiculous given his occupation.

"I smelled your perfume," he said. "It's Beautiful."

"Yes, by Estee Lauder." She felt her neck start to redden.

Jane looked back toward the gents, fearing George would reappear at any moment. Instead, she saw a blonde woman in her early twenties, part of a gaggle of pretty young men and women in designer surfwear, smiling at them. When she turned back she saw the corners of Alex's mouth straighten out. The girl was half his age, yet she was eyeing him off—or was it the other way around? She wondered how many women's hearts he had broken. She was mildly annoyed that he was still glancing at the poppet. "It was good of you to come."

"I'm intrigued," he said. He held his complimentary glass of champagne up to the light, inspecting the company's logo—the letters

RVR. "Nice crystal. I wonder who does the monogramming for them."

She sidled closer to him and whispered, "George mustn't see you. He's still carrying the photo with him."

"I thought he might be. I'll be discreet."

"What are you looking at now?"

He was running his hand along the back of an armchair. "Nice fabric. What do you think of wing-backed armchairs?"

"What?"

"Whenever I travel I look at furnishings, fabrics, wallpapers, carpets . . . for the hotel. How do you think these would look in the bar? I'm thinking the colonial look might be nice."

"Are you serious?" How could he be talking about interior decorating when George might walk out of the bathroom at any second and catch the two of them together? She looked at the chair. "Um . . . I don't know. Too stuffy for a beachside location?"

He pursed his lips. "You're probably right. Here comes your employer. Perhaps I should go get another drink." He left via the French doors.

She turned on her heel and navigated her way back through the crowd. That had been close. Her heart beat faster, but she smiled to herself thinking of Alex standing there admiring soft furnishings and monogrammed glasses while a man who wanted him dead was in the same room.

"Are you all right?" George asked. "You look a bit pale."

"Fine. It might be the heat, or drinking booze so early in the afternoon."

"Speech time, I fear," George said.

A man in a suit had taken position behind a lectern at the end of the hall. The passengers walked or shuffled—some needed walking sticks, Jane noticed—inside obediently. While the speaker outlined the itinerary for the train Jane nonchalantly looked about the room for Alex. He was nowhere in sight.

To her horror, when Jane tuned back in to what the railway company man was saying she realized he was calling passengers out by name. If he said Alex's name George might pick up on it.

"Mister George Penfold and Ms. Jane Humphries," the man said into his microphone.

"That's us," Jane said. "Let's go."

"What's the rush?" George was halfway through his glass of champagne.

"I want to get settled in. Come on," Jane hooked her arm in his, and George grinned and winked at her, setting down his unfinished drink.

As they walked through onto the platform, where their hostess was waiting for her group of passengers to assemble, Jane heard the man inside call Alex's name.

"Mister Alex—"

The rest of Alex's name was drowned out by another loud blast of the steam engine's whistle.

"Christ, I hope they don't keep that up through the whole trip," George said.

Jane forced a laugh and reminded him about the diesel and electric locomotives as she led him down the platform. When she risked a glance backward she saw Alex standing head and shoulders above a group of octogenarians. He was helping an elderly woman into her carriage when he caught Jane's eye, and even far down the platform she could see him wink. Was he scared of nothing?

The hostess for their carriage, a young Afrikaner woman named Liszette, showed Jane to her suite in the second carriage of the train. Liszette pointed out the light switches and the air conditioner's remote control. Jane thanked her and began unpacking for the two-night trip to Cape Town.

The suite was lovely, she thought, though she viewed the permanently made-up queen-sized bed with suspicion. Jane had been expecting a single bed or a bunk, which would need to be made up for her each evening. She wondered if the bigger bed was a sign that George intended visiting her cabin. The rest of the living space was taken up with a small table, beneath which was a cupboard hiding the mini-bar, and two dining chairs. The interior of the carriage was paneled with polished red timber and above the bed-head were prints of watercolor paintings from the 1930s, showing people bathing in a pool on the edge of the Victoria Falls, and a group of overdressed flappers sitting around a bushveld bonfire. The ensuite contained a shower and toilet. There was a knock on her door.

"Are you decent?" George called. She opened the door. "Hey, this isn't bad, not bad at all. Come see mine. You know, it would have been nice if we could share, but as the company's paying I had to get Gillian to book two suites to keep up appearances, for the time being at least."

She frowned at his back, but followed him down the narrow corridor that ran alongside the suites. The train started to move, then slowed, producing a jolt that caused her to reach out in order to stop from careening into George. He turned as her hand landed on his shoulder.

"You saucy minx. Can't you even wait until lights out?"

Jane shuddered.

George slid open the door to his suite. "Ta-dah!"

At one end of the suite was a queen-sized bed, permanently made up, just like hers. The suite was larger, though, as were the two arm-chairs and the table. The main difference that Jane could see was in the bathroom, which boasted a freestanding white claw-footed bath on the black-and-white checkered floor. It would have been perfect for a romantic interlude, though that was now clearly out of the question, despite George's presumptions.

"How about a pre-dinner tub?"

"I've got a headache, George. Maybe later."

"Seriously? I thought you were coming on to me in the corridor."

"I nearly tripped, George, that was all. I'll see you later."

"That you will, gorgeous. That you will."

Jane went back to her suite, slid the door closed and slumped back against it. She kicked off her new shoes, which had been rubbing painfully on her heels, and opened her minibar. She took out a bottle of water and unscrewed the cap. Her mouth was dry from the champagne she'd had at the station. Her mobile phone beeped in her handbag.

Meet me in observation car in 1 hour, read the text message. She recognized Alex's number.

Alex was traveling in a Pullman Class sleeper which, while the cheapest available, was still tastefully fitted out. The trick, he realized as he ran his fingertips over the polished timber paneling, was to make people feel they were traveling first class, even when they weren't. Timber, even varnished, would be hard to maintain in a coastal climate, though. He sat down on the wide couch, which would be converted into his bed in the evening.

He hung his suit in the wardrobe and undid the padlock on his dive bag. The lock wouldn't stop a thief, but it would tell him if someone had tampered with his luggage.

Steam swirled low along the platform. The whistle sounded again and the train started to move. Alex looked out the window. A knot of maids in green dustcoats laughed among themselves, probably glad to see the back of the train once more. Porters smiled and waved.

The staff he had seen in the station building and on board were attentive and friendly—just what one wanted in a top-class hotel. He realized he would need to spend money on training his own people once the resort was up and running. A few of the older people on the island had worked for his mother and father and would recall the etiquette of waiting on tables and dealing with guests, but most of those only spoke Portuguese and Xitswa. He would have to find an English teacher. Perhaps he could offer one free board and meals in exchange for providing lessons to his staff.

He thought about Jane.

He pictured her in the resort, showing a maid where to cut some fresh bougainvillea to put on a guest's pillow; tasting a soup in the kitchen; straightening a waiter's tie; showing Jose how to make the perfect martini; picking up a guest's toddler while the mother gathered up dropped toys.

He'd put on his best cool, calm, collected exterior for her in the departure hall at Capital Park, but inside his heart had been pounding. He wasn't scared of confronting George Penfold, but knew that if he did he would blow Jane's cover and neither of them would find out what was in the hidden package.

It was being in her presence, he realized, that had temporarily unnerved him. Ridiculous. He'd been with almost too many women to remember, and while he loved them all, in general, there had never been one who had so deeply unsettled him. Though she looked alluringly cool and sexy in her business clothes, he knew it was the layer below that continued to attract him to her. She might be nervous, but she was risking her career—and possibly her safety—by plotting to uncover her boss's crooked dealings and, for reasons of her own, seeking revenge on Penfold. She could be principled and ruthlessly calculating at the same time. Danni walked out when she didn't get her way and Kim complained about the fallout from the choices she'd made. Jane went for the jugular of a problem.

Jane's scheming had also nearly got Lisa Novak killed twice. Yet here she was, conning him into shelling out a fortune for a train trip to help her find out if the man who had asked her to marry him was worthy of her. What he should have been doing, he knew, was rendezvousing with his men and planning the most important heist of his brief criminal career. That should have been the focus of his life at this moment, not a girl with strawberry blonde hair and green eyes.

It was irrational.

It was stupid.

It was dangerous.

He checked his watch, left his compartment and walked through the now gently rocking carriages to the rear of the train.

Most of the other seventy-odd passengers were still getting settled into their cabins, and the observation car was nearly empty when he arrived. There was a barman with sideburns and a wispy mustache, and one other passenger, a redhead in an emerald green dress who sat in a deep wing-backed armchair reading a magazine, a glass of red wine beside her. She looked up as he entered and smiled a greeting. The windows here were larger than the suites and golden afternoon light flooded the carriage. The last third of the car, accessed via a sliding door, was open to the elements on the sides.

"Good afternoon, sir. Something to drink?"

"Scotch and ice," Alex said to the barman.

He took his drink to the end of the carriage and opened the sliding door. Stepping out into the open he took a breath of fresh air tainted slightly with diesel fumes, courtesy of the more modern loco that had replaced the Puffing Billy at the front of the train. It was nicer, though, to have the warmth of the sun on his back than the chill air-conditioning inside.

Most of the people waiting on platforms raised a hand in silent greeting or smiled politely as the train passed them by. Some young boys in beanies called out a few angry words, but they were lost to Alex beneath the clicking of the bogies and the occasional hoot of the diesel's horn.

Tactically, it was a bad place to be waiting, at the very end of the train. If Jane showed up with George Penfold and there was a confrontation, he had nowhere to move except off the back of the observation car onto the tracks.

There was no way he would give an inch to that bastard. Part of him wanted the showdown to come sooner rather than later. The Glock bulged reassuringly in the waistband of his jeans. He didn't think Penfold would be armed. Thinking on it, the back end of a train wasn't such a bad place after all for the dispatch of a dead body.

He'd never met the man, but he hated George Penfold already. Hate was a dangerous emotion. Like love, it brought on irrational behavior and compromised one's judgment.

Did he hate Penfold because his men had tried to kill the wife of a close friend? Maybe. He loved Lisa as a good friend and the attack on her had outraged him, though he hadn't confided his concern to Novak that perhaps Lisa's strong will had forced her attackers into a corner. She'd been found with a gun in her hand. If she and her maid had meekly surrendered to the robbers and let them ransack her home, perhaps they would have escaped uninjured.

Alex told himself he would never harm a woman in the course of his work, but then he remembered the torn bodies of women and children after an ill-judged American air strike on a village in Afghanistan. Alex had called for support to neutralize a house where a squad of Taliban armed with two heavy machine guns were keeping his men pinned down. He'd requested Apache helicopter gunships, reasoning that a precision-guided Hellfire missile fired from a low-level hovering helo would do the job, but the only aircraft available was a U.S. Marine Corps Harrier jump jet. The gung-ho pilot had wiped out the machine gun post, and two houses either side of it, with a brace of five-hundred-pound bombs. The pilot didn't have to clear the village and hear the wailing of the surviving womenfolk, or see the cold hatred in the eyes of the young men.

Whatever it was that Penfold was missing was so important to him it was blinding his judgment. He had obviously ordered Van Zyl to track down the pirates at any cost. Alex didn't hate George Penfold for trying to reclaim his property, even if it was stolen.

Jane appeared at the far end of the carriage.

Her hair was down and she'd taken off her business suit. Instead she wore a dress made of stretchy gray fabric that clung to all her curves. He felt himself start to stir, and knew it would be worse when he smelled her perfume again.

And he knew right then why he hated George Penfold so much.

"Where's Penfold?" he asked, forcing himself to be businesslike as he opened the sliding door for her. She walked out onto the observation deck, a glass of mineral water with a wedge of lemon in her hand. She glanced behind herself for the second time since she'd entered the carriage. They sat on the contoured wooden bench seats at the very end of the open-air car, facing each other.

"He's checking e-mails. There'll probably be a hundred or more and he's obsessive about clearing them. I probably won't see him again until dinner."

"You're not in the same suite?"

She raised her eyebrows. "Is it a concern of yours if I am or not?"

He turned to look at the view disappearing behind them. An African woman with a cheap zippered plastic carry bag balanced on her head picked her way carefully between sleepers, ballast and rails to cross the line.

Jane leaned toward him and laid a hand on the sleeve of his black sports jacket. "No, I'm not. And I won't be sleeping with him. That part of our relationship, at least, is over."

Jane explained to him how she had found a prostitute coming out of George's room after she had left Alex. She also said she'd overheard George talking to his wife on the phone, and there was nothing in his tone of voice or words to suggest the marriage was anything other than harmonious. "I feel betrayed."

"I can understand why," he said.

"He's using me. I can't believe I got involved with him. I feel like a right fool; the way I've let him play with my emotions. He only asked me to marry him to string me along a little longer, probably until this trip and his business here in Africa is over. But why?"

"He's not sure if you're telling the truth—about having his stuff. And he's right to be uncertain."

She sipped her mineral water. "Are you telling me I'm wrong?"

"I'm telling you to be careful. You don't know where this is heading, and neither do I."

280   TONY PARK

"Part of me just wants to blurt it out," she said, "to tell him his bloody package is on his bloody ship. I feel like I've backed myself into a corner."

He said nothing, but then her eyes widened, as though a blindingly obvious thought that should have occurred to her had just hit her like a bolt of lightning. "Wait. *You* backed me into this corner."

"I don't know what you're talking about."

"Oh, yes you do, Alex. You're a better charmer than you are a liar. You planted the thought in my head, in Mozambique, that George was up to something criminal. You never asked me directly if MacGregor had given me anything or if I was hiding anything. Why? Because you thought of a way to get me to lead you to it . . . and here we bloody well are!"

She stood and turned to go back inside the observation carriage, but he reached out and took hold of her wrist—firmly, though not enough to hurt her. Nonetheless, she tried to shrug him off, but he held on to her. "Do you think he's up to something illegal?"

She paused, biting her lower lip. "Yes. I do. But so are you. You're just coming with me to steal whatever it is that George has been trading in."

"Hey," he reminded her, "I was on my way back to Mozambique when *you* called *me*. Remember? And here I am, several thousand rand poorer for the cost of a ticket on this train and a new suit and shoes just so I can bloody well dress for dinner."

He smiled at her and her anger seemed to dissipate, but a moment later she had a determined set to her face again. "Yes, yes. All right. But I can't be seen with you again. Not until we get to Cape Town."

"We need to talk through some things before then."

"OK, where?" she asked.

Alex thought about it for a moment. "Does George smoke?"

"No, he hates it. He's a reformed smoker—they're always the worst."

"The smoking lounge is just on the other side of the bar, in this carriage."

She nodded. "I saw it on the way through. That's perfect. He wouldn't even want to walk past that area and there's another lounge car halfway up the train, so he probably wouldn't even bother to walk all the way back here. We're right up the front."

"Good. Meet me here after dinner—say, nine?"

"OK. But one more thing, Alex . . ."

"Yes?"

"What happened between us in Mozambique, in Gorongosa, that was a mistake on my part. It's not going to happen again, OK?"

He nodded.

Jane walked back toward the front of the train. It was a long way, and the trek through the fifteen carriages to hers was slowed by the presence of curious passengers emerging from their suites to check out their surroundings. As she opened her door, George stuck his head out of his. "Oh, good. You're back. Where did you go?"

"Just exploring. I've been right to the back of the train. There's a bar there."

"Well, that was a wasted journey, and one I have no intention of making during the next three days." He ducked back into his suite, then emerged again and entered hers. He carried a bottle of vintage Moët et Chandon and two crystal flutes.

"I'm not sure I want a drink right now," she said.

"Oh, nonsense. I've got a minibar full of this stuff. We've only got another fifty hours or so to get through it all!"

He sat down on one of her two chairs and she moved her jacket from the other so she could join him. Despite her protest he poured for both of them. "Cheers," he said, and she dutifully raised her glass. She took only a tiny sip.

"So, got any plans for the afternoon?" He raised an eyebrow theatrically. "Dinner's not until seven-thirty."

She saw the lust in his eyes. She'd been amused by his caddishness at first, but now that she knew it was actually real, and not a charming act, she was repelled by him. "I've got some e-mails to send."

"I gave up on mine. Stuff it, I thought. I'm on the most luxurious train this side of the equator with the most beautiful girl in the world and I'm sitting in front of a computer screen. Preposterous." He leaned closer to her, placing his hand on her knee as he raised his glass to his lips.

She placed her hands in her lap. "George, I'm not feeling all that well."

"Nonsense. You're just tired." He raised his right eyebrow comically. "Perhaps you need a lie-down."

She shook her head. She placed a hand on his, but before she could move his off her knee, he put his glass down and laid his right hand over hers. He kissed her. She kept her lips clamped shut.

"Are you playing hard to get? Like that time in the company flat? You naughty girl, you."

"No, George, I—"

He silenced her with another kiss and slid off his chair, dropping to one knee in front of her. He moved a hand to each of her knees now and started pushing outward, so that the hem of her dress began riding up her thighs.

"George, *please* . . ."

He leaned his body closer to her, forcing his torso between her legs and pushing them further apart. He lifted a hand to her breast and ran the backs of his fingers across her nipple. The movement of the lace of her bra against her skin caused an involuntary reaction.

She did not want this.

His other hand was moving up her bare thigh, one finger hooking the elastic of her knickers.

"No, George."

"Oh, yes, baby . . ."

"No!" Jane stood, forcing him to rock backward on his knees. He reached up for her, roughly grabbing her by the hips with both hands to halt her.

This was no game. Jane picked up her champagne glass and threw the contents in his face.

"Fuck!" As George stood he flailed about to maintain his balance, the action made harder by the rocking of the train. He pushed Jane's hips away from him, causing her to slump back into her chair.

He wiped his wet, reddened face with his hand and glared down at her. "What the hell do you think you're playing at?"

"Move away from my chair, George."

He stood there, staring at her. She saw the rage on his face and she felt genuinely afraid of him. His hands were bunched into fists, held loosely at his sides. He raised one and she flinched.

He stepped back, opened his palm and ran his fingers through his hair. He took a deep breath and closed his eyes, as if trying hard to regain his composure. "OK. Bad move." He opened his eyes. "I'm sorry, Jane. I just thought..."

"You thought what, George? That no meant yes? I know we've played a few little games, but I expect you to know the difference between coquettishness and a point-blank *no*."

George looked as though he was going to say something else, and opened his mouth to speak, then closed it again. He forced a smile. "Just as well I was planning on dressing for dinner." He brushed the front of his shirt, which was spotted with drying champagne. "Is everything all right between us?"

She wanted to scream at him, to launch herself at him and scratch his eyes and face, and yell and cry and demand to know everything he was involved in, and what he had meant by seducing her in the workplace while he was still happily married *and* shagging prostitutes. The rage seethed in her but she forced herself to stay silent. She needed to get to Cape Town and to the bottom of this mess she'd been landed in. Right then she wished she'd never set foot in the offices of Penfold Shipping, and never met this man.

"I'm fine, George. It's just . . . perhaps it's just a culmination of things. Everything's happened so fast. First the pirates, then . . ." She stopped herself from saying anything about Lisa's shooting, "then the negotiations with De Witt. It's all happened a bit too quick. I'll be fine after a good night's sleep. See you for dinner?"

He frowned. She could see it was clearly not what he'd expected, but he straightened his hair and shirt once more and said, "Of course, my love."

After Jane left the observation carriage Alex finished his Scotch in the open air. The low afternoon sunlight was filtered gold through Johannesburg's cloud of exhaust fumes as they passed the airport, and Emperors Palace, where Alex had met with Chan. His trip to Cape Town might come to nothing, but there was still much work to be done to prepare for the ivory heist.

He was taken aback when the sliding door leading to the rest of the car opened again. The woman in the green silk dress took a seat on the contoured wooden bench opposite him and crossed her legs. "Beautiful, isn't it?"

"Yes, it is."

"We don't get light like this in the concrete jungle."

Her eyes matched her dress and, like the fabric, caught the light's reflection and shimmered in a more than pleasing way. Her accent was American. The diamonds in her ears looked real, just like the ones on the ring finger of her right hand. Only the faint lines at the corners of her eyes, and her mouth when she smiled, told him she was probably four or five years older than he.

He saw the way her glance casually moved to his left hand, as had his. "Traveling alone?"

Alex's first thought was to lie and say no, thinking that he wouldn't want Jane to get the wrong idea if, by chance, she returned to the carriage. That was odd, he realized. Did he consider himself *with* Jane? But he was single, and Jane had made it quite plain that she did not want any romantic involvement with him. "Yes. Though this train seems to be made for couples."

She sighed theatrically. "It sure does. I'm Lesley. Can I buy you a drink?"

He laughed at the joke—all drinks were included in the cost of a ticket on Rovos Rail, but he was pleasantly taken by her forthrightness. "It's the twenty-first century and we're both over twenty-one, so why not?"

She called the waiter over and he ordered another Scotch. His mind was not on sex, though Lesley, who explained while they waited for drinks that she was a widow from Manhattan, had an hourglass figure and breasts that just begged to be seen naked.

"I'm sorry for your loss."

"Morty was eighty-seven, God rest his soul. He had a good life."

"I'm sure he did. Are you dining alone this evening, Lesley?"

"I thought so, up until now."

The shirt had the crisp smell of newness—and scratchy loose threads that pricked his neck. He buttoned it and knotted the dark purple silk tie he'd purchased from the same shop. It had been a while since he'd dressed for dinner, but he looked forward to the day when he'd have to do it every night.

His father had always worn a suit and tie—sometimes a tuxedo—when he'd greeted the guests in the bar or the dining room of the hotel. If a train could bring back formal dining for holidaymakers, then so could a resort. It might keep some people away, but it might also bring in the right ones. He ran a brush through his long hair, slicking it back from his forehead. He'd showered and shaved for the second time that day, and rubbed some moisturizer into his skin before applying just a little Calvin Klein aftershave. He'd swapped his jeans and loafers for the new dark suit.

He fastened his father's gold cufflinks and pulled on the jacket. He decided to leave his pistol in the suite. He took the Glock out of its holster, cocked it and slid it under the pillow of his bed, which had been made up for him while he was in the observation car.

From the corridor outside he heard the low clang of the dinner gong. Alex slid his door closed and walked through the carriage, moving to one side to let a family of four pass. Lesley had given him the name of her suite, Spioenkop—there was nothing as pedestrian as numbers on this train—and when he found it, he knocked.

"Coming right out," she called.

She was still in the green dress, though she'd put her hair up and her slender neck was now adorned with a diamond necklace that would have fetched the same price as his hotel as it stood at the moment.

Alex held out his arm and she said, "Why thank you, sir."

There were two dining cars and the first was already full. Wine waiters in black ties were taking drinks orders as he and Lesley edged their way through. There was no sign of Jane or Penfold yet, but as they hadn't been in the first car he presumed they would eventually show up in this one.

"Wow, this is something," Lesley said as they entered the next car.

She was right. The second dining car was more elaborately detailed than the first which, while still elegant, had a clean, almost minimalist Art Deco look to it. By contrast, the carriage, in which Jane and Penfold occupied the furthest table, was a confection of Edwardian intricacy and detail. Two rows of ornately carved teak pillars ran the length of the carriage, subtly separating the dining tables so that even when fully booked, as the train was now, it seemed like each party of diners had a private space of their own.

Lesley and Alex seated themselves midway up the dining car and Alex deliberately took the seat facing Jane. He could just see the back of George's head. He kept his eye on her and willed her to look up from her menu. Eventually she did, and almost managed to conceal her recognition. By the time Penfold looked around, Alex had raised his menu.

Alex imagined George would have no idea that the leader of the gang his men were hunting would be on the same train as he. He did know what Alex looked like, from a photo, but Alex reasoned the likelihood of him being recognized would be greater if Penfold saw him alone. Lesley added to his cover. The only problem with the tall, elegant redhead was that she attracted the attention of every man in the carriage, and some of their wives.

Alex ordered a Windhoek lager and Lesley a Brampton sauvignon blanc. Once all the guests were seated the train manager took their orders and the food service followed soon after.

Lesley finished a mouthful of her starter, smoked ostrich carpaccio with tempura vegetables, and wiped her full glossy lips with a linen serviette. She glanced over her shoulder and then back at Alex. "Why is that girl at the end of the carriage, behind me, pretending she's not looking at you? Do you two know each other?"

"An old acquaintance," Alex said. "Though her partner doesn't know me, and we'd like to keep it that way."

"Aha. I'm intrigued. I'm sensing you might be what the Brits call a *scoundrel*, Mister Tremain. Is that the right word?"

"It would be ungentlemanly of me to say, Ms. Engels." He asked her more about her background, and she his, while the waiter cleared away their entrée plates. Alex ordered a glass of Zandvliet shiraz and Lesley stayed with the white as the second course, carrot and ginger soup, arrived. Alex held his wine glass to the light of the candle, admiring the etched RVR logo again. It was the little things that sometimes counted the most. He wondered how many glasses were stolen each trip.

"So, I know you're half English and half Portuguese and live on an island in the Indian Ocean, but you haven't actually told me what it is you do, Alex."

He looked out the window, admiring the floral motif embroidered on the curtains at the same time. The train had cleared Johannesburg's sprawling limits and there were no lights outside as they rocked and rolled through the empty night.

"I'm a pirate."

"Really?" She sipped her wine. "Do tell."

Alex thought for a moment, then said, "Sure. Why not?"

22

There were about a dozen passengers in the observation carriage when Alex entered. He ordered a coffee and looked around, but there was no sign of Jane. He checked his watch. It was 9 p.m. He walked out the back into the open-sided compartment. It was cool, but still pleasant.

Jane arrived five minutes later and he felt his heart start to quicken as he watched her thread her way down the length of the carriage, stopping briefly to chat with an elderly lady. She opened the sliding door. "Sorry I'm late."

"No problem."

The waiter came out and Jane ordered a white wine. Alex downed his coffee and asked for a beer.

"Where's George?"

"In his suite. I told him I've got a splitting headache. It's not far from the truth."

"Wine will help."

She laughed. "How can you be so relaxed about all of this? Are you addicted to danger?"

He shrugged. "I'm looking forward to going into detox. I want the biggest threat to my life to be cockroaches in the kitchen and the only risk of dying to come from hardened arteries."

"Are you serious? I'm sure part of you wants to keep doing what you're doing."

"When I thought I'd killed that guy on the *Penfold Son* it made me sick. I don't want to kill any more, Jane."

They were silent as the waiter re-emerged with their drinks.

When the waiter disappeared again Alex asked her about her family and Jane told him how proud her parents had been when she had graduated as a lawyer. "I thought it was all I ever wanted to do."

"Thought?"

"What's happened on this trip, most of it has been ghastly but it's made me realize there's so much more of the world out there for me to explore. There was no excitement in my life, which may be why I fell for George. But I know now that was wrong."

"What I do is wrong."

"There's some good inside you, Alex. You'll make a wonderful hotelier and you seem to be a very good judge of soft furnishings."

He laughed, then looked out at the passing night. "I wonder. I do know it's what I've always wanted. I just hope I'm as good at it as I am at storming ships."

"Well, you're crap at storming ships." He smiled at her and she decided it would be better to stick to something safe. "Tell me about your family."

Alex told her how his father had enlisted in the Rhodesian Army after leaving Mozambique, and how he had been killed in action. "He died doing a job he actually loved, and for a cause he believed in, but it devastated me. I worshipped him."

"I'm so sorry, Alex. And your mum?"

He took a deep breath and a long draft of beer.

"Funny, but I don't talk about her as much as I do about my father."

"Don't, if you don't want to."

"No, it's OK."

He closed his eyes and the visions, the sights, the sounds of that day rushed back over him, making him more light-headed than the drink warranted.

"We were leaving Mozambique. We'd taken our boat to Vilanculos and got into the car my father kept on the mainland. Everything would have been OK, but my dad was in a hurry. It was understandable."

"Alex..."

"No, it's OK. He made the right call. There was a roadblock manned by looters looking to get whatever they could from the people fleeing the country. My father chanced it. It was mayhem. You can't believe what it was like. Everyone wild-eyed. Too much excitement. Too much booze. It was the way he was. Brash. Confident. He floored the accelerator. There was shooting. It was scary . . . but exciting. You know?"

He could see she didn't; not really.

"We made it through and he was laughing—shouting. He asked us if we were OK."

He paused to wipe his eyes, embarrassed by the betrayal of long dormant emotions.

"Only one bullet hit the car. It killed my mother."

Jane raised a hand to her mouth. "My God," she whispered, then lowered her fingers so that they covered his.

Inside the carriage the barman was collecting empty glasses and oh so nonchalantly checking his watch. "I think we'd better make a move," Alex said. "I'll get a bottle of bubbly for the road."

"Are you trying to get me drunk, Captain Tremain?"

"Yes." He was glad that she sensed he wanted no more talk of the past for now.

They went inside to the bar and Alex thanked the barman as he collected the bottle and two fresh flutes.

"I'm afraid I have to lock the carriage now, sir."

"No problem," Alex said, "we'll sit in the smoking lounge." He didn't think it was proper to invite Jane back to his tiny suite, with its two bunks, and hers was next to George Penfold's. In any case, he didn't want her to think he was trying something on.

After the barman said goodnight, Jane took a seat beside Alex on a brown leather settee, in the small smoking lounge next to the observation carriage. The air still smelled of cigar smoke. "We haven't spoken about Cape Town, or how we're going to board the *Penfold Son*."

"That'll sort itself out," Alex said, raising a glass.

"You struck me as the sort of military man who plans everything to the last detail."

"Not everything." He put his glass down, leaned over and kissed her on the lips.

She half-opened her mouth to him then drew back, looking into his eyes. She reached out for him, running a finger down the pitted skin on the left side of his face, where he'd been wounded in the war by the grenade that had taken his fingers. He stared back at her intently.

She took his face in both her hands and held him close to her as they kissed and his hands began their exploration of her body. He traced the line of her spine, from under her long blonde hair to the small of her back, and she shivered in his arms.

"Yes," was all she said.

He moved a hand to her thigh and she parted for him. He felt the softness of her skin and the firm muscle beneath as his fingers continued their trail and found her, ready for him when he pulled the flimsy fabric of her pants to one side. She arched her back in the seat as his fingers circled the hard little bud at the center of so much softness.

"My room?" he breathed between kisses.

"No. Here."

She reached for him as she kissed him again, unzipping his trousers and reaching inside. She wrapped her hand around him and smiled at the look that sprang to his face. George had wanted her to do things for him, to him, but all Jane could think of now was how much she wanted Alex. It was different. She wanted to let go of her inhibitions without the need to discuss it, or to be told what to do. She undid the top two buttons beneath the bustline of her dress. Alex reached for her, but she dropped to her knees on the carpeted floor of the train, tantalizingly out of reach for the moment. She wanted to do this for him. She freed her breasts slowly, one at a time, from her bra.

Alex groaned and she felt the desire well within her like lava. She leaned forward and wrapped the soft mounds of flesh around his shaft. As he moved against her she lowered her mouth to the head of his cock, tasting him at the end of each long stroke. She felt as if she might catch fire from the heat of him against her chest. With the lights on she felt more lascivious, more excited, more aroused and more right than she ever had in her life.

She paused and looked up at him. "I want you."

Alex sighed and ran a hand through his hair. "Jane, I'm sorry, I didn't bring . . ."

She let go of him and reached across for her clutch bag, on the next armchair. She snapped it open, fumbled inside and grinned as she found what she was looking for and tore the foil packet open with her teeth. He closed his eyes as she rolled the latex skin down over him. She loved that he'd tried to do the right thing, and that she, at least, had thought ahead, despite what she'd said to him about there being nothing between them. He opened his eyes and they made her breath catch in her throat.

"Come here," he said to her.

He placed his hands on her upper arms and lifted her to him, kissing her deeply and pulling her closer. She climbed onto the lounge, her knees on the upholstered leather on either side of his legs.

"I've wanted you since I first saw you," he said.

"I know."

She lowered herself onto him and he took her nipples into his mouth, sucking each in turn as she continued her journey. She paused as he filled her, mind, body and soul. She laid her head against his shoulder and he kissed the tender skin behind her ear, lightly.

"Oh, God." She moved faster now and the gentle rocking of the moving train matched their rhythm perfectly. Each judder of the train's wheels on the tracks sent vibrations up through his body and into her, and she rode him with the same stop-start motion of the carriage.

Jane threw back her head and he held on to her, arms clasped behind the small of her back as she abandoned herself. Neither of them would have cared if someone walked in. He looked up at her and when she tilted her head forward again she smiled at him, through glistening eyes.

He raised a hand to her breast and took her nipple firmly into his mouth, drawing it in as she started to come. Alex held her tight as she exhausted herself on him and kissed her hard to muffle the soft cries that nonetheless still escaped.

"Now you," she breathed.

Inflamed by desire he held her hips and lifted her off the seat as he drove up into her. He wanted her more than anything else in the world right then. Nothing else mattered. His breathing quickened as he felt his orgasm building.

Far ahead the locomotive braked and the judder passed down the line through all the carriages. It reached Alex and Jane at the moment he was as deeply a part of her as was possible. The sudden jolt brought on his climax and pushed their bodies into one another.

Jane couldn't help herself and started to laugh. Alex joined in, until they heard footsteps. By the time the barman reached them they were sitting side by side, sipping champagne.

"Everything all right, sir, madam?"

"Perfect," they said in unison, which made them start to laugh again.

23

Table Mountain was draped in a cloth of white mist, the folds of which hung gracefully down the sides of the imposing altar to nature's majesty.

Alex barely spared the mountain a look as he followed the instructions in the rental car's GPS to the Radisson Waterfront Hotel where Jane was staying. It was three in the afternoon on the day after they had left the *Pride of Africa* at Cape Town's railway terminus.

They had fought off the urge to spend every minute with each other and retreated to their separate ends of the luxury train for the rest of the journey, except for a blissful three hours when the locomotive pulled up five kilometers short of the historic nineteenth century town of Matjiesfontein. While most of the passengers, including George, took advantage of a chance to stretch their legs with a walk into town, Jane feigned her headache again, to George's obvious annoyance, and invited Alex to her double suite.

With the bright Karoo sun diffused by the carriage's slatted security shutter Alex claimed every inch of Jane's body with fingers, lips and the tip of his tongue. Before she had to disembark, with George already close by inspecting a museum in the station building, Alex and Jane made love for a furious third time, standing in the shower of her ensuite.

Alex tried to convince Jane to leave the train with him, but she insisted that she needed to find out what was in the package Mac-Gregor had given her. Alex would have gladly left the mystery unsolved if she had agreed to go with him.

He called her mobile phone as he pulled into the Radisson's car park and drummed his fingers on the steering wheel while he waited for her to arrive downstairs. She wore black jeans and a dark long-sleeved T-shirt. She got in the car and kissed him and he accelerated back out into the traffic.

"I didn't know what to bring," she said.

"Swimming costume?"

"Underneath."

"Good. I've got everything else covered."

He wasn't happy about her coming along and told her again that he would have preferred her to simply tell him the location of the package and wait for him to fetch it. "You don't trust me, do you?" he said.

"Of course not," she said. "You're a buccaneer."

Alex drove to the Victoria and Alfred Waterfront complex, one of the busiest tourist destinations in South Africa. He parked in the Victoria Wharf shopping center car park, got out and opened the car's boot.

Jane slipped out of her jeans, but didn't attract too much attention from shoppers moving to and from their cars, as she was wearing a pair of shorts underneath. Alex changed into a sun shirt and produced wide-brimmed floppy hats for both of them. He lifted out the heavy bag, then closed the boot and locked the car.

Alex led Jane away from the shopping complex to a small beach near the start of the main breakwater. "This is Granger Bay," he said. A man stood on the beach next to two sea kayaks. Alex waved to him.

"You need to be back before nightfall," the man said.

Alex nodded as he loaded the dive bag into the front of the larger of the two craft. "Don't worry," he said to the Afrikaner, "with what I'm paying you I can't afford a late fee."

The man laughed.

"Do you need help?" Alex asked Jane.

"I'm fine." She pushed her kayak out a little way, jumped in, and started paddling.

Alex sat in his boat as Jane shot away from the beach, her arms pumping like pistons. Alex dug into the water and was sweating hard before he even got within shouting distance of Jane as she knifed her way across the calm waters of Granger Bay.

"Where did you learn to paddle?" he called.

"Just a natural, I guess." She surged ahead of him and Alex worked his muscled arms hard to keep up. When at last she slowed, near the end of the breakwater, she confessed to Alex, "Actually, I row when I'm back home in England, but I'm a little out of practice. If I was on form you wouldn't have been able to catch me."

When they rounded the main breakwater they turned south and on their right they could see into the Victoria Basin, which was in front of the shopping center where they had parked. They didn't look out of place as Alex had already spotted two other kayaks and a man on a wave ski making the most of the calm conditions and warm weather.

They crossed the mouth of the Ben Schoeman Dock and Alex led the way toward the Duncan Dock, where the *Penfold Son* was moored on the Eastern Mole. They could clearly see the massive container ship now. The bright lights of a welder flashed on and off and Alex noticed a truck with a butcher's logo drive along the long quay to the ship's gangway.

Instead of paddling into the dock Alex turned left and made for the south spur, another breakwater which jutted out from the end of the quay.

There was a port control building about two hundred meters to their north west, but Alex was sure the staff inside would be looking out to sea, not in at the docks.

"We'll stop here," he said to Jane, nosing into the breakwater. "Have you ever dived?"

"Once, on holiday in Teneriffe," she said. "I learned the basics in a cruise ship swimming pool."

Alex pulled out two military scuba kits with rebreathers, and two black wetsuits.

"This works the same way, but uses oxygen instead of air. It's a sealed system so it doesn't produce any bubbles when you breathe, and the tank was small enough for me to hide in the kayak."

Jane was already slipping out of her rash shirt and pulling on her wetsuit. Alex knew that lithe body now and he hated to think of anything happening to her. "I'll ask you again nicely. Please tell me where you hid the package and let me go and get it myself."

"Fuck off."

"So much for the nice approach."

"Where did you get all this gear?"

"I looked up an old friend of mine this morning. He used to be a navy diver and he's more crooked than I am."

Alex showed Jane how to fit and operate the rebreather, then he tied both kayaks securely to the breakwater. "Stay close to me. Hold on to my weight belt." He had his Glock wrapped in a plastic bag secured with rubber bands and he slipped it into the front of his wetsuit and zipped it up. Alex slid into the cold water and together they sank beneath the surface.

The sun had set, but arc lights still illuminated the *Penfold Son* as Jane and Alex surfaced beneath the gangway. The metal above them clanged to the sound of booted feet as workmen came and went. "It's still busy," Jane whispered.

Alex nodded and put his fingers to his lips. He swam on the surface but out of sight in the shadow of the dock to the far end, where a van was parked.

"Wait here," Alex whispered. He reached up and climbed a set of steel rungs set into concrete. Once on the dock he made sure to keep the grocery delivery van between himself and the security guard posted on the gangway. He unzipped his wetsuit and pulled out the Glock. He unwrapped it, opened the rear door of the van and climbed in.

The delivery man opened the door and stared straight into the barrel of Alex's pistol. Alex let the man know, without words, that if he spoke he would die. He beckoned him into the back of the refrigerated van. Once inside he ordered his captive to strip.

"I'll freeze!" he hissed.

Alex shrugged. "Freeze slowly or die quickly. The choice is yours." The man started undressing.

Inside were aprons and capes to be worn when carrying sides of beef and pork. Alex took the drawstring from an apron and tied the delivery man's hands securely behind his back. He then took out his diving knife and cut the remainder of the apron into long strips. He balled one and stuffed it in the man's mouth and tied the gag with another.

Alex had seen two workers so he waited inside the chill of the van until the other arrived.

"Hey, man, where are you? What have you been up—" Alex's Glock and the sight of his colleague bound and gagged silenced the man soon enough. When the second man was also dressed only in his underpants Alex trussed him and moved back to the edge of the wharf. He leaned over the edge and waved to Jane.

Alex and Jane pulled the delivery men's uniforms over their wetsuits. When he was dressed, Alex took the rebreathers and stuffed them under a nearby garbage skip.

"Is this going to work? They know it's two men doing the deliveries," Jane said.

"Put this on." He handed Jane the meat carrier's hooded cape and lifted a side of pork and balanced it on her right shoulder. "Can you carry this much weight?"

"Yes."

"Good. Just keep the meat between you and the security guard on the gangway and follow me in."

Alex hefted the beef and set off, with Jane close behind him.

"Hurry it up," the guard said in a thick northern Irish accent as Alex walked past.

Alex said nothing, but flipped the man the finger with his spare hand. The Irishman swore, but didn't move from his post. He said nothing as Jane walked past.

"Which way?" Alex whispered once they were inside.

"Galley. Follow me."

It was clear to Alex that she knew the ship's layout by heart, which was not surprising given the time she had spent on board. They made it to the galley coldroom without seeing another person. Jane led him through the intricate maze of alleyways toward the stern of the ship.

Cleanliness was next to godliness for Billy Tidmarsh and while he had killed four men in his home county of Ulster it had all been in the name of his religion. The two things he couldn't stomach in life were Catholics and dirt.

And that went for blood, as well. He'd always scrubbed himself thoroughly after a job—not only to get rid of the incriminating gunpowder residue, but also to make sure he hadn't been infected with any filthy Papist blood.

The sight of the drops on the deck irked him. He presumed they'd dripped from the pig or the beef the deliverymen had just brought on board. He picked up a rag lying in a bucket near the gangway and dropped to one knee. On closer inspection, however, he saw the droplets were clear. Looking up he now saw they were spattered all the way down the gangway and, on his other side, into the ship itself. Why would those two men be dripping water?

He would stop them when they came back through. Perhaps a

bottle of water had burst in the last delivery load and Billy had failed to notice it. He paced up and down the deck near the gangway, his eyes continually drawn back to the droplets. They annoyed him fiercely. He checked his watch. The men had been inside for more than ten minutes. What were they doing in there?

He walked down the gangway onto the dock and saw the clearly marked trail went all the way back to the van. He decided to investigate.

"Piet, it's Billy," he said into his radio as he walked along the dock.

"Go, Billy."

"Somethin's not right here, boss. I'm just on my way to the delivery van on the dock to have a wee look."

"I didn't tell you to leave your post. Get back there."

"But Piet . . ." Billy was at the van already. He thought he heard movement so he put his ear to the closed rear doors. There was definitely something alive in there, groaning and moving about. He pulled the pistol from his shoulder holster and reefed open the door. "Jesus *fooking* Christ."

Alex and Jane could hear the shouts across the water, although they were already three hundred meters away, paddling back toward the main breakwater.

"It's a mini videotape," Jane said after she ripped open the package in the car.

"No diamonds?"

"Try not to sound too disappointed. Hang on, there's a USB memory stick in here as well."

After they returned the kayaks Alex drove as fast as he dared back to the Radisson Waterfront. He waited in the car while Jane walked into the hotel, making sure George wasn't in the bar or dining areas, where he might see the two of them walk in together.

Jane called Alex in the car to tell him all was clear and by the time he made it to her room she had her laptop switched on and the memory stick inserted. "It's a video—an MPEG. Could be the same as what's on the tape."

Alex closed the hotel room door and leaned over Jane's shoulder. The screen flickered to life. George Penfold was naked, his back to the camera. A woman was lying spread-eagled across a bed, her wrists tied to the four posts. George walked toward the woman holding a length of rope in his hands. There was no indication that he knew the camera was filming him.

The woman said something that was indiscernible but as he wrapped the cord around her neck she made no further sound and showed no sign of protest. George climbed onto the bed between her legs and began having sex with her.

He appeared to have tied the rope in a single knot. As his thrusts became more furious he began to move his hands wider apart, gripping the rope and pulling it tighter.

The woman began to scream and thrash about on the bed.

"Oh, dear God," Jane said.

"He's killed her."

24

Alex sat on a stainless-steel bench pretending to read a copy of *The Citizen* inside the terminal building of Kruger Mpumalanga International Airport. Although it was cool and gloomy under the soaring thatched cathedral roof he was wearing a baseball cap and dark glasses inside. He didn't want anyone to be able to recall his description, or see it on a security camera video at a later date.

While he waited for the flight to arrive he checked his watch again and thought about Jane, who was at the other end of South Africa. It had gone badly between them.

They had watched the video to the end. The hidden camera had recorded George's behavior when the girl suffocated. He paused, checked her pulse and completed his sexual act with her. Jane had burst into tears at that point and run for the bathroom. He had heard her being sick in there. When she returned she made herself watch the whole thing. Two Asian men—bouncers by the look of them—had banged on the door of the bedroom and George, still naked, had let them in. There had been an argument over the girl, but in the end all three men had seemed resigned to the fact that nothing would be said to the authorities and that their shared priority should be the disposal of the body.

"Don't worry, I will pay your employer whatever is required . . . for the girl," they had heard George say.

Alex guessed that the men's "employer" was Valiant Chan, and that the mid-sea exchange had involved George paying for the original tape, as well as the computer file. Alex had wondered aloud how much George had paid.

It was common knowledge in criminal circles that Chan ran a number of brothels in Cape Town and Johannesburg. He imagined the presence of hidden security cameras in the rooms was primarily for the girls' security, although no doubt the video footage also occasionally came in handy for blackmail.

"It doesn't matter," Jane had said. "He's going to pay for the rest of his life."

Alex had told Jane to come with him, explaining that he had to leave for Nelspruit the next day. He would abandon his pistol and fly, if she would come with him, and if she wouldn't fly then he would drive through the night in his hire car.

Jane had begun to shake and he had tried to put his arms around her to comfort her, but she had shrugged him off, as though she couldn't bear the touch of any man right then. He could only imagine how distressed and betrayed she felt at the discovery of conclusive proof of the evil nature of the man she'd been sleeping with.

"No, Alex. I'm going to the police here in Cape Town. If Chan was involved in this, then the crime took place here, in South Africa. The police will know who this poor woman was. George has been here on business four times already for the preliminary negotiations over the De Witt deal."

"You could drop off the evidence anonymously. The video speaks for itself."

"No. I have to do this. It's the right thing to do."

"Jane, you need to come with me. Now. Once Penfold works out it's you who's gone to the cops you won't be safe. Don't tangle with him, he's a ruthless killer."

"I bloody well know he's a killer! That's why I'm going to the police and not running away. And you of all people can't tell me what's right and what's wrong."

He placed a hand on her forearm, but she shrugged it off. "Why the hurry to get away anyway?" she asked him. "Stay here. Back me up. *Be* with me."

"Jane . . ."

"What? What do you have to do that's so fucking important, Alex? I won't even say 'What about us?' What's more important than bringing a murderer to justice?" Her cheeks were reddening with anger. "Well?"

"Jane . . ." He heard the accusation in her voice, but had no answer for her.

"You're going thieving, aren't you?"

He replied with silence.

"Tell me you're not going to steal something from someone tomorrow, Alex. Tell me you and your band of bloody pirates aren't going to terrorize some good, honest people at the end of your guns. Go on, tell me."

He turned away from her.

"You bastard. Get away from me. I thought you might be different—that you might have been serious about going straight. What a bloody idiot I've been. Get out of my life! You're no better than Penfold."

He'd left the hotel and her words had hurt more than the shrapnel that had carved his body, or his string of failed love affairs. He had left bitter. Now he felt empty. His only hope was that if he pulled off this job he might be able to redeem his wasted life.

It was impossible to miss the South African Army public relations team as they entered the terminal from the arrivals side of the airport, even though they all wore civilian clothes. A soldier could spot another soldier whatever he was wearing.

The one who looked like an officer was a white man and Alex

guessed by the length of his hair and the way he called the other two, a black and an Afrikaner, by their first names that he was probably a reservist.

The African had the muscled physique of an infantryman, but was festooned in gold jewelry. The other white, whom the officer addressed as Dirk, hadn't bothered to shave that morning. He wore elephant-tail and copper bracelets.

Their luggage also betrayed them. There was a precarious mountain of black dust and waterproof carry cases and two sets of tripods. On top of the pile, like an afterthought, were the men's military kitbags.

The officer walked purposefully across the terminal to a car rental agency. Alex wandered past just as the man was taking possession of the keys, and heard the bay number and directions to the team's rental car. It was all he needed.

Outside, heat haze shimmered above the airport car park. Through the shimmering waves came the Nissan *bakkie* that Alex had cached in the storage unit in Nelspruit. It slowed and barely stopped as he jumped into the back and banged on the roof. Novak accelerated away from the terminal.

The green tarpaulin in the back moved and Heinrich's face appeared from under it. "OK?" he asked.

Alex nodded and Heinrich passed him out a camouflage shirt and trousers. Henri sat up as well and fitted a curved thirty-five-round magazine to the R5 assault rifle he was cradling, and cocked it. After Alex struggled into his military uniform, which was no easy task lying down in the back of a moving vehicle, Henri handed the readied weapon to him.

The airport was set in the rolling green hills of Plaston, a farming community near the picturesque regional town of White River. The runway had been laid along a ridge line and the terminal building, from a distance, looked out of place amid the horse studs and macadamia farms.

Alex banged on the roof of the truck again, signaling Novak to pull over. The spot they had chosen was just short of a stop sign, at a quiet railway crossing at the bottom of a small valley. Novak had followed the signs from the airport to the Kruger National Park on the R538. It was the shortest, most logical route to the reserve, and Alex was sure the PR team would take it.

He leaped out of the truck and walked to the front. Novak pulled the bonnet release catch and Alex lifted it. Henri and Heinrich also got out of the back and lifted out a toolbox, which they placed at Alex's feet.

Kevin and Kufa got out of the front seat, where they had been sandwiched in next to the bulky Novak. They took off their tradesmen's grimy blue overalls, as did Novak, to reveal South African Army camouflage beneath. Kevin and Kufa fished their R5s out of the back and lay down in the grass on the verge beside the truck. They laid their rifles beside them and put their hands behind the back of their heads, reclining in the universal attitude of soldiers snatching rest when and where they could find it.

Alex pulled his camouflage bush hat down firmly on his head and put his sunglasses back on. Henri and Heinrich walked across the road and took up concealed positions in a drainage culvert, their faces obscured by a tangle of weeds and shrubs. They held their rifles into their shoulders, pointing up the road in the direction from which they'd come.

Alex looked at each of his men, not only to check their positioning but to try to read their faces. There had been little banter or humor at their reunion in Nelspruit when they collected the cached weapons and gathered for the mission briefing. Mitch's departure had ended the most obvious manifestation of dissent, but Alex still wondered if he could hold their loyalty in the future. He had changed, and they sensed it. The news that there were no diamonds secreted on the *Penfold Son* brought only solemn nods and, in Novak's eyes, a silent "told you so." The good news was that Lisa was recovering well, in a private clinic under twenty-four-hour armed guard, and showed no signs of brain damage.

Alex's life of crime had consumed too much of him. He wanted to prove Jane wrong, that he was not like George Penfold, but the only way he could see out of the mess his life had become was to stage the biggest theft of his career.

"Ready?" he said to Novak.

"That promise I made to God . . . you should make it too, Alex."

A red Volkswagen Golf hatchback crested the rise and slowed as it neared the crossing. Alex gave a thumbs up and waved the driver on. Alex hoped the army camera team arrived soon, as he didn't want too many people seeing and remembering the broken-down military vehicle.

They heard a deeper growl next and a white Land Cruiser came over the hill.

"That's them," Alex said, tallying the make of the vehicle from what he'd overheard at the car rental desk, and then recognizing the driver, the Afrikaner soldier. "Remember, they're not armed, but they are soldiers."

Given the prevalence of carjacking in South Africa, few people stopped to assist others with car troubles. However, Alex had gambled that the team coming toward him would stop for fellow servicemen. Alex stepped out from behind the raised bonnet and waved his hand up and down, slowly, palm facing downward. He glanced to his left and saw Henri and Heinrich tighten the grip on their weapons. If the men in the rented four-wheel drive did not stop, the two pirates would open fire and shoot out the front tires.

The driver slowed, and just as Alex tensed, preparing to draw the pistol from its holster under his shirt, he saw the Land Cruiser's indicator light flash.

Alex started to move forward, then froze as he heard another car's engine. They had reconnoitred the road and knew it was not busy, but a petrol tanker came over the hill and barreled down toward them.

The driver blew his air horn, perhaps checking if all was in order, and Alex waved him on.

By now the Land Cruiser had pulled over and the driver and the leader of the public relations team had got out of the vehicle.

"Howzit?" the driver called. "You *okes* need a hand?"

Kufa and Kevin started to sit up and waved in a comradely way to the new arrivals from their spot on the side of the road.

Alex nodded and reached for his pistol. That was the signal for all of them to move.

Henri stayed in position, still covering the vehicle, but Heinrich leaped from the cover of the bushes just as Kevin and Kufa got to their feet and raised their rifles.

"Down!" Alex yelled. "Down on the fucking ground. Now! Face down!"

Kevin kicked the officer in the back of the knee, forcing him down, and the white soldier complied without argument. Kufa had the back door of the Land Cruiser open and was dragging out the African, who looked totally confused. Alex noted the white ear buds of an iPod and realized the man had probably been bopping along to his favorite tunes in the back of the vehicle, oblivious to any trouble.

"Who are you?" the officer said, then winced as Kevin placed a knee in his spine and jabbed the barrel of his R5 into the back of the man's head.

"Shut it," said the Australian.

Alex dropped to one knee, behind and to one side of the public relations officer, so he couldn't see his face. "Be quiet, man," he said, not unkindly. "Nothing's going to happen to you if you do as we say."

"Shit, you're after the ivory, aren't you?"

"Shut up," hissed the photographer on the ground next to him.

"Listen to what your NCO says." Alex bound the officer's hands tightly with plastic cable ties. "That's the sort of talk that could get you killed. Don't make me do something I don't want to, all right, China?"

The man was silent, but Alex ordered them all gagged with masking tape anyway. Hessian hoods were pulled over their heads and tied at the necks. They lifted the bound soldiers into the back of the *bakkie*, and covered their prone bodies with the tarpaulin. Alex, Kevin and Kufa traveled in the Land Cruiser, now assuming the role of the army public relations squad, while Novak led off in the *bakkie* with Heinrich and Henri riding shotgun in the back. Everyone was in uniform now.

Novak led them through the back roads of White River to the R40. Once out of town they turned right and the road meandered up and down through extensive pine plantations.

Novak had worked for SAPPI, the South African paper manufacturing company, for a while after leaving the army, but had soon tired of a life without action. He'd been based in the Lowveld and was familiar with the plantations around the White River area. While Alex had been in Cape Town with Jane, Novak had rediscovered an old forestry hut. He indicated left and Alex turned off the main road onto a gravel logging road.

At this time of year there was little activity in the forest. Novak rounded a corner and stopped outside a mud-brick shack with a flat corrugated-tin roof. They stopped, offloaded their captives and led them inside the hut and pushed them down onto three metal-framed beds. Working on one man at a time, Heinrich pulled out a pocket knife and sliced through the cable ties binding their hands. Henri then handcuffed each to the welded steel head of each bed. The men would be dry, if not particularly comfortable.

"All of you listen to me," Alex said to the captives as his men filed out. "I'm leaving an armed man outside to keep watch on the road. He will check on you every now and then, so don't try anything. When the time comes, we'll notify the army that you are here. No harm will come to you if you lie still and quiet."

Alex didn't know if the men would fall for his bluff. He was taking all his men with him, but even if the soldiers did manage to escape, or if someone found them, it would be too late for them to do anything.

If all went according to plan, Alex and his men would be safely on Ilha dos Sonhos, and out of the pirate business, by nightfall.

25

Alex took the lead again and carried on to the small town of Hazyview. As he headed into town he turned right and followed his map to the Phabeni Gate.

The detailed orders for the elephant culling supplied by Chan specified that all military and police traffic should enter and leave via this lesser-used entrance to the Kruger National Park, so as to minimize the visibility of the operation to local people, visitors and the media.

The public relations plan for the culling operation called for an army PR team consisting of a video cameraman and a stills photographer, under the command of an officer, to gather footage of the collection and loading of the ivory from the slaughtered elephants on to South African Air Force Oryx helicopters.

Military police would be positioned at Phabeni Gate to check the identities of uniformed people taking part in the operation, and to facilitate their entry to the national park without disrupting the normal flow of tourist traffic. The public relations plan specified a three-man detachment, but there were six men in the two vehicles.

A kilometer from the gate, Alex pulled over. "OK, end of the line," he said to Novak.

Novak, Henri and Heinrich all got out of the Nissan *bakkie* and Kevin took his rifle and webbing out of the Land Cruiser and joined them by the side of the road. All wore military uniforms and carried R5s. "See you at the Albassini Ruins," Kevin said, and gave Alex a smart salute. Alex smiled and waved him off. Kevin checked his hand-held GPS unit and led Henri and Heinrich away from the road, into scrubby bushveld which was slowly reclaiming what had once been a farm on the border of the national park. They would cross into the reserve on foot, cutting through the elephant-proof fence that separated Kruger from the outside world.

Alex took a cigarette lighter from the breast pocket of his fatigues and a plastic soft-drink bottle of petrol from the back of the *bakkie*. After checking up and down the road to make sure no cars were approaching, he lit the improvized rag wick protruding from the bottle and tossed it into the empty cab. An orange-black ball of flame whooshed from inside and soon the vinyl bench seat was blazing fiercely.

Novak climbed into the driver's seat of the Land Cruiser. As an Afrikaans speaker he would play the role of the white photographer from now on, while Kufa, in the back seat, was the video cameraman. As the ranking officer, Alex took the front passenger seat. In his wing mirror he saw the Nissan, now surplus to their requirements, burning fiercely.

At Phabeni a uniformed military police corporal waved them over as soon as he spotted their uniforms.

Novak spoke in fluent Afrikaans before the man could say anything, explaining who they were. The corporal, an African, leaned his head into the cab and looked around. "Let me see your IDs," he eventually said in English.

By speaking English, this young noncommissioned officer was saying that he was of a different generation to Novak, when white South Africans dominated the army and Afrikaans was the official language. Those days were long gone.

"Howzit, my man. Would you like to be in *Soldier* magazine?"

Alex said to the man while Novak searched in his pocket for the stolen identity card of the man whose place he had taken.

The corporal looked at Alex and said, "What..." then added, "sir?" when he saw the captain's rank insignia.

"Pictures! We need photographs of as many SANDF personnel involved in this operation as possible, for your local newspaper, and for our own *Soldier* magazine. You'll be famous, *bru*! Dirk, get your camera, man, and take a picture of this warrior for us."

Novak nodded and reached for the Nikon in the console between them and opened his door. The military policeman stepped back to make room and automatically began straightening out imaginary creases from his uniform shirt and adjusting the red beret on his head to a more rakish angle.

"That's it, man." Novak made a show of checking his camera settings and began snapping away. "Hand up, like you're taking charge of these *bladdy* soldiers. That's it. *Lekker* pose. Work it, work it."

The corporal was laughing now and Novak said, "No smiling!" and this made him double up. When he'd composed himself Novak said, "You're an MP, man. Show the folks at home how you won't tolerate law breakers." The man posed, hands on hips, in front of his military police vehicle for a few more snaps.

"Hey," called a tourist, who had just pulled up at the gate's reception office. "Are you a policeman? There's a *bakkie* on fire just up the road there."

They all turned and saw the column of smoke, dark against the blue sky.

"Hey guys, I'm sorry, but I have to go and report this," the corporal said.

"Duty calls, man. Don't let us stop you," Alex said, clapping the NCO on the shoulder. "Thanks for your time."

"Nice work," Novak said to Alex when they were back in the car.

"He didn't even check our IDs," said Kufa from the backseat.

"It's not over yet."

They entered the park proper, crossing a low-level concrete bridge. Off to their right three old male buffalo wallowed in a puddle of mud, barely lifting their heads to register the passing of the four-wheel drive. "Pull over on the left up here," Alex said to Novak.

Just inside the park was a historical site called the Albassini Ruins. Joao Albassini had been a pioneering Portuguese trader in this part of South Africa in the nineteenth century and the foundations of his home and store were still visible at the site.

Alex got out. This was one of a few public places outside of the main rest camps in Kruger where visitors were allowed to alight from their vehicles. A minute later, Kevin emerged from the bush, followed by Heinrich and Henri. They climbed into the Land Cruiser. With all of the camera gear it was a tight fit, but Alex knew he would need every one of them, especially if their run of good luck came to an end.

From the Albassini Ruins they drove on the sealed Doispane Road, named after an early black ranger who had been given the disparaging name of "Dustpan." The park was busy with local and overseas visitors and it wasn't long before they were passed by open-sided, game-viewing vehicles, converted Land Rovers packed with tourists in an array of designer safari gear and leopard print.

A few kilometers on they found what the radio-equipped vehicles had been racing toward—a pride of eight lions. A black-maned male lay panting in the shade of a marula tree. His four female companions, arrayed around him, were more alert to the traffic jam of private cars and safari vehicles that had stopped to photograph them. Novak edged off the road onto the verge and skirted the phalanx of vehicles. The tourists were too intent on the big cats to pay any mind to the soldiers in the Land Cruiser.

"Bloody hell, I'm glad we've got our guns with us," Kevin said, as the largest of the lionesses, a huge beast with rippling shoulder muscles, stared contemptuously at them through her golden eyes.

"*Ja*," Novak agreed. "A ranger I know says that most of the prides in the Kruger Park have tasted human flesh. They catch Mozambican illegal immigrants coming across the border. More effective than our own army patrols, that's for sure."

It was a reminder that danger awaited them at every turn on this operation. As well as police, soldiers and national parks officers, all alert for theft of the precious ivory and disruption by environmentalist protesters, there was a host of other creatures big and small out here in the veldt that could kill a man.

The others nodded.

"Elephant," Novak said.

All the men looked where Novak was pointing. It was amazing, Alex always thought, how the great gray beasts could sometimes be so hard to spot. But once he saw one swishing tail, and the flapping of a huge set of ears, he was able to pick out the rest of the herd. Novak switched off the engine and they could hear the snapping of branches as the elephants fed, and hear the deep rumbling of their stomachs as they communicated with each other.

They did not have a great deal of spare time to make their rendezvous at the culling operation's field headquarters, but Alex knew they could spare a few minutes to prepare, psychologically, for what they were about to do.

"I could never kill one of these things," Kevin said.

"I could," Kufa said. "In Zimbabwe they trample the maize, and an uncle of mine was killed by a bull that gored him with a tusk then crushed him."

"I hunted one in the Congo once," Henri said. "I tracked him for two days. When it was done, I felt empty."

Alex said nothing, but was transported back with vivid clarity to the misty morning when he was five years old. Again he heard his mother's voice as she warned his father not to get too close to the matriarch. He saw the tiny female with the ragged V notched into her left ear, felt her breath on his hand again.

"You say that this thing that we do, it may stop the culling from proceeding?" Heinrich said.

As military men they had not dwelled on the ethics of what they were about to do, but Alex had voiced the same argument to them that Chan had put to him. It was a thin justification for a crime.

Alex watched a baby elephant, which he knew was less than a year old, as it could still walk easily under its mother's belly. The youngster had not yet learned to use his trunk and it flopped left and right and up and down—a useless but amusing appendage until it could be taught otherwise by his mother. Alex started to speak; the words would not come.

He felt ashamed.

"Start the engine. Let's get on with it."

They passed a herd of zebra and a forest of giraffe heads watched them as they turned right toward Skukuza, Kruger's main camp and administration center. As they drove in through the thatch-roofed gatehouse Alex pulled out his mobile phone and sent an SMS message: *Waiting at reception.*

Alex had Novak park the Land Cruiser away from the main reception building, behind the camp library. Skukuza was a busy place at any time, thronged with tourists, national parks employees, safari guides and, occasionally, police. They opened the doors to let a breeze in and Alex got out of the vehicle when he saw Kobus van Vuuren walking up the main road, from the accommodation area.

The helicopter pilot who had flown them during the raid on the *Penfold Son* had made his own way to Kruger and had been waiting in Skukuza for them to arrive. He walked into the men's toilets, and Alex followed him. They stood side by side at the urinal and, with no one else inside, Alex passed Kobus the sports bag he was carrying. Without a word, Kobus disappeared into one of the cubicles while Alex dallied at the washbasin.

Kobus re-emerged dressed in one of Kim Hoddy's husband's national parks honorary ranger's uniforms. It was a good fit, and Alex was pleased, as he'd judged the two men's sizes from memory.

Kobus's civilian clothes were in the bag, which he passed back to Alex. The soldier and the ranger strode purposefully to the Land Cruiser.

The vehicle was now packed, with two men in the front, three in the back, and two on the jump seats, facing each other over the pile of camera gear and accessories.

Alex directed Novak to drive straight to Satara Camp without stopping. A vehicle crammed with uniformed men was bound to attract attention, but some of them would be getting out once they neared their destination.

Novak sat on close to the maximum road speed of fifty kilometers per hour, ignoring the antelope, elephant, giraffes and zebra they passed on the way. As they neared Satara, the thick bushveld started to give way to more open grassy plains. When they at last rolled through the camp gates they were surrounded by people.

"Holy fuck, what a circus," Kevin said from the backseat.

It was a protest. Men, women and children of all ages emerged from the car park and picnic area at the sight of a four-wheel drive full of men in uniform.

"Stop the cull! Stop the cull! Stop the cull!" they chanted, their voices growing stronger by the second as more and more of the demonstrators found a target for their frustrations.

It was the first glitch in the plan. Alex had intended on dropping Henri, Heinrich, Kevin and Kobus at the camp while he went to the operational control post for the cull, which was located nearby at Satara's dirt airstrip. He'd figured that if he showed up in a rental vehicle with the correct number of people for the public relations team—himself, Kufa and Novak—he would have an easier time getting past the inevitable police and army checkpoint. He knew from the operational orders that he would be issued with a vehicle pass when he gained access to the airstrip. Once he had reconnoitred the area he would leave Novak and Kufa to pretend to take pictures and video, and return to camp for the others. Having passed through security once he would simply claim to have picked up some other men who needed a lift when he returned to the field base.

They were surrounded by chanting people. "I can't move," Novak said. "I don't want to run them down."

"No, lock the doors."

Something thudded on the roof of the Land Cruiser and a moment later red paint trickled down the windows on one side.

A white man with acne, dreadlocks and half-a-dozen piercings glinting on bits of his face pounded the windscreen. "Murdering bastards!"

"Stay cool, everyone," Alex said.

From the direction of the camp reception came the blast of whistles. "Cops," said Heinrich from the back of the truck.

"Move away from the vehicle!" a voice called through a loud hailer in English, then repeated the command in Afrikaans.

"Fascist bastards!" cried the young man. Alex could see he was trying to whip the protesters into a fury. He had a whistle of his own and blew on it loudly in response to the noise coming from the swelling ranks of blue-uniformed police.

"Watch your language, there are children here," said a gray-haired woman who was being pushed into Alex's window by the crush of people around her.

"This is getting ugly. Novak, rev the engine, hard."

A cloud of black diesel smoke belched from the rear of the Toyota, forcing a few people to step back, coughing.

"There's a gap. Slowly now, reverse back toward the police."

"Save the elephants! Save the elephants! Stop the cull! Stop the cull!" Parents moved children out of the way of the moving vehicle, and the crowd of protesters, now at about sixty, regrouped in front of the Land Cruiser to stop it moving forward.

Twenty police moved around the vehicle in a protective phalanx and one jumped on the running board. He rapped on the window.

"What the hell are you doing here, man?" the captain said to Novak as the electric window wound down.

Alex said across the driver, "Sorry. Lieutenant Arno van Dyk from army public relations. I just came in here to get some food for my men."

"Well you should have gone straight to the *bladdy* airstrip. Keep reversing then turn when I tell you to. There's another exit out near the staff quarters. We've been using it discreetly all morning. Hopefully these bunny huggers don't follow us and find it."

The man was red-faced. It was going to get hotter as the day wore on, and tempers were not going to get any cooler on either side. The crowd increased the volume of its chanting, thinking it had a victory.

The police captain jumped off the running board when they reached a white police pickup. "Follow me," he said. He led them past a bungalow that Alex guessed was the warden's house, and through a fence onto a gravel road that eventually joined the main tar road, just outside camp. A short way up the road they turned right, ignoring the red circular sign with a white bar across it that denoted no entry.

"This is the airstrip road," Alex said.

Two soldiers carrying R5s, half-a-dozen policemen and two women in national parks uniforms stood around a makeshift boom gate—a red and white striped pole laid across two two-hundred liter drums. A policeman stopped beside the captain's car, in front of them, and spoke to the officer for a minute. He stepped back, scrawled something on a piece of paper and waved the captain through. The police vehicle did a three-point turn past them.

"He's not having a good day," Kevin said.

"Just think how bad it's going to get for him later," Henri grinned.

"Quiet," said Alex. He didn't want them getting cocky just yet.

The policeman waved them forward and when Novak lowered the window the harried-looking man simply handed them a piece of paper with the words *visitor pass* written on it, followed by the numbers forty-two and seven, with the seven circled. "This is your pass number. Don't lose it. Seven is the number of occupants."

Novak nodded his thanks and slid the paper on the dashboard so it was visible.

"Is it just me or is everyone else nearly *kakking* their pants?" Kobus asked.

"Spoken like a typical air force guy," Heinrich said from the back.

"We can't do this job without you, Kobus. Stay cool," Alex said. As if on cue, a shadow passed over the Land Cruiser and they all craned their heads to see the podgy silhouette of a South African Air Force Oryx helicopter pass overhead.

Novak followed the red dirt road, carved through the brittle yellow grass and occasional knob thorns and leadwoods of the open savannah country.

Alex wondered if the airstrip had ever seen such activity. A row of brown canvas army tents lined half of the length of the dirt runway, and soldiers in camouflage and rangers in khaki darted in and out like mongoose foraging for food. A caravan was serving cold drinks and sandwiches and a line of policemen was queuing for their lunch.

The Oryx, a South African-built copy of the Anglo-French Puma troop-carrying helicopter, touched down. Its rotors stayed turning, throwing out a rolling cloud of choking red dust, grit, grass and stones. Fifteen men, all resting on one knee and holding their balance with long rifles, waited by the side of the airstrip. The lead man had his right hand raised, thumb up. The Oryx's copilot looked like a robot, with a bulbous green head and a lowered reflective visor covering his eyes. He returned the thumbs-up sign and the column of men stood and jogged toward the helicopter. They boarded quickly, showing this wasn't a maiden flight for any of them.

"That must be one of the five culling teams," Alex said. "They're being flown to their positions as soon as a national parks helo confirms the location of a suitable elephant herd."

"Suitable?" Kobus asked. The other members of the team had

been briefed thoroughly on the culling operation and their illegal part in it, but Kobus had been isolated from the others, having only just returned to South Africa the day before from a flying assignment in the Democratic Republic of Congo. If Kobus's flight had been delayed or canceled, the job would have been over before it began.

"They're looking for breeding herds—mothers and young. They need bigger herds of at least fifteen animals and they won't be targeting mature bulls." He didn't have to tell Kobus that elephant herds were generally composed of a matriarch, her daughters and granddaughters and all their children. Young males stayed with the herd only until they could fend for themselves and were then kicked out.

Alex told the pilot the Oryx would return and refuel once the last of the culling teams was out in the bush. Once all of the teams had done their work and removed the ivory, each would stay with the tusks until the helicopter collected them. The Oryx would then head out again to collect the precious harvest.

Kobus looked at the vehicle park behind the tents. "So what are all those armored cars?"

Twenty assorted military, national parks and police armor-plated trucks were lined side by side. Most looked like troop-carriers and the army vehicles had V-shaped hulls perched high above the ground, in order to minimize the effects of land mine blasts. Half-a-dozen had .50 caliber machine-guns mounted on top. Alex viewed the guns with some unease. He'd seen what the finger-length slugs from one of those weapons could do—take a helicopter out of the sky or cut a man in two.

"Redundancy and deception."

"Talk like a civilian, not a marine," Kobus said.

"Partly, they're here in case the helicopter breaks down—that's the redundancy part of the plan. They'll drive out to the culling teams and collect the ivory, load it on board and drive to Skukuza. There's a warehouse there with a reinforced vault under twenty-four-hour armed guard where national parks keep all the ivory they routinely collect from the carcasses of elephants that have died of natural causes or poaching. By the time it gets there a replacement helicopter will have arrived from Air Force Base Hoedspruit to take some of the ivory to Pretoria for the media event."

"Some?"

"Yeah. National parks usually stores all the ivory it collects. They're holding it as an investment for the future. However, the cull has caused so much political division in South Africa and abroad, the government doesn't want to be seen to be doing this for money they might make one day."

"So that's why they're going to burn it."

"Some of it," Alex said. "They'll burn just enough to make a good bonfire for the local and international media in Pretoria. A tonne at least."

"I doubt you'd fit three tonne of ivory inside an Oryx anyway. It'll take the weight, but the volume will be enormous," Kobus said.

Alex nodded in agreement. "After they've picked up about a tonne and a half of tusks the helicopter crew will fly back and unload. That ivory will be stacked into a cargo net. Then the Oryx will top up its fuel tanks and go pick up the rest of the cargo. When it comes back it'll touch down briefly and then the net will be attached. They'll fly to Skukuza, drop off the cargo net and carry on to Pretoria with whatever's left on board."

"Why are they flying the stuff all the way to Pretoria?" Kobus asked.

"The government's playing a clever game. They know the media can't be everywhere at once. They figure if they put on a press conference in Pretoria that will force some of the photographers and journalists to stay in the capital, away from where the action's happening. Same goes for the foreign media. Besides, no politician wants to be anywhere near a dying elephant or men with guns."

"Got it," Kobus said. "But getting back to the armored cars— they're here in case the helo breaks down, but what did you mean by deception?"

"You saw the protesters at Satara. The authorities expect other groups of demonstrators to man the park gates during the day, and to try to blockade the entrance to Skukuza. The armored cars will start leaving here during the day, in packets of three or four, once it's clear they're not needed. They'll leave via the main gates and some will go to park headquarters. It'll give the protesters something to focus on, but there will be no ivory on board. It's supposed to deter and confuse criminals as well."

Kevin laughed from the back of the four-wheel drive.

"So what do we do now?" Kobus asked.

The plan for the pirate gang, Alex explained, was to do the job of the army public relations team. They needed to ingratiate themselves with the people running the operation on the ground, so that their movements wouldn't be challenged. Alex told Novak to drive to the line of tents and they cruised slowly through the dust churned up by an armored car in front of them until they came to one that said *Headquarters.* Someone had scrawled *Operation Jumbo* in chalk underneath. Alex, Novak, Kufa and Kobus got out of the Toyota and Kevin got in the driver's seat. "Go hide in the car park," Alex told the rest of them.

Inside the brown canvas army tent were four rows of folding trestle tables littered with maps, field radio sets, laptop computers, satellite phones and half-drunk plastic bottles of water. Men and women in army, police and national parks uniforms sat in foldout camp chairs. A couple read magazines. A soldier excused himself and edged past them, drawing a packet of cigarettes out of his breast pocket. There was not much going on.

"I'm looking for Colonel De Villiers," Alex said to an African private, who was studying a bikini-clad centerfold.

"Over there . . . sir," he said, looking up and seeing Alex's rank insignia.

Alex tried to remember he was a public relations officer, not a former Royal Marine Commando. If he'd been in his old uniform he wouldn't have brooked the man's casual attitude toward a stranger.

He threaded his way between the tables to the far end of the tent where a short, gray-haired man in army camouflage was talking to a bald-headed African in national parks uniform. The white man was tapping a plastic-covered map pinned to a board on an easel. Both turned at Alex's approach.

"Morning, sir. Sorry to disturb you. I'm Arno van Dyk, from army public relations."

The colonel gave a grunt that Alex took to be a greeting. "Why are you wearing gloves? It's thirty-five degrees out there already."

Alex wore green fire retardant Nomex gloves, the type favored by many special forces soldiers around the world. The way the colonel addressed him sounded like he was accusing Alex of an affectation. "Skin condition, sir."

De Villiers stepped back half a pace. "Very well. You're here to make us all famous, eh?"

"We'll do our best, sir." He introduced Novak as his photographer and Kufa as the video cameraman and Kobus as their national parks public relations liaison officer.

"You've arrived at a good time. All of the culling teams but one have left, and we're waiting for the action to start. The calm before the storm, as they say."

"We haven't met," said the African man. "I'm Jacob Mandile from Corporate Investigation Services." He shook hands with Kobus first. "You're not from Skukuza?"

It was said as an accusation, rather than a question. Alex hoped Kobus would keep his cool. Corporate Investigation Services was the park's elite policing service. CIS operators had a justifiably fierce reputation as hardened fighters in the war on poaching. Its members infiltrated poaching gangs undercover, and tracked illegal hunters through the bush. And killed them.

"I'm an honorary ranger, from Pretoria," Kobus tapped his epaulettes, which showed the national parks emblem of a Kudu's head on a black background, instead of the green of the full-time employees.

"I work as a public relations consultant in my civilian job and was asked to help out."

The bald man nodded, apparently satisfied.

"Well," Colonel De Villiers said, "you know what's required of you better than I do. Go out and take your pictures and your films and try not to get killed by an angry elephant."

"Yes, sir. You would have seen from the PR plan that we need to get some aerial footage as well. I thought this would be best achieved on the last sortie, when the helicopter returns to pick up the net for the trip to Pretoria," Alex said.

The black private who had directed them toward the colonel excused his way into the cluster of men. "Chief of army is on the phone for you, sir. Wants to know how things are going."

De Villiers gave a theatrical sigh. "This will be my lot today. Telling everyone in Pretoria that things are going according to plan. Talk to Captain Steyn, the aviation liaison officer in the next tent. He's coordinating the helo missions."

Alex saluted and the colonel dismissed him with little more than a wave of his hand. He left the tent. De Villiers's lack of interest in the public relation team was a good sign. Better that, Alex thought, than a commander who wanted to oversee every detail.

They filed out of the command tent and went to the next, which had a stencilled sign saying *Air Ops* outside. Alex found Captain Steyn, a red-haired man, sitting at a table talking on a radio. He held up a hand to tell them to wait until he had finished. Over the radio they could hear the pilot of the Oryx talking above the background whine of his engines. They had just dropped off the culling team that Alex had seen board the helicopter.

When Steyn had finished his radio transmission Alex introduced himself and his men.

"Ah yes, the PR man. I've got you on the last sortie—when the helo will go around picking up all the ivory. You'll get lots of nice images of the tusks being loaded. Then, when the Oryx returns here you can get out, he'll hook up the net with the excess ivory, and we can all go for a beer. Is that all right with you?"

That's what Alex liked about the air force. Their idea of issuing orders was to ask if everything was all right. "Almost perfect," Alex said.

"Almost?"

"*Ja*. I've also been tasked to get some vision and stills of the ivory being dumped at Skukuza, when he drops off the cargo net. National parks have asked for it, and it is their operation, after all."

Steyn looked thoughtful, then nodded.

"If it's all right with you, I'd like to stay on board with my guys and then get out at Skukuza. We've got a parks guy with us—an honorary ranger—who has a car at reception. He can drive us back out here to Satara to pick up our four-by-four." Alex pointed a thumb back over his shoulder at Kobus, who was standing at the entrance to the tent. Kobus smiled and nodded.

Steyn scratched his chin. "Hmmm. Hadn't heard about another passenger. Shouldn't be a problem, though. There are two armed airmen on board, riding shotgun. Might be a bit tight for space, but there should be enough room for one more."

"That's great. *Baie dankie*."

"What next?" Novak asked when they walked back outside.

"Earn your keep. Take lots of pictures. Be pushy, and don't take any shit. Kobus, go wait with the others." The pilot nodded and walked off toward the car park.

"Who are you?"

Alex turned around and was confronted by a giant of a man. Alex was six foot two inches and no weed, but he felt dwarfed by the man in front of him, who had three inches on him at least, and had the build of a Cape Buffalo.

"Army public relations," Alex said. "We're here to film and photograph the culling operation."

The man mountain grunted. "You want to see how it's done?"

"Sure," Alex said.

The man introduced himself as Frank Cole. He was an ex-Rhodesian national parks ranger, which Alex guessed must have put him in his early fifties at least, as that country hadn't existed by that name since 1980. Frank had a physique a twenty year old would have aspired to. His bare arms and long legs were mahogany brown and his bushy gray beard was stained yellow around the mouth from nicotine.

He lit a cigarette and said, "Come."

Alex called to Novak and Kufa and increased his stride to catch up with the older man. "What's your role in all this? You're not wearing a uniform of any kind."

"I gave up uniforms a long time ago. And this shit. But they called me back. I used to run the culls up in Wankie and the Zambezi Valley. I came to South Africa when the blacks took over my country. When the same thing happened here and they stopped the culls in Kruger I took the package. I never thought I'd be back here killing elephants again."

"What do you do these days?"

"I'm a PH."

Alex should have guessed he was a professional hunter.

"Tanzania and Zambia, mostly," Frank continued. "Usually rich Americans and Germans, though some Russians as well. Mafia types. They tip well. Here's my crew."

The other twelve men that Frank introduced Alex and his men to were of a similar age—none looked younger than forty. Like him, they had the dark wrinkled skin of men who lived a life outdoors in the African sun.

"Cole?" Colonel De Villiers emerged from his tent holding a piece of paper.

"Sir!" Frank snapped to attention and gave an overly theatrical salute. His men snickered.

De Villiers ignored the mockery. "Parks helicopter has found a herd for you. It's not far, so you can drive rather than fly. Five kilometers from here, on the S100 road. You follow the tar road from here and—"

"I know where it is, Colonel. I know where they'll be drinking this time of the day."

"Yes, well here's a GPS coordinate just in case."

Frank issued his orders with the understated authority of one who has commanded men in the field before. He called an African in national parks khaki over and spoke to the man in fluent Shangaan.

Minutes later Alex, Novak and Kufa were climbing into the back of a South African Army Unimog truck and bouncing along a dirt road that followed the course of an electricity power line.

"We take the back roads," Frank said, standing in the back of the truck, holding onto a tubular metal crossbow that would normally support a canvas canopy. "That way no protesters can stop us, and no civilians have to see the big bad men with guns."

Kufa filmed the hunters and the convoy of vehicles that swung in behind them. As well as the Unimog there were tractors towing flatbed trailers, a truck towing a refrigerated storage trailer, and two *bakkies* with national parks field rangers in green bush uniforms standing in the backs.

"I'd heard elephants were darted with a paralyzing drug rather than shot outright," Alex said. "But I don't see any dart guns."

Frank nodded. "Before the culling ended last time, in 1995, we were using succinylcholine. It brought the elephants down but didn't kill them. We'd still have to go around and give each one a brain shot, but they were conscious throughout the whole thing. Using the drug removed the risk of an elephant being wounded by a bullet and suffering while it was tracked down, but better, I always said, for man and beast alike to end it quickly. If you're a good shot and you know what you're doing, the whole thing is over quick time."

Alex pitied the rangers riding in the open vehicles behind them, as they were soon lost in a growing cloud of red dust churned up by the Unimog and the other vehicles in front of them. But there was no time to waste. Frank spoke on a handheld radio to the pilot of the national parks helicopter, who said the elephants had drunk from the N'wanetsi River and were now feeding in lightly vegetated country.

"OK, keep them in sight but don't spook them," Frank said into the radio. Frank turned back to Alex. "When it starts, you and your guys stay close to me. No one runs, whatever happens."

All three of them nodded.

Novak snapped a photo of Frank looking out over the savannah. "I thought you'd be carrying something bigger than that," he said, pointing at the 7.62 mm FN rifle the hunter carried.

"One of these served me just fine for ten years during the bush war in Rhodesia, and in all the elephant culls I took part in. Wayne over there has a 375, and Jan's got a .458, but they're only in case we come across a big bull. The bulls shouldn't be near the breeding herds this time of year, but you never know when you might run into one. A 7.62 mm round's fine for a cow or a young one, and with a semiautomatic rifle you can put two or more shots in." He snapped his fingers twice to emphasize the benefits of the military-style weapon over a bolt-action hunting rifle.

The truck slowed and Frank leaned over the side of the Unimog and spoke to the army driver through the window, switching effortlessly to Xhosa. The truck stopped and they climbed down.

Frank called them all together. "Right. We set up firm base here." The radio hissed to life and he pulled it from a pouch on his belt.

"*Herd is moving toward you now, Frank, over.*"

"Roger. Let them come."

He gave his orders quickly, telling his shooters to fan out on either side of him. The men took up positions in the shade of knob thorn trees and behind red-earth termite mounds. He pointed to where the herd would come from and Alex could tell they were downwind, so the elephants would not smell them until they were almost on top of them. By then it would be too late.

"Are you filming this for real?" Alex whispered to Kufa.

"Yes. I thought it would be worth something."

Alex nodded. Frank held up a hand for silence, then pointed. Alex saw nothing for a few seconds, then the telltale flap of a sail-like ear caught his eye. The matriarch of the herd was a huge cow who stood as tall as a house. She moved slowly, her head looking from side to side every few steps. She paused and lifted her trunk, sniffing the air, but whatever it was seemed to be a false alarm, so she continued. Her newest calf trotted close behind her. Less than a year old, it was still thirsting for the milk in the swollen breasts between the cow's front legs, which were as thick as leadwood trees.

Behind the queen came her entourage of daughters and grand-daughters. Alex could recognize just three males in the group of a dozen animals. They were juveniles and, like humans of the same age and sex, they were troublemakers. One chased another away from the forest of shuffling gray legs. Alex saw Kufa tense as one of the males let out a trumpet blast. He ran after his brother, but both stopped when they heard a low rumbling noise. It had come from the matri-arch and it sounded like the empty grumblings of a huge hungry stom-ach. Whatever she said, it was enough to calm the unruly youngsters for the moment.

Alex heard the clatter of helicopter blades and looked up to see the green and gold livery of the national parks aircraft glinting in the sun.

"Back off," Frank whispered. "He's going to panic them."

The matriarch lifted her head to the sky. She was old enough to remember the days when the rattle from the skies was a prelude to a deadly symphony of crackling death. She'd smelled the blood and of-fal on the ground and touched the bones of distant relatives once the meat, skins and tusks had been carted away.

"She knows something's wrong," Frank said.

The elephant started to turn. She raised her trunk and blew a high-pitched note that halted her family.

Alex smelled the musty stale odor of elephant on the faint breeze.

He looked at Frank, who was silently shaking his head now, as if he felt the elephant's confusion and mounting panic. He clearly didn't want to get involved in a chase, but what else could he do if the animals decided to change direction?

Frank strode from the shade of the tree that had also hidden him from view of the animals. As he walked he raised the steel-plated wooden butt of the FN into his shoulder and took aim.

The matriarch shook her head furiously, sending out a cloud of dust like a brown halo. She took two paces forward, raised her trunk high between her tusks and spread her ears out wide. It was a classic mock-charge stance, Alex knew. She was giving the man coming toward her one chance to back off and move out of her way.

"On me," Frank called to his men.

Alex, Kufa and Novak moved up behind him.

Frank was moving right, outflanking the elephant. When he had a clear view of her side he fired, twice into the spot where her left front leg met her huge body. She screamed and started to move forward, but the slugs had tumbled their way through her massive heart and the blood gushed from her with each of the four steps she managed.

When she crashed to the ground, first on her knees, she raised a cloud of dust and Alex could feel the vibration in the hot dry earth.

The rest of the herd panicked but did not run away. Their first instincts were concern for their leader, then protection of her and their young ones. The family closed up, all trying to reach the stricken body of the matriarch. The dying elephant's baby was sniffing its mother with its trunk and nudging her lifeless body with its head. He waved his trunk uselessly about in frustration. The young males circled the herd, screaming belligerently and looking for something or someone to vent their rage on. The other females closed in around their mother, backing toward her to meet the unseen threat.

Frank's men, all seasoned veterans of this kind of killing, had already been moving as their leader stepped out. They fanned out into a semicircle and began firing.

The stench of cordite and blood filled the air now and Alex's ears rang to the bang-bang, bang-bang of two well-aimed shots being fired in quick succession—the double tap—and the crack and thump of projectiles splitting the air and driving into flesh.

The animals screamed, though the men were silent. They closed the distance, rifles always up, though the volume of fire that had crackled like dry burning brush at first had subsided to a desultory pop every now and then.

From a circular *laager* of tonnes of protective flesh and bone, an infant escaped. It was younger even than the matriarch's calf. Not even waist high to a man, it was little bigger than a pig, and probably not more than a few days old. It blundered out of the crush of falling and fallen bodies, and the cloud of dust that hung like poison gas over the bodies, straight toward Alex and his men.

"Can't they save it?" Novak asked, although he knew the answer.

Frank Cole lifted his rifle wearily and looked through the sights as the tiny elephant walked closer and closer to him. Alex had no idea why it was drawn toward the hunter; perhaps it was the man's sheer height and bulk.

No one spoke and those of the rest of the herd that had not died in the first few seconds had now been put out of their misery.

There was silence and all eyes turned to Frank.

Alex saw a drop of sweat fall from the hunter's brow and run heavily down the wooden butt of the old rifle. Alex thought he detected a tremor in the brown hands that were spotted with age and scarred from a life full of thorns.

Frank fired twice.

The baby elephant dropped at his feet.

26

Jane looked out over the harbor from the room in the Radisson Waterfront, Cape Town, and wished she could fly.

Why couldn't she be like normal people, who hopped cheap charter flights to Spain or Italy for a weekend or to Australia or the Far East for their annual holidays? Why, whenever she even contemplated the notion of confronting her fear, did she know for certain that she would be counting the minutes and seconds to her inevitable death as the airliner plummeted toward the ground or sea?

She was booked on another ship home and the irony was she had almost lost her life on the high seas when she'd been on George's freighter.

The time and cost of the impending voyage weighed heavily on her mind, too. Now she was out of a job, the price of a last-minute berth on the cruise ship to Portsmouth would hurt even more than usual and would very nearly deplete her savings account. She was pretty sure she would be able to get another job fairly soon, even without references, though she might run out of cash before she could start and that would mean giving up the flat and moving back in with her parents. The thought depressed her. It would be weeks before she could start earning again. At least, she sighed, she could busy herself on the

Internet on board for the next two weeks, emailing off her CV and job applications.

She also wished she could get on an airplane and fly away from George. She wanted as much distance between her and him as fast as possible. But she knew, also, that she could never escape him. At least not until he was behind bars.

Jane looked at the plain manila envelope on the writing desk in her hotel room and shuddered when she remembered the grainy video on the computer. She saw again the sadistic joy in George's face as he strangled the girl, his momentary shock when he realized she was dead, and the cool deliberateness with which he negotiated the disposal of her body with the brothel's owner.

She had tendered her resignation to George that morning over breakfast, but had not confronted him with what she'd found on board the *Penfold Son*.

Something about the way he had handled the news scared her. He had been calm. "I see," was all he had said when she told him she was quitting, with effect from that moment, with no notice.

He'd put down his morning newspaper and coffee and said, "I take it you won't be marrying me then?"

She'd shaken her head.

"Is there any point in asking you why, or if you wish to reconsider?"

What could she have said that wouldn't tip him off about what she was about to do? Had he guessed already that it had been her—with help—who had broken into the naval yard last night and illegally boarded the *Penfold Son*?

There was nothing to say to him and she sensed he knew all too well why she was leaving him and the company.

The luminous numbers on the digital clock radio by the bed read nine fifty-one. It was time for her to check out. She had booked a car for ten. She would be at the Cape Town homicide squad at quarter past the hour, and was due to board her ship at eleven-thirty, for a one o'clock sailing. After that she would be safe.

She'd used the Internet to find the name of the detective handling the investigation into the strangling murder of a nineteen-year-old Cape Town prostitute two months earlier.

Detective Inspector Jan Kruger had sounded distracted to the point of rudeness when she'd called, asking if he was still investigating the death of a prostitute named Susan Hawkins. "*Ja*, but I have another call coming through on my cell phone," he'd said. But she'd heard the musical ringtone in the background cut out as soon as she'd told him she had a video of the prostitute's death.

Jane had refused to give her name, or to say how she had acquired the video, but asked when and where they could meet, so she could deliver it to him. Kruger had told her to come to Cape Town Central Police Station and ask for him.

Alex's parting words lingered in her mind. "Be careful."

She had only one bag with her, containing the new clothes she had bought in Johannesburg at George's behest. She would burn all of them as soon as she got to the UK. She didn't want a single thing in her life to remind her of him. Jane picked up the holdall and left the room, looking up and down the corridor before pressing the "down" button on the lift.

The lobby was busy, but she couldn't see anyone other than half-a-dozen tourists queuing to check out, a couple of porters and a man sitting on a settee reading a newspaper. She couldn't see his face, but he had black hands.

Jane waited impatiently behind a German couple who were disputing their bill in broken English. She kept glancing about and thought she saw the seated man raise his newspaper quickly, as if trying to cover his face, when she turned in his direction.

She was regretting tendering her resignation to George and feeling more afraid by the minute. *I should have just gone to the police and then run*, she thought. "Good morning, ma'am, can I help?" the receptionist said. Jane passed her key card to the young man and looked around again. The man was engrossed in his newspaper.

Jane paid and walked quickly across to the concierge. She was wearing the gray business suit she'd bought for the meetings she wouldn't be attending. Her new shoes rubbed painfully on her heels. "I have a car booked in the name of Humphries, for ten."

As the concierge walked to the door to signal the waiting driver someone walked past them. Jane saw the back of the man she'd been watching, his newspaper now folded under his arm. There was something familiar about his heavyset build and the erect swagger of his walk.

Jane was filled with sudden dread. The car, a black Mercedes sedan, pulled up, and the driver popped the boot and opened his door.

Jane raced past the concierge and thumped down on the boot with her fist, slamming it shut. She opened the back door and tossed her bag on the leather seat. "Stay there and shut the door!"

The driver looked taken aback at being ordered in such a way but closed his door anyway, and Jane slammed the back and jumped into the front passenger seat. "Cape Town Central Police Station. Quickly!"

"*Yebo* madam," said the driver.

Jane looked over her shoulder, scanning the car park, as the driver stopped and put a ticket into a reader at a boom gate. She saw a white Vito minibus reversing out of a car space, but the windows were tinted, so she couldn't get a good look at the driver or passenger.

"Look, I don't mean to be melodramatic . . ."

"What?" said the driver.

"Don't panic, but do you have a gun?"

The driver looked across at her as if she were mad. "Why?"

"I think we might be being followed."

The driver looked into his rearview mirror. "There is no one behind us. But I will keep watch if you wish."

She swiveled in her seat and saw the white van, but then sighed with relief as it indicated to turn right once it cleared the boom gate, taking it in the opposite direction to them.

"I'm sorry for that, it's just that . . ."

As Jane started to face forward again the driver stood on the brake and the Mercedes skidded to a halt. He crunched the gear lever into reverse and dropped the clutch, spinning the wheels. Jane screamed as she saw what had made him stop. A blue Audi had stopped at ninety degrees, blocking their way. Two men wearing black ski masks were out of the car walking toward her, submachine guns in their hands.

Jane ducked her head and looked between the front seats out the back window. The white van that had turned off was now reversing at high speed, weaving crazily as the driver tried to stay straight but then overcorrected. Her driver was closing the distance between them and the van rapidly and she thought he was going to try to ram the larger vehicle.

Jane heard a noise like hail hitting a tin roof, and the windscreen shattered into chunks and fell back in on her. She put her hands over her head and felt the sharp shards bouncing off her skin. The driver braked hard again and she felt herself pushed back into the seat. She saw him reach under his seat and grab a black pistol.

As he started to raise the gun Jane heard shouting from in front and behind, then two shots. She turned to look up and the driver's head seemed to explode, splattering her with blood and brains. Jane screamed and ducked behind the dashboard. She saw the dead driver's gun in the foot well. Almost paralyzed with fear and shock, she nonetheless reached out for it. The pistol trembled in her hand.

"I'm not supposed to kill you now, but I'll gladly do so."

She felt the painful stab of hot metal in the back of her neck. She sat up and tried to look around, but the man who had spoken grabbed a handful of her hair and wrenched her out of the car. "Drop the gun, get out and keep quiet."

Through the pain and frustration that brought tears to her eyes she recognized the voice.

Piet van Zyl.

The slaughtering of the elephants was taking place with gory efficiency in the bush clearing. Frank Cole was supervising the butchering gang and his hands and bare legs were already soaked red.

Alex turned away. He wasn't weak-stomached—he'd spent too much time in war zones for that—but he was saddened by the waste of these great animals. He could understand the logical arguments in favor of culling, but as someone who had invested in the future of Mozambican tourism, he felt the South African government hadn't given nature enough time to work out its own solution to elephant overcrowding in Kruger. He was sure that, given a few more years, more and more elephants would cross the border and populate the Greater Limpopo Transfrontier Park and other reserves further afield, such as Gorongosa.

Vultures were already circling above them, a flock of twenty or more riding the thermal currents while they kept watch on the proceedings below.

Each animal was gutted first, and there were mounds of purple-blue entrails oozing around the men as they worked. Chainsaws were used to cleave off great sides of meat and skin, which were then loaded onto the trailers with a crane on the back of a Unimog truck.

Workers used axes to remove the precious ivory. Each tusk came out with a wet, bloody mass of fat and tissue attached to one end. They were stacked in a growing heap, awaiting pickup by the helicopter.

Kufa and Novak were dutifully pretending to record the event with their cameras. Alex wrinkled his nose at the stench of blood and half-digested vegetable matter.

"Let's go," he said.

Frank walked over to him, wiping his hands on his shorts. "I won't shake your hand. At least you were smart enough to wear gloves. Tell one of the army guys to drive you back to Satara in the Mog. We'll be an hour or so here."

Alex thanked Frank for his time and said he had found the whole experience fascinating. He couldn't wait to get back to his island.

Jane should be three days into her voyage home by now. He wondered what had happened to George Penfold and if she'd taken his advice not to tell her boss that she was quitting, just to not show up for her meeting at De Witt Shipping.

"Alex?"

"What?"

"We're ready, man." Novak had his camera over his shoulder and had obviously been standing next to him for a few seconds unnoticed. "Are you all right?"

"Yes. Of course."

They drove back along the fire-trail road to the Satara airstrip. The Oryx sat in the sun like a huge dragonfly, its rotors still and limp, as if it were sagging in the midday heat.

Colonel De Villiers walked out of the headquarters tent and lit a cigarette. Did you get some film of the cull?"

"Yes, sir."

"The culling teams are all reporting in. We're close to the target already. Eighty-seven elephants killed. Mess tent's over there if you and your guys want to get some food."

"I'm not hungry," Kufa said to him as they walked away. "Not after watching that."

Alex nodded. "We just need to keep out of sight until the chopper's ready to leave."

Alex took a cold drink in the mess and then walked back outside toward the car park. Kevin opened the door of the Land Cruiser and waved him over. It looked like he, Heinrich, Henri and Kobus had been sitting inside with the engine running and the air-conditioning on. He didn't blame them.

"We've been busy while you were off gallivanting about," Kevin said to him.

"Do tell."

"We took a drive down the main road. There's another fire trail closed to public access, not far from here. It looks like a good place for us to wait for the pickup. There's a clearing big enough for the chopper to land—looks like an old road-work quarry that the park guys have been using as a rubbish tip."

"Good." Alex looked back out toward the row of tents and saw De Villiers waving at him. "I'd better go. Head off as soon as we leave in the helo. Come on, Kobus. Stick close to me from now on."

"Get your men saddled up. Chopper's leaving in five," Captain Steyn yelled to Alex as he approached. He heard the whine of the aircraft's turbine engines starting up. When he turned back to call to Kufa and Novak to drop their drinks he saw the rotor blades slowly start turning. "It's all gone much better than we could expect. All the ivory is out and ready for collection and the parks guys have decided to call it a day at eighty-seven."

Alex took a bulky black backpack from the rear of the Land Cruiser and shouldered it. He, Kufa, Kobus and Novak strode through the dry yellow grass to the makeshift helipad.

Kevin started the Land Cruiser and drove past them. Alex held up his right thumb in the air and the helicopter copilot raised his in reply. "Come on!" he called to Novak and Kufa above the growing din of the engines.

They jogged across the clearing, heads bent to make sure they were below the spinning rotors, and eyes down to avoid the storm of dirt and stone and grass that was being blasted out around the Oryx. They hefted their bags into the cargo compartment and a flight engineer in a flying suit helped them aboard.

"Joost," said the crewman. Alex took the man's hand and he pulled him inside. "Welcome aboard!" He was yelling in Alex's ear, his lips almost as close as a lover's. "Captain'll talk to you on the headset once we're airborne. Sorry for the rush, hey, but it looks like we'll be in the pub early this afternoon."

Alex grinned and gave the man a thumbs-up. Joost spoke into his intercom and stuck his head out of the cargo hatch to make sure all was clear. The Oryx rocked a little then lifted off. The pilot dropped the nose to gather speed and they lurched away from the air-strip.

Joost passed Alex a bulky set of headphones and clipped a switch to the front of his uniform. "Press this when you want to speak," he said, and Alex heard him clearly through the earpieces.

"Welcome aboard," said the pilot. He turned and smiled briefly. He was white, a colonel, and looked to be in his forties. An experienced operator. "Sorry for the rush, but we don't waste daylight."

"We'll try not to get in the way," Alex assured the man.

"No problem. We're all looking forward to being famous, although Petrice's used to the limelight, being one of our first African female pilots."

When the copilot turned to acknowledge them with a nod Alex saw for the first time that it wasn't a man, but rather a young woman. She smiled at him. She was very pretty. The surname on the name tag on her flight suit said *Judge*. Alex forced himself to look pleased to meet her over the radio. He heard Captain Steyn, the ground liaison officer, relaying coordinates for the first pickup.

"Confirm you now have four pax on board. Army public relations team plus one parks officer?" Alex heard Steyn ask.

"Roger," said the colonel. "And acknowledge that we are now taking all four to Skukuza."

"That's affir . . ." said Steyn. Alex could not hear the other man's full reply.

"Any word on our guest star . . . for . . . vid . . . ?" the pilot asked.

Alex pressed his left hand against his headphones to try to hear the transmissions, which kept dropping in and out. He jiggled the wires attached to each earpiece as well, and finally was able to hear the conversation, though he had missed most of it.

"It'll be a nice surprise," the pilot said.

Alex pressed the talk switch. "What's that about a surprise?"

The pilot laughed into his microphone. "Well, if I told you, it wouldn't be a surprise. Wait and see. It might not happen."

Novak tapped Alex on the shoulder and pointed out the open cargo hatch. Below them a herd of more than a hundred buffalo was stampeding from the noise of the passing machine. They looked like a swarm of fat black flies from this height, zigging and zagging through the dry yellow grass. Alex guessed plenty of animals had been upset today by the sounds of gunfire and the movement of heavy vehicles and aircraft around them.

Alex was concerned about the pilot's last comment. The only surprise he wanted on this mission was the one he had in store for the helicopter crew and their escorts. Two airmen in SANDF camouflage fatigues sat in troop seats at the rear of the cargo compartment, R5 rifles resting on their knees. One of the men grinned and raised his rifle into his shoulder and aimed out the open door when Novak pointed his stills camera at him.

Both were young—one white, the other African—and Alex was sure he would be able to best them when the time came. Airmen received basic weapons training, like all members of the military, though they would not be as adept in hand-to-hand combat as the ex-special forces soldiers on board. Both wore bulletproof vests, which Alex guessed was more for the benefit of the news cameras waiting in Pretoria than in acknowledgment of any real threat to the helicopter and its cargo.

"First collection coming up," the pilot announced for the benefit of Alex and the helicopter's crew.

Alex looked out between the pilot and the copilot. Ahead he saw two tractors towing trailers loaded with gray hide and raw meat and fat. The bones of a dozen dead elephants were showing white against the brown of the bush. A man in national parks field green stood with both hands above his head.

The crew conversed among themselves as the pilot descended. Joost the flight engineer craned his head out the door and gave a commentary on vehicles below them and their distance from the nearest trees.

"When we touch down, your cameraman and photographer can get out to photograph the loading, if you like," the copilot said to Alex over the radio.

"Thanks, will do. I'll let them know."

Alex relayed the orders to Novak and Kufa in a shout. It was important for them to win the confidence of the airmen around them. As the Oryx's wheels touched down the flight engineer gave the men a thumbs-up and yelled, pointing to the rear of the helicopter, "Stay clear of the tail rotor!"

Novak and Kufa jumped down and were almost stampeded by a chain of national parks staff who were already running toward the Oryx, laden with tusks. Joost grabbed one of the rangers by his epaulette and motioned for him to get into the helicopter and help stack the ivory. Alex, Kobus and the two armed airmen joined in. The uniformed men at first slung their weapons, but when one jabbed the other painfully in the side of the head with the tip of his barrel, both decided to unsling their rifles and stow them under their seats. Alex moved to the extreme rear of the fuselage and motioned to the two guards to pass the tusks back to him, where he began stacking them.

Alex's gloves were soon wet with blood from the uncleaned ends of the tusks. He pulled off his right glove and stuffed it in the pocket of his fatigue shirt, which made handling the yellowed shafts a little easier. Sweat was pouring down his face by the time the last of this first batch was on board.

Novak grinned and winked at him as he climbed aboard. He held up his camera. "I could get used to this job. Point and push the shutter button!"

Alex reached down to help Kufa aboard, as he was burdened by the unfamiliar bulk and weight of the video camera. Kufa nodded his thanks then wiped his bloody hand on his shirt, giving Alex a look of genuine distaste.

The engines whined and the rotors kept turning the whole time.

After the third pickup Alex told the pilot that Novak and Kufa had shot enough stills and video and would now be happy to help load the tusks on board for the final two collections.

"Great, thanks," the colonel said. "That'll save us some time."

The airmen who were supposed to be guarding the ivory were now chatting and laughing with Novak and Kufa as though the four of them were old friends. Kufa told a dirty joke that had all of them roaring.

Alex took off his headset and handed it to Kobus. Cupping a hand around his mouth, in case the flight engineer could lip-read, he told Kobus to listen in to the chatter between the air force pilots and those on the ground. He would need to learn the call signs and verbal procedures they were using.

Kobus nodded, and licked his lips. He looked pale, Alex thought. Kobus had been fearless in landing them on the *Penfold Son* under fire, and while he was a good pilot he was not a soldier. No doubt he was nervous about what was to come.

The next two collections of ivory went without incident and, with Alex and his men helping with the loading, were completed quickly. The Oryx had traveled a circuitous route and now skimmed the trees at the edge of the Satara airstrip.

On the ground they all sweated in the midday heat as they unloaded the ivory from the helicopter and stacked it in the cargo net laid out in the dirt. The pilot had shut down the engines and a refueling truck pulled up next to them.

"Petrice?"

"Yes?" said the copilot.

"We need to get some pictures of you for the army newspaper," Alex said.

"OK," she sighed. "It's not the first time, and it won't be the last."

Alex chatted to Petrice while Novak posed her first at the nose of the helicopter, then sitting in a copilot's seat with the door open.

"It can't be easy for you, being one of a few women in a mostly male environment."

"Don't take this badly," she paused to smile for Novak's camera, "but it's only people like you who make my job difficult. The other female pilots and I get more publicity than the males and it makes them jealous. We get ribbed about it."

"Well, you're more photogenic than the colonel over there." Alex gestured to the older pilot, who was chatting to Captain Steyn out on the airstrip, and smoking a cigarette the regulation hundred meters away from the refueling bowser.

"Are you flirting with me?"

Alex raised his palms and shrugged. She laughed. "You work a lot with the police, don't you?" he said, changing the subject. He'd wanted her relaxed and felt he'd succeeded.

"Yes. We fly special weapons teams to incidents such as sieges and armed farm invasions."

"Sounds dangerous. You don't carry a gun yourself?"

"Sometimes, but not on PR jobs like this," she said. "The colonel's old-school, though. He always has a pistol on him. He was shot down twice in Angola during the border war."

The pilot, who Petrice referred to only as the colonel, was probably the squadron commander, Alex thought. He saw the man stub out his cigarette and place the butt in a zippered pocket of his flying suit. He couldn't see a pistol belt or shoulder holster, but as the officer swung his arms out and around as he walked—he looked like he was stretching away a muscle ache—Alex caught sight of a bulge under his left armpit.

"OK. Finished your photo shoot, Petrice? Good. I know it's a chore, but someone's got to do it and they don't want an ugly old white man like me in the news, do they?"

A circle of men was now raising the sides of the wire cargo net and linking them to one another with snap hooks. The mouth was pulled close and tied tight with cord.

The engines whined and the rotors started to turn slowly above their heads. Alex looked at each of his men and they all nodded back to him. It was nearly time.

Alex looked out the hatch of the helicopter, watching a herd of giraffe loping away from the noise of the helicopter as they raced along above the dry gray-green carpet of bush. The wind coming in through the opening provided a welcome relief from the day's heat. Alex felt a tap on his shoulder and looked up. The flight engineer was standing beside him, pointing to the black nylon backpack Alex had brought with him from the four-wheel drive.

They had just completed the fourth pickup of tusks on this trip—the ninth in total. There was one to go.

Joost leaned closer to him and yelled, "Give me your pack—I've got to move it!"

"I need the stuff in there!" Alex shouted back.

The flight engineer shook his head. "We're going to be nearly full after the next pickup. Let me stow it in the rear. It'll be safe." The helicopter started to bank.

He was right—there was barely enough room for Alex, his men and the two security guards as it was, and there was still one more load of tusks to come on board. Nevertheless, he could not risk handing over the pack. Joost grabbed the bag but Alex held tight.

"Give me the bag, please, *sir!*"

Alex wavered and was about to comply, thinking he could get to the backpack when they next touched down and the flight engineer was busy manhandling ivory, but then Joost reached across with his other hand and accidentally grabbed a nylon tab attached to a zip. As he pulled, the flap came undone, exposing the butt of an R5 assault rifle.

The flight engineer stared at the weapon, his mind trying to process the information his eyes were sending him. The public relations team were military people, but why would they be carrying weapons with them as well as cameras? He reached for the press-to-talk switch clipped to the front of his flying suit.

Alex jerked the bag violently back toward himself, pulling Joost off balance. As the man fell toward him, Alex shot his right fist up hard and fast, punching the man in the Adam's apple. He lurched backward, reaching for his neck with one hand.

Alex reached behind his back and pulled the Glock from the holster under his shirt. He leaned forward and grabbed the leads connecting the press switch to Joost's helmet, put his foot on the man's chest to hold him on the deck and ripped the cables free.

Novak and Kufa had needed no orders to spring into action, or warning that the plan's timing had suddenly been brought forward. Novak king-hit the black airman in the face, bringing forth a spurt of blood from his nose, while Kufa had the white man covered with his pistol, which he'd been wearing in a shoulder holster under his camouflage shirt. The African airman dropped his head between his knees, blood pulsing through his fingers, while Kobus dragged the men's R5s from under their seats. Novak moved to Alex's side and covered the flight engineer, still lying on his back. He was alive, though breathing was clearly a difficult task for him, for he was bright red in the face.

As Alex spun around he saw Petrice, the copilot, looking over her shoulder. She was open-mouthed with shock at the scene unfolding behind her. Alex had been scanning the helicopter cockpit instrumentation during the flight and had identified what he thought was the radio, judging by an illuminated display of numbers that looked like a radio frequency. He hadn't confirmed it with Kobus yet, but he prayed he was right as he raised his pistol and fired a bullet into it.

The Oryx banked sickeningly to the left as the pilot flinched away from the noise of the gunshot—still brutal even over the whine of the engines—and the shower of sparks that erupted from the console in front of him. Alex grabbed the rear of the pilot's seat and thrust the

barrel of his pistol up under the colonel's chin to reinforce the point
that the machine was now under new management.

Alex motioned to Kobus, who passed him his headphones. Awkwardly, Alex put on the headset one-handed.

"Mayday, Mayday, Mayday . . ." he heard Petrice saying. That
meant the internal intercom was still working, but was the woman's
message being transmitted to anyone else?

"Shut up or your colonel dies," Alex said to her.

Petrice looked at him, wide-eyed, and nodded.

"Who the devil are you?" the pilot asked.

"None of your business. Give her control of the aircraft. I want
her flying, not you." Alex pushed the pistol harder into his throat. The
pilot gave a slight nod and told Petrice to take over.

The helicopter lurched.

"Steady, Petrice. You're doing fine."

Alex reached around and undid the zip of the colonel's flying suit
enough for him to get his hand in and pull out the man's concealed
pistol. "Just keep flying straight and level," he said to Petrice. "I want
to hear if the Mayday message is acknowledged. If you say a word
without me telling you to, this man dies. Understood?"

Alex saw the copilot start to form a word with her lips, then think
better of it. She nodded her head instead.

"Clever girl. Hush now while we listen."

A few seconds later Alex heard a burst of static, then Captain
Steyn's voice. "Tiger One-Three, I say again, pickup five is ready.
Acknowledge?"

"Tiger One-Three this is ops, I say again, pickup is ready, Acknowledge?"

"Acknowledge his message," Alex said.

"Ops, this is Tiger One-Three, affirmative, over," Petrice said, her
voice quavering a little.

Alex held a finger to his mouth, telling her to say no more. She
stayed silent and kept the chopper straight and level. Alex glanced back

quickly over his shoulder and saw that Kufa and Novak had the two airmen on their knees, their hands fastened behind their backs with plastic cable ties. He looked back to the pilots.

"Tiger One-Three, this is ops. Assume you will return to base to get the comms problem sorted. Nothing heard this end, out."

Alex nodded to himself. His bullet in the radio had cost the helicopter the ability to transmit messages, but they were still able to receive. It was a lucky shot.

Alex pulled a piece of paper out of his shirt pocket and handed it to the pilot. "Program this waypoint into your on-board GPS, Colonel." He had to press the barrel of the pistol even harder into the man's neck to make him obey.

Once the colonel had entered the figures, Alex told Petrice to change course and head to the new destination. Kobus was standing beside Alex now, looking over his shoulder at the cockpit instrumentation. The Oryx banked to starboard, heading northeast. When Alex looked at him, Kobus nodded that the copilot was following the new course.

"When we get to that point you'll see a white Toyota Land Cruiser in a small clearing. You will land next to the vehicle and you two, the flight engineer, and the two airmen who were supposed to provide your security will get out. The cruiser will be disabled, but you can sit inside it for protection against animals and the sun. There is water in the vehicle. Your location will be given to the relevant authorities in due course. Do you understand what I have just told you?"

The pilot nodded, as did Petrice.

"Good. No one needs to get hurt. Do as ordered and all will be well."

"Get up, out of your seat now, please, Colonel." The man unbuckled his safety harness, unplugged his intercom leads and clambered out of his seat. Alex saw his face was scarlet with fury as he obeyed. Kobus quickly took his place and pulled on the bulbous flight helmet that Alex took from the colonel, while Novak covered him with an R5. Kufa tied the pilot's hands and had him kneel on the deck of the cargo compartment, next to Joost, who now seemed to be breathing easier, even though his face mirrored his superior's hate-filled rage.

Kobus's eyes and fingers roamed the instrument panel as he identified the myriad switches and readouts. Next he transferred his hands to the cyclic and collective controls, resting them there while the copilot flew the machine, ghosting her movements in order to get a feel for the helicopter.

Petrice turned to look at Alex, her mouth opening and closing, pantomiming speech. Alex nodded.

"This is a terrible thing you're doing. Profiting from the death of all those elephants," she said into the boom microphone extending from her helmet.

"This is a terrible day," Alex agreed. "Now just fly the bloody helicopter and shut up."

They crossed the snaking N'wanetsi River and Alex saw the white of the Land Cruiser starkly visible from far off. As they approached, Heinrich, Kevin and Henri emerged from the vehicle.

"Steady now, no heroics. Think of your commanding officer and your crew," Alex said to Petrice. He felt bad about manipulating the young woman, but he was concerned that if he'd left the senior pilot in charge the man might have done something rash—perhaps even deliberately crashing the helicopter to thwart their plan. He trusted that Petrice would do as ordered because she was younger and less experienced than the combat-hardened colonel.

As the helicopter slowed and began to descend, Kevin disappeared back inside the truck and popped the bonnet. Heinrich opened it fully, reached inside and yanked out a handful of leads, which he held aloft, grinning, as the Oryx touched down.

"OK?" Alex asked Kobus.

"I've got it," Kobus nodded.

"Treat her kindly," Petrice said.

"She's more responsive than the Russian beasts I usually fly, but I've got the hang of her."

Alex slumped forward as something or someone fell hard against his back.

He rolled to one side and Kufa slipped by him and landed on his side between the two pilots' seats.

The colonel had broken free after Novak hauled him to his feet and launched himself forward, head-butting Kufa and knocking him backward into Alex.

"Go, Joost, now!" the pilot yelled. The flight engineer then leaped out through the cargo hatch before Novak could strike him with the swinging butt of his R5. Unable to steady himself with his hands, Joost pitched face-first into the dirt as soon as he touched the ground, but scrambled up to his knees, then feet.

Novak raised his rifle to his shoulder instinctively, to fire on the man, but the colonel charged him, knocking him to one side as he fired. The bullet missed its mark.

Petrice hauled on the controls and the Oryx rose again into the air. Ten meters off the ground she banked viciously to port in an aggressive move that almost had the rotor tips scraping on the dirt. Novak slid out of the cargo hatch and landed hard in the bare dirt of the abandoned quarry site a few meters below.

Heinrich, Henri and Kevin were running back to the shelter of the Land Cruiser, away from the crazily jinking aircraft dancing above them.

Kobus was frantically trying to regain control of the aircraft, but all he was succeeding in doing was overcorrecting Petrice's maneuvers, which made the ride even rougher for those in the back.

Kufa had a hand on each of the pilots' seats and was dragging himself up to meet the two air force security guards, who had been left on board and had now gained the courage to stand and rush forward. Alex regained his balance, raised his pistol, aimed at the nearest man's thigh and fired. The man dropped to the floor and his companion either fell or decided to drop to the other man's side. The colonel had fallen onto his back thanks to Petrice's flying, and as he tried to stand Alex planted an army boot hard on his chest, pinning him down. He pointed the pistol between the colonel's blue eyes but saw no fear there.

He swiveled at the waist and pushed the gun into the back of Petrice's neck. "Take your hands off those controls. Now. Kobus, take control of this helicopter," he said through the intercom.

Alex felt the Oryx wobble and lurch a couple more times as control was transferred, but Kobus soon had her hovering steadily, and brought her back to terra firma with only a slight bump.

A flick of his pistol hand was all Alex needed to get Petrice to unbuckle and ease herself out through the cargo hatch.

Novak was standing at the opening ready to lift down the wounded airman, and Heinrich and Henri took charge of the other security officer. Kevin had run into the bush after Joost and had been easily able to catch the flight engineer, who was more used to flying across the hot thorny bushveld than running through it. He had him covered at gunpoint in the swirling dust of the makeshift landing zone.

Alex unclipped a green canvas bag emblazoned with a red cross from a bulkhead in the helicopter and tossed it out, so that it landed at the feet of the uninjured airman. He grabbed the colonel by one arm, lifted him to his feet then gave him a shove in the small of his back.

"You put the lives of those under your command at risk for nothing," he yelled at the colonel as the man climbed down from the helicopter, slowly and with dignity, finally surrendering his machine.

The pilot stopped and turned, looking back up at Alex crouched in the open hatchway. "I think you probably would have done the same thing."

Alex couldn't stop the hint of a smile from curling the corners of his lips. "That man's not badly wounded, but bandage him and keep him inside the vehicle, in the shade. Someone will be with you in the hour."

The pilot nodded, turned and walked away toward the Land Cruiser.

Alex ran a hand through his sweat-dampened hair. "Let's get moving."

The rest of his men climbed aboard the helicopter and Alex followed. He sat in the open cargo hatch, an R5 across his lap, watching the stranded air force personnel milling about the Land Cruiser as the helicopter climbed skyward.

It had a been a close call. He didn't want anyone killed on this operation, which he still hoped would be his last. He stared out at the brown bush racing beneath his boots and breathed deeply, waiting for the adrenaline to subside. What would have happened if Novak had shot and killed the flight engineer; or if the colonel's near-suicidal antics had led to the death of Petrice, or one of the two airmen who were supposed to have been providing security? He had aimed for the airman's leg, with the intention of wounding him not killing him, but Alex knew that if his aim had been even slightly off he might have nicked the man's femoral artery and he could have bled to death in minutes.

Risks.

It was what had driven him as a pirate. As much as his need for cash and building materials, he knew he was a junkie, still addicted to the rush his body was now recovering from. He stripped off his gloves and flexed the two remaining fingers on his left hand. The air crew would be able to provide a good description of him, Kufa, Novak, and Kobus, but it would be a little thing, like his disability, that would narrow the search inexorably to him.

The injury had never hampered him from doing anything—apart from typing or playing the piano with more than one finger—but it had ended his military career. He had been bitter at first, but later he'd realized that if he hadn't been injured in Afghanistan then he might never have fulfilled what he had believed had been his destiny since his family had fled Mozambique.

He needed Africa. It was as much of a drug as combat action or crime. He looked eastward over the horizon. The country of his birth, his home, was out there, not twenty kilometers distant. He would reclaim his birthright. He would commit no more crimes. He would live out his days, sated with the simple joys of living on this continent that was as beautiful as it was ugly, as peaceful as it was battle-scarred, as healing as it was deadly.

"Alex!" Novak tapped his shoulder and passed him the spare headset.

He put the headphones on and Kobus told him Steyn had just radioed them with a new message.

"He says that another herd of twenty-three elephants was spotted by the national parks helicopter a little while ago heading for a waterhole near Frank Cole's team. The parks helo had to return to Skukuza to refuel. Steyn wants us to find the herd and drive them toward Frank's team. He can't get to them by vehicle as the bush is too thick."

Alex scratched his chin. He wanted the ivory Cole had already harvested from the elephants he'd shot that morning. If they drove the herd onto his guns, Cole and most of his hunters would be busy shooting. He might only leave a couple of laborers to load the ready tusks.

"Let's do it." He explained what was going on to the rest of his crew.

Kobus found the elephants without any trouble. They were strung out in single file, walking across a wide-open grassy vlei. Ahead of them was an expanse of mopane trees that stretched on toward the Lebombo Mountains and the border with Mozambique. Frank would want them to make the herd turn left and move down the vlei, instead of heading for the waterhole in the middle of the floodplain and then disappearing into the thick mopane beyond to feed. At the far left-hand end the grassy expanse gave way to thinner scrubland. Frank's team, according to Kobus's reckoning, was about two kilometers in that direction.

"Concentrate on the big cow at the front," Alex said. He knew the rest of the herd would take its cue from the matriarch.

Alex climbed into the copilot's seat and found a pair of binoculars in a pouch on the side. He focused on the elephant as they circled the *vlei*. She was enormous, and sported a pair of long, curved yellowed tusks, each nearly the length of a man's body.

27

Not many things frightened her, but today she was scared.

It had been many years since she'd heard the clatter and whine of the machine that close above her. It swarmed around her like a huge angry bee. While she could fend off an attack by a pride of lions with her trumpet-blast scream and a flick of her mighty trunk, she hated bees.

She turned her face to the sun and spread her ears wide, then raised her trunk to sniff the air and scare it with her silhouette. She caught the oily stench of it, but it wasn't scared by her display.

She'd heard the popping in the distance earlier. It was something else she associated with the coming of the noisy flying beast. After the noise had died, in those years gone by, she had visited the bones of the others. She had sniffed them, rolled them with her huge padded feet and mourned for them. She had learned, from an early age, to associate those noises with death.

Her mother had taken her and her brothers and sisters and aunties on a tiring, arduous journey. Death had plagued them at every step and the popping and the clattering had filled most days of her early years. Her mother had taken them across the wide open grass and swamplands where she'd been born into a strange land.

Her mother had not known where to find water every day, and all of them felt the stress of her uncertainty. Yet still they trusted in her judgment. It was their way. They had passed the blood-soaked dirt and bleached white bones of more of their kind, but always her mother had kept them a step ahead of the rattle and hum of the killers.

They walked all day and all night, feeding on the move and stopping to slake their massive thirsts whenever they chanced upon water. The end of each day found them heading unfailingly into the setting sun.

Fires sometimes raged, racing through the parched mopane, leaving treats behind in the form of cooked, caramelized sap, which was one of the few pleasant memories she had of that long trek west. In time, they reached the mountains. Not the isolated peak she recalled from her birthplace, but a line of blue-green hills that stretched as far as she could see from left to right as she walked toward the red ball falling through the dust.

Her mother led them into those hills and it was an effort for all of them. One of her aunties gave birth one night, a long, painful affair made worse by the climb and the days without water. The tiny baby was stillborn and they all paused to touch and mourn it, but not for long. Her mother ushered them forward, with a prod of her tusks or flick of her trunk if needs be.

When they came to a stout fence she thought her mother would have to give up, but she summoned the remainder of her failing strength and rested her forehead against a post. She pushed, and one of the young bulls—a noisy, annoying beast, as most young males were—joined her at the fence. Soon another took up the challenge and slowly but surely the steel poles and wire mesh yielded to their combined weight. The little ones, as she was then, had to climb up the diamond patterned wire and drop off the other side.

It was a long, long time since she had come to her new home, but she had been safe here.

Things were different on the western side of the mountains, and they had all had to learn how to survive here. There were more humans, and more of their noisy, rolling, smoke-belching conveyances but, unlike the country of her birth, these did not always bring death.

She remembered the first time she saw one, on the floodplain beneath the mountain, how it had emerged, like an apparition, from the morning mist. She had screamed in terror, and heard something almost as fearful from inside the steel beast that confronted her. Her mother had nudged her little backside with her trunk and she had sniffed the creature inside the box. Not long after that time the truce that had existed between the elephants and the two-legs had ended. Every vehicle was a threat, every man a killer. They had learned to fear and to run.

But those days were gone and by the time she had taken over as the matriarch, after her old mother passed away silently one night, the herd had lost its fear of people in cars and trucks. They were an occasional nuisance, but nothing to fear.

The large angry bee, however, was different. Even here, west of the mountains, it was the harbinger of death. Not on the scale of her youth, but there was still the pop-popping in the distance, and the flensed bones and blood-soaked grass in its aftermath.

Her own daughter—her fifth surviving offspring—ran to her and huddled beneath her legs. She made a soothing sound that belied her own fear. She turned her head and watched the bee reach the far end of the vlei, then turn around and head back toward them. It was lower this time. Never had one come this close to her. She knew what her mother would have done. She would have run for the trees. The water could wait. She raised her trunk and sounded a shrill note, but the deep rumblings from her stomach gave her real orders to the herd.

She set off, her baby's tiny legs flashing in a blur to keep up, toward the mopane trees on the far side of the vlei. Behind her, the others needed no further encouragement. Instinctively, they raced to catch up with their leader and to crowd around her. They moved as a group now, a great gray mass thundering through the golden grass, rather than a straggling line of individuals. Safety lay within the family. They were as one in the face of danger. It was the same when the lions circled in the evening, looking for stragglers or wayward youngsters. Stay together and survival was possible.

"She's leading them past the water to the trees. Head her off," Alex said to Kobus through the headset's microphone.

Alex hated that he had to drive this herd of elephants onto Cole's guns. More than enough animals had been killed already, but if he ignored Steyn's request for assistance then the people on the ground would become suspicious. They needed to buy themselves as much time as possible. Also, if Cole was busy slaughtering this new herd then he and his men would pay little attention to Alex's men as they loaded the ivory from the animals the professional hunters had killed earlier.

Kobus overtook the herd and banked hard to the left, forcing Alex to reach out and grab the top of the instrument panel to steady himself. They were low now, close enough to the ground for the rotor wash to flatten the long grass of the vlei.

"She's turning."

"Good job," Alex said, though his face was grim.

The matriarch had veered left short of the trees, startled by the helicopter hovering not a hundred meters from her.

"Stay this side of them, between the herd and the trees, and slightly behind."

"Roger," Kobus said.

Alex could see vehicles at the far end of the flood-plain now. It had to be Cole and his team waiting in ambush. He guessed they hadn't traveled out in the grass in case they spooked the elephants into running away from them. Better to let the helicopter bring them onto the guns, like an airborne beater.

The matriarch lifted her trunk on the run. Alex couldn't tell from inside the chopper which way the wind was blowing, but perhaps her keen sense of smell had detected the men on the ground ahead of her.

"She's making for the trees again," he said into the microphone. "Head her off, Kobus."

The pilot dropped until the wheels of the big helicopter were almost skimming the long grass stems. Alex guessed that this work was best done by smaller, more nimble machines. He admired the way Kobus had gotten the feel of the aircraft so quickly. He increased speed and they edged up alongside the elephant. When she raised her trunk again it reached almost as high as the spinning rotors above. For a moment, Alex thought she might actually charge the Oryx.

She slowed and flared out her ears, flapping them in a vain attempt to scare off the thing that was tormenting her family.

Alex stared at her.

Kobus flared the nose upward, as if challenging the mighty cow.

"Hold steady," Alex said.

"She's stopped. I need to get her moving again," Kobus replied.

"I said hover here, damn it."

Novak had moved between the pilot and copilot's seats. He had been monitoring their conversations on the spare headset and he placed a hand on Alex's shoulder. "What is it, man?"

Alex opened his mouth to speak, but couldn't form a word. He was staring at the distinctive V-shaped notch in the elephant's left ear.

He was five years old again, sitting on his father's lap, his hands on the black steering wheel of the shiny new Land Rover.

"She's a little female," his father had said. He heard his British accent again, as clear as if he were sitting beside him now, in the helicopter. "She's about your age, Alex. She doesn't mean us any harm."

The elephant shook her head again. The thing wasn't moving now. She gave up her quest for the trees. She turned and headed along the vlei.

She smelled danger in front of her, in the trees, and the humans were on foot. She might have a chance at charging through them. She would let nothing stand in the way of the safety of her family. If only she could outrun the buzzing bee.

"Get in front of her," Alex said.

"What? Why, Alex? Cole and his men are up in the trees ahead. Can't you see them?"

Alex turned to stare at the pilot. "Yes I can bloody well see them. Get past the herd and get in between that cow and Cole."

Kobus turned to look at Novak, who just shrugged.

"Don't look at him. Just do as I tell you. Turn them back. I want you to chase them into the mopane bush, away from the culling team."

"All right. You're paying the bills."

The herd started running and Alex knew they would soon be in range of Cole's rifles. He took off the flying helmet and climbed out of the copilot's seat as Kobus drew level with the charging cow. She looked across at them but did not slow her stride.

Alex told Novak to give him his headset, then grabbed an R5 off one of the cargo seats and cocked it. He sat in the open hatchway, his legs dangling out. The ground rushed up to meet him as Kobus turned again and Alex was face to face with the charging elephant.

"She's not stopping, Alex. For fuck's sake, I think she's going to try to ram us!"

The elephant had her trunk down, curled between her tusks, and her ears pinned back—a sure sign, Alex knew, that she meant business and was ready to kill. He felt his stomach drop and Kobus increased power and climbed in a straight hover.

Alex pulled the rifle into his shoulder and flicked the selector switch to automatic. He squeezed the trigger and emptied the thirty-five rounds into the ground, just meters in front of the elephant.

She stopped.

Frank Cole strode from the treeline, his FN rifle up. His team of hunters emerged on either side of him. They were walking forward.

The elephants jostled each other, those in the rear of the herd colliding into those who had stopped on the matriarch's signal. There were trumpet blasts of confusion and two juvenile males ran around the group in a circle.

"Magazine!" Alex yelled back into the cabin of the helicopter. Kevin tossed him a fresh one and Alex ejected the empty mag and thrust home the new one. He yanked back on the cocking handle. "Drive them into the trees, Kobus."

"OK, OK."

The Oryx lurched, nose down, and Kobus flew a tight half-circle around the confused animals. He flared the nose up, facing down the matriarch again. She raised her trunk to sniff the air and must have seen the line of men walking toward her. The smell of gunpowder wouldn't have escaped her either. With the helicopter now on the other side of her, she headed away from the men on foot, toward the shelter of the trees she'd originally been making for.

"That's it," Alex said. "Come on, come on . . ."

The matriarch lengthened her stride and the herd stepped out to match her. She thundered eastward down the vlei then veered left into the mopane. Coppery leaves and small branches were shredded as the huge creatures charged into the foliage.

"Give her some space now," Alex said into the intercom.

Kobus climbed and Alex could see the elephants continuing unchecked toward the distant blue-green haze. He allowed himself a private smile. It was good to do the right thing for a change. Out in the clearing, he saw Frank Cole raise a fist to the sky. "Let's go pick up his ivory, before the old man gets back to it."

She ran until her big heart and lungs almost gave out. Behind her was her family. They were tired, scared, but alive.

The incline of the first row of hills slowed her. All was quiet now. There was no buzzing in the sky, no popping, no acrid chemical smell to scare her.

It was time for her to do as her mother had done and to lead her charges to safety, although this time she was going east, back toward the land of her birth.

She had expected to find the fence her mother and the other old ones had pushed down all those years ago, but it was gone. In time, they crested the final ridge and below them, spread out forever, was a forest. For the last few years the trees where she lived had never seemed to grow taller. In the bad years, when water was scarce, it was sometimes hard even to fill the bellies of all those who depended on her.

But the trees on this side of the mountains were taller than her. There were seed pods and leaves in the uppermost branches that not even she could reach, and shade for all of them from the hot afternoon sun. There was food for a lifetime here.

She felt safe, for she had come home.

"When we touch down, keep your sun visor down in case any of them get close to the helicopter," Alex said to Kobus. "There's a chance someone on the ground might have met one of the pilots."

They were coming up on the remains of the herd Frank Cole and his men had slaughtered in the morning. Just two African hunting scouts had stayed with the heaped ivory to guard it and help load it onto the helicopter.

Alex moved further back in the cramped cargo compartment to where Kufa was and shouted in his ear that he should climb into the copilot's seat and put on Petrice's helmet and pull the darkened visor down.

"But I'm not a woman!"

"I know, but at least you're the right color!"

Alex was first out the open hatch when the Oryx's wheels settled in the grass near the pile of tusks. The clearing looked like the abattoir it had become. The dry earth was soaked dark in patches and a pile of tusks was waiting for them.

They sweated hard loading the ivory and were nearly done when a Toyota Hilux emerged from the trees and bounced across the clearing, stopping a few meters short of the tips of the spinning rotors. Frank Cole got out, slammed the driver's door and strode across to Alex, who was passing tusks to Novak inside the helicopter. Kevin stood by with an R5 held loose in front of him.

"What the hell was that all about?" Cole yelled. "I want to talk to that fucking idiot of a pilot. The word around the camp this morning was that there was a black woman flying this thing. Was it her fault?"

"There was a bit of confusion on board. They hadn't done this sort of thing before," Alex said, hoping to calm the hunter.

"Well that was bloody for sure! And who opened fire? I'll throttle the stupid bastard myself. Couldn't they see we were down there? We could have been shot!"

Alex shrugged and passed the second-last tusk inside to Heinrich. He motioned to his men to get on board.

Undeterred, Cole walked to the cockpit and banged on the perspex.

He must have sensed someone was behind him for he turned around and saw Alex. "Hey! Something's not right, man. That copilot won't take off her helmet, but her body doesn't look like a woman's. All the guys were talking about her this morning."

Cole looked at Kobus now, cupping his hands on the windscreen to cut out the sun's glare. "The pilot's wearing national parks uniform, with honorary ranger tabs, and the copilot's got camo on instead of a flying suit. What's—"

Alex reached under his shirt and pulled out his Glock as Frank pulled the walkie-talkie out of the pouch on his belt.

"Give me the radio, Frank."

The hunter turned from the cockpit to Alex and shook his head. "Shit. I thought you looked too bloody hard to be a PR officer."

Frank was three meters away and he tossed the radio at Alex, perhaps expecting him to try to catch it and become distracted for a

TONY PARK

second. Alex ignored it and let it fall to the ground near his feet. "Back away. Slowly."

Frank raised his hands and looked over his shoulder, no doubt hoping one of his men would see something was amiss. "This'll cause a shit storm for the government and national parks. They won't be game to cull again, you know."

Alex kept his face impassive, but just waved the pistol a little.

Frank's face split into a grin. "I saw you during the shooting this morning. I watched your face when the butchering started. You're no poacher. You looked like you felt something for those elephants. What are you, some kind of animal rights activists or something?"

Ignoring the question, Alex reached into his pocket and pulled out a piece of paper. He balled it and tossed it at Cole's feet. "Give that to Colonel De Villiers. It's got GPS coordinates for the locations of the real PR team and the helicopter's crew. There's an airman with a bullet in his leg not far from here who'll need medical attention, but he'll live."

Cole nodded and Alex backed around the cockpit. He raised his free hand and twirled his finger in the air. At the signal he heard the engines reach a higher whining pitch. He lowered the barrel of his pistol, pointed toward the walkie-talkie and fired a shot. Frank was still grinning, hands up, as Alex sat in the open cargo compartment.

Across the toes of his boots, as the helicopter rose, Alex saw Frank break into a run toward his *bakkie.*

28

Alex could see Satara airstrip ahead and made out the cargo net full of the morning's ivory haul sitting waiting in the open. Two soldiers in camouflage fatigues were sitting on the ground next to the tusks, but they got to their feet at the sound of the approaching helicopter.

"I have to touch down before they attach the net to the hook under the helicopter," Kobus said into Alex's headphones.

"Why?" Kufa asked. He was still sitting in the copilot's seat, wearing Petrice's helmet.

Alex answered for Kobus, who had flared the nose to bleed off speed as they started to descend toward the airstrip. "The rotors build up static electricity while we're flying, particularly in dry dusty weather like this. Kobus needs to ground the helicopter to discharge the energy, otherwise when those guys touch the hook they'll get a shock that will knock them off their feet."

Kevin, wearing the flight engineer's helmet, lay on the floor of the cargo compartment watching the ground beneath them. "All clear," he said. Kobus had told him to take the position as he would need to relay instructions to him when it was time for the men on the ground to attach the cargo net to the hook. Kevin would have to direct Kobus left or right or backward or forward. It was called pattering, Kobus had told them.

They touched down about twenty meters from the two soldiers, who wore goggles to protect their eyes from flying debris, and helmets in case they bumped their heads on one of the Oryx's wheels while it was hovering above them. One man would attach the "donut," a looped nylon sling at the top of the net, to the hook, while the other man was there to hold on to the hook-up man's belt, steadying him against the massive downwash of the main rotor.

All the army, police and national parks officers who had been inside the base camp tents had come out to watch the helicopter pick up the ivory. Some had small digital cameras raised. Alex could make out the short, gray-haired figure of Colonel De Villiers. He felt sorry for the grief he was about to cause the man.

"OK, here we go," Kobus said.

The hook-up man was standing, holding the donut above his head to signal he was ready. Kobus would hover above him and Kevin would give minute directions to bring the helicopter's hook as close to the man as possible.

"Move right five meters ... four, three, two, one," Kevin said into the intercom, counting off the distance as Kobus brought the machine down out of its hover. "Forward. Three, two, one ..."

Kobus worked the controls gently and the helicopter responded.

"Over the load ..."

Alex saw a cloud of red dust on the road. "Cole's coming. Hurry it up."

"Going as fast as we can," Kobus said testily.

"Bring her down, Kobus, five ..." said Kevin.

"Shit, he's pointing his rifle out the window," Alex said.

Above the whine of the Oryx's twin turbine engines they heard the pop, pop of two gunshots fired in quick succession. The men and women who had been standing on the side of the airstrip watching the hovering helicopter now turned at the sound of gunfire. More than one reached for a sidearm. Alex saw De Villiers and a couple of staff officers break from the crowd and move to cut off the approaching *bakkie*.

"These blokes are looking nervous," Kevin said into the intercom.

Alex dropped to his belly and stuck his head out into the rotor wash to look underneath the helicopter. As Kevin had said, the two soldiers who were supposed to be hooking up the cargo net had been distracted by the noise of gunfire and the commotion near the tents. Kevin waved to them and pointed furiously at the hook.

Alex looked up and saw De Villiers, Cole and two other men in army uniform sprinting toward them. De Villiers was waving his hands above his head. Cole had his FN in his hands and the other two soldiers carried R5s.

The soldier holding the donut sling still had his arms raised, though he was watching the approaching officers. "Nearly on," Kevin said. "Go forward, Kobus, and you'll snatch the bloody thing out of this idiot's hands."

Kobus nudged the helicopter forward.

"Nearly on the hook," Kevin said. "Don't stop now."

The hook-up man felt the sling twitch in his hands and looked up at Kevin and Alex, startled. He glanced back at the running men and then snatched the sling back off the hook. He shook his head furiously.

Frank Cole stopped halfway across the width of the airstrip and raised his rifle.

"Shit, they're firing at us!" Kobus jerked back on the stick and the helicopter rose a couple of meters and banked to the left.

The two soldiers needed no further explanation. They dropped the slings, disentangled their feet from the pile of tusks and the wire mesh of the net, and sprinted away.

"This is bullshit. I'm getting us out of here," Kobus said.

"Wait!" Alex got to his knees, grabbed his R5, slung it over his head and across his body and vaulted out of the helicopter.

"Bloody madman," Kevin said.

Novak tapped Henri and Heinrich on the shoulders and lifted his own rifle to his shoulder and pointed it out the open hatch. "Covering fire! Aim short, don't kill anyone unless you have to!"

Colonel De Villiers had stopped Frank Cole from firing more shots, forcing down the barrel of the hunter's weapon with a slap of his hand. He wanted the hook-up team safely away from the helicopter first; but now the men were clear, Cole and the other two armed soldiers took up firing positions.

Alex hit the ground heavily and rolled, the rifle digging painfully into his back and side. Bullets raised geysers of dirt on the ground around him, and he crawled to the far side of the net full of ivory. He didn't think the tusks would provide great protection against copperjacketed lead, but he would be out of sight for a few moments. Spent brass cartridges rained down around him from the helicopter overhead and Alex could see the winking muzzle flashes from Novak, Heinrich and Henri's rifles. He looked up and Kevin, still peering over the rim of the cargo compartment floor, gave him an urgent thumbs-up.

Alex clambered up onto the pile of ivory. He slipped and felt the sharp point of a tusk jab him painfully in the right calf. He carried on, groping in the choking, blinding dust for the mouth of the net and the nylon slings attached to it.

Cole, De Villiers and the other riflemen had dropped to their bellies in the long grass in response to the fire coming from the Oryx, but they were still trading bullet for bullet. On the edge of the airstrip police and soldiers were climbing into *bakkies.*

Alex found the round donut sling and stood, raising it above his head. He heard the whine and zing of bullets cleaving the air around him. Come on, come on, he willed Kobus. He could see Kevin talking into his mouthpiece and slowly the helicopter leveled out and started coming down toward him. The sheer bulk of the mechanical beast eclipsed the sun and Alex stretched up to meet the oncoming hook. Kevin guided the pilot to him.

As Alex slipped the ring over the point of the hook he heard three or four bullets strike the metal skin of the bird, followed by a scream of pain. The ivory under his feet shifted as another fusillade ripped into the precious cargo.

Alex gave Kevin a thumbs-up to confirm the hook was securely attached, but the Australian was pointing over Alex's shoulder. He turned and saw trucks full of police and soldiers bouncing across the dirt and grass toward them.

"Go! Go!" Alex screamed, pointing upward. Kevin relayed the order and the Oryx started to climb.

Alex unslung the rifle from his shoulder and held it with his good hand. He opened fire with a wild burst in front of the oncoming trucks and one swerved. The driver overcorrected and the rear of the *bakkie* slid hard to the right. The second truck was just behind him and the driver couldn't brake in time to miss him. The two vehicles collided and the one that was already sliding spun three-hundred and sixty degrees. Two policemen who had been standing in the tray were thrown into the dirt. Alex wrapped his left arm around the now taut nylon sling that attached the cargo net to the hook. He dug his feet into the holes in the net's mesh, and the jumble of shifting tusks below.

Muzzle flashes winked at him from the ground, and though the seconds dragged like hours, they were soon sixty meters off the ground, heading toward the Lebombo Mountains and Mozambique.

Alex screamed with a mix of relief, elation and the wild, terrifying euphoria that comes from being shot at and surviving. As he swung below the helicopter, the slipstream flapped his clothes and tousled his dark hair.

It was the ride of his life, and it was taking him home.

29

Jane came to, in darkness.

It was hot and stuffy. She heard the continuous dull throb of an engine somewhere, and the vibration it sent through the bare metal springs of the bed she was lying on mirrored the steady pounding in her head.

She raised a hand to her forehead and wiped away perspiration but not the pain.

She sat up and felt dizzy, so she lay back down again for a moment. Her back felt scored by the imprint of the surface she'd been lying on. She was wearing the same business suit she'd had on when she'd left to meet the police detective in Cape Town, though her shoes were missing, along with her belt, watch, rings and bracelet.

Taking a deep breath she raised herself again, slower this time. When she placed her feet on the floor she felt warm bare steel. She let her body adjust to the change in position and, resting her hand on the railing at the foot of the bed, she stood. She swayed a little and at first thought it was another case of lightheadedness, but then realized she was not the only thing moving. She was on board a ship and could feel a mild swell. Not as it might have been on a small boat, but more like the gentle rocking she'd experienced during her weeks on board the *Penfold Son.*

Jane walked slowly away from the bed, hands outstretched in the blackness, until she came to a wall. She felt the steel and confirmed by the number of paces it had taken her what she had begun to suspect—she was inside a shipping container.

In one corner was a steel bucket, which she discovered by painfully stubbing her toe against it. It was empty. In another corner was a full bucket. She dropped to her knees. It smelled odorless so she guessed it was water. She realized then how thirsty she was, but she wasn't sure if the water was safe. Jane got back down on her knees and scooped some water into her mouth. It was lukewarm, but she gulped down several handfuls. She was perspiring, so she shrugged off her cropped gray jacket.

Jane sniffed the air as she stood. It was dank inside the container, but there must be airholes drilled somewhere. If so, that meant it was either nighttime or she was inside the hold and the lights were turned off. She listened closely, and above the engine noise she heard the slight hum of wind rushing along the metal sides of the container. She was on deck. She had no idea how long she'd been unconscious after she'd been dragged into the van and drugged. What she did know, however, was that she had to urinate.

She counted her paces back to the bucket, found it and undid the button and zip on her suit pants and lowered them.

Cooler but saltier air flooded the container and she squinted, holding one hand to her eyes, as a powerful torchlight blinded her. Acutely embarrassed, she tried to stand and pull her pants up at the same time.

"Stay still! Don't you fucking move a muscle, bitch. Keep squatting there for us." The accent was American and she knew, with dread, who it was. Mitch Reardon. "Remember me, cunt?"

Jane bit her lower lip to stop from crying. She didn't want to give him the satisfaction. She remembered how she had left him crying in pain on the floor of the basement of Alex's hotel. She shivered.

"That's quite enough of the name calling, Mitchell."

"George..." she started to stand.

"No. Do as Mitchell says, Jane. Stay where you are."

She was confused. "For God's sake, let me pull my pants up, George."

He said nothing and she couldn't see either man, but the one with the torch strode across to her as she started to rise, and swung the long-handled light against the side of her head. She dropped to one knee, knocking over the bucket. The dull thud in her head turned to blinding pain and as she righted herself she saw glints of light at the periphery of her vision.

"You'll fucking learn to do as you're told," Mitch said.

"Indeed she will," George said from behind the blinding light. "She's a smart girl, aren't you, Jane?"

"What..." she coughed. "What do you want, George?"

"Aha. No games now? No misdirections? No one to blame for your predicament but yourself, now, Jane, is there? Good. We'll come to the point then. The boys found the original tape and memory stick in your handbag, along with a copy on a disk in an envelope addressed to your parents. Very clever, but too bad you didn't make it to the post office. Did you make any other copies I don't know about? Did you send or e-mail it anywhere?"

"YouTube."

At an unseen signal Mitch moved forward and grabbed a handful of Jane's hair. She screamed and he half pushed, half dragged her so that she rocked back and fell on her bottom, her pants still around her knees. Mitch flashed the torch down on her nakedness and she pressed her thighs together. When she looked up at him she saw he was carrying a compact assault rifle in his other hand. He was also wearing some kind of headset with a cylindrical object attached to it that looked like a small telescopic lens. She guessed it was a night-vision device.

"Don't bruise her too much, Mitchell. It won't look good on camera." Mitch retreated, holding the light up into her eyes again.

Jane knew her worst nightmares were coming true. "You got the only copy I made when your thugs grabbed me. Who was it, Van Zyl, or this small-pricked psychopath?"

The light moved and Jane heard the squeak of Mitch's rubber-soled combat boots on the bare steel floor. "No, Mitch. Ignore her insults. We've got several days' grace."

"You're going to kill me, aren't you?"

Jane heard the groan again as the container door started to swing shut. Mitch switched off the light and the two men stood there, in silence. Jane was too scared to move in case she was hit again. After seconds, or minutes, George spoke, so softly she had to strain to hear him above the throb of the diesel engines. She couldn't see either of them in the dark, though she could smell Mitch's sweat and George's aftershave. She'd never liked either.

"I may do, Jane. But whether I do or not is very much up to you. Certainly, you won't ever see London, or your family, again."

A sob escaped her, despite her best attempts to show him no weakness. The sound of his footsteps echoed off the steel walls as he walked around her. She thought about making a move on them. George might be carrying a pistol, or she could try to grab Mitch's rifle in the dark. It would be better to go down fighting, quickly, she thought, than endure whatever they had planned for her.

"But if you cooperate with us, you will save your own life, Jane."

She moved silently to her hands and knees and started to crawl toward the sound of George's voice. Her eyes probed the darkness, then she saw the movement of a tiny red light.

Mitch laughed. "Hey, George, your bitch is down on her knees coming toward you. Maybe she's hungry for some cock."

Jane froze and looked toward the sound of the American's voice. She saw the pinprick of red light again and cursed. He must have switched on his night-vision monocular and he'd been watching her every move. Dejected, she sank down on her haunches.

"She's still now," Mitch said.

"Thank you, Mitchell, and, as I said before, keep the obscenities to a minimum—for now, at least. As I was saying, Jane, if you are completely honest with me, I will let you live, if you wish, or I will kill you quickly."

"And if I live?" she whispered into the impenetrable gloom.

"A Chinese business associate of mine has expressed a desire to purchase you from me."

"What? You're fucking crazy, George, I wouldn't—"

"Hush. White slavery is not a thing of fiction, Jane. There are men in the Middle East who would pay good money for a European woman—blondes, especially. Who knows, you may even be well treated."

"You're sick. I'd rather die."

"As I said, that's also an option. If you tell me what I need to know, I'm happy to kill you quickly, instead of selling you. If not, I'll let Van Zyl and his men use you for a few days. Mitch has expressed a desire to be first."

"Yes, ma'am!" Mitch laughed out loud again.

When silence filled the shipping container again George continued his measured monologue. "If you still refuse to cooperate, I'll have your mother and father abducted and I'll let you listen, on the satellite phone, while a man who specializes in extracting information and money from people begins severing their joints, starting with the first knuckle joint of each of their little fingers."

Jane swallowed her tears. She knew, then, that he had won. He would live, as a free man, and she would die, her body tossed overboard into the Indian Ocean.

She wished, now, with all her might, that she hadn't been so

harsh on Alex, hadn't forced him out of her life, and not just because he might have protected her from these men. The truth, which
she would never be able to tell Alex, was that she was fairly sure she
loved him.

30

Colonel De Villiers looked around the tent for someone to blame.

As commanding officer of the military component of the operation, the buck stopped with him. He'd thought it would be a good way to end a thirty-five-year career in the South African Army—a high point that would set the benchmark for future culling operations. Instead, it was his ticket to ignominy. He had summoned all the senior police, army, air force and national parks representatives to a crisis meeting. People were talking on cell phones, their frantic reports filling the tent with nothing more than hot air. De Villiers ran a finger around the neck of the T-shirt under his camouflage battle-dress shirt. He looked at Jacob Mandile, from national parks' investigative services, raising his eyebrows hopefully as Mandile snapped his mobile phone shut.

Mandile shook his head. "Our helicopter is still at Skukuza refueling. It's doubtful they'd catch the Oryx, even if Mozambican radar is able to pick it up."

"Thank you, Jacob." De Villiers turned to a female African staff officer. "Winnie, where the hell is Captain Steyn?"

"I'll—" Before the officer could give an excuse, Steyn strode into the tent, threading his way through the crush of men and women in blue, khaki and camouflage.

"Sir! Good news."

"It had better be, Steyn," the colonel said. "Where the hell have you been, man?"

Steyn fought to slow his breathing. He wiped sweat from his forehead and eyes. "Sir, I regret that there was something I didn't tell you, something the air force was planning today"

De Villiers gritted his teeth and balled his fists. "Get. On. With. It."

"Yes, sir, sorry, sir. When I found out that the army camera team was going to be traveling with the Oryx to Skukuza, I made some calls to a friend of mine who's the operations officer at Air Force Base Bloemspruit. I knew that one of their helicopters was going to be arriving at AFB Hoedspruit today, to refuel, after taking part in an exercise with Seven SA Infantry Battalion at Phalaborwa, and—"

Everyone in the tent was silent now, watching the red-faced man. "Steyn, you're wasting valuable minutes. We've just heard that the parks helicopter wouldn't be able to catch up with the poachers from Skukuza, so how can another Oryx catch up with them from further away?"

"It's not an Oryx, sir. And it's already on its way here. In fact, it should be here any minute now. It was going to rendezvous with the aircraft carrying the ivory, so the cameramen could get pictures of it in flight, over the Kruger Park. I thought it would be good public relations for the air force and I was going to tell you, but then . . . well, all this happened."

De Villiers could feel his cheeks reddening with rage. He was going to throttle this air force *poephol* if he didn't give him some good news soon.

Steyn drew a deep breath and held up both hands, palms outward, as if trying to ward off the salvo he knew the colonel was about to fire. "Sir, it's a Rooivalk!"

De Villiers's mouth opened and he stared at the air force captain, but the younger man had stopped talking. He was beaming at him like a child who thinks he has just done something monumentally impressive and is awaiting a word of praise. "Tell me it's armed, Steyn."

The captain nodded, still grinning broadly. "Eight Mokopa laser-guided antitank guided missiles and an F2 twenty-millimeter cannon in the nose with seven hundred and fifty rounds, sir."

"How far away is it?"

The air force officer looked at his watch. "It should be here any minute now. I ordered the pilot to divert here to Satara immediately. I hope that's all right, sir."

De Villiers's face showed the merest hint of a smile for the first time since the Oryx had taken off toward Mozambique. He started issuing orders to half-a-dozen staff officers, telling them to contact a general in Pretoria and the office of the Minister for Defense, among others who would need to authorize the action they were about to take. He was asking Mandile to find out from his superiors what would happen if the ivory was destroyed when the whine of turbine engines and the *thwap* of rotor blades cleaving hot air silenced all conversation.

The canvas walls of the tent were snapping and billowing against their poles as the colonel walked outside, a hand shielding his eyes from the glare of the afternoon sun and the stinging wall of dust. He looked up. Ordinarily he would have cursed the pilot for such a reckless, ostentatious show, coming in low over the headquarters to land.

Now he could have kissed him.

Steyn and De Villiers ran, heads bent, to the Rooivalk. The name was Afrikaans for "Red Kestrel," but the colonel thought South Africa's homegrown two-seat attack helicopter looked more like a shark. Long, sleek, fast and deadly, the Rooivalk had had its detractors over the years it had taken to get the aircraft from the drawing board to the air, but De Villiers now thought it the most beautiful thing he'd ever seen.

A refueling truck pulled up beside the gunship and two airmen got out.

The pilot who opened the cockpit hatch was a tall, broad-shouldered African man who looked no older than twenty-five. He had a narrow mustache and perfect teeth and he gave crisp, authoritative orders to the refuelers before turning his attention to the two officers.

"Howzit," the pilot said to Steyn, extending a hand.

"Colonel De Villiers," Steyn said, "this is Lieutenant Oliver Msimang. He's one of the finest helicopter pilots we've got."

Msimang ignored the compliment and shook the colonel's hand.

"Steyn's explained the situation?" De Villiers asked.

"Yes, on a secure back channel," Msimang yelled above the noise of the still-turning engine.

"I'm waiting on final approval from the powers that be," De Villiers said. "But if it comes through, can you shoot down the Oryx, Lieutenant? Can you pull the trigger and down one of our own helicopters?"

"I've been waiting all my life for the chance, sir."

De Villiers ran his eyes along the camouflage panels of the helicopter. Msimang had clambered down from the pilot's cockpit, which was situated above and behind the weapons officer, a white man who was busy checking displays and instruments in front of him. Hot exhaust gases from the twin Makila turbo-shaft engines billowed around them. "Can you catch them, though? I've read that the Rooivalk and the Oryx have the same powerplant."

Msimang nodded. "That's true, sir, but we're lighter and sleeker than he is. Also, from what Steyn tells me, they're carrying a tonne or more of ivory in a net. That'll increase their drag and reduce their speed dramatically."

De Villiers pointed to the stubby wing on their side of the helicopter, from which four missiles hung. "What about those?"

Msimang shook his head. "They're antitank missiles—air to ground only. We can carry air-to-air missiles. If we had those I'd be able to blow this guy out of the sky before he even saw me." Msimang walked to the nose of the aircraft and slapped a palm on the long bar-rel of the twenty-millimeter cannon that jutted forward from a tur-ret mounted in the helicopter's chin. "It'll have to be this baby. And Jaco—that's my weapons officer—never misses."

The white man knew they were talking about him. He looked across at De Villiers and grinned, giving him a thumbs-up.

"The 16 Squadron motto is *Hlaselani.* It means "attack," sir. We'll find that Oryx and we'll slaughter it like a lion taking a buck."

De Villiers nodded, but his face remained grim. He'd spent enough time in the bush to know that the desert-dwelling oryx with their long pointed horns were dangerous when attacked, and that lions often shied away from them.

Jose drained the dregs of his bottle of Manica beer as the chartered twin-engine turboprop executive aircraft taxied under the control of the African marshaller and pulled up outside the Vilanculos Inter-national Airport terminal building.

Jose left a crumple of Meticas notes on the table and winked at the pretty waitress, who scooped up the generous tip and stuffed it into the lacy bra poking out from the open top of her white blouse. Jose would have liked to linger longer, but business was business.

He excused himself as he stepped over the bucket of the cleaner who was kneeling scrubbing the steps which led to the terminal's roof-top bar and restaurant. He moved through the small terminal with confidence and greeted the customs and immigration officials with a friendly "*Ola.*" One was his brother-in-law, the other a cousin. As he shook hands with each man he palmed them green fifty-dollar bills, which were secreted as hastily and expertly as the waitress had done.

Jose pulled on gold-rimmed aviator sunglasses as he stepped out onto the baking black tarmac of the runway, which simmered under the unforgiving midday sun. "Welcome, Mister Chan, or *Bom dia*, as we say here."

The gangster wore a lightweight beige cotton suit with a black open-necked shirt. He was followed down the stairs by a shaven-headed bodyguard. Jose noted the bulge under the man's navy blazer and assumed his boss, Chan, would be armed as well. Jose's own Glock was in a shoulder holster under his loudly patterned beach shirt. He could handle these two if there was trouble. Alex had warned him to be vigilant.

"Is the *Peng Cheng* ready to sail? Where is Captain Wu?"

Jose's African blood was instinctively offended at the gangster's abruptness. He wondered if Chan hated black people. Criminals such as Chan and the Chinese government were pillaging his country's lands and waters to feed their greed and their people's hunger for resources and possessions. If Chan despised Jose for being African, then it was nothing compared to Jose's dislike of the mobster. "Your ship is moored at Ilha dos Sonhos, fueled and ready. Captain Wu and two of his crew have been shopping in the markets for fresh fruit and vegetables for your voyage. We're joining them just now."

Chan nodded and looked around him. He spoke rapidly in Mandarin to his bodyguard, who turned back to the aircraft's copilot and relieved him of a briefcase and a green canvas and brown leather safari carry bag.

Thanks to the gratuities Jose had paid his relatives, Chan and his bodyguard, whom Jose learned was also called Wu, passed through the customs and immigration formalities in a matter of seconds. Jose got into the driver's seat of his black BMW, leaving Chan's sour-faced bodyguard to open the back door for his master. Jose would be damned if he was going to kowtow to the bastard, even though Alex had told him to treat Chan civilly.

Mitch held the body of Angel Guitterez over the dhow's starboard gunwale. He lowered her head until her frizzy black hair kissed the turquoise water. He thought her face looked serene, almost beautiful, now that he had closed her eyelids.

When the waters washed over the gash in her throat he had to grip her sequined red top even tighter as her body literally started to fill. He watched, fascinated, as the blood coagulated and curled into a fluttering submerged streamer of red that tailed the wooden boat and mixed with its wake. It would, he hoped, attract the sharks.

"Goodbye, babydoll," he said as he released his grip on the prostitute. Angel's body, weighted with water, sank quickly from sight. He thought of her writhing and thrashing under his grip, after he had killed the dhow's captain in front of her. What a shame there wasn't time to satisfy his sexual thirst. He'd slake it soon enough on the Island of Dreams, which was growing with every second, from speck to blob to enticing mound on the horizon in front of him. He adjusted the tiller then unceremoniously dragged the muscled body of the skipper, his throat also slashed, from the pink bilge waters, and tossed him over the side.

In the center of the dhow was a wooden box lined with heat- and salt-corroded corrugated iron and filled with sand. This served as the ship's galley and a mound of charcoal glowed in the center. Mitch finished the job the captain had begun, just before Mitch had killed him, and poured tea into a tin mug. He blew on the hot liquid and sipped it. Life was good, he said to himself.

That morning, Angel had brought him the news he'd been waiting for. Jose and a couple of the Chinese sailors from the *Peng Cheng* had arrived in Vilanculos and the crewmen had gone shopping. Jose, he knew, would be heading to the airport to wait for Chan, just as George Penfold had predicted.

Angel missed nothing of what went on in town, particularly near the small port where she plied her trade, and she had advised him when Jose had ferried Kevin, Heinrich, Henri and Kufa to the mainland, and of their departure on the Pelican Airways flight to South Africa.

It was time for him to strike. The island and its arsenal would be unguarded.

Mitch steered his way through the gap in the coral reef and lowered the dhow's ragged, patched sail. When the keel shushed home on the sandy beach he jumped off, not bothering to anchor or tether the vessel. He wouldn't be needing it again. It drifted slowly out from shore, riding the strong current with just the ghosts of a man and woman as crew. His spine tingled, but in a good, exciting way.

He walked up the beach carrying his docksiders in his left hand and his fishing knife in his right. "Hi, honey, I'm home!"

George Penfold scanned the horizon with his binoculars. It was good to be back on the bridge of a ship, in his rightful place, as master. Even though he owned the entire company and its fleet, there was nothing quite so satisfying as being addressed, once again, as "Captain."

Beside him, Piet van Zyl buckled the black nylon pistol belt around his waist and zipped up his combat vest. He carried enough ammunition in the magazines in his chest pockets, and strapped to his left thigh, to kill more than three hundred human beings. They were only hunting six today, but they were through taking chances.

"Any further news from Reardon?" George asked Van Zyl.

The mercenary fitted a magazine to his M4 assault rifle and cocked it. "No. Just that he had taken control of the armory on the island, as planned, and had armed the *Peng Cheng*'s crew and taken care of Tremain's man who'd brought Chan to Ilha dos Sonhos. Reardon's staying on the island, as planned, and the *Peng Cheng* sailed an hour ago. She's in international waters by now."

George nodded. "Reardon worries me. He's a psychopath. What are you smiling at, Van Zyl?"

"Nothing. Mitch is the right man for the job. He's betrayed his comrades and given us the location of the pirate base. With us on board the *Peng Cheng* and her crew carrying weapons, there's no way Tremain and his men will escape now."

It wasn't only politics that made for strange bedfellows, George mused as he stared out to sea. He'd had a long, profitable and illegal business relationship with Valiant Chan for many years. The late Iain MacGregor had rendezvoused with the *Peng Cheng* on many occasions, usually transferring drugs to the smaller freighter, which Chan's man Wu would then land in Mozambique or on isolated spots on the South African coastline.

When George had killed the prostitute Chan had told him that his men would dispose of the body, and that George would have to "compensate" him for his men's efforts, the risk involved, and Chan's loss of earnings because of the woman's death. Chan didn't threaten, verbally, to do anything with the tape, but he did tell George that he would hand it over once he'd received his compensation. Chan was too polite to rise to George's accusation of blackmail, but they both knew what was going on.

Following the pirates' raid on the *Peng Cheng* and the *Penfold Son*, Chan had told George, via a secure phone, that Wu had confessed to telling the pirates that the package he had handed over to the *Penfold Son*'s engineer was worth a million pounds. In fact, George had paid only two hundred thousand. Chan had apologized for Wu's actions and said he'd thought the man had made up the figure to tempt the pirates into letting him and his ship go, while they went in search of a juicier target. Wu's strategy had backfired, as he had ended up incarcerated at the pirates' base and would at some time in the future, Chan promised George, pay for his ill-thought remarks to the hijackers.

The pair of them had talked at length about the growing number and increasing audacity of pirate attacks along the coast. In a previous meeting Chan had floated the idea of stealing several tonnes of ivory from the South African National Parks board once the authorities reinstated their controversial elephant cull. George had admired the boldness of the idea, but agreed with Chan that neither of them had the people or the logistics to steal the tusks and get them to the coast. "I'm a smuggler, not a thief, Valiant. There's a fine line."

Chan had told George that he had received a ransom e-mail from the pirates and had a mind to see if they were interested in getting involved in the ivory heist.

"Interesting," George had said. "You want them to do your dirty work and I want them dead." At the time he'd thought the pirates had stolen the tape from MacGregor's safe, as well as killing the roguish old Scot, kidnapping Jane and damaging his beautiful new ship. There were plenty of reasons why he wanted them eliminated. Even though he now knew Jane had hidden the tape and betrayed him, he still wanted this Tremain and his crew wiped out. He gripped the binoculars hard in his hands, his knuckles showing white. Jane had obviously been helped in getting the tape back and it seemed she had been in cahoots with the pirates all along. If she knew what was on it, then so would they.

"Perhaps we can both benefit from me forming a temporary alliance with these pirates," Chan had said, reading his mind. "It will not be in my interest to have these men roaming the seas at will, and armed with the knowledge of my role in a massive theft of ivory. I will want them gone as much as you, once I have my ship back and the ivory loaded on board. It seems you have your own small army at your disposal, George. Perhaps between us we can do our bit to stamp out maritime crime?"

George shifted his gaze from the horizon back to Van Zyl, standing beside him. Tremain had outwitted them all more than once, and he hoped the South African's confident optimism wasn't misplaced. "Don't come back to my ship until the job's finished. Understood?"

Van Zyl nodded.

"After you've disposed of Tremain and his gang, and the ivory's safely on board the *Peng Cheng*, I want you to go to Ilha dos Sonhos and kill Reardon."

"I'll do it, but why?"

"I don't want some murderous nutter setting up another band of buccaneers on that island. I've got ships to run up and down this coast. Also, I can't trust him not to double-cross us in the future."

Van Zyl nodded again. He waved his hand in the air, signaling his men to board the RHIB. Five minutes later they were laying a swathe of furious white foam on the waters of the Indian Ocean.

They stayed low, following the ribbon of white-gold sand that ran like a highway, south to north, dividing the emerald inland from the indigo ocean. Alex checked his watch.

"Turning now," Kobus said, and Alex gripped the back of the pilot's seat as the Oryx banked to the right.

Novak had lowered the winch cable soon after they crossed the Lebombo Hills and Alex had taken the green canvas satchel attached to the rescue loop and buried the bag as deep as he could beneath several layers of tusks. It had been a tricky job, but with the safety harness now looped around his torso and under his arms he'd been safe enough.

They were right on time, but Alex still had to wipe the sweat from his brow with the back of his gloved hand. "How's the fuel?"

"Tight," said Kobus, "but we'll make it. Just. What was in that bag?" he asked over the radio as Alex moved behind the pilot's seat and looked forward through the cockpit.

"An insurance policy."

The pilot was too busy to query Alex any further.

"Up ahead," Kobus said into his microphone, and pointed.

Alex blinked and refocused his eyes. He saw the speck and pointed it out to Novak. "Get everyone in the doors. Cover all angles, all approaches."

Alex took off his headset, as they all knew the plan from here on in. Novak helped him fasten the padded yellow rescue sling around his body once again.

Alex checked the rifle slung across his chest. It was cocked and he flipped off the safety catch. He felt the nose of the helicopter lift, and the airspeed bleed off as Kobus approached the ship.

Kevin was lying on the floor of the cargo compartment, in the same position he'd occupied during the hook-up of the net full of ivory. He was counting off the meters between the chopper and the ship, speaking into the flight engineer's headset.

Alex braced himself with a hand on the hatch and leaned out. Two Chinese crewmen stood on the raised teak-and-plywood platform that had been added to the stern of the *Peng Cheng* by Wu and his crew during their last few days of internment on Ilha dos Sonhos. Around the landing pad hung a net made of knotted rope, wide and strong enough to catch anyone who might have to leap off the structure in case of an emergency. It was an idea Alex had borrowed from U.S. Navy aircraft carriers. One of the men on the makeshift helipad held up a bamboo pole insulated with thick rubber and anchored by a cable to the platform. As the net descended above him he touched it with the pole, discharging the static.

Kobus settled into a hover and the two crewmen retreated to the edge of the structure, holding hands up to their eyes to protect them from the downwash. The helicopter slowly turned, the net hanging a couple of meters above the wooden deck. Alex could see Captain Wu and Chan standing in the open wing of the bridge. Chan was waving at them, pointing downward with his thumb, like a Roman emperor giving a death sentence.

Alex stepped out of the cargo compartment, letting the winch cable take his weight. He nodded to Novak, who pressed the button to lower him. Alex turned slowly through three hundred and sixty degrees as he descended to the platform, giving him a chance to survey as much of the ship as was visible from the outside. He noted a couple more crewmen in baggy shorts and grimy off-white singlets. None of them was armed.

Odd, he thought.

With so much ivory and so much money at stake Chan would

have been as wary as Alex was of a double cross. Chan was scurrying down a ladder. As Alex unclipped himself from the harness Chan jogged across the open cargo deck between the helipad and the bridge. He lurched slightly from side to side. Although the swell was negligible the gangster had not been on board long enough to find his sea legs.

Alex stood still, ignoring the rotor downwash that flicked his long hair about his face.

Chan cupped his hands on either side of his mouth. "PUT MY IVORY DOWN ON THE DECK!" He gestured furiously at the laden net.

Alex shook his head. "HALF! UP FRONT!"

Chan mouthed something in Mandarin.

Alex looked up at Kevin, whose head was hanging over the edge of the cargo floor. He raised his thumb. Kevin spoke into the intercom and Alex reached for the swinging rescue harness and started to put his head through it.

"WAIT, WAIT! I GUESSED YOU WOULD DO SOME-THING LIKE THIS!"

Alex gestured up at Kevin with an open palm and removed his head from the harness again. Chan waved at Wu, who dispatched a young crewman from the bridge. The boy carried a black nylon sports bag and ran with it across the hot metal of the deck. He handed it to Chan who threw it at Alex. He caught the bag one-handed and used his other to unzip it. Inside were stacks of banded U.S. dollars. There was no way to tell if they were counterfeit.

Alex unsnapped a metal carabiner from his assault vest and used it to fasten the two loop handles of the bag to the rescue hoist. He gave a thumbs-up and the bag whizzed skywards.

"NOW!" yelled Chan.

Alex nodded and Kobus started to lower the helicopter. Chan took Alex gently by the arm to steer him away from the descending net, toward the bridge, and allow the two crewmen to move in closer, but Alex shrugged him off and backed away in the opposite direction, toward the stern.

Two kilometers away, out of sight of the men on board the *Peng Cheng* and those hovering above it, Lieutenant Oliver Msimang watched the stolen Oryx helicopter on the video screen in his cockpit. He keyed the radio: "Command, this is Kestrel One. Target helo is lowering the ivory onto the suspect vessel. Request permission to engage, over."

"Hold, Kestrel One," came the voice of the naval captain at the Joint Operations Center thousands of kilometers away in Pretoria. The irascible Colonel De Villiers had been sidelined by the chain of command.

"He's cut away the net, Oliver," Jaco Kronje, his weapons officer, said into their private intercom.

Msimang returned his gaze to the screen as he held the hover. He checked the fuel gauges. They hadn't miraculously climbed out of the red since the last time he'd looked, two minutes earlier. "Control, this is Kestrel One. Target has released cargo net and is climbing." So, too, was the note in his voice. He took a breath. "Target helo is holding above suspect vessel. Request permission to engage, over."

Come on, come on, Oliver said to himself.

"Cargo is being loaded into the ship's hold. Request permission to engage, over."

"Hold, Kestrel One, damn you. I said *hold.*"

The weapons officer was intent on his display screen and systems readiness. "Look, they've got the net stowed. The Oryx is coming in to land. We've got two, three minutes at the most, and not enough fuel to chase him *and* stay with the ship if he gaps it for the coast."

Oliver pushed the stick forward and started flying toward the ship.

"Hey, where are we going?"

"To war, Jaco."

• • •

Alex's men had a rhythm going now, passing tusks from man to man and finally to Novak, who stood on the wooden deck, overseeing the transfer to a stream of Chinese crewmen. Alex stood back, his R5 still slung but the barrel covering the operation. Chan, he saw, stayed on the far side of the helo, with Wu next to him. The pair started to back away, toward the bridge. Novak had noticed the movement as well and looked over at Alex, who raised his eyebrows in acknowledgment.

The helicopter was nearly empty now. Alex hoped Chan and Wu were going to collect the balance of his money. There were thirty or forty tusks lying on the deck next to the Oryx, but the antlike flow of crewmen had stopped and none had returned from the hold amidships, where they had been ferrying the ivory down a series of ladders. Up until now they had been efficient, jogging to the hole in the deck with full loads and sprinting back empty-handed for more.

Alex raised his hand to get Novak's attention. "GET ON BOARD!"

Novak backed up to the helicopter and sat in the open hatchway. He had unslung his rifle and held it at the ready.

"Kestrel One, this is Command. You are to engage target helicopter and destroy. Repeat, engage and destroy target helicopter. Suspect vessel is not to be engaged. SAS *Talana* is closing on your position. Make best speed. Acknowledge, over?"

"Yes!" Jaco called from the front seat of the Rooivalk.

The South African Ship *Talana* was one of four frigates bought from the Germans a few years earlier. It had a big fat landing deck and fuel just waiting for him. Oliver pictured them arriving on the ship, with nothing but fumes in his fuel tanks—he and Jaco climbing down from the cockpit and being carried on the shoulders of cheering sailors, just like Tom Cruise in *Top Gun*.

"Closing," Oliver said.

"Roger."

Oliver felt the sweat dampening the fabric of his flying gloves as he gripped the stick tight. His heart was clunking in his chest and he took a breath to steady himself.

"I've got visual on the ship," Jaco said. "At one o'clock."

Oliver peered out into the near-blinding haze coming off the ocean and made out the dark speck.

"Selecting guns. Guns armed," Jaco said.

Oliver couldn't see the target vessel and helicopter now, because of the haze that blurred the line between water and sky. He was banking on the ship's crew being similarly blind to their approach. Until it was too late.

Alex looked around for Chan or Captain Wu but neither was in sight. He unslung the R5 from his shoulder and started backing toward the Oryx. He wasn't going to leave without the balance of his money.

He turned and looked at Kobus through the Perspex and waved his hand in the air in a circling motion. The rest of the men were on board. "Take off!"

Kobus hesitated, but Novak was inside the chopper now and Alex saw his bull-necked head appear next to the pilot's. He yelled something into Kobus's ear and the Oryx started to lift off.

Novak knew the drill for such an eventuality. They would hover a short distance from the ship and at the first sign of trouble, or a double cross, they would return and start raking the decks with automatic fire. If Alex were still alive they would try to rescue him.

As the Oryx's fat wheels left the deck the gunfire started.

"Seven hundred, six hundred," said Jaco, counting off the meters. "Guns hot, target acquired."

"Fire when ready," Oliver said.

"Target's lifting off. Adjusting aim."

Control of the Rooivalk's twenty-millimeter cannon was slaved to Jaco's flying helmet and the monocular sight attached to it. Simply by tilting his head a little the long, lethal barrels rose. Jaco started to squeeze.

"Incoming!" Oliver was watching the whole of the, ship rather than focusing on the other helicopter and saw the winking muzzle flashes before his gunner. Instinctively he pulled back on the stick.

Jaco swore, but pulled the trigger home even as the Oryx disappeared from his sight. The Rooivalk shuddered as thirty of the long fat projectiles erupted from the rotating barrels of the cannon. There was another sound, too, like hail on a tin roof.

The tracer rounds in the mix glowed red, burning an arcing path through the afternoon haze, but flying harmlessly past the Oryx and over the bow of the ship.

"We're taking fire!" Oliver yelled, his earlier cool all but gone.

Oliver saw the ship flash away, below and to his left. The Oryx was disappearing from view on the far side of the ship, staying low, the pilot keeping the nose down to gather speed.

Alex leaped from the wooden deck but instead of hitting the water below he was caught in the cargo net surrounding the landing platform. In his mind, when ordering its installation, he'd thought of many things that could go wrong during the exchange of ivory for cash. A full-scale war wasn't one of them, but the ropes had saved him for the moment.

He heard shouts on the far side of the *Peng Cheng*, in English.

The unannounced arrival of the helicopter gunship had taken them all by surprise, and that, too, had probably been a major contributing factor to his continued existence. He craned his neck and saw the sleek helicopter wheeling around. He had little time to worry about Novak and the others in the Oryx, because copper-jacketed lead slugs were tearing through the timbers above his head.

Cradling his R5 in the crook of his arms, he leopard crawled his way awkwardly along the netting. At the very stern of the ship he slung the rifle around his neck, grabbed the edge of the rope with both hands and rolled forward. Dangling two meters above the deck, he let go, and landed hard but intact.

The gunfire had slowed to the occasional shot now. Reconnaissance by fire, the Americans called it. It was a simple "pray and spray" technique designed to get him to fire back, but guile and silence would be the only things that would help him now, unless he had a man's head in his sights.

How many had there been? Seven? Eight? Nine? Wu only had five crewmen on board the small freighter. Others, English-speakers, had joined them, and they must have come by sea.

Alex heard a noise like a buzz saw in the distance. The sun glittered off spinning rotors and a cockpit windscreen as the helicopter gunship chased his men in the Oryx. The noise was another deadly spurt from the long-barreled cannon in the turret under the Rooivalk's chin.

He moved slowly, unlike his beating heart. He smelled rotting food and saw the stains on the rails and the stern of the hull where the cook tossed his waste. Alex peeked around a corner of the ship's superstructure and saw two Chinese crewmen creeping aft. Both were armed and Alex had time to register that the lead man carried a stubby green plastic Steyr carbine, the same weapon he used on his pirate raids. Odd, as it was an unusual weapon in Africa. Beyond them, of more interest, was a rope ladder, dangling amidships, and tethered to a bollard in the same location was a rigid-hulled inflatable boat. The boat bounced alongside the *Peng Cheng*. The name of the rubber tender's mother ship was painted in bold white—*Penfold Son*. Things started to make sense. Chan had blackmailed Penfold, but now they were in cahoots. The tender was Alex's only means of escape, and he had to get to it.

The sailors moved with exaggerated caution, their weapons held high. He saw the fear in their faces. These were not warriors. He took a breath, stepped out fully, dropped to one knee and raised his R5 to his shoulder, all in one fluid, well-practiced move.

The lead Chinaman fired his Steyr. As Alex expected, the man had jerked the two-stage trigger hard enough to fire the rifle on full-auto and, just as predictably, the carbine pulled high and to the right. Bullets pinged off the deck head above the starboard walkway, ricocheting over his head and out to sea behind him. Alex fired two aimed shots into the man's chest, which threw the hapless sailor back onto his crewmate.

The other discharged his AK-47 into the air out over the railing as his friend's body knocked him to the ground. Instead of throwing down his weapon he raised it, one-handed, and aimed at Alex, who was on his feet by now, moving toward them, his weapon pulled tight in his shoulder. Alex didn't give the man time to fire. He put one round into the man's neck, and the other between his eyes.

He felt nothing. Chan and Wu had laid an ambush to kill him and his men. This was war.

He stopped and knelt by the bodies. He didn't need to check if they were dead. He picked up the Steyr. He didn't need to check the serial number to know that it was his. Slinging it over his shoulder would only make his movement more awkward and there was only the one magazine, now half empty, in the rifle. He tossed it, and the other man's AK, over the side rail into the Indian Ocean. His R5 was warm and had tasted blood. Its aim was true, plus he had plenty more magazines full of ammunition.

Alex stepped over the bodies and ran toward the rope ladder. Two meters short, Piet van Zyl rounded the forward edge of the superstructure and opened fire.

A bullet tugged at the camouflage sleeve of his uniform. Van Zyl was no amateur and his first snap shot had nearly found its mark, even though Alex was moving. He dived left into an open hatch and pulled the steel door shut behind him. Alex grabbed a crowbar lying nearby and wedged it into the hatch's locking dog.

"Shit." He'd been almost in reach of the ladder and freedom. Now he'd have to make his way through the stinking bowels of the *Peng Cheng.*

As the rubber soles of his boots squeaked on the metal decks he navigated his way inward, moving by instinct and memory. In addition to the usual smells of a freighter—diesel fumes, sweat, disinfectant and engine and cooking oils—was the lingering reminder that this ship had once been a floating zoo, and not all the animals had survived. Behind him he heard the frustrated swearing and clanging of rifle butts on the jammed hatch. They'd soon find a way in.

As he moved, he thought about his rifle, which he had thrown overboard. The fact it had turned up on board this ship was ominous. Either Chan, together with the freed Wu and his ship's crew, had overpowered Jose and gotten into the armory in the boatshed on Ilha dos Sonhos or, perhaps worse, Van Zyl and his men had been to the island.

Jose, his brother in all but blood, would not have let them take weapons off the island without a fight.

He also feared for Jane's safety. If she had made it to the police in Cape Town with the evidence of Penfold's crime there was little chance his flagship would have been allowed to leave port. The surest way for George to stop Jane would have been for him to kill her.

A door opened beside him and Alex turned and sidestepped as the silver blade of a meat cleaver swung in an arc. The tip of the honed metal passed millimeters from his nose. Alex reversed his rifle and smashed the butt into the face of the *Peng Cheng*'s chef. The gray-haired man reeled backward, in a clatter of pots and pans, and fell to the greasy floor of his bug-infested galley. Alex stamped mercilessly on the man's right forearm and felt bone shatter under his boot. The cook yelped like a dog. They were determined to stop him—even the ones who couldn't be trusted with a rifle. Alex had hijacked their ship, but when he thought of the meals Henri had cooked for the crew when they were hostages he felt nothing but contempt for this gang.

There was more shouting. Van Zyl and his mercenaries were behind him. Alex pulled another hatch closed and stopped. He was breathing hard, sucking in great gulps of air as he opened one of the pouches on his vest. From it he took one of the fragmentation grenades the crippled gun dealer had sold him in Alexandra. He took a small roll of trip wire from another pocket, quickly tied one end to the ring, then pulled the pin almost completely out. Gently, as the slightest disturbance would free the pin, he wedged the green orb in between a fire extinguisher and the metal bulkhead to which it was mounted. He pulled the wire taut and tied it off to the locking dog of the hatch. The footsteps on the other side were loud, as were the orders barked by Van Zyl.

Alex ran down the companionway and through the next hatch, which he closed and locked just as he heard the one behind him being opened.

The next door led to the cargo hold. It was empty bar the net full of elephant tusks, which had been lowered down via the ship's crane.

"Grenade!" someone shouted.

The ship vibrated with the explosion. Those who survived the blast would have been deafened in the confines of the closed compartment. Alex clambered up onto the mountain of yellowed, bloodied ivory and began shifting tusks, unstacking them as he dug down into the core of the white gold.

31

"Here he comes again," Novak said into his headset. He and Heinrich sat side by side in the open cargo hatch of the Oryx, their rifles ready, full magazines loaded for the Rooivalk's next pass. Novak thought it would probably be the gunship's last.

Henri screamed through gritted teeth as Kevin tied the tourniquet around his right thigh. The inside of the helicopter was spray-painted with blood. One of several twenty-millimeter cannon shells that had passed through the fuselage walls had all but severed the Frenchman's leg. The pulpy mess was studded with the bright white of shattered bone and the leg rested at an obscene angle. Kevin's quick work might just save his life. It was probably wasted effort, Novak thought. The weapons officer on the gunship had his eye in now and had steadied his nerves. Death was coming up behind them.

"Fuel state critical," Oliver Msimang said.

"Roger," Jaco said. "I've got him. He won't survive this pass. We hit him last time. There'll be *okes* bleeding on their ivory in there now."

Oliver nodded to himself.

They were chasing an unarmed whale of a troop helicopter. There was no way he could fail. The consequences of letting these men escape were not worth considering.

"Kufa," Kobus said into his mouthpiece, "get on the satphone and call Jose on the island. Give him our location off the GPS on the instrument panel. Tell him to come to us in the *Fair Lady* and—"

"But what about Alex? This isn't part of the plan, Kobus."

Novak cut in on the chatter. "We're about to fucking die, Kufa. Do as he says, man! If any of us survives it'll be the only chance we have. Fire!"

On Novak's command, he and Heinrich each emptied a magazine of bullets in the direction of the Rooivalk, which was now in range, at about three hundred meters. They aimed high, hoping the other helicopter might fly into one or two of their rounds. Even if they did score a hit, though, the projectile would bounce off the armored cockpit windows. By a fluke, they might sever a fuel line or damage some other vital component through the aluminum skin.

Kobus threw the Oryx hard over to the right.

Cannon shells ripped through the tail boom and Kevin laid his body over Henri's.

"Kobus, we're smoking!" Novak yelled into the microphone. Behind them, the Rooivalk had veered off to avoid flying into the thick cloud that was pouring from their engine exhaust.

"Fuck. Right engine's gone. I'm shutting it down."

Novak felt the loss of speed. Through the hatch he could see the Rooivalk standing off, just out of rifle range. It slowed its speed to match theirs, waiting out there like a vulture waiting for a stricken beast to die.

"We can keep going. I've still got control," Kobus said.

"Put her down," Novak said.

"What? Are you crazy?" Kobus replied. "They'll slaughter us."

"I said, put us down."

•   •   •

Jaco said over the internal intercom, "I'm going to finish them off."

"No," Oliver replied.

"What do you mean, no? I'm well within range for the twenty-millimeter."

Even though the Rooivalk was hovering, it was still pointing in the same direction the Oryx had been traveling. Jaco turned his head to the left and Oliver knew the multi-barreled cannon was moving, following his weapons officer's eye.

"Jaco, they've got a wounded man down there. They wouldn't have put out the raft if they could take off again. I'm not going to let you murder them in cold blood."

"All right. We wait until it looks like they're all clear—until the raft has moved a safe distance away—and then if that fucking helicopter is still afloat I'm going to sink it."

The captain's voice over the radio stopped further debate. "Kestrel One, good work. You are to disengage and proceed to a new rendezvous. I'm told you won't make the *Talana*, but we have contacted a civil vessel which you can land on."

"Roger control," Oliver said, swinging the nose of the Rooivalk to the south, away from the Oryx. "What's the name of this ship, over?"

"The MV *Penfold Son*."

Alex found the canvas satchel he had buried in the mound of tusks after the helicopter had picked up the cargo net. It was time to cash in his insurance policy.

He opened the bag and checked the home-made bomb. Four thermite grenades were bound together with duct tape and wired to a detonator and a satellite phone. If Chan had tried to double-cross Alex, or ambush him—as he had, then Novak would have called the satellite phone once they were all clear of the ship. Receiving the signal would activate the detonator and the grenades. Alex knew Novak wouldn't make the call while there was a possibility Alex was still alive.

The firebomb in Alex's hands would ignite the ivory around it and punch through the hull of the *Peng Cheng*. It would be like using an oxy-acetylene torch to cut tinfoil. Alex knew the smoke and flames from the burning tusks would make it impossible for the ship's crew to reach the hole and attempt to repair it. The *Peng Cheng* would sink.

Alex didn't have a phone of his own, so he set the alarm for twenty minutes' time. He replaced the bomb in its bag and tucked it under half-a-dozen shafts of stained ivory.

Alex couldn't feel bitter toward Chan, because even if the gangster had stuck to his end of the bargain he would have called tactical headquarters and relayed the *Peng Cheng*'s last known position. He'd phoned Silvermine, anonymously, using the same codeword he always did when he was reporting an illegal fishing vessel or a ship he suspected was carrying illegal immigrants.

For months the South African Navy had been apprehending wrongdoers on Alex's information and he'd often imagined their puzzlement at who the source might be. No doubt the staff officers would have a fit if they knew the information was coming from a pirate with a conscience. To lure the *Talana* out he had hinted that the *Peng Cheng* might be carrying arms and explosives as well as ivory and rhino horn. He wanted to make doubly sure that while the elephant cull would go down in history as a disaster, the ivory would never make it to Asia.

"Drop your gun, Tremain."

Alex looked up. "Van Zyl?"

"You can call me 'Death' if you like." The South African grinned across the sights of his M4. "I said drop it. Don't make me kill you now—my employer wants that privilege for himself."

Alex stood slowly, laid down his R5 and unholstered his pistol.

"What were you doing in the ivory?"

"I was going to hide under the tusks."

Van Zyl laughed. "That's pretty stupid."

Alex shrugged and started to move away from the ivory. He

wanted to draw their attention away from the explosive device. "So who's your boss—Chan?"

Van Zyl followed him toward the shaft of light that shone down from the open cargo hatch above. Alex moved to a ladder, unbidden, and started climbing.

"You'll meet him soon enough, but I sense it'll be a pretty brief chat."

Alex looked down at the South African as he climbed. "Why not do me a favor, as one soldier to another, and shoot me now?"

Van Zyl shook his head. "As one soldier to another, you'll understand orders are orders. Don't worry, though, you won't be alone. You'll have someone else there to talk to. An old friend of yours."

Alex swallowed. "I don't know what you mean."

"Five six, strawberry blonde, nice legs . . ."

Jane heard the changing note of the diesel engines somewhere below her and felt the ship slow. She sweated profusely in the hot, stuffy shipping container that was her cell. She had prayed to God—something she hadn't done since she was twelve—and hoped that her parents wouldn't suffer too much. She wondered if the change in pace of the vessel signaled her end.

She looked up and the beams of light that penetrated the airholes at the top of the container were momentarily eclipsed. She placed a hand on a warm metal wall and felt a different hum. It was louder now, the buzzing noise increasing in volume as the ship's engines slowed even more.

A helicopter.

She allowed her hopes to rise, though told herself to stay calm. Was it a rescue force, or something yet more sinister, related to the fate she had all but resigned herself to? Someone was yelling outside, shouting instructions. She couldn't make out the words.

Jane started banging on the walls of the box with her balled fists. The sound was puny and not even she could hear it over the competing mechanical notes of the aircraft and ship. She tried yelling, but her voice was lost too.

Jane looked around her. The only thing in the container was the steel bucket full of her own waste. She grimaced as she grabbed it and emptied it in the furthest corner of her jail. She retched and swung the bucket with all her might against the wall of the container. It made a satisfyingly loud clang, so she did it again.

George Penfold walked down the stairs from the bridge wing. Sitting on a tightly packed row of shipping containers was a Rooivalk attack helicopter.

To ignore the distress call from the South African National Defense Force would have simply drawn unwelcome attention to the *Penfold Son*, but having a stranded helicopter gunship on his vessel was tantamount to the same thing.

He tensed his face into a grin and moved closer to the aircraft as its blades finally stopped turning and began to sag. The Rooivalk looked less like a kestrel and more like a giant resting dragonfly. He eyed the rocket pods, cannon and wing-mounted antitank missiles. There was enough hardware here to stop a troop of tanks or a company of infantry.

The pilot and gunner opened their cockpits.

"Welcome aboard," George called over the last dying groans of the engines. "I'm George Penfold."

"Lieutenant Oliver Msimang and this is my weapons officer, Warrant Officer Jaco Kronje."

George shook hands with the two airmen as they stepped down onto the deck.

"I can't tell you how grateful we were to see your ship on the horizon. We were on fumes," the black African said.

George laughed politely. "So, what exactly are you guys doing out here?" The panicked satellite phone call from Chan had told him already, but he needed to feign innocence.

Msimang explained they had been tracking a smugglers' ship and a stolen helicopter full of ivory. "We splashed it," the pilot said proudly.

"Wow," George said. "That must have been quite a sight, seeing another aircraft go down in flames."

Kronje shook his head. "They ditched in the ocean, but the helo was still afloat. You'll hear rescue traffic on your radios soon. The *Talana* will be looking for survivors, and we'll get back into the game once we're refueled."

George processed the new information. Tremain was being brought to the *Penfold Son* by Van Zyl and his men. He'd hoped the gunship would have killed the rest of the pirates, but they were possibly still at large.

Chan was making for Ilha dos Sonhos, the nearest landfall, where he would stash his cargo. With Mitch Reardon in charge of the island and the pirates out of action, Chan could hide out on the resort for as long as required. The *Peng Cheng* would sail on, in international waters, and if it was boarded by the South African Navy its crew would say the stolen helicopter had tried to force a landing on her deck.

"How will you refuel?" George asked the pilot.

"We've got just enough left for one takeoff and a short hop, to the SAS *Talana*, when she gets close. To be honest, she'll need to be almost alongside, as we're just about dry."

George nodded. "They have aviation fuel on board?"

"Yes, and they're equipped to take helicopters too."

"Well let's get inside out of this heat. We'll get you a cool drink and there's even an indoor swimming pool if you'd like to cool off."

Kronje smiled. "*Lekker.* This beats the navy any day."

George led them along the walkway beside the stacked shipping containers.

The loud clanging of metal on metal stopped the military men.

"Hey, what was that?" Msimang said.

"Probably something coming loose, falling over or banging into something."

"It's smooth as glass on the water," Kronje said.

"Quiet! I can hear a voice," Msimang said.

"I'm sure it's nothing," George replied. He reached behind his back and lifted his shirt. Tucked in the waistband of his jeans was a .44 Magnum pistol. He liked the feeling of power a big gun gave him.

The pilot moved to the container and his stocky warrant officer planted himself in the center of the walkway, watching both his superior and George.

"It's a woman!" He leaned his head closer to the hot steel of the box. "She's calling for help. How do you open this thing?"

"My God, perhaps it's a stowaway," George said, hoping he sounded surprised enough.

"Show me your hand, Mister Penfold, sir," Kronje said, hands on hips.

"Oh, all right, if you insist. But I wish you hadn't said that."

George pulled the pistol and shot the warrant officer in the heart.

"HELP!" Jane rattled the stinking bucket over and over against the container's side. "Help me!"

She stopped when she heard the shot. She sensed there was no longer any point, and she slumped to the floor, tears filling her eyes.

A while later she heard the hum of outboard engines. The noise grew louder and when it stopped she heard the ebullient voices of Piet van Zyl and a couple of his men. George was talking rapidly, but his deep, low tones were harder to decipher.

When the door creaked open she retreated, like a night creature, from the flood of light that invaded her prison.

The first man who came through the door was dead. She cowered at the back of the metal box as a booted foot rolled the body over. The dead man wore a green military flying suit that was drenched with blood, front and back.

The next man in walked like a zombie. He was an African, dressed the same as the first. He barely registered Jane's presence when he blinked, his eyes finally finding her in the gloom. She said nothing.

With the door open she could hear George's voice clearly. "We've got to get that helicopter off the deck," he said.

"How?" Van Zyl asked.

"Push the fucking thing, I suppose."

"All right, but let me lock this bastard up first," Van Zyl said.

Jane watched the black man. He looked around the container, his nose wrinkling at the smell of her.

Three men were silhouetted in the doorway of the container, against the blindingly bright outside light. One was pushed to his knees and the door slammed shut.

The sudden appearance then loss of light ruined Jane's vision and she blinked in the gloom, waiting for it to return. "Who's there?"

"Jane?"

She got to her feet and stumbled toward the sound of his voice as he said her name again. When she bumped into him in the dark she lost her footing, but he wrapped his arms around her, holding her tight.

"Jane," he said, and she felt him bury his face in her hair. She clung to him and fought back the sobs.

"Alex, I didn't want to die without seeing you again."

He kissed her cheek and her forehead. "I know how you feel. But we're not going to die on this ship."

32

Captain Gert Fourie sat in his padded leather chair in the air-conditioned bridge of the SAS *Talana*, sipping a mug of coffee.

He projected an air of calmness in the face of the mounting excitement building in the voices of the officers and sailors around him. They had listened to the radio transmissions between Tactical HQ and the Rooivalk crew, and the men and women on the bridge had cheered when the news came through that the hijacked Oryx had been downed.

A suspect vessel was out there somewhere ahead of them, and their job would be to intercept and board it, as soon as they had taken the Rooivalk on board and refueled it. With the help of the gunship they would also have to search for and apprehend the pirates who had left their downed aircraft. It would be a busy day and the first real test of the *Talana*'s crew against an armed foe.

The *Talana* was already off the coast of Mozambique, thanks to an anonymous but supposedly reliable tip-off that a ship smuggling arms was in the area. Fourie didn't know if the report was linked to the stolen helicopter and the ivory heist, but one thing was certain—they were now in dangerous waters.

The ship needed a win. The air of controversy over the government's purchase of four new frigates from the Germans had never entirely cleared. Opposition parties and the media had criticized the ships as too costly for a country where too many people still lived in poverty, and there had been questions over the transparency of the tender process.

But Fourie was a navy man through and through. Third generation. Every day of his life had been preparation for this one and he was determined every man and woman under his command would be going home safe to their base at Simon's Town.

The screen set high in front of him showed their position in relation to the MV *Penfold Son*, which was ahead. They would soon have visual contact.

"XO, what's the position of the suspect freighter?" Fourie asked his executive officer, Commander Mishak Kumalo.

"Target is bearing zero-four-two degrees, twenty nautical miles, sir. He's making a steady eight knots further into international waters," Kumalo replied from his place behind the captain.

Fourie looked across at the framed photograph of his ship. He would miss her when his posting ended in a few short weeks.

"SAS *Talana*, this is the MV *Penfold Son*, over," came a voice over the loudspeaker on the bridge.

Commander Kumalo acknowledged the call and the captain listened intently to the exchange. The voice of the *Penfold Son*'s master sounded anxious.

"We've got an emergency situation here," the Englishman said. "Your air force helicopter has just crashed into the sea!"

Fourie craned his head to look back at Kumalo, who held the radio handset by his side. "Sir, the last report from the Rooivalk crew was that they had landed safely on board the *Penfold Son*."

"I know, XO, I heard it too." Fourie could feel his stress levels start to rise.

"*Penfold Son, Penfold Son*, we heard they had arrived safely, over," Kumalo replied.

"I know that," said the worried voice from the freighter. "It's just . . . I don't know how it happened, but something . . . something exploded just after they touched down, while the rotors were still turning. My God . . . it was . . . it was horrible. The blast threw the helicopter on its side and over the edge. The explosion seemed to come from one of the rocket pods and . . ."

Fourie processed the information. The voice had tailed off into silence. "Maybe a missile malfunction?" he said out loud. He left his seat and took the handset from his executive officer. "MV *Penfold Son*, this is the Commanding Officer of the SAS *Talana*. To whom am I speaking, over?"

"George Penfold, master of the *Penfold Son* and MD of Penfold Shipping."

Fourie had heard of the man—no one at sea had not. The millionaire's position and standing meant little now. "How long ago did this happen, over?"

"Only a few minutes ago, Captain. We've launched a boat to look for survivors, but the helicopter went down fast."

Fourie turned to Kumalo, but before he could speak the African officer said, "Should I launch a RHIB sir? It will get there much faster than we will."

Fourie nodded. "Send both of them, XO."

Kumalo moved to the *Talana*'s broadcast system and issued the orders.

"Mister Penfold, hold in place and continue your search. We're sending two boats to help you. They'll be there soon and we won't be far behind. Have you suffered any casualties?"

"Negative, Captain. Hurry, please. I just hope we can find those brave airmen alive."

Van Zyl paced the bridge of the *Penfold Son* like a caged lion. "We've got to kill them, now. Those sailors are going to want to board us to talk to you. If the prisoners start banging on the walls of that container again we're finished."

George frowned. "Agreed, but keep the woman alive."

"Forget her," Van Zyl said, shaking his head. "She's your weakness, George."

"Shut your bloody mouth. I will keep her alive as long as it suits me. Take her below decks and chain her somewhere in the engine room."

"What about Tremain and the pilot? Do you want to do it, or shall I?"

"I'll do it. I want to make sure the job's done properly."

Van Zyl ignored the implied insult and looked out over the deck. His men had barely shifted the Rooivalk helicopter. Pushing it over the edge was easier said than done. The Rooivalk sat on a three-wheeled undercarriage, with two at the front, beneath where the crew sat, and a tail wheel. The containers on the *Penfold Son* were stacked close together, but there were still narrow gaps between them and every time one of the Rooivalk's wheels hit a gap it required a strenuous effort from the men to dislodge it and get it rolling again. "Well, you can come and give me a hand to move that helo as well. And summon some more of your crew or else it'll still be there when the navy arrives."

Van Zyl slung his M4 over his shoulder and joined his men, who were clustered around the helicopter, panting in between efforts as they leaned against the fuselage. "Come on, you bastards, get your backs into it."

It seemed Van Zyl was incapable of getting anything right. He'd told George that he and his men had held their fire on board the *Peng Cheng* until he had all the pirates in his sight. But by waiting for Tremain to get into the stolen helicopter—Van Zyl's plan was to kill all of them and destroy the aircraft machine in one go, before it took off—he had allowed the bulk of the pirate crew to escape. But at least George had their leader.

George walked over to the container which housed the prisoners. He was looking forward to killing Tremain, but wished it hadn't been necessary to finish off the innocent airmen.

He didn't underestimate the cunning of a pirate and a pilot, so when he opened the door he stood back. He'd brought a powerful Maglite flashlight with him from the deckhouse and he raised it with his left hand and used it to scan the darkened interior.

Jane cowered in a far corner, sitting down with her knees drawn up to her chest. Tremain, in his South African Army camouflage fatigues, was next to her, in a similar position, although his head was resting on his knees. The man was broken. The black pilot of the helicopter was in the other corner, standing, and the dead crewman lay in a pool of his own blood where Van Zyl had dropped him.

"On your feet, Tremain."

The man said nothing.

"Leave him alone, George. For God's sake leave us all alone, or just kill us," Jane screamed.

"Get up, Tremain. Now!"

Jane leaned over to him and put her arms around the sitting man. "He's finished, George," she said softly. "Can't you see he's no threat to you now?"

George laughed, long and loud, his peals echoing off the inside of the steel box as he stepped inside. "Not such a big man now, are you, you bastard."

"What of me?" the pilot asked. "Are you going to execute me or set me free?"

"You, my friend, have become an inconvenience. I really wish you hadn't landed on my ship."

"So do I." He took two paces toward George.

"Stop! Sit down, where you are." The pilot complied and slid to the floor, his back against a side wall.

George licked the sweat from his top lip. It really was like an oven in this box. He stepped over the body of the helicopter crewman.

"TREMAIN! Get on your feet or I'll shoot you where you're sitting."

"George, no, please," Jane cried. "Can't you see he's beaten? He's no threat to you. You could let him go and leave him on his island. Please, let him live."

George laughed again. This really was very amusing. "And tell me, why should I do such a ridiculous thing?"

"Because I love him, George. Let him live and I'll do whatever you want. I'll be whatever you want. I'll be your slave, George, if that's what you want . . ."

He shook his head. "Too late, darling. You had that chance, only you could have done it in style, as my next wife, but you rejected me for this burned-out loser. And now you'll pay for your treachery." He raised the pistol and pointed it at the seated man. "At least be a man and face me, Tremain."

"No!" Jane screamed.

George wanted the pirate to look him in the eye, but he felt the rush anyway. The man deserved to die for his cowardice alone. Jane was showing more balls than this pathetic creature. He squeezed the trigger.

The noise of the .44 was deafening. He'd aimed the first shot low, into Tremain's gut, because he wanted to hear him cry, but the man was silent. Amazing. He fired the next into his head and when the bullet struck it flicked the skull back so that the face was visible. "Shit . . ."

While George was talking Alex had closed his hand around the handle of the metal slop bucket, which he and Jane had positioned close to him. The helicopter gunner's drying blood was all over him, on the dead man's clothes and plastered to his face and hands from the sticky pool on the floor of the container. He looked like a red-streaked creature from hell as he unleashed a war cry and swung the bucket at George's head.

George fell to his knees, but then dropped to his belly and rolled, avoiding Alex's backswing.

"Run!" Alex yelled at Jane and Oliver.

Oliver lashed out at George, kicking him hard in the ribs as he tried to crawl away. George loosed another shot, which would have struck Jane if she hadn't dodged to her left. Alex stomped his booted foot down on George's wrist and the other man cried in pain and dropped his pistol. Alex scooped the weapon up and pointed it at George.

"I should kill you now."

"I'll kill him for you, man," Oliver said.

Alex shook his head. "No. Not yet, at least. We need him."

George got to his knees, nursing his wrist. Alex guessed it might be broken.

"On your feet." He grabbed the Englishman by the collar of his shirt and hauled him upright, eliciting another cry of pain. He checked Penfold's pockets and relieved him of a speed loader fitted with six rounds of ammunition for the pistol.

"What now?" Oliver asked.

Alex held the pistol under Penfold's chin, his free hand locked around his neck. "Why did you land your helo on the ship?"

"Fuel," answered Oliver.

"How much have you got left?"

"Enough to start it and make a short hop. The tanks would be dry soon after."

"How far could you get?"

"I don't know. A kilometer, maybe two?"

"That's enough. We're going to go out there and you're going to take Jane, get off this bloody tub and fly toward the *Talana*. Ditch if you have to. They'll pick up your emergency rescue beacon."

"How do you know about the *Talana*?"

Jane looked at him.

"Long story. The short version is I put a call into Tactical Headquarters to tip them off about the *Peng Cheng*—that's the freighter we landed the stolen ivory on. I didn't want that ivory leaving Africa and ending up in China or Taiwan."

"I don't get it," Oliver said. "You stole millions of rands worth of ivory and you were going to hand it back again?"

"It's complicated."

Jane smiled.

Penfold's face showed his disbelief and outrage. "It's a bloody double cross is what it is. You prick. You were going to take Chan's money and then shop him."

Alex shrugged. "You and Chan set me up and ambushed me. I'm a pirate—what's your excuse, George?"

Piet van Zyl stormed away from the Rooivalk. His men rested in the shade of the drooping rotor blades. They were all strong guys, but they would need more muscle power to tip the helicopter overboard, and time was running out. He'd heard the shots from inside the container and assumed George was executing all of the prisoners.

"Christ, what a bloody mess," he muttered to himself, ruing his decision to take Penfold's money. Still, he told himself, they were all in it up to their necks now. There was no going back. He climbed the stairs to the bridge. He would get the first mate to broadcast a message to the rest of the ship's crew over the PA system, summoning every spare man to the helipad.

"What's going on down there?" the mate said as Piet opened the door.

He turned and held a hand to his eyes to shield them from the glare reflected from the deck and the containers that crowded it. "Fuck."

Piet unslung his M4 and, staying low, moved out onto the starboard bridge wing. He rested his rifle on the rail, switched the selector switch to single shot and took aim.

"Unsling your weapons and put them on the deck," Alex commanded Van Zyl's thugs. Seeing their paymaster, Penfold, with a pistol at his head, the men slowly, reluctantly, complied. "Jane, Oliver, grab a gun each. Toss the rest overboard." What worried him was that Van Zyl was not with his men. Alex scanned the decks and faraway bridge, but couldn't see the South African.

Jane hurled the small arsenal into the blue waters of the Indian Ocean below while Oliver frisked each of the men. He liberated concealed pistols from two of them and stuffed one in the breast pocket of his flight suit. "All clear."

"Oliver, get in and start up."

The pilot needed no convincing. He tossed his assault rifle into the cockpit and climbed up into his seat.

"Jane, give me the rifle and get in the front seat."

"No, Alex. I'm not going to leave you. I've got a gun and I'm going to stay here with you, until the navy comes."

"I'll face the music—God knows it's time—but I want you out of here, safe and alive. You're better off with Oliver in a life raft than on this death ship."

She shook her head. "I'm staying with you."

There was a whine from the Rooivalk's engines and the rotors above them slowly started to turn.

"Get in the chopper! Oliver, close your hatch. There's still one of the gunslingers unaccounted for. Keep an eye out for him."

The pilot cocked his head, unable to hear Alex over the growing noise from the turbojet engines.

Jane looked from Alex to George, who glared back at her malevolently. She stared into the eyes of the monster she had very nearly married, then looked into Alex's. She saw the resignation there, and something else. "I love you, Alex."

Alex opened his mouth, but the report of the gunshot silenced him.

The first bullet passed through Oliver's throat. The second took off the top of his skull. Unrestrained, he toppled sideways, and hung half in, half out of the cockpit.

Alex threw George to the deck, his pistol still at the shipping magnate's head. He was unwilling to give up his only bargaining chip. Van Zyl's men made a run for it, scurrying amidst the mass of stacked containers like fleeing cockroaches.

Van Zyl's third, fourth and fifth shots went into the air intakes in front of the Rooivalk's twin engines. Thick smoke billowed from one exhaust, but the rotors still turned steadily above them.

"Alex!" Rounds zinged off the metal containers around Jane, sparks and bare metal gouges showing the path of ricochets.

Alex knew they would be picked off soon enough, and Jane would be the next to die. Penfold was the only thing stopping Van Zyl from shooting Alex. The mercenary was toying with them. He'd told Oliver to close the canopy on the chopper as he knew the Rooivalk's crew stations were protected by armored glass. "Jane, when I start firing, climb up into the gunner's seat . . . in the front, OK?"

"OK."

Jane looked at him, eyes wide with fear, but she nodded.

"On three. One, two . . ."

Alex's third count was drowned out by a short burst of five rounds on automatic from Van Zyl's rifle. Alex countered, emptying the revolver at the bridge. He had little chance of hitting the man at this range, but all he wanted to do was keep his head down. Jane leaped from the container top and climbed into the gunner's seat. As she slammed the cockpit closed a bullet bounced off it, starring the glass.

Alex had to release his grip around George's neck to reload and as he did so Penfold elbowed him hard in the ribs. He knew it was coming, so he rolled out of the way. George sprang to his feet and ran off toward the bridge. Alex rammed the speed loader in the empty chambers of the six-shooter. He fired alternately at George and the bridge wing as he used his free hand to haul Oliver's body down from the pilot's seat.

Alex climbed in and slammed the cockpit hatch closed as a fusillade of shots bounced off the glass. Alex surveyed the array of gauges, switches and buttons in front of him. He'd watched plenty of helicopter pilots over the years but had no idea how to fly. He found the throttle and revved it hard. Above them he heard the engine note change and saw the blades turn faster.

Jane was on her knees, looking up at him from the front seat. She winced every time a bullet bounced off their glass cocoon. "Can you get us off the ship?"

"I don't know, but I'm trying."

Above the noise of the engine Alex could hear someone talking over the loudspeaker. The words were unclear but, glancing around, he saw Van Zyl's men start to emerge from their hiding spots, and crewmen in overalls appearing, more tentative than the trained killers, as they climbed up onto the top stack of containers. The men moved toward the helicopter.

"Hurry, Alex!"

Alex increased the throttle further and pulled up on the lever by his side. He felt the pressure ease off the Rooivalk's landing gear. He toyed with the cyclic stick.

"We're lifting!" Jane squealed.

Jane had dropped her rifle in her rush to get aboard the helicopter. Washington, Van Zyl's hugely muscled African-American sidekick, scooped the weapon up.

"Come on baby . . . Please . . ." The Rooivalk lifted a meter off the deck and rocked sickeningly from side to side as Alex wrestled with the unfamiliar controls.

"We're flying!"

The hired gun raised the M4 to his shoulder and opened fire, emptying thirty rounds from the curved magazine into the one functioning engine.

The Rooivalk dropped like a dead bird, jarring Alex and Jane in their seats.

Alex looked out and saw Van Zyl and Penfold, side by side, returning to the helicopter. If he opened the armored glass cockpit to shoot at the men he would be cut down in less than a second by the black man standing guard, his rifle pointed straight at Alex. There was no way he could be quicker on the draw.

Van Zyl's men and a dozen of the ship's crew surrounded the Rooivalk and the two people trapped inside it. They laid their hands on the hot metal and, at Penfold's shouted urging, began pushing.

Alex checked the instrument panel in front of him. Even though both engines were dead, the lights on several gauges and monitors were still illuminated. That meant they still had electrical power. "Jane, put on the gunner's helmet."

"What? It's like plastic, it's no good for—"

"Jane, just put the bloody thing on."

Alex found the weapons selector switch and moved it to "guns."

"Pull the monocle on the side of the helmet around so you can look through it. Tell me what you see."

Jane did as he asked, then said, "It's a sight of some sort."

Below them, Alex felt the vibration of something mechanical moving.

"Turning your head moves the guns in the turret under the nose."

With the extra manpower the Rooivalk started to slide. It was sitting crossways on the container stack, its nose pointing out to sea on the starboard side of the ship. Looking over Jane's head Alex could see the front of the chopper was now overhanging the edge. They'd be lucky to survive the long drop uninjured, and if they couldn't get out they would suffocate once the helicopter went under. He was sure that if they did get out, Van Zyl and George would pick them off in the water.

"Jane, aim at something and pull the red trigger on the control stick."

"OK."

He watched her shift in her seat and turn her head as far to the right as she could, until she was looking back at the bridge. Alex could just glimpse the tips of the cannon's multiple barrels. Jane squeezed the red trigger and the whole aircraft shuddered. Men around them scattered when the guns roared into life and spewed hot spent brass onto the containers.

Tracer rounds flashed brightly past the bridge and others slammed through steel plating and shattered even the thick glass in front of the helm.

"Whoo-hoo!"

"Keep firing, Jane. Short bursts, though. Keep their heads down."

For a minute they stayed there. Alex looked around him. The crewmen and gunslingers were slowly edging back toward the Rooivalk. Jane turned her head as far as she could to the right, then shifted position to turn to the left and the guns moved with her. However, it was impossible to get them to face rearwards. Van Zyl was quick to spot the weakness and he and most of the men disappeared out of sight under the Rooivalk's tail boom.

Alex felt the rear of the aircraft start to lift.

"No!"

"Shit," Alex said. He pounded the instrument panel in front of him. "We've got a helicopter gunship full of missiles and rockets and nothing to shoot at."

"What's that on the radar?" Jane asked.

Alex looked at the screen and checked the name next to the blip. "The SAS *Talana*! Jane, I could kiss you."

33

The voice on the radio being broadcast throughout the bridge of the SAS *Talana* was distorted by the hum of the sea boat's engine, wind and the slap of the RHIB's hull on the water.

"Say again, Ironman," Captain Fourie said into his microphone.

Petty Officer Bruce Irons—Ironman to all ranks on his ship—was coxswain of one of the rigid-hulled inflatable boats racing toward the *Penfold Son* and the reported location of the crashed Rooivalk.

"Sir, we've just heard what sounds like gunfire coming from the direction of the *Penfold Son*. Request further orders, over."

Fourie turned to Commander Kumalo. "XO, get onto that bloody freighter and find out what's going on." To his small boat crew he said, "Ironman, cut your engine and hold your position. Tell the other RHIB to do the same. Await further orders."

Jane looked out of the cockpit to the stubby wings on the right-hand side. A pod of a dozen air-to-ground rockets hung there, along with two larger Mokopa antitank missiles. One of Van Zyl's henchmen stood behind the wing, out of the arc of fire of the cannon under the nose, and pushed forward as the other men lifted the tail another few degrees higher. She felt the helicopter start to slide.

"Now, Jane. Fire!"

"Oh God, please forgive me," she whispered. At rest, the Rooivalk had been sitting slightly nose up, but with the men lifting from behind, the rocket pod was now sitting close to parallel with the sea surface. She could see from the radar display in front of her that the blob electronically marked as *SAS Talana-F 149* was dead ahead of them. Alex had told her that in the unlikely event the unguided antipersonnel rocket hit the *Talana*, it would bounce off the ship's thick hull. It had been her idea to fire at the *Talana* and get them to do something—anything—in a response that might buy them some time. She prayed there were no men in exposed positions, then switched the selector to "rockets" and pulled the trigger.

The single rocket shot from the pod and Jane glimpsed its sleek menacing shape for an instant before her view was clouded with smoke. Over the noise of the launch, though, she heard an agonized scream.

Fire and more smoke had burst from the rear of the pod as well, and the back blast had engulfed the man who'd been pushing against the wing. He spun and dropped to his knees, his face and hands blackened, his hair and fatigues on fire. Jane shut her eyes to the horror, but his piercing yells easily penetrated the armored glass.

The rear of the Rooivalk dropped with a thud as Van Zyl, Penfold and the others moved away from the new threat.

"Missile inbound, missile inbound!"

The *Talana's* klaxon sounded throughout the ship.

"Hands to action stations. Launch countermeasures," Fourie ordered.

"Sir, missile's splashed into the sea, at five thousand yards by radar," Kumalo said.

The captain picked up his binoculars and scanned the shimmering water. He saw the plume of spray. "There. It's dropped short." The other officers of the bridge looked where Fourie was pointing.

"Not much bang in it, whatever it was," Kumalo said.

"Damn it, that's not the point. Someone just fired at us!" The words had come out harsher than he'd intended, but Kumalo nodded anyway, suitably chastised.

"We're closed up at action stations now, sir," Kumalo said, steadying himself after the rebuke. "Still unable to make radio contact with the *Penfold Son*, sir."

Petty Officer Irons's voice came through on the loudspeaker again.

The captain picked up the radio handset. "What have you got for me, Ironman?"

"Sir, it looked like an air-to-ground rocket passing over us a short while ago. Detonated somewhere behind us, by the sound of it. Permission to close on the *Penfold Son*, sir, and investigate."

"Permission denied." Someone was firing guns and rockets at his ship. He admired Irons's bravery and dedication, but a RHIB could be shredded by that kind of weaponry. "Return to the ship."

"Yes sir," said an obviously reluctant Irons.

"Guns, this is the captain. Fire two rounds from the number one gun, two hundred meters off the *Penfold Son*'s bow. Let's show them we mean business, whoever they are."

Alex had been fiddling with the radios inside the Rooivalk and had picked up the frequency on which the executive officer of the *Talana* was trying to reach the *Penfold Son*. Alex had keyed his radio "send" switch several times and tried to explain their situation. He wanted the *Talana* to send a boat to them at the double.

He looked outside the cockpit. Van Zyl and his men had retreated, scared off by the force of the rocket's back blast. He could make out only two of them now, both armed—one with a pistol and the other with the M4 Jane had dropped. Every now and then they fired a round into the Rooivalk to deter Jane and him from making a run for it. Though quite where they would run to, he had no idea. He wondered where Van Zyl had gone.

The ship itself was turning and from the radar display it appeared they were heading toward the *Talana*. He looked up at the bridge. There was no one to be seen through the shattered windows. He wondered if one of Jane's earlier bursts of fire had killed the helmsman. The fact that there were no answering radio messages from the *Penfold Son*'s deckhouse firmed his suspicions.

Even though he couldn't radio the frigate, if they could sit tight the *Talana* would be in visual range in a few minutes and would see the Rooivalk was on the deck and not lost at sea. That should prompt the captain to send a boarding party.

"Alex!"

He looked up at Jane's call and saw eight figures striding toward them across the top of the shipping containers. They looked like they had come from the set of a science fiction movie. "Fireproof suits," he said.

"That means the rocket blasts won't stop them," Jane said.

Alex looked at the radar screen again. The *Talana* was closing the gap, but was still beyond visual distance. They wouldn't see the Rooivalk hit the water, or even hear the gunfire as he and Jane were murdered. He couldn't be sure, but it seemed like the naval ship might even be slowing its course or standing off. Not surprising since it had come under attack, however ineffectual, from the small air-to-ground rockets.

"Alex, we're moving again!"

The mercenaries and crewmen, clad in their firefighting gear, were putting their backs into pushing again. The Rooivalk was slightly skewed and its front left wheel went over first and the helicopter's fuselage grounded onto the metal top of a container with a sickening thud.

"Alex! There's a speck on the horizon. I can see a ship."

The tail of the helicopter started to rise as the men got underneath it and lifted.

The *Talana* was on her way, but she was still too far away for its captain and crew to see what was happening on board the *Penfold Son*. He needed to show them.

"Jane, lock onto the ship with your sight and select the Mokopas."

"The whats?"

"The antitank missiles."

Jane moved her helmeted head and scanned the horizon to their left. He strained his eyes and made out the speck in the distance. He heard a high-pitched tone as a missile locked on.

The nose of the Rooivalk started to tip forward, and Alex could see the waters below them. He gripped the cockpit walls on either side of him. Through the scarred armored glass he heard two explosions in quick succession.

The helicopter thudded back onto the deck on its tail again as seawater thrown up from the two geysers washed over the men pushing them and coated the chopper.

"The *Talana*'s firing on us!" Jane said. She sounded happy about it.

"Strap into your seat. Pull your harness as tight as you can."

The men renewed their effort and the tail of the Rooivalk began to rise again.

Jane finished securing herself and grabbed the instrument panel in front of her with one hand, the other still on the gunner's joystick. "We're going over!"

The missile tone still buzzed in their ears. "Fire, Jane. Shoot all four missiles!"

Jane pulled the trigger.

The first Mokopa missile leaped from the bracket under the Rooivalk's port wing and, because the helicopter was facing downward, as if in a dive, it splashed into the sea a short distance from the *Penfold Son* and exploded, sending up a huge bubble from far below the surface. While the men lifting the Rooivalk were spared most of the force of the back blast, the roar and noise of the big missile's launch caused them to falter and the tail fell once more.

The missile lock tone still buzzed in Jane's ears. "Fire, Jane. Shoot them all!"

The men on the containers were lifting again and didn't stop this time, even as the second and third missiles left their racks, engulfing the suited mercenaries and crewmen in smoke and fire.

"Alex! They're not stopping. We're going over!"

The Rooivalk's fuselage scraped on the edge of the outermost container and they started sliding forward. The right-hand wheel went over as the men slewed the tail around.

"Hold on!" Alex yelled.

Jane fired the fourth antitank missile, but like the first, this one flew straight down, and the helicopter followed it into the sea.

The alarm sounded on the *Talana's* bridge. "Two missiles inbound!" said Kumalo.

"Launch countermeasures!" Fourie ordered. "All guns, fire!"

Super Barricade launchers on either side of the ship sprayed out a storm of chaff away from the *Talana*. The small strips of metallic foil were designed to confuse and attract incoming missiles. Gunners manning the thirty-five and twenty millimeter cannons fired in the direction of the oncoming missiles, hoping a lucky shot might detonate one or more of the warheads.

One missile went wide, homing in on the chaff cloud and exploding in a fireball a hundred meters from the port side of the ship.

The second hit the hull at an oblique angle and penetrated, its armor-piercing warhead punching through the steel to enter the enclosed fo'castle.

Fourie grasped the sides of his padded chair and turned his face from the glass in front of him as the blast rocked the ship and a cloud of smoke obscured his vision.

"Damage control party to the fo'castle," Kumalo ordered over the ship's main broadcast system. "Damage control! Report."

Smoke billowed from the vents on either side of the compartment that housed the anchor winch.

Fourie clenched his fists to control his anger. He was livid, but would not let his officers see his emotions. "Commence firing procedures for missiles one and two," he said.

Kumalo looked at him, the intercom handset poised near his ear. The African's eyes were wide with astonishment. "The Exocets, sir?"

"You heard me, XO. Don't just stand there staring at me."

"But sir, she's a merchant freighter . . . one of the largest afloat and . . ."

"And she just fired two missiles at us." Fourie repeated the order.

Kumalo licked his lips and gave the order. "I'll keep trying to contact them, sir. In the meantime, damage control reports no casualties, although the anchor winch is damaged. They're assessing now. The RHIBs are back on board, with all hands safe."

"Very well, XO. Maintain present course. I want to see what's going on with this ship. If she fires on us again, I'm going to shoot."

Alex shook his head to clear his vision. His head had banged against the armored glass of the cockpit when the helicopter hit the concrete-like surface of the water. His chest ached where the restraint straps had cut into flesh and muscle. He would be badly bruised, but he was alive. "Jane?"

"I'm OK. What do we do?"

They were floating, but listing hard over on their right side. Alex looked down and saw water entering the cockpit. Within seconds it was swirling about his ankles. A bullet zinged through the metal of the fuselage. "They're trying to keep us inside, or shoot us as we get out. Open your cockpit a little."

"But won't that flood us?" Jane asked, looking back over her shoulder at him.

"Yes, but if we go under with the cockpit locked the water pressure will stop us from opening the hatches. We'll flood ourselves. Take a deep breath as the water comes in, and get out before we touch the bottom. Swim as far as you can underwater toward the stern of the *Penfold Son.* If we can make the overhang we can hide underneath for a little while."

She nodded. "Let's hope they don't start the engines again or we'll be caught in the propellers."

He knew she was right, but they had no other choice. The ship had come to a stop just as they were being tossed overboard. That meant someone was back on the bridge again. The electrical systems on board the Rooivalk were still working and Alex heard again the executive officer of the *Talana*, who had identified himself as Commander Kumalo, trying to raise the *Penfold Son.*

Alex opened his cockpit a fraction and a rush of water flooded over the side. Jane did the same.

"Jane?"

She turned again and looked at him. "Yes?"

"I didn't get a chance to say it to you before."

"What?"

"I love you too."

An explosion beside and beneath them silenced her reply and rocked the Rooivalk further onto its side, raising the cockpit out of the water a little and slowing the inflow of water. "Grenade!" Alex yelled. He looked up through the bullet-starred glass and saw Van Zyl pull the pin from another orb, hold it for a few seconds and then drop it over the side. The mercenary was counting off the fuse's timer, trying to judge it so the next grenade would detonate just as it reached the helicopter.

"Second vessel approaching from the northwest, sir," said an able-bodied seaman seated at a screen on the *Talana's* bridge. "It's small and fast—a motor cruiser. Speed twenty-eight knots, range seven miles, sir."

"Keep an eye on him," Fourie said. "Ready the guns." He wiped his brow.

They were in visual range of the *Penfold Son* now. "She's stopped, sir," Kumalo said, holding binoculars to his eyes. "Explosion below the waterline, sir! Maybe she's launching something?"

The radio on the bridge squawked to life. "SAS *Talana*, SAS *Talana*, this is the master of the *Penfold Son*, Commodore George Penfold, over . . ." The voice had a distinct British accent.

"Damn fool's promoted himself now." Fourie stood and snatched the microphone from Kumalo's hand before he could reply. "This is the Captain of the SAS *Talana*. Go ahead, and what the hell do you think you're playing at?"

"This is Penfold. My ship has been taken over by armed terrorists. They are carrying explosives and missiles on board. I suspect they are planning on attacking a port facility or another vessel, over."

Fourie looked at Kumalo, who shrugged. "Patch in Tactical Headquarters."

"The hijackers killed the crew of your air force attack helicopter and tossed the aircraft overboard. Two of my crew and I escaped. I am broadcasting from a private motor cruiser that picked us up."

Fourie checked the radar screen and saw the smaller boat approaching. "I see your vessel, Penfold. If you got away, though, why the hell did you come back?"

"Saw you on the radar, Captain. Thought I'd better come back to warn you, in case the terrorists opened fire on you."

"Well, that they did. Pirates or terrorists? What about your earlier radio transmissions?"

"I am George Penfold and this is the first time I have contacted you, Captain. I don't know anything about any other transmissions, and if you were talking to another George Penfold, I can assure you he was a fake."

The voice sounded different. Fourie rubbed his chin. The presence of terrorists on board the *Penfold Son* fit with the intelligence he had received from Tactical Headquarters.

"Sir," Kumalo interrupted. "I can see a rotor blade sticking out of the water. Looks like the Rooivalk is still floating. Another explosion just went off . . . They must be trying to sink it. What will we do, sir?"

"Sink my vessel, Captain," said the cultured voice over the radio and the words stilled even the murmured conversations going on around the *Talana*'s bridge. "I am requesting that you sink the MV *Penfold Son*, at my request, over."

"Gunfire, sir!" called a seaman, also keeping watch on the *Penfold Son*. "I see muzzle flashes from the freighter."

The voice from the radio came back, loud and clear. "Captain, there are no friendlies left on board that ship. It's packed with explosives and weapons and it's looking for a target to sink. It's only cargo on board, and it's all insured, as is the ship. I could never forgive myself if my vessel caused a loss of life. Sink it, Captain, sink it."

"Ready the missiles. Guns, target the engine room unless otherwise ordered."

The shock wave from the second grenade caught Alex's cockpit hatch from underneath and blew it open. A torrent of seawater flooded the chopper immediately. Alex's left side was scorched by the explosion and he felt tiny pieces of crimped wire—the grenade's shrapnel within its casing—pepper his arm. He was exposed as his head started to go under, and bullets sent up geysers of water around him.

The Rooivalk sank and Alex undid his last restraint strap and swam clear. He held his position, two meters below the surface, and watched the nose of the helicopter point downward. He could see Jane pushing and punching the cockpit glass from within. He dived and kicked his legs, following the sinking chopper.

His ears started to pop. He saw Jane's mouth pressed against the top of her hatch, sucking in the last of the air. Alex touched the glass and kicked hard, pushing himself down faster than the sinking machine. He hooked his hands under the open lip of the hatch and turned. He kicked for the surface, in the opposite direction to which the gunship was slowly falling.

Jane pushed from inside, holding her breath as the water filled the cockpit. The hatch slowly started to budge and as the last of the air inside was expelled by water she felt it move. It came open with a burst of bubbles and Jane kicked free. Alex pointed toward the stern of the ship and they swam. The Rooivalk disappeared into the gloom far below.

Behind them, another grenade exploded beneath the water's surface and the shock felt to Alex as though he'd been kicked from behind by some invisible sea monster. It made him gasp and he automatically drew in some seawater. His reserves of air were gone. Jane looked back at him, but he pointed for her to continue swimming toward the aft of the *Penfold Son.*

Alex headed for the surface.

When his head broke the waters he retched and sucked in a lungful of warm air. He heard a shout above and behind him and then the rattle of gunfire.

"That bloody frigate's almost on top of us," Van Zyl said to George, who had just come from the bridge.

"The Rooivalk's cannon killed the helmsman and buggered the radios. Can't hear a thing, or transmit. I don't know what the navy will make of this, but we'll tell them pirates came aboard and killed the helicopter crew. We'll say we turned on them and they jumped ship." He paused to draw his breath.

Van Zyl looked out at the approaching warship and nodded at what George had just said. "We need to kill Tremain and the woman now, though. We don't want them being picked up and interviewed by the navy."

"Agreed. Where are they now?"

"Heading aft, underwater. We just saw the woman break surface and just missed her. I've positioned my men all around."

"They'll be trying to take shelter under the overhang of the stern," George said. "I'm going back to the bridge to start the engine. That should flush them out."

Van Zyl nodded. "What about the *Talana*?"

George looked back at the menacing gray lines of the frigate. "He's hardly going to fire on a merchant ship, is he, even if a few rockets did go off in his general direction."

Alex surfaced just after Jane and swam to her, near the *Penfold Son*'s massive rudder. "Hear that?" she said. "Look! It's a boat."

He looked where she was pointing. Even from afar he recognized the clean lines of the *Fair Lady.* "That's who I could hear on the radio. Kevin, putting on an appalling British accent." He laughed. It was good to know at least one of his men was still alive, and on his way.

"I heard him, too, just before we went under, trying to impersonate George. Do you think he got away with it?"

A blast of automatic gunfire from above raked the water around them, telling them that whatever the navy thought of Kevin's charade, George Penfold was still very much in control above.

Something splashed in the water nearby. "Grenade!"

They duck-dived under the surface and swam away from the slowly sinking orb. The water slowed the shrapnel, so that it didn't reach them, but the shock wave pummeled their chests and tortured their ears. They swam back to their position, under water.

"I hope they hurry," Jane said. "I don't know how long we can last down here."

Alex heard shouting above them and then three weapons opened fire on the approaching luxury motor cruiser. He watched the tracer fall short and heard Van Zyl's command to cease fire and save ammunition. He knew that Kevin and whoever else was on board would have come armed. There would be a fight, but at least it wouldn't be as one-sided as it had been so far. All they needed to do was hang on for a few more minutes.

"What's that rumbling, Alex?"

He felt the vibrations emanating out from the steel-hulled monster. Ominous, shaking growls filled their ears and he was aware of movement below them. "Shit! They're starting the engine. We'll be washed out into the open. We'll be sitting ducks."

"What do we do?" Jane said, wiping plastered hair from her eyes as she clung to the rudder with her free hand.

He wrapped his arms around her. "Pray."

"Keep watch. We'll see them soon," Van Zyl said to his men. "Once we get them, we'll give those bastards in the cruiser a welcome they'll never forget."

"What about the navy?" one of the men asked, gesturing over his shoulder with a thumb.

Van Zyl spat into the Indian Ocean. "Fuck them."

"Fire," said Captain Gert Fourie.

34

The Exocet's solid fuel jet engine propelled it at three hundred and fifteen meters per second, skimming two meters above the ocean's surface.

Weighing more than six hundred kilograms, it punched a hole three meters by four amidships of the *Penfold Son*, just above the waterline. The missile had traveled only a fraction of its one hundred and eighty kilometer range, so when the warhead detonated, the fireball it created was fueled and expanded by unburned fuel. Aided by the impact of round after round from the *Talana*'s main gun, the *Penfold Son*'s fuel ignited and an explosion ripped through the ship.

After the second Exocet added to the inferno, the *Penfold Son* began to sink.

Alex and Jane were pushed aft, away from the stricken ship, on a bow wave caused by the force of the blast.

Several of the ship's crew and Van Zyl's men, Billy and Tyrone, were vaporized by the fireball.

Van Zyl jumped overboard as the freighter bent like a banana, the stern rising high as the ship started to fall in on itself. The screw, which had not yet started turning, was lifted clear of the water. Shipping containers, freed from their restraints by the explosion, cascaded into the water like a steel waterfall. Enrico screamed as he watched a six-meter box block out the sun before it crushed him.

On the bridge, the force of the explosion knocked George Penfold off his feet. On the way down to the deck he cracked his head against a control console and lost consciousness. The warm translucent waters of the Indian Ocean revived him and he came to, finding himself floating, on his back, his face inches from the deck head of the bridge.

"Help!" he screamed. Water was gushing in through the window that had been blasted out by the Rooivalk's cannon fire. As he swam he found the water around him was stained with the blood from his head wound.

Around him the light was fading, but there was still a pocket of air and he flailed his arms and legs in order to keep his mouth and nose clear of the water. Floating next to him, just a few centimeters from his chin, was a soggy brown envelope. He recognized it immediately. It was the one his men had intercepted—the tape of him killing the prostitute. It had all been for this. He started to weep.

George composed himself, took a deep breath and duck-dived. He groped his way toward one of the shattered windows and managed to squeeze out. The stern of his ship slid deeper into the blackness. George's ears hurt from the pressure but he forced himself to exhale slowly as he floated toward the surface. When he broke free he greedily gulped in air before taking stock of his surroundings. The gray-hulled frigate was in sight and he could hear a motorboat somewhere close. The body of a Filipino mess steward floated by, face down. None of them had even had time to find their life jackets. He touched his aching head and saw he was still bleeding.

Something brushed against his foot and he screamed.

He ducked his head underwater and saw the sleek, menacing shape glide by. It turned and headed back for him.

"No!"

The shark began by taking his right leg, just below the knee.

•   •   •

Valiant Chan had been monitoring the radio transmissions between the *Penfold Son* and the *Talana* from his position several nautical miles away.

He was smiling. He might only have half the ivory, but it was still worth a small fortune. The sports bag he had given to the pirate, Tremain, had been mostly filled with bundles of newspaper. It was a shame not knowing for sure if Penfold had killed him, but if he was still alive it would not be for long.

The podgy Captain Wu looked no thinner as a result of his captivity on the Ilha dos Sonhos. He was on watch, staring blankly out through the glass of the wheelhouse.

An alarm sounded.

"Captain!" a breathless able seaman burst into the bridge, but Chan and Wu could already see the smoke curling from chinks in the poorly sealed timber covering the main cargo hold.

As well as the ivory the hold contained boxes of explosives and grenades that Chan had ordered removed from the boatshed on the pirates' island. He'd reckoned he could turn a nice profit from those military stores in some tinpot African dictatorship or another.

By the time Wu's crew had their fire hose connected and the pump working, it was too late. The ivory was burning with such intensity that the seamen could barely get close enough to hit it with the hose.

The wooden boxes containing the C4 explosives and grenades smoldered at first, then caught fire.

Chan was decapitated by a flying sheet of metal after the first explosion.

Captain Wu was blinded by shattered glass and was crawling, in agony, on the bridge of his ship as the cluster of four thermite grenades burned their way through the hold and dropped, still glowing, in the waters of the Indian Ocean. Secondary explosions were still going off and the ship was ablaze as it sank.

•   •   •

The *Fair Lady* coasted up to Jane and Alex and willing hands reached over the back of the swimming platform and hauled them aboard.

"My God, I've never been so glad to see a bunch of pirates." Jane took the towel handed to her by Heinrich and rubbed herself dry.

Alex saw that Kevin was at the helm and the Australian waved down to him. "Lucky we got here when we did—we just passed the biggest great white I've seen in my life."

"Go Kevin. Don't spare the horses. The navy will be here any second."

"You got it, Skipper." The *Fair Lady* leaped away like a thoroughbred leaving the gates.

Novak handed Alex a towel. "We ditched to fool the Rooivalk, but Kobus was able to restart the one good engine and take off again after the gunship left us. That *oke's* a *lekker* pilot. We left the Oryx on a remote beach on the mainland. The air force will get it back, more or less intact. Henri's hit bad, but he'll live. He's in the hospital at Vilanculos and Captain Alfredo's keeping an eye on him. It's not all good news, though."

Alex looked around at the faces of his men and saw there were no smiles. "Where's Jose?"

"Van Zyl and the others must have hit the island. He put up a good fight, Alex. Two of the Chinese seamen were dead. Jose had run out of ammo at the end, by the look of it. We found him with a knife in his hand and a single round through his forehead."

"They executed him."

Jane moved to his side and took his hand. "I remember him. He wanted to be a barman, not a fighter."

Alex nodded. "Or a pirate. He was my brother." Alex looked away from his men and swallowed hard. He felt the tears pricking at his eyes. Jane squeezed his hand harder, then wrapped an arm around his waist and drew him closer. He drew a breath. There would be time to grieve later, but it wasn't over yet. "Has anyone seen Mitch? Jane says he was in on the whole thing."

"No sign of him," Novak said. "He must have got away"

Alex simply nodded again.

"There's a survivor up ahead!" Kevin called from the bridge.

Alex and Novak went forward and each picked up a pair of binoculars. "Ease off, Kevin. Let's check him out."

They moved to the starboard side, along with the others, and Jane joined Alex again, standing by him.

The man was white, though his face was blackened by burns or spilled oil. He was waving to them. As Kevin put the engines into neutral, and then reverse, to further slow the cruiser, they got a better look at him.

"Well, this is ironic," Piet van Zyl called out.

Alex looked at Novak and then at Jane. "He tried to murder your wife, twice, and kidnapped Jane so that Penfold could rape and kill her. Plus, he tried to kill us today—several times. What do you think?"

"Come on, man, take me aboard," Van Zyl called. He was grinning. "I'll come join you *okes* if you like. I'm sure you could use another crewman."

Alex called back, "Why, because you killed Jose, on the island?"

Van Zyl waved a hand in the air. "It wasn't me, but there are plenty more of those *munts* where he came from, man."

"Give me your gun," Alex said to Novak.

"No." Novak drew his nine-millimeter from his shoulder holster, cocked it, aimed and fired twice.

Alex turned to Jane and wrapped his arms around her as Van Zyl's lifeless body slowly sank beneath the water's surface. "Are you all right?"

"If he hadn't done it, I would have. Can we please go back to dry land now?"

Alex called a meeting of the crew after they landed at Ilha dos Sonhos and cleaned themselves up. "It ends now," he said. "There's food and board and whatever I can afford to pay you, if you decide to stay here and work with me on the hotel, but the piracy stops today."

"I have to be with Lisa, always, from now on. I'm out, too," said Novak.

Kevin looked at Alex. "Wouldn't be the same without you, mate. I'll stay, for a bit, and give you a hand." Kufa and Heinrich had also agreed to lay down their arms, though Heinrich said he might look for more work in Iraq or Afghanistan. Kufa said he would stay, as there was little prospect of a job for him in Zimbabwe.

They buried Jose at sea that evening, in the deep waters out past the reef. Alex said a few words and the rest of the crew fired a five-gun salute as the sea claimed his body.

Alex looked at Jane, who was wiping a tear from her eyes. She smiled, though, when he picked up the M4 he had just fired over his friend's body. He walked to the *Fair Lady*'s stern and tossed the weapon overboard. Next, he reached under his sports jacket and pulled the Glock from its holster. This, along with his spare magazines, he also dropped into the water.

One by one Kevin, Kufa, Novak and Heinrich all filed aft and tossed aside their own tools of a trade they had all agreed to forsake.

Jane respected Alex for his decision, but was still fearful about what might happen to him. She sipped a glass of chilled wine and Alex used a bottle of Dois M beer to take the cap off another. He clinked it against her drink and said, "Here's to whatever may come."

"To the future."

He laughed. "Do you really think we have one?"

"As a group, I don't know. Your men might still decide to leave the island, and—"

He took her free hand in his. "No, I mean you and me."

Jane had given the matter some thought already. Her life had changed beyond all recognition since the rain-swept day she had boarded the *Penfold Son* at Southampton.

Here she was with a man who until five minutes ago had made

his living by terrorizing innocent merchant sailors at the point of a gun. Yet he was willing to change, and to admit his mistakes and learn from them.

"You could always leave Africa," she said.

"I can't. This is my home. It's the only one I've ever known." He looked out over the sparkling ocean.

"Well," she said, taking another sip to calm her nerves, "I don't have a job to go back to in England. And whatever happens to you, you're going to need a lawyer, either to keep you out of jail or to help you negotiate the Mozambican tax system."

Jane lay on her back on the big beach towel and held Alex's hand. She could feel the warmth of the white sand on her back, through the weave, and the afternoon sun blanketed the front of her naked body.

When she opened her eyes she saw he was up on one elbow, looking down at her and smiling.

"What?"

"What, nothing. I just like looking at you," he said.

"Pervert."

"Guilty," he said. He lowered himself and kissed her and she felt the fire rekindled, as though he was blowing on hot coals.

There had been some whistles and laughter from the others when they had slipped away, on the pretext of going for a swim, but as yet they hadn't made it to the water. Alex had told her that they wouldn't be followed and she believed him. Of Mitch, they had found no sign. His gear and weapons were gone, as was one of the rigid-hulled inflatable boats. Although she was exposed, on a beach, and could occasionally hear the thump of music or a hoot of laughter from the wake at the beachside bar, she felt perfectly safe in Alex's arms.

"I love you," he said.

"I gathered."

He laughed. "We should go for that swim, otherwise the others might get suspicious if I come back covered in sand."

"A pirate protecting my reputation? How nice."

"Ex-pirate."

He stood and she looked up at him, marveling at his body and his complete lack of embarrassment. She could still feel him inside her and she wanted him again. She wanted him to never leave her. He reached down and pulled her effortlessly to her feet. Jane looked over her shoulder when she heard another raucous chorus of laughter coming from the bar, on the other side of the point.

"It's an odd way of showing their grief over Jose."

Alex took her hand as they walked down to the sea. "It's the way they are—we are. We've all lived with death too long. You know it can happen, and when it does you try and remember the good times. Jose called you my 'new wife' when he first met you."

They waded into the water. It was warm and clear and when she looked back at the shore the palm trees and sand made it look like paradise.

"It was a joke," Alex added, filling the silence.

"I get it," she said, but didn't know what to say next. They embraced and she felt his cock stir against her. It was enough, Jane told herself, just to be with him for now. She put a finger on his lips and led him into the deeper water. He put his hands under her bum and lifted her, and she floated, like a mermaid, up and onto him.

"I love you," she whispered into his ear as she wrapped her legs around him.

"I gathered."

Afterward, as they followed their long shadows up the beach, he asked her if she was hungry.

"Famished!"

They dried off and dressed and folded their towels, and he kissed her again, as greedy for her as she was for him. They walked back, hand in hand, across the spit of land on the track through the bush that brought them back to the main beachfront and the hotel. The other men waved to them from the beach bar.

"I'll go to the boatshed and get some firelighters for the *braai*," he said. "That's South African, by the way, for a barbecue."

"Then I suppose it's the woman's work to make the salad?"

He shrugged, but she blew him a kiss and set off for the hotel.

Mitch stood in the shadows, holding his breath, in anticipation.

When the pirates, minus Alex, had returned to Ilha dos Sonhos in the helicopter and hurriedly departed again on the *Fair Lady* after finding Jose's body, Mitch knew Van Zyl would not be coming to get him. He'd methodically made his preparations for revenge. The others hadn't had time to conduct a thorough search of the island, and Mitch had watched them come and go.

Mitch had packed his kit and hidden it in the bush, then taken one of the two RHIBs out to sea and scuttled it. He'd then swum back and gone into hiding, waiting for the moment that was about to arrive. He was almost aroused at the thought of it. If Chan and Van Zyl and Penfold had failed to wipe out Alex and his men en masse, then that was OK. Mitch would do it one man at a time, and he'd save the woman until last. She'd be freaking out by the time her turn came. Maybe some of the men would beg him to spare their lives, in return for swearing their loyalty to him. Mitch liked the thought of that. He might be back in business sooner than he thought.

Alex stepped into the boatshed via the side entrance and paused for a moment to let his eyes adjust to the dark. Mitch moved behind him, raised the pistol and brought it down hard on the back of Alex's head.

Mitch dragged the unconscious Alex up and over the rubber gunwale of the inflatable boat. He sagged against the craft, breathing shallowly. He looked down at the crumpled form. The others wouldn't dare follow him if they knew he had a live hostage, and later, out of sight of the island he would kill Tremain, slowly.

Mitch opened the double front doors of the boatshed, released the chock and pushed the RHIB so that it rolled down the twin rails to the water. Nothing could stop him now.

The men were still at the bar when Jane came out of the kitchen with a bowl of salad. She looked for Alex but couldn't see him.

"Where's Alex?"

"Probably still messing about in the boatshed," Heinrich said.

She set the bowl down on the bar and wandered, barefoot, along the beach to the shed. "Alex?"

The black bow of the RHIB rolled out into the sunlight. Jane saw Mitch at the helm and screamed. He fired a shot at her and she dived into the sand.

Jane was aware of shouting behind her, but she knew she had to get to her feet. She pulled herself up just as the boat was entering the water. Mitch was preoccupied with the starter as the twin engines were sputtering, failing to start.

She sprinted for the shed. Mitch was drifting out further from shore as she ran inside the musty hut. She looked around. The racks that once bristled with assault rifles were now empty. There were no pistol belts hanging from hooks and even the boxes of grenades were at the bottom of the Mozambique Channel.

The RHIB's outboard motors caught and Mitch revved them hard.

Through the shed door Jane could see the other members of Alex's crew, all drunk, were trying to organize themselves. She felt helpless, and terrified for Alex's safety. Mitch was a madman, bent on revenge. After all she and Alex had been through, she felt like screaming. She hadn't endured all this to see him taken away from her and executed.

Jane looked out and saw Alex getting to his knees in the front of the boat. Mitch sent him sprawling face-first into the deck with a vicious kick in his back.

Jane saw one of the ALM line launchers lying on a workbench.

It was the closest thing to a weapon still in the empty racks of what had once been the pirates' armory. A grappling hook was loaded in the barrel and a yellow compressed air container was attached.

Jane picked up the launcher and ran down to the water's edge.

Mitch turned and saw her. He raised his pistol but didn't fire. She stood her ground, aimed the launcher and pulled the trigger.

The grappling hook hissed from the barrel and sailed in a high arc, passing over Mitch's head.

"Ha! Missed me!" he yelled.

He was turning to look at her as the line continued to shimmy and snap out of the plastic holder beneath the barrel.

Jane dug her feet into the sand and held tight as the last of the nylon rope drew taut.

The hook had landed in the boat and Alex rolled on his back and saw the rubber-coated grapnel. He grabbed it and aimed at Mitch, who was off balance with his pistol hand on the helm as he continued to look backward.

With Jane holding firm on the other end of the line, and the boat accelerating furiously, the hook left Alex's hand of its own accord and snapped viciously into Mitch's face. One curved prong wrapped around his throat and he was yanked off his feet backward. His back bounced against one of the outboards and his body slammed into the water.

Alex crawled back to the helm and knocked the throttles into dead slow. He turned the RHIB around and headed for shore. The force of the hook catching Mitch had pulled Jane off her feet, but she was standing now, waving to him.

Mitch floated face-down in the water and when Alex coasted up beside him it was clear immediately that his neck was broken.

Epilogue

One year later

Alex looked into the mirror, lifted his collar, and ran the black bow tie around the back of his neck. "We should get a new boat some time. I miss the *Fair Lady*."

As much as it had pained him to do so, Alex had scuttled the *Fair Lady* a few nautical miles out to sea, the day after Jose's funeral.

When the South African Air Force made some low-level passes over Ilha dos Sonhos, presumably looking for the vessel which had been spotted on radar near the sinking of the *Penfold Son*, he was pleased there was nothing in the bay for them to photograph.

The South African Navy's board of inquiry had found that Captain Gert Fourie had acted properly, sinking the *Penfold Son*. Fourie confirmed, under oath, that Penfold had told him he had left the ship and was on a motor cruiser, which had never been seen or heard from again, and that the Englishman had ordered him to sink his ship.

"Well, you might not need to steal one this time. Here, let me," Jane said, moving behind Alex.

He smelled her perfume and took her slender forearm in his hand and kissed it as she encircled him. She pushed herself against his back and he found the sound of her silk dress rubbing against his dinner jacket almost as sexy as her.

"Why are men rubbish at tying bow ties?" She peeked over his shoulder, looking in the mirror of their suite as she tied it. "There, now you look more like a hotel owner and less like a cutthroat."

"Half-owner of a hotel," he corrected her.

"Half is better than nothing," she reminded him. She kissed his cheek, then wiped the lipstick away with her thumb.

Two floors and forty-eight rooms of the hotel were finished— enough to declare it open. Alex poured them each a second glass of vintage French champagne.

"Hey, go easy on that," Jane said. "You've got a speech to make."

"Dutch courage," he said, "and every pirate needs his grog."

She frowned and he mouthed "Sorry." He got down on one knee and reached into the pocket of his tuxedo.

"What the bloody hell do you think you're doing?" She put a hand over her mouth as the realization dawned on her.

"Jane . . ."

"No!"

"What?"

"I mean, yes, if this is what I think it is."

"I've lost a cufflink and I was just getting down here to look for it."

She punched him on the shoulder and got down on her knees so she was eye to eye with him.

"So, will you?" he asked.

"Help you find your cufflink?"

"No, you know what I mean."

"Yes, and I will."

Lesley Engels, the American widow Alex had met on the *Pride of Africa* en route to Cape Town, was waiting for them downstairs. The diamonds around her neck glittered with reflected candlelight. A string quartet played in the background and the hundred and fifty guests parted as Alex and Jane walked arm in arm along a red carpet.

"Those two look like they've stepped off a bloody wedding cake," Kevin joked to Kobus as Alex and Jane passed them.

All of Alex's men were there. Kufa, looking dapper in a white suit and black tie, chatted to a German travel journalist who laughed at something he said. Henri, now fully recovered from his injuries, was staring into the eyes of a South African Airways flight attendant whose dinner suit couldn't hide a body builder's physique. Heinrich drank beer instead of champagne and was discussing the merits of the AK-47 over the G3 with an American travel agent from Dallas. Mark and Lisa Novak danced slowly in front of the quartet, paying attention only to each other.

Alex made his way to Lesley and kissed her on the cheek. She was a stunningly beautiful woman, and the first, that he could remember, from whom he had ever turned down an offer of sex. He'd thought that he would never hear from her again, though she had seemed to understand why he declined her offer when he told her he was in love with another woman. It was the first time he'd realized how he truly felt about Jane.

In the days after the sinking of the *Penfold Son*, his initial elation at having survived had worn off when he realized they were all broke and living on an island with little food and no source of income. He, Jane and the others had worked the bars and backpacker joints of Vilanculos, trying to drum up business for fishing and diving trips, but they were competing with other, better established operators. The future looked grim, until one day when Alex checked his e-mails on the computer at Smugglers and saw the message from Lesley in the U.S.

The music ended and when the crowd eventually hushed itself Lesley began her speech.

"When I came to Africa, on my last trip, I knew I wanted to invest some of my late husband's money in a hotel property, preferably on a beach, but I had no idea where to start looking. I didn't even know where Mozambique was." She paused until the polite laughter subsided. "And then, on a train, in the middle of the Karoo Desert, I met this gorgeous fellow, Alex Tremain."

"If she lays a finger on you, I'll shoot her," Jane whispered in his ear.

Lesley held up her hands to drown out the wolf whistles from the men. "Alex told me about this beautiful hotel on this beautiful island in this beautiful country that I knew nothing about. When I looked into his eyes I saw that this was no conman trying to fleece me; this was a man who truly believed that he had paradise within his reach, but there was something keeping it from him, just beyond his grasp. I wanted to help him catch that dream and make it a reality."

Alex looked at Jane and put his arm around her and squeezed her tight. She smiled at him. Whatever happened from here on with the hotel didn't matter. He knew now that happiness wasn't tied up in concrete and fine china, or in the sands of an island or the memories of a long-gone colonial era. He'd betrayed his honor and himself to fast-track his dream, but with Jane by his side he felt more complete than he had in a long time. With Lesley's money and a great deal of hard work, he might just have the life he wanted, but he'd never steal or put the lives of those he loved at risk again.

"Anyway," Lesley continued, "I say to this stranger on a train, Alex Tremain, 'So what do you do for money, to finance your grand plans to reopen your hotel?' He kind of sighs, looks all world-weary, and says, 'I'm a pirate.'"

The crowd laughed, egged on by Alex's men, who were slapping each other, cheering and spilling drinks on each other and some of the perplexed-looking guests.

"And I ask you, what girl can resist a pirate?"